Blood Harvest:

The Hidden Amongst Us

Michael Louis Weinberger

Published by Purple Mountain Publishing

International Standard Book Number: 978-0-9837683-0-2

Edited by Dan Hankison

Cover Art and Formatting: Bill Kutcher: www.pbase.com/ibill

Printed in the United States of America

Second Edition

Dedications

To my parents, Beth and Bill, who taught me the beauty and depth of the right side of the brain, the wisdom and logic of the left, and despite some of my more eccentric behavior, had the understanding and patience to allow me the exploration of both.

To my brother Matt, who has always given me the inspiration, humor and insight that brought this book to life. This book would not have happened without you.

To my wife Rebecca, simply for willing to be my wife. For pushing me forward, when I am floundering, as well as giving me meaning and reason in my adulthood.

To my girls Mikayla and Natasha, now the greatest adventure and joy of my life.

And to my grandmother Jessie, who is my reason for believing in all things good, fair, right, spiritual and magical.

Contents

Part I: Exsanguination

Chapter 1

London, England 1528

Count Alphonso Diemo pushed his long white hair out of his eyes as he watched the patient in his barber chair begin to nod off, as if falling asleep. This, he knew, was not as a result of fatigue, it was as a result of the patient having been bled, and in an amount where her ability to maintain consciousness was difficult. Alphonso recognized this syncope, or sleep caused by a diminished amount of blood getting to the brain, as an indication that the proper amount of blood had been drained from the body, so he removed the glass suction cup from the lacerations that his Phleam, the main cutting tool of the barber's bloodletting craft, had produced. Alphonso then folded a clean linen towel into a square and applied direct pressure to the wounds as he called one of his assistants over to monitor the stabilization of his patient.

"Make sure that when she wakes she begins to drink both water and wine constantly to replenish what she loses in the perspiration."

The assistant nodded as Alphonso lifted the collection bowl and carried the blood-filled vessel carefully into a back room of his majestic home/office. Due to his large frame and unusual height he had to duck under the top of the six foot doorway to keep from hitting his head and shoulders on the molding. There he transferred the blood he had just drawn, approximately three pints worth, into a five-gallon ceramic jug via a wide-mouthed funnel and replaced the cork in the top.

Returning to the great hall, Alphonso looked out over the rows of cots that made his London home into a makeshift hospital, reflecting on the difficulty the recent times had brought upon him. The plague, known as the English Sweate, was again ravishing all of England, however the current manifestation of the disease displayed a severity and lethality that had increased exponentially from its previous manifestations. Alphonso had taken in as many sufferers of the disease as he could manage, and performed his bloodletting service to the victims with varying results but, on the whole, London was being devastated. King Henry VIII had fled London in fear of the disease and, for the first time, the illness had spread outside the borders of England and was extending into Europe.

Furthermore, the conflict between King Henry VIII and the Catholic Church was reaching a fevered pitch, after Pope Clement VII refused to grant King Henry a divorce from Catherine of Aragon. The Catholic faithful were at odds with the new Church of England, which in turn put Alphonso and all of the other barbers in England in the middle of the conflict, as their practice of bloodletting was highly frowned upon by the Vatican.

Still, Alphonso did what he could. He had met the disease head on, having a small degree of success in healing some of its sufferers during the previous outbreaks, which was more than any of the other barbers or physicians could claim. There was also the added benefit of collecting large quantities of the drawn blood, and, given the needs of both his people and himself, this made every extended effort invaluable.

Alphonso stood in the entryway and pulled his snow-white hair off of his face and tucked it behind his ears. Looking down to his hands he noticed that some of the blood he had just drawn and stored in the cellar had stained his alabaster skin. Being an albino, his pale flesh made for a sharp contrast with the crimson that he worked with on a day-to-day basis. It was also somewhat disconcerting to his patients when they first came to see him., After all, who wouldn't be a bit ill at ease when the barber of choice looked as though he, himself, had been drained of blood. It took years for Alphonso and his staff to earn the trust, respect and admiration of the community. He had persevered and succeeded, despite the occasional rabble-rouser, and had even become a personal advisor for King Richard, King Henry the VII and the current King Henry, VIII.

Now Alphonso watched as his staff moved among the mass of patients he had taken in, all of whom were in various stages of suffering, caused by the English Sweate, when his eyes fell upon a woman lying in one of the cots who looked to be suffering from a dramatically different malady. The woman was strapped down to the cot as her body convulsed in the throes of a violent tremor. She also appeared to have lesions that covered all areas of her exposed skin. His recognition of the woman's condition shocked Alphonso into action. Running to the closest of his assistants he asked, "Where did this one come from?"

The assistant, a small woman named Abigail, who had worked with Alphonso since he had taken her in over twenty years ago. A former prostitute, she had a toughness that living on the streets had given her, and it served her well as a senior member of his staff. Abigail was also exceedingly beautiful in a way that neither her former profession, nor her age could strip away. Her hair was so blonde it was almost yellow and her eyes were the color of blue ice. She wore a white dress in a loosely fitting fashion, but it couldn't completely disguise a near flawless figure underneath. She was an incredible sight indeed, and one of his most trusted staff.

"She was brought in last night. Apparently she was out in the streets raving like a mad woman and getting more and more potentially violent until the local constabulary brought her down. They were going to take her to the asylum but decided to try us first, since we were so much closer to them at the time."

Alphonso looked down on the woman, who had grown very quiet and still as the seizure faded.

Abigail whispered, "Thank God they brought her here."

Alphonso looked to Abigail and back to the woman on the table. "Take her upstairs and begin a direct transfer."

Abigail looked shocked, "A direct...?"

"She's too far gone for the tonic. Let us pray that her system is resilient enough to make use of a pure dose."

"As the Master says." Abigail bowed her head and hurried off to make the arrangements.

Alphonso turned back to the woman on the table and guessed

her age to be around twenty, however, the lesions on her face gave her an appearance of being much older. Her face was sunken and her eyes bulged in their sockets. The poor girl was emaciated to the point that her body was mostly skin and bones. Her skin had a slight bluish tinge to it, and to the untrained eye the girl appeared to have the life of a corpse. Alphonso knew differently. He knew what ailed her all too well. Indeed he and everyone on his staff and in his household, suffered the same condition as the strange young woman on the table. Alphonso had been gathering them to him as best he could, and he shuddered to think how everyone he was close to could end up in a similar state, should they ever be separated from the blessed tonic that he had created and stockpiled for all these years. Gently he placed a hand on the girl's forehead, as she moaned softly and oscillated back and forth on the cot, for as much room as her restraints would allow.

Whispering, Alphonso said, "I pray that your mind is still capable my dear."

A voice from behind made Alphonso jump: "The Master did not give up on me when I was in far worse a state. The girl will survive."

Alphonso turned to see William, the most senior member of his staff and his dearest friend, looking down on the woman in a state of contemplation similar to his own.

"You always give me a start when you do that silent entrance and exit of yours."

"Sorry sir. Old habits and all."

Alphonso chuckled. William was such an enormous man that he might have been the only person in England who could make Alphonso look like a small child. How such an entity could move so swiftly and silently, despite his enormous size, was one of the great mysteries that Alphonso could never fathom.

"Well, it is also somewhat comforting to know you would always be close at hand."

"That would be because I always am."

"I know old friend. I know. So, was there a reason for you

revealing yourself just now, or did you simply want to see the latest addition to our family?" Alphonso gestured to the woman on the table.

"Assuming she survives intact you mean?"

"Didn't you just say that I brought you back from far worse a state?"

"Indeed I did. Then again, that was me."

Nodding, Alphonso knew that every time a new case like this was found the results of the tonic were different. Sometimes the mildest cases turned out to be incurable, while others, as was the case with William, who seemed to be lost causes, instead became strong survivors.

"Actually sir, there is a gentleman awaiting you in the parlor. He says his visit is of the utmost urgency."

"Is he in need of treatment?"

"No sir. This has the feel of a more 'official' visit." William emphasized the word "official" heavily enough for Alphonso to get the point.

"Official? Has Henry returned to London?"

After a pause William replied, "No sir, I believe the gentleman is here on business of the Church."

Alphonso grew very serious, "England or the Vatican?"

"He is wearing King Ferdinand's standards."

Now Alphonso's breath caught in his throat and, once the initial shock wore off, he had to struggle to keep his voice down.

"Are you telling me there's a damned Inquisitor in my receiving room?"

"Actually M'Lord," William began without a hint of alarm in his voice, "there's a damned Inquisitor and at least four of his guard in your receiving room."

Alphonso moved to a washbasin and quickly dipped his hands in the clean water.

"Have you checked the grounds?"

William nodded. "I took a quick look around and it seems as though they came alone."

William was quick to add "But you never know with the Inquisition."

Alphonso lowered his head as he dried his hands on a torn piece of bed linen that had been set aside for use as a towel.

"I don't like this. How in God's name are they in England in the first place?"

"I don't know M'Lord." William brought up one hand, in which he held a particularly long and wicked looking butcher's knife. "Shall I dispatch them for you?"

Alphonso quickly placed a hand on William's wrist and lowered the blade. "If he is only here with four guards then it is likely he is here to talk."

William looked skeptical, but shrugged his shoulders and sheathed the knife into a makeshift scabbard attached to the rear of his belt.

"See to things here while I meet with our guest. Did the gentleman give his name?"

"Yes sir. He said his name was Don Leon Amonbagada."

"All right, help Abigail get this girl upstairs and see to it that both she and her treatment are undisturbed."

The tone of voice Alphonso used set William into motion and he immediately untied the girl, lifting her effortlessly over one of his large shoulders and carrying her upstairs.

Alphonso hurried downstairs to his receiving room, but stopped short of the parlor doors and composed himself with a deep breath before turning the doorknob and entering the room.

"Gentlemen!" Alphonso said warmly, "So good to see you."

The guards immediately turned toward Alphonso each with a hand over the grip of their swords, the Inquisitor sat calmly in one of the large leather chairs and made no attempts to rise.

"Ah, Alphonso Diemo, the Comte De Navarre himself. I see there is no rest for you this evening. I do hope that my unannounced visit does not put you out."

"My home is always welcome to receive such vaunted guests as your selves." Alphonso inclined his head in a polite nod

11

appropriate in such a casual setting as opposed to the more formal bow that would have been proper on a more formal occasion.

The Inquisitor inclined his head, but to a far less degree, which was highly inappropriate for a guest in another man's home, regardless of how casual the occasion might be. Silence filled the room as the Inquisitor and his guards seemed to assess Alphonso and his reaction to the blatant insult.

Alphonso stood to his full height of six and a half feet, pulled his long hair off of his ears and let it fall to the middle of his back. Then he looked the Inquisitor directly in the eyes and his voice lost any pretense of hospitality as he said, "You honor me with your presence, however, I am very busy tonight. Perhaps you would be good enough to explain how I can be of service?"

The chill in Alphonso's voice accompanied with his intimidating countenance made the guards step back in apprehension. Alphonso had expected the Inquisitor to hesitate as well, however, the man jovially rose up from the chair and bowed deeply to Alphonso. When his head came up out of the bow he was wearing a smile across his face.

"Forgive me Sire, I tend to forget myself when out of Spain. I am here only to request your help and would be horrified if I were to offend you when I so desperately need your aid."

Alphonso was taken aback by the rapid change in the Inquisitor's demeanor and his entire body relaxed ever so slightly at the Inquisitor's words.

"Count Diemo, we have traveled a great…" Don Leon's words caught in his throat as he looked past the open parlor door and into the great hall where so many people lay suffering and dying.

"Are…are they all suffering the Sweating Sickness?" Don Leon asked nervously.

Alphonso turned to see the door ajar. "Ah, yes. We call it the English Sweate, however, I believe it has crossed the ocean to France and Spain this time around."

Terror covered the Inquisitor's face as he spoke. "My dear sir, would it be possible for us to speak outside of your home? I fear that I have not been blessed with the capacity for enduring the ill."

Alphonso didn't relish the idea of going anywhere with the Inquisitor alone. On the other hand it would get them out of his home and away from William before his aide decided to act on his earlier murderous intent.

"Very well gentlemen, after you."

The group walked out the front doors and down the cobbled path leading to the street. Once on the street the guards all picked up torches from where they had apparently left them on the ground as they had arrived. They ignited them by striking flint stones and the oil soaked rags around the tips of the torches immediately caught and illuminated the street as they walked.

When they had traveled a few paces away from Alphonso's home and makeshift hospital the Inquisitor said, "I appreciate your understanding."

Alphonso thought the man looked genuinely relieved to be out of the immediate presence of the ill, as did his guards.

"My honor, sir, now, can we discuss what brought you to my door in the first place?"

"Of course. As you so aptly said moments ago, the Sweating Sickness has indeed crossed the ocean from England to Spain and I have a few questions that I would like to ask of you regarding the illness."

Alphonso nodded. "Certainly, but that does not explain why you sought me out. After all there are numerous doctors in England that you could speak with, not to mention the fact that the Church has officially frowned on those in my profession for a great deal of time now."

"Indeed, it is as you say. There are several doctors around London, some of whom have direct ties with the Holy Father himself that we could have contacted, however, from the journals provided to my office by your King Henry it would appear you are the only person in all of England, perhaps in all of Christendom, that has any…ah…experience with the plague, the only one still alive in any case."

Alphonso's blood chilled at the thought that King Henry might be acting in collusion with these Spaniards. Alphonso had always enjoyed the protection of the throne of England ever since he had done an investigation into the death of the prior King Henry's son.

"True, the illness had come around twice before, and it was particularly devastating in 1485, , when it had hastily taken the lives of a multitude of individuals. At the time King Richard had gathered nearly one hundred physicians to search for a cure for the malady."

The Inquisitor paused to look directly into Alphonso's amber-yellow eyes. "As I recall there were one hundred physicians…and one barber." The Inquisitor paused and watched for any reaction from Alphonso. When none came he continued, "This journal mentioned you by name as having been the only one of those enlisted able to move freely among the ill, with no fear of the sickness, while all others who came into contact with the sick, became sick themselves. Any and all of the physicians who tried to emulate your ability to move amongst the ill perished after only a few days. How is it you were able to remain steadfast, while all your counterparts succumbed?"

Alphonso remembered the time the Inquisitor spoke of vividly. "Indeed the plague was extremely virulent at the time, and often would kill its victim mere hours after the first manifestations of the disease. Then, only a few months after it began, the disease seemed to disappear on a grand scale with only a few cases being spoken of per year since that time. Even now, years later, no cause or cure has ever been found.

"As far as your question is concerned regarding my apparent immunity, the ability for a healer to not become ill around the sick is simply a trait which all in our profession share to some degree, , and apparently it is a trait stronger in me than in most."

The Inquisitor's gaze never veered from Alphonso's, but his body shifted uncomfortably as if he knew that Alphonso was holding something back.

"Either you are a wonderful liar, or you've only told me a part of the truth."

Alphonso's face was a mask of stone as the Inquisitor continued to study him looking for any telltale signs of deceit. After nearly a minute the Inquisitor seemed to deflate as he spoke again.

"Count Diemo, this Sweating Sickness has traveled to France and Spain as you have said, and your presence has been requested by both countries in order to assist their physicians in an effort to stem the tide of the disease. My King Ferdinand has already petitioned Henry VIII of England to have you taken directly to Spain." With that the Inquisitor produced a parchment from his belt and held it out to Alphonso.

"I would assume these are the King's commands for me to travel to Spain with you?"

"Something like that."

As Alphonso looked down to the parchment and read the words written across the page he didn't notice that the guards had quietly moved from their positions around the Inquisitor in order to block the path in both accessible directions.

Then shock and disbelief registered on Alphonso's face as he read. "This...this cannot be right! This is an arrest warrant!"

Suddenly the guards to the rear grabbed Alphonso's arms and held him fast while the remaining two drew their swords and placed the tips at his throat. The Inquisitor sauntered around his men to face Alphonso.

"Corrupt heathen, did you think that it would go unnoticed that of all those physicians employed to treat the disease only you survived? The Holy Father in Rome and King Ferdinand agree that this plague has been set upon us by Lucifer to strike down God's most devout. Clearly you, and all of those in your household, are in league with the Dark Lord who has made it possible for you to have survived. Well your reign has ended Demon, for you and your lot. Even now the faithful are moving 'en masse' to your doorstep to purge your presence from their city."

The Inquisitor inclined his head in the direction of Alphonso's home where an orange glow from multiple torches burned an incandescent aura in the night sky. Alphonso felt the sword tips lower from his neck as the Inquisitor moved in even more closely. He was about to say something when he felt an explosion in his chest.

The Inquisitor sneered as he felt his dagger slide between Alphonso's ribs. "I was supposed to arrest all of you and put you on trial in Barcelona, but I think we both know what your fate will be once we reach Spain. I would prefer to keep the gold, which would have been needed to be spent in order to feed you and yours on the voyage home."

The guards released Alphonso's arms and allowed his body to fall to the road in a lifeless heap.

Chapter 2

"I cannot allow you to enter as the Master is not at home." William's voice was hard as he faced down the mob that had gathered suddenly outside the house. Almost one hundred of the Inquisitor's followers had arrived at the doorstep a few moments prior and appeared as though they might force their way in until William had suddenly swung the front door open and placed his enormous frame in between the entrance and the people outside. William knew no one was going to want to be the first to rush at him and he used the intimidation to momentarily stifle the hostility. He also knew it wouldn't last, but it might give him a few moments to evacuate the staff. "Now I would thank you to leave us to our work. We have many suffering…."

The closest and most vocal of the mob stepped forward and spoke commandingly to William: "You will grant us entrance to this residence immediately, or we shall force our way in and burn the building down around you."

William hesitated, looking out on all of the faces that stood before him, many of whom had previously received treatment and been healed by Master Diemo. The betrayal from such previous "friends" was heartbreaking, and all William could do was shake his head in disgust.

He looked the speaker right in the eyes. "Give me a moment, and I will give you what you ask."

The speaker tried to respond, but William shut the door in the man's face. Quickly, William moved to a fireplace, picked up a hatchet from a block and made his way into the cellar. The barrels lined neatly across the floor contained a combination of oil of roses and turpentine. William knew that, if this mixture was combined in the right proportion with fresh egg yolks, then an incredibly effective healing poultice for open wounds would be created.

William also knew that in its current state the mixture was highly flammable. Moving to the barrel closest to the door he swung the hatchet in a wide arc, shattering the wood at its midpoint. Spray exploded from the rupture and began to saturate everything in the room as the mixture also gushed from the broken slats of the barrel. He then proceeded back up the stairs to the parlor where other staff members tended the sick. William beckoned one nurse over and spoke in whispers.

"How many patients are still alive?"

"Of the eight we were trying to save only three remain and I don't think they will last more than a few hours."

"Is there any chance of saving them?"

"You know how lethal the sickness has been this time around. No, I fear they will be gone before long."

William nodded. "What I am about to ask of you, it may seem contrary to what we have always practiced. However, I believe it is the only solution open to us if we are to survive this night."

When William told the woman what he had planned the woman's face lost all of its color.

"But...but how will any of us survive?"

"There are horses waiting at the livery, use the back stairs and escape with the rest of the staff. Make your way to the Dover house and gather all you can. Hopefully the Master will see my signal and be warned away. He will make his way to Dover as well. That has always been the plan should we ever find ourselves in such a dire situation."

Tears began to well in the woman's eyes. "And you?"

"I will be close behind you, of course."

The woman knew full well it was a lie, but she agreed all the same. Quickly she gathered the other members of the staff, and each of them sprinted to their rooms to collect whatever items were necessary for the journey to Dover.

William made his way upstairs to the room where Abigail was tending to the young woman with the special needs. The young girl was now sitting upright with Abigail, who was holding a large chalice and helping the young woman drink the contents. Abigail looked up from what she was doing to see William watching her. Then the smell of the turpentine struck her nostrils and her eyes went wide.

William asked, "Is she able to travel?"

"Not even close, you'll have to carry her."

"No Abigail, I need to distract the crowd outside and draw them away from the rear of the building so you and the others can escape unmolested."

Abigail shook her head. "I will distract them, your strength is needed to get them all away safely."

"Abi-" he began.

"I'll hear no more of it. Go make the final arrangements."

William knew it was pointless to argue with Abigail when she was like this. He decided to go as she requested, but when he returned he would "strong arm" Abigail out with the rest of the staff and lock the door behind her.

He ran back down to the first floor and grabbed a mop before he started back toward the cellar. Along the way William saw the thirty or so staff members hurrying to the rear exit with small bags filled to capacity with their personal items. Each looked to him beseechingly before continuing to the rear of the building. William smiled, as each sad glance reminded him that he was part of a family brought together by Master Diemo over all of the intervening years. He knew what he would do to *anyone* who would try to bring harm upon this family.

William saw one of the women holding a small bundle in her arm. He took one shaky step toward her. Gently William's huge hand pulled one of the linens off the bundle and he stared at a soundly sleeping infant, looking as content as if nothing in the world mattered more than the thumb he silently suckled. William's hand was nearly twice the size of the infant's head, and it trembled as he stroked the baby's downy hair, feeling the warmth of the softest skin he had ever touched. "See to it that everyone is ready. We will only have one chance at this."

The woman nodded as William forced himself to turn away and descend the cellar stairs where he submerged the mop into the several inches of the turpentine that had flooded the floor, He then backed his way up the steps leaving a wet trail as he climbed. The oil of roses combined with the turpentine prevented the trail from drying out, while William continued to mop the slick all the way up the stairs and into the parlor where, to his horror, he saw the front door wide open. Dropping the mop he scanned the house to see the three remaining living patients being carried out by some of the mob that had formed outside. William could easily have stopped them but he was actually relieved to have them out of the building.

Apparently, the Inquisitor and his guards had returned and hadn't waited to rush the door. William couldn't see any sign of the Master, but he couldn't waste time wondering as the sounds from the angry voices of people echoed down from the highest point of the stairwell. He knew it was coming from outside the room where Abigail had been tending the girl.

"Oh, bloody hell!" William cursed, knowing he only had a few moments before the entire mob would work their way into the building. He ran back to the rear exit to see the rest of the staff by the door waiting for a signal that it was clear for them to escape.

"It should be clear. GO!!!" William hissed and the entire staff burst through the door and into the night, without anyone seeing them or accosting them in any way. He had gotten them all out safely. Now there was only one thing left to do. William ran to the parlor and picked up a flint stone and striker off of the table where he had left it and, careful not to ignite his sodden clothes, sent sparks into a bed sheet saturated with the turpentine and oil mixture. The sheet immediately ignited and William hurled it at the wet streak he had created with the mop earlier. He watched the fire travel along the path and into the area by the cellar. William indulged himself with one more look around the building, which had been his home for so many years. Then he turned and walked toward the front door. A loud "whomp" echoed as the flames ignited the pool of turpentine and oil in the cellar.

Chapter 3

"Here!" one of the guards called out. "This door is locked and I can hear voices inside."

"Force the door!" The Inquisitor called back. "We have God's work to do this evening!"

But when the guards opened the door they were met by the countenance of the girl, looking gaunt and eyes bulging with blood from the chalice encircling the sides of her mouth and wetly staining the front of her dress.

"Mother of Christ!!!" The Inquisitor screamed as the four guards drew their swords. Then the Inquisitor screamed the word that had followed Alphonso Diemo and all of his staff members for the entirety of their lives.

"VAMPIRE!!!"

Abigail spun toward them as they entered, dropping the chalice holding the collected blood that the girl had been drinking, and stood defiantly between the girl and the armed guards.

The Inquisitor completely lost his nerve in that moment. "Kill them! Kill the vampire and the whore who protects it!"

The guards charged, eyes wild with fear and hatred, but Abigail had been brought up on the streets, was no helpless victim. The first guard never saw the blade she withdrew from beneath her clothes, Abigail opened the man's throat with a single cut as she side-stepped his charge. The dying guard panicked and blocked the other guard's path, as he flailed about, hands at his throat, trying to staunch the flow of his life's blood.

Abigail then stepped up to the bed and bounced, launching herself at the Inquisitor shrieking as she sailed through the air. Not being a warrior himself the Inquisitor screamed and covered his face at the sight of her literally flying at him. Before Abigail could reach him one of the guards had stepped in between them and caught her in mid-air. The guard slammed her to the ground but Abigail tensed as she hit and countered by placing her foot on the

21

man's chest. With a mighty heave of her leg she flung the man back and righted herself in a crouch, turning her face back to the Inquisitor.

"Mary, Mother of God!" The Inquisitor shrieked and Abigail nearly burst out laughing as the pompous fool held a cross in front of him, as if it would offer any protection from her wrath. Abigail smiled at the sight of the extreme fear in the eyes of the Inquisitor. The girl began shrieking behind her and Abigail spun to see a guard run a sword through her chest.

The scream Abigail let out was so bloodcurdling everyone in the room recoiled at the sound. Forgetting the Inquisitor, Abigail charged at the guard who had struck down the girl, driving him back toward a window. The two slammed into the wooden shutter, which gave way under their combined weight, they fell through, plummeting twenty feet to the ground below. Initially, the stunned mob crowded close to the two writhing bodies on the ground, but all staggered back as the guard began bellowing in pain, grabbing at his right leg that was bent in a way it was not supposed to bend. Abigail, who had landed more on the guard than on the ground, recovered and scrambled on top of the helpless guard while brandishing her dagger overhead. Shrieking, she stabbed the man repeatedly with such violent intent that the entire mob cowered at the sight and sound.

"Seize her!!!" The Inquisitor, appearing in the ruined window above, screamed his panicked orders at the mob below.

Hesitantly, a few men began to move toward Abigail but she noticed their advances and began hacking and slashing wildly at the incomers. Abigail drew blood on the first few, but she was soon overwhelmed by the numbers as more of the mob swarmed in upon her, holding her fast. She kicked and thrashed and tried to bite anything that passed near her face, while attempting to break free of the multiple hands holding her. The faces of the crowd were a mixture of hatred and anger. She couldn't see that the majority of the onlookers had expressions of uncertainty and, in some cases, outright revulsion at what was happening. Unfortunately, it would have also been apparent these people were not going to come to her rescue, as, they backed away from the Inquisitor and his two remaining guards who had exited the building and stomped toward her with swords drawn.

Abigail flailed and kicked as strong hands tried to hold her down while the head Inquisitor shouted something while holding a small crucifix in one hand inches from her face and his rapier sword in the other. With a final resonant "Amen" the Inquisitor thrust with his sword arm and Abigail felt a searing hot flash of pain as the slender rapier blade passed through her side. The blade was exquisitely sharp and she felt no resistance by her flesh as the cold steel entered her and was then pulled free. The pain and fear of being stabbed caused her to surge with all her effort and she managed to free one hand, grasping out desperately for anything solid.

Abigail was surprised as her hand closed around the hilt of a small dagger that had been attached to the belt of one of the men trying to restrain her. She pulled the knife from its sheath and plunged the blade into the nearest body. A man screamed and Abigail felt her other arm come free. She swung the dagger in front of her toward the Inquisitor but felt the blade slice only air. Again she felt the white-hot pain of the rapier's point enter her, in the fleshy part between her shoulder and neck. Again the wound did not strike anything that would be instantly mortal and Abigail grabbed the base of the weapon with her free hand and drove the dagger forward toward the man wielding it.

The Inquisitor saw the attack coming and abandoned his weapon in order to stay out of reach of the knife Abigail was guiding. Most of the mob had moved to a safe distance at this point, and as the Inquisitor tried to do the same his feet became tangled beneath him and he tumbled to the ground only a few feet from the demon woman who was approaching him.

Abigail knew she was losing blood quickly as she used the pain she felt to keep going. Sliding the rapier out of her shoulder was excruciating, but the pain also gave her clarity, as she stalked toward the Inquisitor with murder in her eyes.

She was about to drive the blade home when another of his guard stepped in front of her and thrust the point of his rapier at her chest. With uncanny ease Abigail spun her dagger up and parried the thrust to one side of her body then thrust the Inquisitor's rapier, which had only moments ago been lodged in her shoulder, into the heart of the guard, killing him instantly.

The Inquisitor let out a whimper as he watched another of his guard fall, and he let out a high shrill scream when Abigail turned her attention back in his direction.

"Stop her!!! Force her down!!!" The Inquisitor was screaming to the mob, but no one moved as Abigail began taking pained and tremulous steps toward the begging man. Abigail could feel the strength draining from her with every step she took. She knew she wasn't long for life, but before she closed her eyes for the last time, Abigail would will herself to get revenge on this murderer, begging so pathetically before her eyes.

All at once she stood over him, as the Inquisitor wept and covered his eyes. Abigail raised the rapier for a final killing thrust, but before she could act a tremendous force exploded in her back as she was suddenly struck by an overload of pain followed by... nothing. She watched the world moving in slow motion, as she felt herself fall and land, painlessly, on the grass of the front yard. All the pain had left her body, as did all of her fatigue, all her worries, and then all life, as Abigail felt herself drifting as if she were being carried up and away on a cloud in a dream.

Chapter 4

Confusion overwhelmed fear as the Inquisitor got to his feet and moved to see what could have fallen this…this…beast in the guise of a woman when cold steel seemed to have no effect on her. He cautiously approached the body and saw that a jagged slat of the window shutter had been thrust through her back in precisely the location where her heart would lie. Next to the body the last of his guard lay, breathing heavily and holding another of the wooden slats that had broken into jagged points.

"The wood pierced her heart and killed her instantly," the Inquisitor said aloud. The man was about to say a prayer when a scream from the crowd directed everyone's attention back to the building, which was now becoming engulfed in flames. A lone, large man stood in silhouette by the front door with both of his hands pressed into fists and trembling with rage at the site before him.

William had walked out of the building at the precise moment for him to witness in disembodied disbelief as the guard had struck down Abigail in the most cowardly manner he had ever beheld. As he walked over to where Abigail's body lay prone on the ground, the mob parted at his approach. William bent forward and wrenched the wood from the corpse then he put his large arms around her still form and hugged her fiercely.

Tears welled in his eyes as he roared a curse at the mob and then the Inquisitor.

"Cowards! Murderers of women and children! I will see you all burn in hell for this!" William turned to the Inquisitor, "And you!" He pointed his finger at the man. "You, I will send you to hell. Even if it means my own end I shall see you there tonight!"

The Inquisitor, now encouraged by the death of the woman, stood defiantly and held his silver crucifix before him.

"Heathen! Demon! Your words strike no fear in me, for I and all here do the Lord's work!"

William gently caressed Abigail's cheek and then set her limp form back on the ground. With a flash of movement, he closed the distance between himself and the Inquisitor, so quickly that the remaining guard didn't have time to flinch before William had the Spaniard by the throat.

The Inquisitor made gurgling, choking sounds as William squeezed with all the strength he could muster. The Inquisitor's face had just begun to turn a light shade of blue when the remaining guard came up behind William and struck him on the head with the window shutter. As William fell some of the mob regained its courage, several hands grabbed at William holding him fast in a kneeling position as the Inquisitor coughed while trying to get in as much air as he could.

The Inquisitor was screaming some prayer about heathens, heretics and demons as he touched the crucifix to William's forehead. At first, the gesture struck William as humorous, he was about to overwhelm those who were attempting to hold him down when a small flicker of orange light caused him to freeze. It was a small ember still ablaze with the remnants of flame from the inferno that had been his home. William watched the ember float on the wind and carry it straight toward his head. Realization flooded William's mind and he quickly accepted his fate as the ember landed lightly in his hair.

Hair that was still soaked with the turpentine and oil mixture.

William's hair and head ignited at the same moment the metal of the crucifix touched his forehead. The fire on top of William's head spread rapidly to his clothes, covering William in a deadly blanket of flame. The men restraining William let go immediately, but the Inquisitor was not as lucky as his own sleeve ignited before he could pull his arm away.

Panic now overwhelmed the mob and people began to scatter. Turning away from William, the Inquisitor desperately tried to douse the flames on his sleeve. It was a sight akin to a demon rising right out of hell to see William stand. His entire body had been saturated by the turpentine mixture and the flames instantaneously engulfed him, but William acted as if he didn't even notice. He grabbed the remaining guard, completely ignoring the fire that was burning him alive.

The Inquisitor had extinguished the flame on his sleeve in time to see the horror unfolding before him. William's skin blackened and sizzled, his eyes began to boil in their sockets but he held on, undaunted, as the guard's clothes ignited. William's face was no longer recognizable, his mouth was spread in an insane smile. With an effort derived from sheer will, anger and hatred William dove to the ground, taking the guard down with him.

The guard's fanciful uniform and other personal draperies became kindling, the man screamed as his clothes caught fire and the smell of his own burning flesh filled his nostrils. The Inquisitor could only watch, helpless as his charge and their quarry burned together in a deadly embrace, until the flesh of both men had completely blackened and smoldered. The guard began to convulse as William fell limply on top of him, still alight and burning. A few moments later the guard stopped thrashing and lay still along with the others who had died this evening.

The Inquisitor whispered a quick prayer underneath a hand raised to his nose, attempting to quell the nausea threatening to overwhelm him. Suddenly he realized he was completely alone. The mob had run off, leaving the dead strewn about the property. The only sound was that of the roaring fire still engulfing the house.

The Inquisitor hugged himself fiercely as he looked around nervously. He needed to return to the road that would take him to the docks where his ship was moored, a road that would take him directly past the place where he had left Alphonso's body, but arriving at the location, all he found was a small puddle of blood.

Fear grabbed hold of the Inquisitor as he desperately began to survey the grounds for any sign of tracks indicating whether someone had taken the body away or… Finding no telling sign of what might have happened, panic replaced fear and the Inquisitor broke into a run for the docks and his ship. He arrived with a face completely white from the fear and exertion, and yet he still managed to give the orders to launch for Spain immediately. When the Captain protested they hadn't had time to take on enough provisions for the journey home, the Inquisitor insisted he leave behind however many members of the crew that weren't necessary for an immediate departure. Reluctantly, the Captain complied and the Spanish galleon set sail for Spain.

Two days later the Spanish galleon passed less than one hundred yards from an isolated sandy beach near the cliffs of Dover. The blood drained bodies of the Inquisitor and the majority of the crew were all heaved over one side of the ship while a lone passenger dove into the water and swam toward the beach. The relieved crew immediately turned the ship for open sea and headed home.

When the ship finally made it back to Spain the remaining crew members were immediately taken into custody. All spoke of a stowaway who slaughtered and feasted on the blood of the officers and many deck hands, and had tortured the Inquisitor for nearly two full days before he let the man die. When asked for details about the stowaway, the terror in their words revealed superstition. Some spoke of a demon, others described a vampire, while several spoke of Lucifer himself. The one consistency among all of the descriptions, was that the stowaway was very tall with long, snowy white hair.

\

Part II: Stasis

Chapter 5

Los Angeles. The Sunset Strip. 11:23 P.M.

The night was cool, dry and pleasant. Another perfect evening in Southern California where a slow, steady breeze flowed in from the ocean pushing the day's automobile exhaust out of the LA basin and into the San Fernando Valley. The sulfurous cloud would rise like a phantom, waft over the hills, and take one final bite at the Earth's ozone layer, before it disappeared into the upper atmosphere.

The city was alive at this hour with neon and otherwise illuminating lights pulsing like a nervous system. Expensive cars acted like red blood cells carrying their cargo of people through arterial freeways toward their various organic destinations. As in any living body system, the city too had a core or "heart", the only difference being this city's heart could be found at a different location every six months or so.

The heart in this concrete and steel carcass would be whichever nightclub was "in" or the "place to be." Lines of people and limousines would extend for city blocks waiting for the opportunity for passage into its hallowed chambers. For the past eight months this centralized hot zone was *The Inferno*. The entrance was controlled religiously, with celebrities and high rollers given instant access. Single women who were dressed to impress, which really meant "stripper formal with loose morals", were scrutinized by the various bouncers, but also given immediate access. These were not absolute entrance requirements, rather they were the subjective perceptions of the four well-dressed and highly imposing men who blocked the passageway into this modern-day cathedral.

Unnoticed by most were two ferocious looking gentlemen, also serving as security for the club, at a rear entrance. Through this door another group of people gained access to the club. Enter here the drug dealers, high priced prostitutes and other vice peddlers who preyed upon the rich and privileged. This element was controlled and encouraged by the operators of *The Inferno*, even though the management vehemently denied the fact. The operators of the club understood they were in the business of entertainment and fulfillment and, as the patrons were slaves to their vices, it meant money to the club if the patrons were given access to their needs and desires.

The entire spectacle was the brainchild of Phillip Devereaux, a former concert promoter for some of the most successful musical groups of the nineties. Tired of the constant travel and the need to deal with the immature ravings of the addicts he pushed into superstardom, Phillip decided to use his exceptional talents at creating something based within his home city of Los Angeles. He already knew most of glamorous Hollywood, so LA seemed to be the right location for his enterprise. The biggest hurdle in the creation of his personal Eden was the extension of the life expectancy of the nightclub beyond the six-month to one-year limit, which was the norm within the nightclub industry.

The solution, Phillip knew, was balance.

Phillip believed *The Inferno* had to contain the high profile glitz of glamorous Hollywood, while making the low profile grime of Hollywood, available to the people who attended his establishment. The club crowd has always lived the "sex, drugs and rock and roll" lifestyle. Prohibition had its Speakeasy, the '70s had Studio 54, and the new millennium had *The Inferno*. By providing both the glamour and the grime, Phillip achieved a high gloss environment where the stars of the moment came to be seen, while he also was allowing the shadows of humanity to work their sticky fingers into those who had gained admittance. The main targets were the rich and the beautiful who wasted hundreds and thousands of dollars on a regular basis, lest they be considered "out" of the "in" crowd. This ostracism was as unacceptable a fate to the ego-laden socialites of Los Angeles as mortal sin was to the devout.

Despite an otherwise dreary exterior, *The Inferno* had an air about it, especially at night when the whole structure would vibrate from the thunderous booms of the sub-woofers inside. Heavy soundproofing kept all audible noise from spilling into the streets, despite the steady rhythmic pulsations that could be felt through the soles of your shoes. The outside revealed nothing of its lush interior, since the building was remodeled from a former office and storage facility near the center of the high rent district of Sunset Strip in West LA. The ceiling and walls of *The Inferno* were covered with multi-million dollar lighting and sound equipment that would be the envy of some of the greatest productions on Broadway or any concert venue. *The Inferno* had been gutted of all non-structural walls and columns, resulting in an enormous dance floor, with a spectacular ceiling four stories high. Extending from the south wall were enclosed balconies on the second and third story levels. The main floor was accessible to all who entered the club. The DJs, house dancers, roving security, and, especially the customers, all gyrated to a cacophony of music, sound, sight and sweat on this level.

There was also a basement level, uncreatively nicknamed "Hell" by those who knew of its existence. This area was accessible first by invitation, then by membership, to only the most hardcore of players. This below-ground realm was a club within a club, the dark side of not only *The Inferno*, but of human nature itself. The "members only" entry allowed a select group into this realm where they "enjoyed" the delights of all things fetishistic to carnal. All behavior, with the exception of violence, was tolerated. The rules were few and existed only to maintain the marginal legality of the club. This was a dangerous place, but not because of threat of physical injury. Phillip's Gestapo-like security took all the necessary precautions to protect the clientele. No, here the danger lurked for those who were ill-prepared for the vices available. These vulnerable souls were often tangled into webs that could not easily be unwound, not without a sojourn into some rehab at the very least.

Despite the risqué atmosphere of the basement, its existence was a little known secret. The entrance to Hell was located on the second story balcony above the main floor. Here was where the VIPs, celebrities and special invitees made their way and the unknowns and wannabes paraded themselves before those who had access to this second level, because invitation by a celebrity or VIP to this sacrosanct area would equivalent to, or at least be the start of, becoming a celebrity or VIP. High priced liquors, cigars and gourmet food were all served by professional waiters and waitresses. The entire floor was illuminated by candlelight from an immense number of candles giving the space a regal feel. The privileged sat in leather and velvet loungers, viewing the action below from the darkened balconies, as each was deciding the right moment to "descend into Hell." Once ready for their descent, they would gain access to a spiral staircase that led down past the main area and into the earth.

"Abandon all hope, ye who enter here" ala Dante's Inferno.

The one constant within all of these levels was the connection to the sound systems and lighting. True, candles illuminated the second level, however the lights of the main room could be seen and the sounds felt, by those on the second level. This was done for a variety of reasons. First, to keep the uniformity of the music and lighting, lest they otherwise clash, and second, to allow all levels to act in unison should any emergency occur. Fire was the greatest threat to any club, and therefore, if one area were compromised, the activation of an emergency switch would cripple the noise and lights for all three levels, enabling everyone to reach safety within a short time-frame. Even the restrooms were "plugged in" adding a sense of continuity to the call of nature. Phillip loved this feature of his club. Although it was done for the same safety reasons, he often joked of urinating by strobe lights.

The third story balcony held the offices, where Phillip Devereaux sat tonight, as he did every night. His desk was made from black granite and was almost invisible in the darkened room.

Working in the relative darkness kept the crowd below from seeing through the one-way glass, which enclosed the third floor balcony like box seats at a football stadium. The only illumination came from the black and white security monitors on the far side of the room and the computer monitor mounted on the left side of the black granite desk. Sharing the space with Phillip were two security guards who kept a constant watch over the monitors, and therefore over the entire inner workings of the nightclub.

Phillip sat with his back to the glass walls as he studied the accounts, computing the profits and losses for the club through the current date. The club was ten months old at this point, and the profits continued to increase and surpass each previous month. This was extremely encouraging. Most nightclubs began to plateau, and experience a drop in their profitability by the sixth or seventh month in existence, due to another more grandiose club opening. *The Inferno* had set the bar so high that nothing short of a Las Vegas mega resort could hope to topple it. This was the goal Phillip had set for the club, and it seemed to be working.

Breathing a sigh of relief and pride with regard to the final numbers, Phillip sat back in his leather office chair. He loosened a button on his black silk shirt and spun toward the one way glass for a look down into the crowd below. Stretching his arms out, he gazed down and locked his eyes on a young woman who danced in a powerful undulating fashion on the main floor. She was wearing a fluorescent green, one-piece spandex mini-dress that gripped her body like a second skin. The dress was so short that each time she raised her hands above her head the dress would hike up over her body and reveal her naked hips and pelvis. Feigning embarrassment, she would slowly pull down the fabric, which glowed brightly in the black lights. Then she would "adjust" her perfectly out of proportion, surgically-enhanced breasts. Phillip watched as she giggled slightly while dropping her head to one side and looking up into the eyes of her gawking audience.

Her flamboyance was quickly making her the center of

attention on the main floor. Phillip had noticed her earlier when he had arrived at the club, and made a mental note to congratulate the front door security for covertly getting her into the club in spite of her "under the legal limit" age. He could almost hear the cash registers "chi-chinging" all of the money being spent by her would-be suitors buying highly overpriced champagne, in an attempt to get into her missing panties.

He chuckled to himself as he stood up from the desk and stretched his legs. Smoothing out his linen pants, he walked away from the window toward the one quiet room in the entire building , his own little spot of contemplation away from all external noise came in the form of a private executive restroom. This room was the one area in the whole building not subject to the music and lights of the club.

* * *

Outside on the street the line to get into the club extended two blocks down Sunset Boulevard. Eric Sims had been the head bouncer for *The Inferno* since it opened ten months ago. He was the one responsible for making the decisions regarding who gained admittance, and how much money it would take to change a rejection into an approval. Eric pocketed the money a group of eight women had slipped him as they entered the club, replaced the velvet crowd-control cord on the pedestal, and looked out among the crowd to inspect the next customers in line. A familiar face replaced the spot in line where the last of the women had stood. Although familiar, the face immediately sent tangible rage and frustration into his core.

"Awe no, not you again!" Eric managed in a frustrated laugh.

The lanky figure standing in front of him was smiling and, as opposed to the shy and nervous disposition displayed on previous nights, seemed unnervingly confident.

"Listen man," Eric said in an exasperated tone to the figure in front of him, "don't make us throw your ass off the property again. Your money's no good here so let's not make a scene, all right?"

The figure behind the velvet rope was a spindly fellow. His skin was extremely pale as if he had been indoors too long. Actually, it appeared as though he had been locked in a dark room too long. Way too long. Running his hands through his greasy, unkempt black hair, the man closed his eyes and inhaled deeply, as if savoring the air as it filled his lungs. Reaching into a pocket of an oversized denim jacket he removed a metallic object that reflected in the lights of the club. Thinking it was a weapon, Eric was just about to call out a warning for the other bouncers and rush the man when he realized the object was a small digital camera.

Breathing a sigh of relief Eric said, "What's this? Candid Camera?"

Slowly, methodically, the man raised the camera up to his right eye. Then, in a voice far deeper than would be expected for such a frail man, he said…almost hissing…

"Smile…."

It was at this point that the whole world went insane.

* * *

Phillip washed his face in the marble sink at the far end of the restroom. He relished the feeling of the cool water running over his face, which never failed to revitalize him in the early hours of the morning. He patted his face and hands dry with the expensive terry cloth towels embroidered with his initials in gold thread. Strange to love a restroom he thought, but he did love it. It was his sanctuary after all and he loathed leaving it, but there was work to be done. He had to make an appearance and 'case' the joint. Pressing the flesh is paramount to the success of any business, and this club was no exception.

Turning the doorknob, he took in one last moment of quiet before exiting the washroom and re-entering his office. As he surveyed sparkling sinks and other décor of the washroom, he caught the briefest shimmering of white light from the corner of his eye. It was in his peripheral vision where he perceived a distorted flickering of shadows as if someone had turned on an overpowered strobe light. Following the pulsation, or whatever it was, Phillip felt momentarily dizzy, as if getting a head rush from a rollercoaster. The feeling passed almost as quickly as it had come over him. The moment Phillip opened the door the peaceful serenity of this sanctuary restroom was stripped away as the pumping bass of the music rushed in with its dissonant sound. Moving over to his desk, Phillip opened a small office refrigerator, removed and popped the top off one bottle of Blackened Voodoo beer. The small New Orleans brew was his favorite, and the one thing he treated himself to on a nightly basis. The public could wait. He was feeling good and he felt he had earned this moment of relaxation. Lifting the beer to his lips Phillip anticipated the fizz, foam and flavor of his beer when the club fell completely and hauntingly silent.

Phillip paused, the beer millimeters from his lips, and he looked up in wide-eyed confusion. Putting his beer onto the desk, Phillip dashed to the window overlooking the club, and gasped.

The partygoers, all of whom were dancing and cavorting as usual mere seconds ago, were now strewn across the dance floors in every manner of disarray. Some lay as if dead, others were quivering as though in the middle of some sort of seizure.

"What the hell?" Fear was quickly turning Phillip's spine into jelly, but his mind went into action.

"Figure out the cause and react to control the situation." This was a mantra Phillip used in times when he had to keep his wits about him. It had always helped him concentrate in order to make the best of any bad situation.

"Actually," he thought, as reality came crashing in, "the first thing I should do is get the hell out of here."

This wasn't the first time the unexpected or unbelievable happened in Phillip's career. Of course, he never envisioned anything like this. Who could ever expect anything like this? He turned to leave and nearly fell over the two security guards who were previously watching the scene on the main floor. The two men were lying on their backs with their eyes open. One was drooling from a corner of his mouth and the other had fouled himself. The odor was beginning to seep through the office making the bile in Phillip's stomach rise into his throat.

Turning away from the bodies, Phillip raced to the exit from his office to the first floor. As he ran down the stairs and through the doors the stench of sweat, urine and feces slammed into his nostrils like a slap across the face. He practically reeled backwards, but regained his composure and pressed forward.

Stepping over bodies he raised the lapel of his shirt over his nose in an attempt to block out some of the smell. The scene was the same downstairs as in his office. People were lying on the floor, most had fouled themselves in some fashion and all had their eyes open and fixed on some faraway place.

Transfixed by the sea of bodies, Phillip forced himself to scramble through the club moving, forward to the exit. His current position gave him a clear view of the soundstage where the DJ had evidently collapsed over his equipment. This, Phillip thought, was most likely the cause of the music system shorting out while leaving the club lighting intact. The animated lights still circled in kaleidoscopic patterns around the walls and floors. The black lights still illuminated bright colors in an electric fashion, as if the music was still playing and nothing out of the ordinary had happened.

Phillip pressed the lapel of his shirt tighter across his face as the smell was becoming almost palpable. He continued to hurry across the floor to the exit. The doors were only about fifty feet away at this point and Phillip was desperate for a lungful of clean night air, free of the fetid stink enveloping his Eden. He moved faster toward the exit doors. Only thirty feet or so now before he was free of the one place in the world he had, only moments before, felt most liberated and at home. The irony was not lost on him. He felt the crushing pang of sorrow and regret as he moved, his drive to escape overwhelming his sentimentality.

Suddenly, not ten feet from the exit doors, he noticed a familiar green glow to one side of the dance floor. He froze in place, then slowly turned toward the glow as all thought had left his conscious mind. Phillip lowered his hand from his face allowing the lapel of his shirt to dangle loosely to one side of his chest. As he moved away from the exit doors and headed toward the bright electric green glow on the floor he didn't notice the smell anymore. His subconscious mind quickly erupted in fear, urging him to turn around and flee the scene, yet something drove him forward to that green glow on the floor.

He stared…at her.

It was the young woman he had seen from his office window in the fluorescent green spandex mini-dress. She didn't look so alluring anymore. He was embarrassed at himself for having looked at her the way he had before. She looked so young now as she lay prone across another woman. He didn't see her breasts anymore, or her body, or her dress. No, now all he could see was a little girl who had been the victim of some undetermined accident.

Unable to restrain himself, Phillip knelt down and placed two fingers to her neck. He felt a very slow and shallow, but steady pulse. She was alive! He quickly stood up and glanced over all the people in the club. They were all alive! He was sure of it.

The need to get help for all of these poor people sent him into motion. He stood, intending to sprint for the exit, and turned head on into another man who had been standing quietly behind him. The man was frail, but not short, and had a camera in his hands. Placing his index finger to his lips as if to "shush" him, the man turned from Phillip and glared down at the girl in the green mini-dress. Raising the camera up to his eye he began to take pictures of the girl like a photographer on a fashion shoot. Uncomfortable and confused, Phillip looked back down at the girl. Each flash exposed her flesh as her dress, which was not made to truly cover any of the more private areas of her body in the first place, completely revealed her to the man's camera lens.

Rage welled up in Phillip. He lunged for the man grabbing his shoulder and spinning him around. The force of the spin practically sent the frail man into the air, but Phillip caught him before he could fall away.

"What the hell do you think you are doing?" Phillip screamed into the man's face.

The man showed no fear. Only mild amusement flickered in his eyes.

"Now, where were you when the lights went out...or in this case, on?" the man chided in a deep guttural voice.

"Who the fuck...."

Phillip's words caught in his throat as he frowned at the man, searching a face which he now felt he should recognize. The man looked somehow familiar, but he couldn't place him.

Unseen by Phillip, the man slipped his index finger over a small button on his camera switching the setting from "flash" to "red eye reduction."

"I know you, don't I?" Phillip stammered.

"Not really," the man returned in that too-deep-for-his-frail-appearance voice. The inflection in those two words made him sound cocky and confident.

Nothing made sense but somehow Phillip's knees, which had been weak from fear the moment the sound turned off, were suddenly bolstered with strength born of anger and adrenaline.

"Are you responsible for this you bastard!?!"

"You want to know what happened?" the man calmly responded.

"What have you done!?!"

After a brief, yet incredibly uncomfortable pause the man said in a frighteningly deep hiss: "You'll never know."

"What...?" Suddenly fear returned full force along with confusion as the man raised the camera up and into Phillip's face. "What the hell are you doing?"

"Nothing…Smile." The deep voice sang the word out in the same manner a grandmother would while taking pictures of her grandkids. The man quivered with what seemed to be orgasmic delight as the red eye reduction strobe illuminated Phillip's face.

Phillip saw the strobe and began to speak when he suddenly realized he couldn't get any words out. He tried to protectively raise his arms, but his muscles failed him and they fell slack to his sides. He began to feel himself lose his balance, he couldn't use his legs to catch himself as he began to drop. As he fell he was still able to control his eyes enough to look at the man who stood before him. He had lowered the camera from his face and was smiling with an ugly, wide-toothed grin. Phillip's mind raced. All thoughts, words, memories, emotions flashed through his consciousness with such speed he couldn't register or comprehend anything. His vision began to blur and fade to dark, with the last sight he would ever see being that of the lanky figure with the wide-toothed grin.

Chapter 6

Los Angeles. 2:30 A.M.

California weather never fails to disappoint in its ability to be spontaneous. The cool, dry night had developed into an unseasonable downpour three minutes earlier. By the time Steve Jacobs arrived on the scene at *The Inferno* the rain had stopped, leaving a clean but humid feeling to the surrounding area. Steve was not the first investigator from the LAPD to arrive. He may have, in fact, been the very last, as the immediate surroundings were now at least two cars deep in rows of flashing red and blue siren lights. The accumulation of ambulances along with marked and unmarked police cars forced Steve to park his old (or as he liked to say "unpretentious") Toyota Celica half a block away. At least this way he didn't have to worry about any of the city vehicles scraping its faded but still good looking paint job.

Steve parked in an alleyway perfumed by the garlicky smell of the Korean restaurant, whose back door was left open to the alley, not as an entrance for customers as much as a reprieve from the heat of the kitchen for the staff. Above the door a yellow electric sign cast a sulfurous glow.

Steve ran his fingers through his wavy dark brown hair, which hadn't been combed since he got out of bed half an hour ago. He had received the call a couple of minutes before 2:00 A.M. and was shocked that the Captain had called him personally. Despite enjoying a close, and more often than not supportive relationship with his superior, he knew the Captain had other experienced detectives who he communicated with in a more official manner. It was the strain and unease in the Captain's voice that concerned Steve, and which preempted any of his questions about the call. Without a second thought, he raced to the scene from his home, arriving at *The Inferno* on the Sunset in a record 30 minutes.

Exiting his car, Steve did a quick inventory of the detective gear he had so rapidly pushed into his pockets, before rushing out the door. His firearm was now securely settled into its holster and attached to the side of his belt with his gold detective's badge clipped to the front so he wouldn't have to constantly retrieve it from his pocket, as every uniformed officer would try to block the entrance to the crime scene. Not that he would blame them of course, since he was dressed in the very civilian looking apparel so common to most Los Angelinos, including denim pants, brown hiking boots, and a T-shirt inscribed with the artistic renderings of the tribal tattoo patterns popular in today's slacker-style fashionistas. He felt the small Steno notepad in the right rear pocket of his pants, along with the small mechanical pencil he knew he would need to make notes, on whatever important information he might come across.

It was only when his left hand grazed the hard rectangular object in his rear left pocket that he hesitated. The flask held slightly less than eight ounces of fluid, but it would be enough to get him through the evening in case his hands started shaking and he needed to calm his body in front of another bloody spectacle. Steve knew that in the years since he had joined the force his constitution had improved somewhat, in the face of the gruesome and senseless violence committed on a regular basis in the city. Still, whipping out a flask, while on duty, made his fellow officers uncomfortable. It wasn't as though they didn't understand. God knows they all needed some alcohol after witnessing the aftermath of the carnage the city seemed so eager to produce. It was Steve's blatant disregard for discretion that actually made them so ill at ease. Most of the policemen knew, or at least had heard about Steve's needs, and were sympathetic enough to allow him this one major breech of protocol, as long as he didn't get sloppy of course.

Steve never got sloppy, or drunk, or even tired when he was doing his job.

Ever.

Steve looked from the alley to the cascade of flashing lights less than one hundred yards away, nodded and pulled the flask from his pocket. He unscrewed the top and sniffed the contents,

43

which sent a shiver throughout his entire frame. One swallow would be all he needed, and as the spiked concoction burned its way down his throat he felt his whole body release the tension that had been building since he had been summoned from his bed over half an hour ago.

He replaced the top of the flask, shoving it back into his pocket and then engaged the car's alarm while walking toward the commotion of red and blue flashing lights. Uniformed policemen circled the outskirts of a ring of paramedics who seemed to be continually wheeling bodies out of the club and placing them into a row near multiple ambulances. The entire area was sectioned off with the yellow plastic "Police Line, Do Not Cross" ribbon, while detectives and forensic specialists mulled over the victims and the surroundings at the entrance to the club.

The closer Steve approached the more he began to detect an odor getting seemingly stronger. The odor was mild, but reminded him of his childhood visits to the zoo, specifically, his visits to the elephant enclosures. He stopped momentarily to allow his badge to be identified by the uniformed officers, who quickly let him pass under the police tape. He made his way toward the entrance to the club. As he passed through the castle-like double doors he froze in his tracks, as the full weight of the scene came crashing down on him from his first clear view of the club's ballroom.

The special effects lights had been switched off and the general fluorescent lights switched on. Under normal lighting the mystique of the club vanished, leaving something akin to a school gymnasium with wet bars. Bodies turned the scene into a surreal war zone. Most of the people had been moved onto makeshift triage cots, while others had been neatly aligned in side-by-side rows, with attending medical personnel hovering over a few individuals. Clearly the number of victims was more than the current number of medical professionals could handle.

"My God," he thought. "What the hell could have happened here?" Unconsciously Steve began to reach for the flask in his rear pocket, but caught himself as a voice called out to him.

"Hey, Steve!"

Steve knew the voice. It belonged to Chris Barnes, a longtime friend who worked for the LA County Coroner's office.

"Chris," Steve said warmly as the two slapped hands together in a familiar handshake. "What, they've got you out working nights now?"

"Nope, still on days, but Peterson's got the flu so I'm pulling a double for the next few days…and nights."

"I hate to say it, but you may be pulling a triple from the looks of things," Steve said while scanning the area.

"What'cha mean?" Chris laughed with a frown of confusion.

Steve looked at Chris, now confused as well by the response his statement had received.

"Well, with all of these bodies, you and your crew are going to have your hands full."

"What?!? They better not expect me to…" Chris paused, "Oh, you don't know? Did you just get here?"

Concerned, Steve acknowledged, "Just now and no I haven't a clue what's going on."

"Oh, well let me tell you. None of these poor souls will be meeting me in the basement anytime soon."

The "basement" Steve knew was Chris' nickname for the Coroner's personal office and autopsy, where he spent most of his working hours. Steve could tell by the excitement in Chris' eyes that something extraordinary was going on. Chris wanted him to ask. He seemed almost giddy with the knowledge that he was privy to information Steve didn't have yet. Steve played along. He always liked Chris' sense of humor and the two of them were fast friends. Steve often thought that spending all day and night with the dead made Chris…well…eccentric would be the polite way to put it. Chris seemed to stop breathing, in anticipation of the question he knew Steve would ask, and he appeared hardly able to contain himself.

Steve let the silence drift a moment longer, wondering briefly if Chris was really holding his breath, and if so, would he soon turn blue. Finally he relented and guessed, "None of these poor souls will be seeing you because...they're dead and can't see?" Steve thought this might have been the punch line Chris was looking for.

"No!" Chris said abruptly, "and frankly I am shocked... SHOCKED... that you would say something so cold and callous in relation to these poor people," Chris blurted with what Steve was almost certain was mock indignation. He then turned his back to Steve and stared at the ceiling in a pose of maximum offense.

Taking in a deep breath Steve tried to calm himself.

"Okay! You're right, I should be more sensitive. I'm sorry." Steve gave in with a slightly mocking apology.

"And you should be. Stealing one of my best dead person punch-lines is tantamount to a stoning offense, amongst us ghouls." Turning back to Steve with a smile on his face, Chris continued, "They won't be seeing me because they are NOT dead."

Stunned and wide-eyed, Steve spun to the multiple supine figures, looking again at their apparently lifeless bodies strewn all over the floor of the club.

"None?" Steve stammered, feeling a little guilty for not being more uplifted by the news of the lack of death in the room.

"Not a one. As far as I can tell they all seem to be physically fine with strong vital signs and no apparent trauma."

"Then what?"

"Can't say as I know, but the Captain and Commissioner are trying to keep a lid on the whole thing. You may have noticed the lack of the press and paparazzi."

Steve nodded, too dumbfounded to speak.

"Anyway, I was pretty much dismissed as soon as I arrived. After all, there's no need for a coroner when there are no dead bodies. I was on my way home when I ran into a paramedic friend of mine and decided to hang around and help out. I guess curiosity got the better of me."

"I can certainly understand why."

"No kidding. Well, my friend left me alone with one of the victims long enough for me to do a basic vitals exam."

"And?"

"And if all of the victims here are in the same condition as the one I examined, then we have some rather diabolical happenings going on."

Steve's breathing was getting faster, "Well! Don't keep me hanging! What...." Steve broke off in mid-sentence, "did the Captain dismiss you?"

"Yeah, why?"

"Then you'd better go. The Captain is making a bee-line right for me and considering the history between you two...."

"Oh man, I am so gone." Without another word Chris turned on his heels and walked off in the opposite direction from the on-coming Captain.

Calling after him, "We'll talk tomorrow, all right?"

Chris waved the back of his hand at Steve without turning around.

"Jacobs." The Captain addressed everyone by his or her last name.

"Captain." Steve returned the greeting.

"Was that Barnes you were talking to? I sent him home half an hour ago. What's that weirdo still doing here?"

"Yes sir, but you know those guys from the basement have to be a bit off in order to do what they do."

Steve watched the Captain as he stared off into the direction Chris had gone. The Captain was medium, just medium. Medium height, medium weight, medium build and coming from a Mediterranean background, he looked more like an Italian mobster than the half-Greek, half-Portuguese all cop, man he was raised into by his parents. He hunched over slightly when he walked, even though he had no physical impairment.

The rain continued to fall, but had subsided into something more like a mist than the previous downpour, and the Captain ignored it completely as he stood seemingly mesmerized by the night. A couple of times Steve averted his eyes from the Captain to scan the area, only to look back at him in confusion.

"Sir?"

After a few more awkward moments of silence the Captain finally spoke in a shaky, broken whisper. "Have you ever felt Jacobs, that when you stare into the darkness... I mean... is it possible on any level... that the dark is staring back at you. I don't mean someone in the dark watching from the shadows. I mean the dark itself."

The Captain's words had an eerie seriousness to them and completely out of character for this hard-edged, tough-as-nails veteran of the homicide division. The Captain had seen more than his share of incomprehensible violence, gore and subsequent death to the point that he had become sufficiently numb to such things. He wasn't being cryptic with his question and Steve knew that something, perhaps something inside the club, had spooked him. He had seen it happen only once before, and the Captain had philosophically questioned Nietzsche's aphorisms on that occasion as well.

"No sir, not really, I always seem to find someone or something tangible when I look for it." Steve continued, "In all the cases I've closed and all of the many more you have closed, haven't you always found that there tends to be an unremarkable, albeit often disturbing, resolution."

The Captain waited a few moments, considering Steve's words.

"I used to believe the same as you." He sighed deeply and shook his head, almost as if in resolution to some forgone conclusion.

Steve was perplexed. He knew the Captain was a man of facts. Theory had its place in police work, but the reality of the work was the dredging up of tangible evidence against individuals who had committed crimes. No jury could convict on speculation, theory or informed guesses.

"I'm not...what exactly are we talking about, sir?"

"I guess what I am trying to say to you Jacobs, is that despite my better judgment and experience, despite everything I have been through…"

The Captain drifted off as if lost in a daydream. Steve shifted uncomfortably, waiting for the Captain to finish his thought. Blinking rapidly the Captain shook himself out of the daydream. Turning quickly he put his arm around Steve's shoulders as he led him toward the club entrance.

"Has anyone briefed you on what happened inside?"

"I have no details other than the fact that everyone is still alive."

"Well, they seem to be catatonic, whatever that means. All their vital signs are stable and strong with no signs of any injury, except for some bumps and bruises in those areas where they hit the floor."

"Hit the floor?"

"Whatever happened here happened so fast that no one had time to react. There are no signs of panic, struggle or violence. It's as if they were all plugged into a light socket and someone simply turned the switch to off, and they fell where they stood."

The description the Captain relayed was beginning to weigh on Steve.

"Who called this in?"

"A couple waiting outside the club said a fight broke out in line and the bouncers locked the doors to keep the skirmish from filtering into the club. The couple had friends inside and called the police. A black and white responded. Locking the doors of the club is an extreme violation of the fire laws and one that most clubs wouldn't risk, so the officer decided to check it out. Eventually he forced the doors open and found everyone inside to be in their current state."

A long moment passed before Steve spoke.

"Everyone?" was all he could manage.

"Not a single person inside isn't in this condition. Everyone!"

"Damn," Steve sighed under his breath.

"The Feds have got wind of it and want the whole area contained. It seems they are all afraid of something."

"Something?" Steve repeated questioningly.

The Captain looked at Steve with the direst of expressions.

"Something, maybe biological."

Steve's breath caught in his throat. There it was, laid out in plain words with more underlying meaning than could ever be spoken out loud. Terrorism. Insanity. Chaos. A hot zone of biological weaponry. All things which were out of his control and that should have been affecting him right now as he inhaled the night air. Like an unbidden thought intruding on his anticipation of impending doom, a wave of doubt entered his mind. He embraced the steadily growing doubt.

Pressing, the Captain asked, "Could they be right? About the biological stuff?"

"I'm no scientist or expert so I don't really know, but...I mean... if it were what they're supposedly afraid of, wouldn't we all have dropped by now?"

Steve smiled to himself as the Captain had eloquently stated the exact doubt having entered his mind a moment ago.

"Has anyone else who arrived after the initial incident collapsed?"

"Nope, not even the officer who forced the doors earlier. Honestly, this feels more like some kind of federal spin factor, as opposed to any continual danger."

The two crossed the threshold of the club. Steve caught his breath as he saw the sheer number of alive, yet inanimate, victims strewn throughout the interior of the nightclub. The smell was worse than the dumpster of rotting Chinese food he had parked next to earlier. More accurately it smelled like a morgue without proper ventilation. Steve had to constantly remind himself that the victims in this situation, despite all appearances to the contrary, were actually alive.

"How many?" Steve asked as the two began to step over bodies while crossing the dance floor.

"Nearly one thousand and well over the capacity set by the Fire Department. About three quarters of them were on this level, the rest are spread out among the second floor, the kitchen, and the basement. Don't even get me started about the kind of disarray the people in the basement were in—looked like a cross between Sodom and Gomorrah meets the Hefner mansion. Oh, and there were the odd few in the restrooms and offices on the third floor."

"Have the owners been notified? Can they shed any light?"

"One owner, no silent partners and he's...." The Captain stopped, turned to look down at a group of bodies, spun around to another set across the room, then glanced ahead of where they were walking. "Over there, in that group of poor souls. He's Phillip Devereaux, former concert promoter to the stars turned nefarious nightclub owner.

"I knew him," Steve said. "Because he would call me when he wanted some undesirables to stop darkening his doorstep."

The Captain seemed taken aback not only by the revelation, but by the candor with which Steve spoke. He grasped Steve's arm and halted him in his tracks.

"You knew him officially or unofficially?" the Captain asked with a seriousness that might have turned anyone to stone who was unfamiliar with his intensity.

"Officially," Steve grunted his reply while returning an indignant glare back at his superior. The response was, perhaps, a bit too aggressive, however, Steve knew his record while on the force was beyond reproach. The Captain knew it as well, which was probably the reason the insubordinate tone was overlooked as the Captain released his arm.

"Of course." The Captain actually looked abashed. "Of course, it was official. Look who I'm talking to, after all."

Anxious to change the subject Steve postulated, "It may be a stupid question, but does this have to be something sinister? I mean, could this have been an accident, like a broken gas pipe or something?"

"No. Gas, carbon monoxide or any toxic fumes have other symptoms, manifestations and ultimately will end in death. This bizarre comatose catatonia, or whatever it is, is just plain weird."

The two stood in place and watched as paramedics from all over the city examined the sea of humanity, noting each victim's health status and identification. It was all so repetitive that Steve began to feel overwhelmed.

Finally, his head seemed to crest the pinnacle of the scene, and he fell squarely into his detective mode.

"Why isn't anyone being taken to the hospital?"

"Rule number one in Federal containment: 'Don't spread the contamination beyond the hot zone.' The Feds say they're shipping doctors and equipment here, and instructed us to set up a basic triage area, for when their docs arrive.

Steve nodded. It would have been a sound strategy if it were some sort of biological outbreak or attack, yet Steve felt almost certain that it wasn't.

"All right, let's say this was a deliberate act. What is the motive? Why would anyone do this?"

The Captain's face turned instantly from its melancholy muse into a challenging grin, as he slid comfortably into the professorial mode Steve knew so very well.

"What reason can you think of Detective?"

This was a type of game they played. Actually, it was a very effective way of sorting through the mountains of information, in order to come up with some working theories, but the two of them had turned it into an exercise long ago. Steve closed his eyes and took in a deep breath of foul air. His mind raced through the possibilities, motives, rationales, until finally he found what he felt to be the most likely answers.

"Terrorism, revenge, or ransom, I believe the most likely of the three would be ransom."

"Ransom??!" Apparently the Captain hadn't thought of that one. He had nodded along with the first two suggestions and looked eager for an explanation regarding the third.

"Terrorists would have a new way to affect the well-being of huge groups of people. This technique would eliminate the need for primitive car bombings, however, where there is life there is hope. Terrorist goals involve the taking away of hope to replace it with fear. The otherwise apparent well-being of the victims makes this an ineffective vehicle for terrorists."

The Captain nodded absently with the explanation.

Steve continued, "Revenge kind of makes sense except the act is too general with too many unrelated people involved."

"What about revenge against the club or its owners?" The Captain interjected.

Steve could tell the Captain was testing him.

"A direct shot at the club through arson or demolition could have been accomplished when the club was empty, thereby, not endangering such a large number of people. This wasn't an attack against the revenue production of the owners. This was an attack directly on the people who work and frequent the club. In fact, I get the impression that the person or persons responsible for this wanted the club intact, maybe to move in and pick up the pieces now that the owners are incapacitated."

"As in a hostile takeover of a sort?" the Captain sounded doubtful.

"Yeah, I think that sounds a little far-fetched too."

"Okay, so what about the "ransom" theory?"

"Well, let's suppose someone did loose a biological agent in here. It dispersed quickly or broke down into something harmless in seconds after its release, but was in a viable state long enough to knock everyone into a catatonic state."

"Go on." The Captain began to look intrigued.

"Well, if this is something new, like an anesthetic or something, maybe whoever developed it has some kind of reversal agent."

"Reversal agent?"

"I know that may be an overdramatic term, but you understand what I mean."

"So you think the doctors won't be able to revive these

people?"

"No. I don't see this case coming to such an easy ending."

"But you do think we will ultimately hear from someone who will provide the antidote for a price?"

A moment passed as Steve seemed to think about his answer.

"Yes, that is pretty much what I think is going to happen. The thought of over 1,000 people being held hostage inside their own bodies would make a lot of friends and relatives very adamant about the city paying whatever it takes to get the antidote. Whoever did this wants something so they left everyone alive. Why do that? Why go to all the effort of doing this without any benefit to yourself?"

"Maybe they did it for the thrill?"

"No, I think there was a method to their madness. Look who was in the club. Celebrities, yuppies and well-to-do people in general are here nightly. Even if there were no direct target, any given night would have delivered famous and affluent patrons. These are people who have the means to buy their way out of a predicament faster than we can figure it out."

The look of interest dissolved from the Captain's face, replaced by a look of concern.

"Jesus. We have to make sure we keep a lid on this. If word gets out that this whole thing is about money then whoever did this will probably get privately paid off and be inspired to repeat himself."

A whole new weight seemed to drop squarely on the Captain's shoulders. He forced himself to scan the club. Steve thought he was trying to get a feel for the sheer size of the situation when he saw the Captain's face turn to intense rage.

"You!" he screamed as he launched himself forward, vaulting over catatonic club goers.

As he ran, the Captain pointed at a paramedic across the dance floor from where he and Steve had been standing. Steve erupted into motion as well, although for the moment he wasn't sure why.

When the paramedic saw the Captain charging at him his eyes

bulged in fright and he began to move quickly toward one of the rear exits.

"Officers, stop that man! Bring him down now!" the Captain bellowed.

The few uniformed officers who had been standing near the dance floor hesitated slightly before springing into action. The medic tried to run as the officers closed in around him.

Steve made a break to the right in order to cut off a potential escape route. He still didn't know what was going on, but he trusted the Captain's instincts. It was then that he saw the medic was holding something small and metallic in his closed right hand.

Steve was about to yell "gun" when an officer dove for the medic, reaching for his ankles, missed by centimeters and came crashing down on the hardwood dance floor. The medic's face resembled the mask of a trapped animal knowing it was about to get caught. Without warning, and with considerable effort, the medic threw the metallic object against the nearest wall. The object cracked into the wall and broke into a few large pieces.

"I guess it wasn't a gun," Steve thought.

Two officers tackled the medic with brute force, taking him to the ground. The rest of the uniformed officers swarmed on top of the three men on the ground as Steve slowed to a walk and stopped just outside of the violent dog pile of men. He turned on his heel and walked over to the area where the metallic object had been thrown.

The Captain stormed angrily over to the medic who had been seriously roughed up in a matter of seconds by multiple officers who already had him in handcuffs and back on his feet.

"Who were you talking to?!" the Captain roared.

The question surprised Steve. He never heard the medic say a word. Then he looked down at the large metallic pieces that lay in close proximity by his feet and understood.

There were about five pieces of what used to be a cellular phone. Steve collected the pieces and walked back over to where the Captain was hollering at the medic.

"I said, who were you talking to?"

Terror filled the eyes of the medic who looked as if at any moment he might start to cry. The Captain had that effect on people when he wanted.

"No one! I swear!" the man begged.

"Listen asshole, this isn't second grade and the 'I don't know' answers aren't going to fly. I saw you with the cell phone to your ear and I saw you talking into it. This area has been sealed off with no information to leave the scene!" The Captain ripped the I.D. badge off of the lapel of the medic's white paramedic shirt.

"Josh," he read. "Okay Josh, right now your job with Mercy Ambulances, whose people I know always respect crime scenes and the need for confidentiality, is over. Now if you don't want to be brought up on charges I want to know who you were talking to and I want to know now!"

Before Josh could answer the Captain heard a sound behind him.

"Bleep-boop."

Turning, he saw Steve handing over to him a reassembled cell phone. The sound was the cell phone powering up.

"No cell phone I ever owned could have survived that. Mine seem to be permanently damaged if they fall out of my pocket." Smiling, the Captain accepted the phone from Steve.

"The display screen is broken, but I have a friend who owns this model phone. Hit the menu button, then the down arrow twice, then press "OK" and hit send."

The Captain did as he was instructed. "What am I doing?"

"Redialing the last number," Steve said with a grin. "Would you mind also hitting the speaker phone button on the bottom right of the keypad?"

"Wait! That's my phone! Don't you need a warrant or something?" The medic protested vehemently as he was systematically wrestled to the ground again by the multiple hands holding onto him.

Those still standing leaned in, attempting to hear as the line connected and began to ring. Before the third ring the line was answered by a voicemail system.

"You have reached the *Los Angeles Times* Crime Reporting Division. If you know the extension of your party, please enter it now."

A collective groan escaped from everyone in earshot of the cell phone.

Chapter 7

"I do not take kindly to this lack of cooperation with law enforcement. Let me give you some forewarning. If your paper releases anything before I give the go-ahead, I can assure you that any previous privileges your company has enjoyed in the past will disappear. I don't care how important you think this story is or how important your editor is supposed to be!"

The Captain slammed his folding cell phone shut reminding Steve how he probably would have slammed the receiver down on his office phone into its cradle if they were back at the precinct.

"Well, some disease control or biological agent type crew is en route. The *Times* is threatening to run the story as some kind of biological terrorist attack unless the LAPD makes a claim to the contrary. This is the kind of thing that puts me in a position to get bitten however I move."

The Captain was hot, really steaming and twice as animated. Steve wanted to get into the game, but was unsure how the Captain wanted to proceed.

"Where do you want me on this Cap?"

The Captain had been pacing furiously across a fifteen-foot expanse of dance floor, stopping short with Steve's use of "Cap."

He glared at Steve for a moment, then looked away, shook his head and chuckled as if responding to a personal joke.

"I want you out of here," the Captain said when he finally spoke to Steve. "I want you to start building the case with that useless grave robber friend of yours."

Steve started to protest involving Chris in the case. Although the two had been friends for years, and there was no one Steve trusted more, he also knew Chris could, at times, be so eccentric it would become downright unnerving. Besides, it felt like he was being sent away from the crime scene and, after all, there was a huge amount of information still waiting to be collected from the surrounding area. Before any words of protest passed his lips,

Steve felt the Captain abruptly grab his arm and pull him toward the exit.

"I know what you're thinking Jacobs, but you're gonna have to trust me on this one. Whenever the feds get involved, and they will be involved in this case, things tend to get sticky. I like Special Agent Macintyre and I'm really hoping he is in charge of the team being sent here, but something about this isn't sitting right with me. I spoke briefly with Macintyre before you arrived and he seems as lost as the rest of us. In my book when the arrogant know-it-alls at the FBI are ready to admit they don't know something, *then* the situation is serious enough for major concern."

The Captain's voice dropped to a conspiratorial whisper and Steve had to strain to hear him.

"I want someone on my team investigating this thing, but I have a hunch the LAPD is going to be taken off the case. I want you to stay on it covertly. I don't mean undercover, I mean completely off the radar. I am going to brief everyone that you and Barnes have other priorities, working on another case maybe, I don't know. Regardless, you'll officially be indisposed. Understand?"

He didn't, and the idea actually disturbed him. Sure he had worked undercover before, but this was a lot more like Hollywood spy stuff. Steve began to feel the onset of a nervous tremor as his hand reached for the flask, but he felt the Captain's eyes on him and casually let his arm fall away from his pocket, willing the tremor to subside.

"I take it, Detective, that you will be able to handle the assignment *and* comport yourself in a professional manner?" The Captain had given him an over-abundance of leeway, with regard to his unprofessional "quirk," but tonight was obviously not the night to push the subject.

"Yes sir."

The Captain nodded as they made their way past the final line of stacked bodies. Together they stopped and watched as four different gurneys were rolled out of the club, with an immobile victim on each one. They made their way to the yellow police line ribbon, and the Captain lifted the yellow ribbon with one hand, pushing Steve under and past the line with the other.

"Go! Now! We'll talk later." Without another word the Captain turned his back on Steve and headed toward the club.

Stunned by the urgency in the Captain's voice, Steve absentmindedly began walking backwards, and away from the scene. He became aware that the smell of the night air was becoming cleaner, the further away he moved from the club. He had gotten used to the putrid odor of the air inside and relished the damp, but clean smell of the air around him. After a couple of deep cleansing breaths he turned his back on the club, and slowly started to walk in the direction of the alley where he had parked his car. He briefly considered going back inside the club to confront the Captain because in his opinion the man was acting weird, and totally out of character, Steve knew going back inside would not be received well. He had known the Captain a long time and the man could be as immovable as a mountain if he wanted to be. Clearly, he wanted to be that way now. A final mind-clearing breath removed the remainder of the desire to confront the Captain. So Steve stretched his arms and shoulders, getting the tension out, and then continued the walk back toward his car.

Chapter 8

Steve felt his body relax as he pulled the car into his parking space at the apartment complex where he lived. Nonetheless, all that he had witnessed left his mind spinning and no matter how hard he tried to concentrate on what his next move was going to be, he couldn't shake the images from the whole insane night. The Captain had asked him to work with Chris. Why? he wasn't sure, but getting another person involved was probably a good first step.

God, he felt tired. The adrenaline of the evening was wearing off and as it left his body the remaining feeling was one of being totally drained. All Steve wanted to do was get inside and go back to sleep, although he knew his mind was racing far too fast for that to be a possibility.

"Ah screw it!" Steve pulled the flask from his pocket, draining the contents in a succession of rapid swallows. Instantly he felt energized, as the lethargy left his mind and body, totally washed away by the contents of the 'cocktail.'

The thought that Chris would share in the investigation actually made him feel better. Sometimes Steve would forget how much of a friend Chris was to him. Okay, so the guy had become eccentric during the time he had spent as a M.E., but no truer friend could ever be found. The two used to spend most of their free time together, when they had any, since neither of them ever managed to have any lasting romantic involvements. Any psychological distance between them that currently existed, Steve knew was a result of his not being available, after he made the rank of Detective, far more than Chris being an eccentric.

* * *

Unbeknownst to Steve, as he approached his building, an

61

intense pair of eyes watched from her hiding place. She shrank back into the shadows, at her first glimpse of him and once Steve came further into view she could make out his face and the fact that he seemed to be smiling at some personal joke written on the ground in front of him. Was he drunk? Maybe, but he seemed to have good balance, and was generally in control of himself. The woman wondered how he would behave, as she stepped fully out of the shadows, revealing her presence to him.

* * *

Steve laughed out loud at one particular memory, regarding a practical joke he and Chris had pulled on some unsuspecting friends. As that scene materialized in his mind, a motion to his left returned his attention to the present. A woman appeared to flow out of the darkness, pausing under one of the few operating lights in the parking garage's ceiling.

Steve froze.

This was not just a woman. This woman was the personification of every man's adolescent, and probably adult, fantasy brought to life. Steve squinted to get a clearer view of her in the faltering light, as she turned to face him and continued slowly walking forward.

"Oh…my…God!" Steve barely uttered under his breath as she came fully into view. The strength had been sapped from his bones, and the breath from his lungs.

The woman looked young, maybe in her early twenties, and definitely of a multicultural descent, with predominant influences of Asian and Caucasian origins. She was wearing all black, or at least the little she was wearing was all black. Fishnet stockings exposed her thighs above knee-high boots and below her body hugging patent leather "extremely mini" skirt. Her flat abdomen was fully exposed with barely visible striated abdominal muscles

62

twisting with each movement. She wore a black patent leather jacket, polished to the same high gloss shine as her boots and miniskirt, and her jacket remained unzipped, revealing a black see-through lace bra worn in place of a bikini top.

She was deeply tanned and lean, without an iota of extra fat anywhere on her five foot seven inch frame. Her arms and legs were extremely muscular, giving her a streamlined look that was well-defined, but allowed her to keep all of her femininity intact. Her waist and hips were small, solid, round and smooth, with breasts of a size disproportionately large for her frame and residing high on her chest. Her lips were puffed and her Asian eyelids had been widened to give them a slightly more Caucasian appearance, while still retaining their exotic "Far East" look. In fact, her face and body had that "too perfect" look, enhanced to a point just before exaggeration, by what must have been the world's best cosmetic surgeons.

Steve knew some people would argue that she had been altered too far, to the extent she was no longer beautiful, but this was not an attempt at beauty, it was a huge success at becoming "ultra-alluring", with the specific intention of conquering those who might otherwise resist her sexual overtures. Her long hair was typical "oriental-style" straight, jet-black and flowing down to her waist. As if this weren't enough, another striking add-on feature included colored contact lenses, which tinted her eyes into a radiant and completely unnatural shade of royal blue.

As the woman approached she tilted her head down slightly while raising those incredible blue eyes upward. The look appeared innocent and extraordinarily conniving at the same time. She put her arms behind her back, forcing her jacket to open. Steve gasped, without being subtle, as he caught full sight of her breasts. She ran her hands through her hair on both sides of her head and gave her lips a half smile, half pout as she closed the final distance between them.

Steve breathed in the smell of her perfume, which increased

63

his sense of vertigo. His eyes crudely scanned her whole body, which was absolutely flawless. He was ashamed of his gawking even as he did it, but he couldn't stop himself, especially since he knew her.

"What the hell are you doing her Lei?"

Steve could now feel the heat coming off of her body as Lei held out her arms and walked into him, embracing him tightly. Steve returned the embrace but kept it to a gentle pat on her back instead of crushing her into himself as he really wanted to do. When she finally released him she reached out to hold and caress his face with her soft hands, it took every ounce of Steve's concentration not to roll his eyes back into his head and succumb to her touch. He had been longing for this every night since he'd left home, so many years ago. The fact that she was here, now, couldn't be coincidental, nor without ulterior motives. Steve knew that was how she and the rest of his "family" operated, and ultimately why he had left home. Memory of the betrayal came crashing back into his mind, rudely stirring him out of the momentary bliss that seeing her had given him.

Lei felt his hesitation, it was enough to stop her seduction in its tracks as her face melted into an expression of regret. "Still haven't forgotten that terrible day I see."

"How could I?" His words smacked of malice and more so than he had intended.

Lei shook her head in disappointment. "You don't understand what it was you saw, you never did and, until you face that day and talk to him, you never will." Lei reached out to lay a hand against his face again, but Steve brought his own hand up and lightly gripped her wrist before she could touch him again.

"Enough with the seduction—it won't work on someone who knows what you are doing and doesn't want to be taken in."

"Of course, I know that. Maybe I hoped you wouldn't want to stop me."

She was right. Steve couldn't believe how difficult it was to make himself stop her, but he continued to gently push her hand away from his body.

He released his grip and Lei let her hand fall to her side. "You should talk to him Steve, patch things up and come home where you belong." Now Lei spoke with the authority and control Steve knew she possessed. "He's here in Los Angeles."

"What?!?" The shock of that final statement caused Steve to take a step back.

"I said…"

"I know what you said! What do you mean he's here? Is he responsible for what happened tonight at *The Inferno*?!?"

"You know better than that. He's nothing if not subtle."

Steve was still fuming, even though he knew that it was true and overtness of any kind was not part of "his" makeup.

A shape sped past them, and with it Steve could feel a certain amount of heat diminish from the surrounding area. Being startled invoked his reflexes and he instinctively drew his gun. He could hear Lei take in a gasp of air as she saw the weapon.

"What are you doing?!? Put that away!" Lei commanded, but Steve ignored her as his eyes scanned in between rows of parked cars for any sign of the figure that had flashed past him and Lei. He heard the sound of footsteps and when Steve turned back, he saw Lei running off toward the parking garage's exit stairs. He looked at the firearm in his hand, then up at Lei running from him, all the old feelings came rushing back to him and filled his core with regret. Just as he was about to holster his gun and call out to Lei, the shadows came to life all around him.

The shape that emerged was a man, large and coming quickly from the side. Steve whirled around and brought his gun up to fire, but the man launched himself over an impossible distance, landed next to Steve and wrenched the gun from his grasp. Steve immediately sent a right-cross to the man's face which was effortlessly parried and countered by a powerful sidekick to Steve's ribs, sending him reeling, and briefly airborne, as he was propelled from the impact of the kick to about fifteen feet from where he'd been standing. He didn't feel any ribs snap, but he did have the wind knocked out of him. Landing prone, Steve righted himself and rose to one knee, hoping the man would be cautious before charging in to finish the job. Steve placed a hand on his knee, trying to regain his breath as he looked up and directly into the face of his assailant. The one especially distinguishing feature about the man was a full head of snow-white hair, extending down to the middle of his back.

"Ah crap Alpha," Steve complained, "did you have to hit me so hard? "The man called Alpha stood about twenty feet away with his side to Steve looking at something he was holding with both hands. When Alpha turned to face him Steve could see his flask gently resting in the grasp of Alpha's left hand.

"It was you who drew the gun on me, boy. You know how I feel about those things." Alpha's voice was unnaturally low and Steve had never known if it was an affectation the man had adopted or if it were genuine, but regardless, the eerie effect remained the same.

Steve rose to his feet and the man abruptly straightened to his full height. The two simply stared at each other for a moment before Steve let out an exasperated sigh.

"Didn't work much when I asked Lei, but what are you doing here Alpha?"

The man called Alpha cocked his head as if confused by the question. "Last time I checked, this was a free country where people could go as they wished."

"Don't be evasive, just tell me why you're here. And I mean why you are here now, at this moment, and did you have anything to do with what happened tonight."

Instead of answering, Alpha unscrewed the top of the flask and sniffed the contents. His face screwed up into a look of disgust then he looked back to Steve.

"Please don't tell me you are using French wine."

"Just as you taught me…"

"I didn't teach you that. I used to use that swill because it was all I had available to me at the time."

"It's not all bad."

Alpha seemed to consider this. "True, but apparently the type you can afford on a Detective's salary turns the mix into something more akin to hog piss." Alpha tossed the flask away and then pulled a large syringe out of a lining in his black jacket. "There's an easier way you know."

Rage filled Steve as he recognized the syringe and the contents within.

"Never! You son of a bitch! How dare you even show that to me!"

Alpha smiled. "Still upset I see?" Alpha rolled up his sleeve, pushed the needle into the fleshy part of his forearm and injected the entire contents of the syringe into himself. Steve caught himself staring at the entire process and felt his body writhe with longing for the now empty syringe's former contents.

"God's eyes boy, I don't know why you do this to yourself. Your stubbornness will only ruin you in the end."

"I know your secret Alpha. You may have fooled the rest of the clan into believing you are some kind of benevolent leader, but I saw how you make your little cocktail and what you will do to keep it safe."

Alpha's demeanor deflated when he heard Steve's words. "I have wanted to explain to you what you saw that night for years, but you've never given me the opportunity. At first I thought it was simply because you were afraid of me, but now I see that it isn't fear that keeps you away."

"No?"

"No. You feel betrayed. If for nothing else, then for that I am terribly sorry."

Steve was struck by the apology because he hadn't expected it, but the rage he felt overwhelmed all other emotions welling up inside him.

"It's a little too late for apologies, and even if it weren't, it certainly doesn't change anything."

"No it doesn't," Alpha agreed. "So where does that leave us?"

"It leaves me as a Detective with the Los Angeles Police Department and you a suspect in an ongoing investigation."

Alpha tilted his head slightly, almost as if to stifle a laugh, then he began to turn his back and walk away.

"Don't you move!" Steve tried to say with authority, but it came out more like a request than a command. Alpha froze. His back was now to Steve. As he looked over his right shoulder Steve spoke. "You can't just leave."

"Oh?"

"No. You need to answer some questions."

"That would be fine. After all, I came here to talk…"

"No, not about our past Alpha. You are not under arrest at this point, but I need you to answer some questions specifically about what you and Lei are doing here, at this particular time, and I am well aware it isn't simply to talk to me."

Alpha apparently had no response as he remained silent and motionless.

You can tell me here or back at the station." Steve began to reach for his back-up pistol, the one he had in an ankle holster.

"No. I don't think so." The man's head shifted slightly as Steve silently drew the revolver and pointed it at Alpha's back.

"It isn't a request," Steve said calmly as he fingered off the gun's safety.

"It should have been," Alpha said angrily in a voice that had changed into something more primitive and guttural.

Alpha suddenly spun and jumped toward the left of the garage wall. Steve didn't want to shoot, but realized he might not have a choice as Alpha now leapt off the wall and launched himself directly at Steve. Before Steve had a chance to comprehend what was happening Alpha had closed the gap between them. Using his left hand, Alpha slapped the revolver out of Steve's grip. With his right hand he snatched Steve by the throat. Alpha's grip was incredibly strong and Steve felt as though he had been grabbed by some kind of hydraulic vise, as opposed to a man's hand.

Steve brought his hands up to his throat but Alpha slammed

his left fist into Steve's solar plexus forcing all of the remaining air from his lungs. An incredible pressure had built up under his lower jaw as his entire body weight was being supported by the one-handed grip around his throat. He couldn't breathe and his vision was getting blurry. He scratched, kicked and clawed as best he could, but he had already grown so weak he doubted the effort was going to help.

"You are going to have to start respecting your betters, boy," Alpha hissed softly as he bent his arm to pull Steve in close.

Though his voice was little more than a wheeze Steve managed, "Let me know when they arrive."

Steve struck Alpha hard in the throat with the webbing between his thumb and index finger, pressing upward and forward directly on the cartilage below Alpha's Adam's apple. In any other case Steve knew the strike would have been lethal, crushing the cartilage and collapsing the trachea, such that the person on the receiving end would suffocate, but Steve knew that in Alpha's case it would only be a mild annoyance. Truly, Steve was aware of just how out-classed he was when it came to confronting Alpha. Even with everything Alpha had taught him, and all he had since learned at the Police academy there was no comparison between them.

But that didn't mean he wouldn't fight back.

Alpha had regained his footing and held his arms out at his side.

"So this is what we have come to?"

Steve didn't answer as he quickly glanced in each direction to see if there was anyone who might be a witness to what was happening. Not seeing anyone, he dropped to the ground and lifted a cinder block which had been lying in a pile of garbage next to the parking garage wall. As Steve rose he threw the concrete block at Alpha with considerably less difficulty than it should have taken to cover the ten yard separation between the two of them. Alpha didn't try to duck out of the way or dodge, instead he looked bored as the projectile closed the distance on its deadly path. Then, at the last possible moment, Alpha raised his fist and struck the airborne cinder block as it reached him with such force it caused the block to explode in a cloud of small fragments and grey dust.

Initially, Steve felt a surge of panic when Alpha wasn't trying to get out of the way of the block. He had hurled it in anger and the reality that it might actually strike Alpha sent a terrifying concern through him. After Alpha had shattered the block, Steve felt slightly relieved and frankly impressed at the sheer spectacle of power his one-time mentor showed…until reality set in that the fight was not yet over.

Steve lunged forward and began landing blow after blow to Alpha's body and face with a determination that should have been bone-splintering with every impact. Steve had always had to hold back whenever he trained with the other members of the Police Department. He possessed enough strength to cripple a man with a single well-placed punch, and now he held nothing back. Steve let loose with everything he had, but Alpha's body barely rocked as each fist landed.

Steve kept the punches coming, but soon realized he was tiring. His knuckles had begun to bleed while Alpha looked no worse and even seemed to be bored. Less than a minute later Steve knew he didn't have the remaining strength to keep his arms up. He looked into Alpha's eyes, glowing in their bright yellow amber color.

"So," Alpha said mockingly, "you done?"

Steve was completely out of breath and could hardly speak.

"We…we haven't…even started…yet" Steve barely managed.

Alpha shook his head in what seemed to be more disappointment than anything else.

"No boy, we're done…at least for tonight." Alpha balled his fist and held it up next to Steve's cheek. "Sleep well."

"Oh crap," was the only thought passing through Steve's mind before the blackness enveloped him.

Chapter 9

Pain was the first sensation to return as Steve regained consciousness. It was as if the entire physical world was comprised of nothing but pain. He believed even his thoughts were hurting him as he strained to open his eyes and realized that he was lying in a large pile of garbage. Unfortunately, the next sense to return was the sense of smell which, in combination with the pain, created an extremely nauseating reality.

Instinctively, Steve rolled away from the putrid odor although the action didn't diminish the smell all that much. It did, however, successfully increase his pain to the point where he couldn't hold back the nausea. He managed to clamor to all fours before the violent contractions sent what little he had in his stomach into the mound of trash surrounding him. When the spasms finally stopped he extended one groping hand in search of something he could brace himself with and support his attempt to climb to his feet. Most of his bodily pains had subsided to only a mild roar after the retching, although his head was still throbbing explosively. In his disorientation the word "concussion" flew across his mind a couple of times, but in this tenuous state he didn't pay it much attention.

Touching his face and the sore spots along his jaw and cheekbones, hazy memories began to return. Carefully trying to stand, the pain and nausea came back with flooding swiftness. He placed the flat of his back against an unexpected wall and slowly slid down to a seated position so as not to fall. That's when Steve realized he was in a dumpster, probably the one outside his apartment building.

"Yep, concussion," he softly spoke out loud, understanding why the word had been flying around in his head the entire time since he'd regained consciousness.

Searching his pockets the best he was able, Steve located his wallet, keys and cellular phone. He opened the flip phone and scrolled down the contact list until he found the one he wanted.

Depressing the send button he waited until the line connected to the other end.

"About time you called ass face!" came over the speaker end in a volume far too loud for Steve's condition. Chris Barnes was in his usual jovial mood, playfully reproaching Steve in his own humorous way. "What, were you planning to keep me hanging all night? Dude, that is so not cool and I have half a mind to…"

"Chris…" Steve's voice was so cracked and so slight he was barely able to get the word out.

Silence followed on the other end of the receiver.

"Chris…" Steve spoke again and this time his voice was marked with the pain that accompanied the effort to speak.

Chris' voice and attitude changed to a deadly seriousness.

"Hurt or sick?" Chris said gravely as if he already knew the answer. Over the phone Steve could hear Chris' footsteps hurrying over hardwood floorboards and the sound of keys being scooped up from a countertop.

Steve tried to reply but his head started swimming and his eyes began to lose focus.

"Steve," Chris spoke calmly and directly into the other end, "Tell me where you are."

Steve could barely focus enough to respond, he was only able to utter an unintelligible sound as he slumped to one side.

"Steve! Concentrate and tell me where you are!" Chris almost hollered in a commanding voice.

Using every last ounce of effort Steve managed, "Dumpster. My place I think."

"You're in the trash?!?" Chris sounded panicked. "Can you climb out?"

"No." Every word seemed like a full physical effort so Steve limited his answers as best he could.

"Holy crap dude! What days do they collect at your place?"

Steve tried to think but his thoughts were muddy.

"All right, never mind, I'm on my way. Stay with me, keep talking and I'll be there before you know it."

Steve couldn't stay awake anymore as his body slid into the filth that lay beneath him. He gave a silent thanks that his head landed gently on something soft and dry as opposed to a used diaper or some other such nastiness.

"Steve!" Chris urgently yelled from the other end of the phone line. Steve looked to his left hand and was amazed to see he was still holding the device.

"Chris…" Steve managed.

"I'm coming bud, stay with me."

"I'm still here," Steve whispered into the dark as the shadows danced around him swallowing him whole into a sea of black.

* * *

Welcome to KTLA Channel 3 News. Our top story this morning:

The United States division of the World Health Organization has declared a state of emergency surrounding what appears to be a biological or chemical agent let loose inside the popular nightclub "The Inferno" last evening at approximately four minutes past midnight. Officials on the scene are reporting that a serious contaminant, used primarily in biological or chemical warfare, was released into the ventilation system of the trendy nightspot and has resulted in several casualties. The officials are not releasing the names or the exact number of victims, nor are they stating the mortality rates among the victims, however, they do feel the threat has been contained and the surrounding area is free of any danger of exposure. Lead officials on site had this to say:

'Currently we are detecting absolutely no residual traces of the suspected agents outside the nightclub.' We are in the process of performing sterilization procedures to the interior of the club, at

the completion of which we are confident all remnants of the agents in question will be eliminated.

Clean up continues at this time and all traffic has been re-directed around the area. Gridlock has been kept to a minimum, due to the light Sunday traffic in the immediate vicinity, but commuters are cautioned to take alternative routes for the majority of the day. We will update this story as information is made available.

Chapter 10

The Pharmanetics Building, Downtown Los Angeles
Corporate Headquarters, Pharmanetics Corporation

Alex Daniels loved working the weekends, particularly on Sunday since the building was so quiet and peaceful he could actually relax inside his executive office. He would look out the floor to ceiling windows, see the ocean on a clear day and read the Sunday paper while drinking a decadently heavy cream café latté and eating a scone.

His company had struck it rich with two different patents on new cancer drugs evidencing the same success rate as traditional chemotherapy without all of the side effects associated with normal cancer treatments. Not that there hadn't been a few problems along the way. Rival companies had released similar drugs first, which caused Pharmanetics' cash flow to plummet to the point the company had declared a Chapter Eleven bankruptcy.

Alex scrambled and found a group of investors who were willing to infuse substantial amounts of capital into Pharmanetics. The group's only stipulation for the investment, aside from a significant amount of ownership in the company (which Alex had been reluctant to part with), was for Alex to employ one of their handpicked executives to oversee their interests within the business. This liquidity of cash enabled Alex to "grease the wheels" within the FDA, the drugs passed through the human trials in half the time it would normally have taken to have the substances legally approved. The money also funded a massive PR campaign for the drugs once they were available to the public and the drugs sold at unbelievable rates. Now Pharmanetics was one of the leading pharmaceutical companies in the world and one of the largest in America.

As Alex scanned through the Sunday paper, CNN played on the 60" plasma TV from the wall across from his desk. He had been paying partial attention when the news of the incident at *The Inferno* had been announced on the national news. Details about the condition of the victims were now being released:

Eyewitness reports state the victims were in a comatose or catatonic state, but there appeared to be no fatalities.

Alex lowered the paper and stared off into the distance of Los Angeles. The news broadcast now commanded his full attention:

Apparently, the list of casualties includes most of the members of the Los Angeles Police Department who arrived on the scene soon after the outbreak of what people are calling the worst biological attack in the history of the United States.

Alex spun toward the television as he swallowed hard and tried to control his breathing, his hand shaking as he reached for the phone and pressed a speed dial button.

"Where are you?" Alex spoke into the phone as the line connected. "You're in the building? Good, come to my office immediately." Alex nervously set the phone down on its cradle. He began to pace the room, something he had not done in years, a clear indication of just how agitated he had become.

It had been such a perfect Sunday. Now Alex wondered if this latest development could ruin the whole project. If the Press were to get any leads which pointed back at Pharmanetics the whole world would find out what they were working on. This would spark other pharmaceutical companies trying to beat them to the Patent Office. Industrial espionage would become so rampant the company would be spending all of its resources trying to prevent it instead of finishing current projects.

Pharmanetics had been trying to develop a new form of anesthesia, without the negative side effects from being anesthetized. The number of patients who have complications, including death, as a result of adverse reactions to anesthesia is staggering. The development of a side-effect free, surgical anesthesia, would be worth billions of dollars to the company able to patent it. Pharmanetics' latest research, spearheaded by their incredibly eccentric head researcher, had taken the company into a direction they had previously never been fathomed.

The research was so cutting edge that they would gain a head start of at least five years on their competition, assuming that this idea had even occurred to them, which Alex doubted. The only way for another company to compete would be to steal the research, reverse engineer it and then get the patent, first. It was a technique Alex knew well, having used it in the past with significant financial success. He would not allow someone else to beat him at his own game, he could still control the situation. He simply had to reign in a few loose ends. Ironically, his investors had saddled him with the perfect man for the job.

Alex heard a slow knock on his large oak office door. Before he could call out "Enter," the latch turned and Kenneth Kunnert walked into the office unbidden, in that arrogant manner of his. Kunnert was a big man, standing six foot four inches tall, with sharp facial features and long, seemingly unnatural blonde hair and equally strange blue eyes. He was in incredible shape, carrying his frame with an effortless and confident air. He was the man the investor group had requested, demanded actually, to be employed within Pharmanetics. At first Alex was highly put off by the man being given such free reign, within the company he had developed. However, as time went by Kunnert proved himself to be a tremendous benefit to the company in several different ways. Security was the man's specialty. Alex had come to respect and rely on Kunnert for the various operations within the company that required extremely secure or "deniable" solutions.

"You called?" Kunnert spoke with the slight trace of an accent. He was an American, born in Philadelphia, but his grandparents had raised him in Johannesburg, South Africa from the age of three. At age 18, he was awarded a scholarship to West Point and graduated with honors four years later. He entered the military immediately after, excelling at all duties to which he was assigned. Two years later Kunnert filled out an application for Special Forces, and completed the training necessary to become a Green Beret. He'd extended his tour of duty beyond the mandatory requirement, attendant to graduating from West Point, and was later recruited by Delta Force, leading his own team on several "Black Ops" missions, for three additional years.

Alex knew that was where the man's file ended and the mystery began. There were rumors of a covert team Kunnert had led for a couple of years, but outside of the normal military channels. Alex had some of his best sleuths investigate this unknown period of time, but all leads turned cold shortly after the inquiries had started.

"Have you seen the news this morning? What the hell is going on and why wasn't I informed?"

"I have been controlling the situation ever since I was made aware of it," Kunnert replied calmly.

"Controlling it?" Alex exploded. "The goddamn World Health Organization is all over the scene! If they find out…"

"Who said the WHO is on the scene?" Even Kunnert's accent couldn't hide the emotionless quality of his voice.

"It's all over the news for Christ sakes!"

"Yes…and?"

A thought slowly crept into Alex's mind, too incredible to believe. "You…you mean to tell me those are actually all our people?" Alex lowered his voice, completely lost in the grandiose dimension of what was being presented before him.

Kunnert gave Alex an expectant look.

"You? How?" Alex managed.

"That is the reason you pay me the extremely large sum of money you do." Kunnert spoke calmly as a slight half smile broke through the right side of his mouth. "Do you want to know the details?" Kunnert asked, with no expectation of having to reveal any details.

"I want to know everything and anything you do on behalf of

the company. This is not a request. What if someone was actually trying to call the WHO?" The air of authority returned to Alex's voice, and he could see Kunnert's physique shift to a more submissive demeanor.

"They will be told Pharmanetics is acting as the duly appointed representative of the World Health Organization, and that we have been given full authority to function on their behalf within Los Angeles," Kunnert spoke calmly.

Stunned, Alex said "You have a contact within the WHO?"

"Yes, within the WHO's main headquarters in Europe. This enables our credentials to be confirmed at the highest levels of the organization."

Alex was impressed, but moved quickly on to other matters. "Right now I want to know if we are safe. Have our plans in any way been compromised?"

"We have not been compromised. All equipment at the location was collected and returned to our research facility. The witnesses have been dealt with and the Press has been misled."

"That's quite a mass of witnesses Kunnert, including the majority of them being LAPD. Are you sure their abduction was wise?"

"Wise or not, it was necessary. If need be, we can always say our efforts to save their lives were ultimately in vain. I have already stockpiled enough Anthrax to create the corpses necessary to substantiate our story."

Alex nodded. "Good." He stopped pacing behind his desk and sunk into his large leather chair. He calmed himself and gestured for Kunnert to sit across the desk from him. Kunnert obliged and sat in the guest chair.

"How do you plan to proceed from here?"

"I would say we should move to the next phase, however Dr. Whelan feels another test is in order."

"Another!" Alex quickly picked up the phone and hit another speed dial number.

"Put the doctor on the line—now!" Alex tried to take a deep

breath before the sound of Dr. Whelan's voice came over the line.

"Hello?"

"Didn't you have enough fun during the first test at *The Inferno*? What is this I hear about needing a second test?"

The doctor's unusual voice answered after a long sigh. "I'm sorry to say the first test was not a 100% success. One person didn't succumb to the device."

"Only one out of nearly one thousand is an overwhelmingly good percentage."

"True but it shouldn't have been possible, and I haven't been able to determine why the man wasn't affected."

"Still Doctor, only one…"

"What if certain individuals are immune due to their particular brain chemistry, or other genetic predisposition?" The doctor waited as Alex considered in silence.

"Is that possible?"

"I don't know, but if you have any plans on selling this in a military application then it would be a good idea to find out."

Alex let out a long exasperated breath. "Yes it would. Hold on, I'm going to put you on the speaker phone so Kunnert can hear."…"there."

"Hello Ken," came the doctor's disengaged voice through the phone's speaker.

"Doctor."

"I must commend you Ken. That bit with the WHO is absolutely brilliant."

Alex could hear the smile in each of Dr. Whelan's words as he spoke them, and he thought the doctor might be enjoying the entire process a little more than he should.

"On to business, Doctor, if you please." Alex was anxious to get the details squared away for this "second test" as quickly as possible. Every day they were delayed was a loss of money, a loss of potential opportunity and Alex was not one to leave such things behind.

"Of course," the doctor began. "Ken, how soon before I can

initiate another test run?"

"What did you have in mind? Same as last time?"

"Well…similar. I have an idea that would be far more mobile and would spare the need for any equipment removal afterward."

Kunnert gave it some thought, it would make things easier, but…

"We can't do this in Los Angeles again. If you are as mobile as you say then I would recommend an alternate city." Alex turned to Kunnert: "Any particular preference?"

"That would depend. Doctor, am I correct in assuming that if this second test proves 100% successful then we can move immediately to phase two of our operation?"

"That would seem logical and prudent, as everything is ready here," the doctor's voice grew slight colder, "even with the sudden addition we accepted recently."

"You disapprove?" Kunnert asked.

"Disapprove of what?" Alex seemed bewildered.

"Not really, I simply don't like surprises." The chill in the doctor's voice became more apparent.

"What are you two yammering about?!" Alex was practically hollering at this point.

"Our trusty senior security advisor here thought it acceptable to bring all of the 'test subjects' from *The Inferno* to this location for storage," the doctor finally revealed.

"ARE YOU OUT OF YOUR MIND?!?" Alex was yelling now, "You abducted over one thousand people and brought them HERE???"

"Where did you think I was going to take them?"

"I didn't know or care! Dig a deep pit and bury them all in it or put them in a cargo container and sink it in the ocean for all I care, just make sure it can't be tracked back to us."

"You do remember they are all still alive, yes?" Kunnert's crooked smile belied his concern for the victims.

"So? As long as we are safe what difference does it make?"

"We are safe, believe me. If anyone gets wind of their presence here we will say we had to bring them to our facility in order to cure them. Unfortunately, none of them will survive if our plans fall completely apart, but if things plays out as we expect we can spin this into an excellent PR campaign as we 'cure' them."

Alex shook his head. "That's a big risk you are taking."

"True, but the reward will greatly outweigh the risk. Besides, it gives the good doctor more test subjects to play with."

The speaker on the phone mused, "Hmm, yes I like that part."

"Do we still have enough space for the other "guests" we are hoping to receive after phase two?"

"Oh yes and then some." The doctor once again sounded cheery. "Space and supplies were never in question. It was simply a case of my not liking surprises, as I said."

"All right," Alex concluded, "I think we can move forward. Ken, where do you want the next test to take place?"

"It would stand to reason that if we run a second test and immediately move on our target date for phase two, then we should run the test in the city closest to our quarry. That way the entire unit will basically be in place, and we can readily move out as soon as the test results are in."

Again the voice from the phone hummed a happy sound. "Ooooh! Excellent idea! I will get prepared." Then the connection closed as the doctor hung up the phone on his end.

Alex reached over and disconnected the call. "What's he so happy about?"

"Think about it." When Alex didn't respond immediately, Kunnert added "The city closest to the target."

Alex still didn't get it. Another moment passed and then he did.

"Oh!" Alex sighed, "Of course."

Chapter 11

Steve shot up in bed to a seated position. His right hand instinctively went to the pain on his head where Alpha had struck him. Groping, Steve felt his temple as he surveyed the area and recognized that he was in Chris' apartment on a pullout sofa bed. It was only then he looked to his left, and realized Chris was sitting on the side of the bed shaking a cold pack.

"That was some kind of nightmare." Chris pointed out.

"It was?" The tremor in Steve's voice was unmistakable. Chris quickly caught on to the seriousness of Steve's state of mind.

"Steve, you have a grade +1 to +2 concussion. It's going to take you out of circulation for a little while. I've shot you up with some anti-inflammatory medications, which will help you feel better, but the only way to really heal from a concussion is to rest. In the meantime, you may have some unusual experiences—memory loss, hallucinations, nightmares."

A moment of silence passed before Chris spoke again.

"Do you want some Valium? I've got a whole medicine chest filled with goodies if you need it," Chris said with some mild cheer.

"No thanks," Steve replied while letting the political incorrectness on Chris' part slide without comment. "I just need a minute to get my wits back."

"You want some quiet time? I can get out of your hair for a little while if you want to try to sleep some more."

Steve was still struggling to remember and talking seemed to be helping quiet his nerves.

"No. I don't think I want to sleep, even if I need it. I would rather relax and talk if you don't have to be anywhere."

An unusual look crossed over Chris' face, but whatever it was, he dropped the subject rather than bring it up.

"What?" Steve asked.

"Nothing we can't talk about later." He said as he handed the ice pack to Steve. "I was bringing this to you. Put it on your head wherever it hurts."

"Thanks."

"Sure. So I guess I should ask if you got the license plate number of the truck that hit you," Chris said with a smile. "Or is this a 'You should see the other guy' scenario."

"You have no idea how well the second one applies."

"You get your licks in?" Chris seemed eager for a story. He certainly deserved it after all he had done. Steve looked down to see he was wearing the most God-awful pajamas, with small pictures of SpongeBob SquarePants emblazoned all over the fabric. He was also clean and smelled of Ivory soap as opposed to rancid garbage.

Steve looked up at Chris and raised an eyebrow.

Catching on, Chris replied, "Yeah, I stripped you. Washed you, shaved my name in your chest hair, put you in my favorite PJ's and then I put you to bed. What of it? Are you being ungrateful or something?"

Steve stared wide-eyed at Chris. He had flashed him that look solely because of the pajamas. Now he had to seriously resist the urge to look down and open the pajama top to check his chest hair.

"No. I really can't express how much I owe you. Thanks for finding me."

Chris was shaken by the overly sincere tone in Steve's voice and his own voice faltered.

"Oh...Well... No problem, I mean, how long have we known each other? Fifteen years?"

Steve nodded, "Over a decade for sure."

"So it's nothing. I know you'd do the same for me."

Steve knew that was true, but he wondered if he would be more reluctant than Chris had been. Being a cop had hardened him. Being a Medical Examiner was no picnic either, but Chris seemed able to cope with it. Far better than Steve was able to deal with his job's insanity, in any case.

"Sometimes I forget myself Chris. I know it's the job but I

don't want to make excuses…"

Chris cut him off with a wave of his hand, "Stop. Stop. Stop. This is starting to sound way too sappy, sentimental, and just a little bit gay. Not that I don't find you attractive, or that there is anything wrong with that. I just don't bend that way."

Steve smiled at Chris' comeback.

"And stop staring at my ass," Chris finished.

Steve actually laughed out loud at that one, and his head throbbed in time with his laughter.

"Okay Chris, I give up. Don't make me laugh."

"All right, well this should sober you up. This fight you found yourself in, was that before or after you lost your guns?"

Steve's face melted into a mask of concern as he suddenly remembered Alpha having disarmed him.

"Oh no!" Steve let out an exasperated breath and closed his eyes.

"Easy Wild Bill, I didn't say they were gone." Chris rose to his feet and opened a drawer of the bed stand to Steve's right. Steve sat up and looked inside to see where his Glock and spare revolver rested.

Chris said, "They were lying nearby when I found you. Whoever took them from you wasn't interested in keeping them."

Steve reached for the Glock, and as he grasped it a familiar feeling came over him. The weapon felt cool and comforting in his hand. He had owned this Glock 17 automatic pistol for over ten years. So far the weapon had never failed him, and it had saved his life a number of times. He checked the magazine and found it had been emptied of its ordinance. Pulling back the slide, he found the lone bullet in the barrel had also been removed.

"Did you empty it?"

"No. Honestly, I didn't even look to see if it was loaded or not." Chris spoke tentatively when he asked his next question. "Steve, where's your flask?"

Memories began to materialize and Steve remembered Alpha having removed it from his pocket at one point during their confrontation. Steve looked back at Chris but said nothing as the realization set into his mind.

"Okay," Chris said, "How much do you need?"

"Chris...I can't ask you..." Insecurity tainted every word Steve had uttered even though he knew he didn't need to feel that way around Chris. Chris had been his best friend ever since he had fled from Alpha and the rest of his people, and more importantly, Chris knew his secret.

"Stop!" Chris spoke with a rare tone of uncompromising authority. "You don't realize how long you have been out. You are seriously in need. I can see the early stages of the symptoms in your pallor already."

"What?" Steve suddenly felt a little panicked. "How long was I out?"

"Two days, almost three actually, and as I said that's nearly a grade 2 concussion you're sporting."

"Damn, he really clocked me."

"Who?' Chris asked as he began rolling up his left sleeve.

"Wait Chris, I don't want you to do this."

Chris ignored him.

"I'm serious Chris."

Chris looked up from his sleeve. "I'm sorry, did you hear something? It sounded a little bit like one of those not-so-rare Los Angeles mules. You know...Hee-Haw....Hee-Haw...I'm a stubborn Jackass...Hee-Haw."

Steve tried not to, but he began to laugh as Chris went to the nightstand and pulled out a large gauge syringe used for drawing blood, tape and some surgical tubing. Chris tied the tubing around the exposed part of his left bicep and slapped at the "eye" of his elbow a couple times until the veins swelled. Chris plunged the syringe into one of his veins and taped the needle down. With his free hand he reached back into the drawer and removed a four-ounce collection test tube.

Chris waggled the tube at Steve. "This is going to be enough to get you back on your feet?"

86

Steve nodded grimly. "It will bury the symptoms until I can get a larger dose from my apartment."

"Do I have to mix it with wine or can you take it straight?"

"Straight is better, the wine is just a preservative." Steve thought about that for a moment then relented, "I suppose the wine is also for appearances sake as well."

"Better for people to think you're an alcoholic than to realize you're a vampire, eh?"

The word struck Steve like a punch in the guts. "Chris…"

"I know. I know. Not REALLY a vampire, still, give me my indulgences."

"Which indulgences?"

"Specifically, the one where I tell myself my best friend is a vampire. I have to admit I find that so absolutely and completely awesome! I mean, you're as strong as three men, and until the other night I thought you were unbreakable. I've never seen you sick a day in your life. I have seen you beaten, stabbed and shot, but each time you recovered in hours when any other man would have been hospitalized for weeks."

"Pros and cons of my Porphyria and the way I was raised as a result of it."

Chris' smile faded. He knew Steve's vampire nature was the result of a medical condition called Porphyria. And he knew the condition is such that the "heme" part of his hemoglobin cannot be properly synthesized by his body. Unlike the essential amino acids a "normal" human being needs to consume in order to survive, Steve must consume what his body cannot make. Chris understood the supplementation required would be the drinking of raw human blood. The "cons" Steve was referring to were those of a person with Porphyria going too long without consuming that part of the blood his or her body is unable to synthesize. Then the red blood cells start breaking down leading to excruciating pain, madness and death. As far as his strength and rapid recovery were concerned, well, that was a bit more complicated to explain.

"Sorry. Sometimes I forget it's not all super powers." Chris removed the collection tube from the syringe and held it out to Steve. "Here"

Steve still wore an uneasy look on his face although his body was practically quivering with anticipation of the tube's contents.

Seeing his friend's reluctance Chris said, "It's not like this makes us engaged or anything, just take it already."

Steve reached out with a trembling hand and carefully plucked the tube from Chris' fingers. He immediately put it to his lips and downed the contents in two quick swallows as if throwing back a couple of fingers of tequila.

Steve felt the beneficial effects of the blood instantly, his headache quickly diminished from an intense throbbing to an almost imperceptible drone. The aches in his body disappeared completely and the sense of emptiness in his core now felt partially sated.

"Better?" Chris asked as he finished securing a bandage over the area on his arm where he had drawn the blood.

"Much. Thank you, Chris."

"Not a problem. So you want to tell me what happened?"

Truth be told, Steve's stomach was still unsteady and the now more subtle thrumming behind his eyes threatened to make every spoken word resonate with pain inside his skull. In spite of all of this, Steve managed to relay everything that had happened. Afterward, he could see a familiar look on his friend's face as Chris' analytical mind switched to the "on" position.

"Okay, we have an unexplained trauma affecting an entire building's worth of people. Then your…uh, 'family' shows up and Alpha gives you the big beat down, without giving you any rhyme or reason as to why they are hanging around."

Chris paused as Steve confirmed everything with a gentle nod. "Well, I would say you had quite an evening!" Chris concluded.

"Thank you Captain Obvious." Steve chuckled.

"So what's our next move?" Chris asked unexpectedly.

Steve was caught off guard. "What?"

"Where do we go from here? You're the detective, what's

next?"

"You actually still want in on this?"

"I believe you said the Captain wanted you to bring me in on this one. Why? Hell... I don't know, although I do know that the Captain and I have a tolerant relationship at best. He knows my skills and I respect his instincts. Maybe he knew or suspected something whereby I would prove myself to be useful in the long run."

Steve thought about it and nodded again. "All right, you're in. Do you have the morning paper?"

"Yeah, Why?"

"I want to get up to date on what's currently happening with the case. I know it's been two days, but maybe there's something in the paper that could give me some insight."

"Oh, in that case I have something even better."

Chris walked over to where the television sat on a flat entertainment unit. Pushing a videotape into the VCR, Chris switched on the TV and returned to Steve's side. The TV played the end of a teeth whitening toothpaste commercial, which sang a catch phrase, and then faded out. When the picture returned it was of the early morning news from two days ago. The heavily made up anchor announced the headline story.

Our top story this morning revolves around the ongoing investigation into the possible terrorist attack on the local nightclub and hot spot, The Inferno. Bringing us the latest information is Carrie Sanchez reporting from The Inferno. Carrie:

Thank you, Marc. Just after midnight last night police were sent to the scene of the nightclub, The Inferno, to break up a disturbance out on the street. That's when the officers on the scene noticed the locked doors of the nightclub, a serious violation of the city fire codes. The officers eventually forced the doors open and entered the club only to succumb to what authorities believe is the first biological terrorist attack on American soil.

Authorities believe the biologic agent was spread though the ventilation system by whoever initiated the attack. All persons including club owner, Phillip Devereaux, were affected by whatever agents were released.

What makes this story even more frightening is what followed, as emergency crews arrived on the scene and rushed in to administer aid to the victims. They too, succumbed to the effects of whatever still lingered in the air. All police and medical personnel who arrived early on the scene collapsed as well, and needed to be evacuated by federal emergency crews arriving shortly thereafter. Currently, at the request of the World Health Organization, the biohazard unit of the Pharmanetics Corporation is overseeing the clean-up procedures. Their report, for now, claims the danger is over. In charge of the clean up is Pharmanetics CEO Alex Daniels.

Alex Daniels:
We have been, and are currently registering, zero levels of any biological or other contamination in the club, or in the surrounding area. At this point in time, there is no further danger and it is clear that whatever was used, in this instance, was a self-limiting material, which dissipated over time. Our efforts shall now turn to the aid of the victims, and to their recovery. We at Pharmanetics are ready and willing to assist Federal and State law enforcement agencies, in any way we can, to help in the apprehension of those responsible.

No word has been released at this time regarding the state of the victims or if there have been any deaths. The only word is, that the victims have been placed in quarantine and every measure is being taken to assist in their recovery. Pharmanetics is attempting to identify each of the victims, so that friends and loved ones can be kept apprised of the latest developments.

Carrie Sanchez, Channel 3 Morning News, reporting.
Anchor:

No group has claimed responsibility for the attack on..."

"Turn it off Chris." Steve was dumbstruck by the report. The cover-up was so huge it boggled his mind.

Chris walked to the TV and switched the power off.

"Jesus! None of the officers on the scene collapsed that night!" Steve said in exasperation.

"At least not while I was there. When the hell did that happen?"

"I don't think it did," Chris acknowledged. "You and I were both there. I feel fine and whatever happened to you was the result of the run-in you had, not as a result of some kind of gas attack."

"So whoever is involved in this has the ability to influence the press." Steve thought out loud, "and that means...what?"

"As I said, you're the detective, you tell me."

Steve thought for a moment.

"Chris, what do you know about Pharmanetics?"

Chapter 12

Walking into the Police Station, Steve was overwhelmed by the scarcity of officers and the high level of activity of the few who remained. With the disappearance of almost an entire shift of officers, those remaining were spread so thin the city was running on a skeleton crew. Phones were frantically being answered and most callers being put on hold. Desk clerks were filling out forms, answering phones and taking statements, all at the same time. Uniformed personnel were doing the best they could, however it was clear that such an immediate shortage of people was taking its toll on the whole of the police force. Both the Mayor and the Governor had called for neighboring cities to lend personnel, and for the Academy to send new recruits to temporarily help with the load. The trainees were working the office and performing guard duties, while the active officers patrolled the streets and investigated new crime scenes as best they could, until some relief from the neighboring cities arrived.

Fortunately the news of the lack of law enforcement personnel was a relatively well-kept secret from the public. In the interest of public safety, and to suppress the fear of rioting and the emboldening of the criminal element, the various press agencies were cooperating, for the time being, and holding back releasing a full story, until the relief for the Police Department had arrived.

Steve felt a surge of pride in his city, as people came together to work toward a common goal. This city of plastic appearances, self-glorification and solipsistic ideals could surprise you every now and again, with its ability to reach out in a time of need. Los Angeles could truly become a City of Angels when the need arose.

A few veterans stared in surprise as Steve made his way to his desk. Steve was the only officer, who was on site, and who hadn't "disappeared" that night. He was sure more than a few of his brethren were wondering how he had accomplished that feat. Steve felt as if he wanted to cringe under the scrutiny of those accusing eyes, but he pressed forward until he reached his desk. No sooner had he sat down then the buzzer on his phone rang. Steve answered it on the third ring.

Steve figured this call was coming. The Captain was missing and, in true military fashion, his temporary replacement had already been assigned. Paul Meyers had been a lieutenant and lead investigator in the Internal Affairs division of the LAPD. Steve knew of him only by reputation, and as a tough, but fair investigator, who did his job well and didn't abide by any of the "Big Blue Wall" code of silence, which was prevalent in most police precincts. Meyers was a 40-something, athletic, and always wore a sports coat, never suits. And that was about all he knew of the man. What disconcerted him about Paul Meyers was the fact that as close as he had been with the Captain, Steve was an unknown to Meyers. This normally wouldn't have been a problem, assuming he could adequately explain the last two days, which of course, he couldn't. Steve had no explanation for what may or may not have happened for the two days he'd been "out."

"Jacobs here," Steve spoke evenly into the phone.

"Jacobs, Paul Meyers here. I need you in the Captain's office now. Don't keep me waiting." The acting Captain hung up the phone.

Steve didn't think the tone Meyers had taken with him was too brisk and he really appreciated the fact that Meyers had said "the Captain's office" and not "my office" when he told him to report. Maybe this wouldn't be so bad after all. Whatever the case, he was out of his chair and heading toward the Captain's office before he'd hung up the phone.

Steve knocked on the glass door as he entered the Captain's office. Meyers was on the phone trying to speak to the screaming voice on the other end. It sounded as if he was being called to task by whoever was having the one-sided conversation. Finally the hollering stopped and the line went dead on the other end.

"What an asshole," Meyers sighed as he hung up the phone. "Our Chief of Police certainly has a knack for making as loud a scene as possible."

Steve smiled as Meyers spoke. Yeah, he seemed okay Steve thought, even if he was I.A.

"I guess there's no reason to enlighten you with the information the Chief had to impart. He's begun to put the pressure on me regarding this whole debacle."

Steve nodded and continued to listen as Meyers spoke.

"All right now. Since I never had the unfortunate pleasure of reading through your current file while I worked with Internal Affairs, I read through your personnel file this morning after your call."

Steve waited patiently as the acting Captain thumbed through his file.

"You do realize that prior to your call requesting information we had all assumed you had disappeared with the rest of our men. You have missed two shifts without explanation, and then you call requesting information on the case, to which only a few people have access. You have to know how this looks. With all of the pressures and people watching this case, it's not as if we can allow any potentialities to fall through our fingers."

Steve didn't like it, but he could understand the skepticism. Maybe he had gotten spoiled with the amount of leeway the Captain had always given him. Whatever the case, an explanation was due so Steve started talking. Meyers, to his credit, listened through the whole story, excluding the run in he had with Lei and Alpha, and blamed his absence on investigating the crime as the Captain had requested him to do, which led him to Pharmanetics.

"Why Pharmanetics?" Meyers asked with what appeared to be genuine interest.

"It just strikes a strange chord with me that a major pharmaceutical corporation is doing the clean-up of a potential biological attack for the World Health Organization. Maybe I'm being a conspiracy theorist, but the thought occurred to me this might actually be some manufactured new party drug like 'Ecstasy.' Maybe they're looking into producing something with a legitimate medicinal purpose, but with the bigger profit margin of an illegal substance. I've been to a few raves and I can tell you, that as a police officer, if I were to bust one person I would have to bust everyone. I have nothing to back this up but, could Pharmanetics have hired someone to pass out samples of a new drug to see if a clientele could be formed? *The Inferno* would be the best place to start, in that instance."

Steve finished and waited for the incredulity from Meyers he was sure would come.

"All right, follow-up on Pharmanetics, and see if you can dig anything up from their history, shareholders and so forth. Check in with me via phone and email. You have my numbers."

"Excuse me, sir?" Astonished at the ease at which Meyers absorbed all of the information, Steve had to shake himself to break the spell he was under.

"I am expecting answers from you and soon. Do I need to remind you that we have a lot of people counting on you not only to figure out what is happening in our city, but to find our missing people as well?" The air of authority was building in Meyers' voice.

"No, of course not, it's just that I'm having a hard time believing what happened, and I went through it." Slightly embarrassed Steve continued, "I guess I expected some skepticism and doubt on your part."

"I really don't like any of this," Meyers continued. "I am somehow giving the go-ahead to something I would otherwise be investigating, if I was still a lieutenant in Internal Affairs."

"I understand. We won't let you down, Captain."

"See that you don't. Dismissed."

Chapter 13

Steve looked directly into the eyes of the security chief stationed in the front lobby of the Pharmanetics building. He was making an unofficial and unscheduled call upon the CEO and founder, Alex Daniels. He had politely requested to speak with Mr. Daniels for a few minutes regarding *The Inferno* clean up, which had been completed, but was still being monitored by Pharmanetics employees. When the security guard abruptly told him to forget it, Steve pulled out his credentials, flashed his badge, and said he would come back with a court order, yadda-yadda...the usual routine. The eyes of the security guard got bigger and darker as he restrained himself. Speaking into a landline phone on the desk, the security fellow called Alex Daniels' office. Whoever answered the phone asked for a few minutes, and said he would come down directly and escort Steve to Mr. Daniels' office.

After the security guard explained all of this to Steve the staring contest had begun. As Steve watched this man's eyes he realized this was no ordinary security guard. The eyes, truly being the window to the soul, do reveal a great deal about a person. Steve recognized the look in this man's eyes. This guy was probably a soldier or a mercenary who had been hired as muscle for the company. The troubling part was how young this man appeared to be. He couldn't have been out of his twenties, yet he had that same unyielding look that comes only from battle experience. Far more experience than he should have at his age.

Steve's gaze did not falter, nor did he back down under the scrutiny of the security guard. Seconds crept by like minutes as he waited until finally, Mr. Daniels' assistant emerged from the elevator. The woman was tall, lean and very blonde. This was the kind of woman you would expect to have a supermodel contract along with a professional beach volleyball career. She was wearing a smart charcoal black business suit with classy shoes and sparse but elegant jewelry.

"Detective Jacobs?" She had no detectable accent to her voice, which was contrary to what Steve was expecting. Steve answered without breaking his gaze with the security officer.

"Yes."

The assistant looked from Steve to the security officer, then back to Steve.

"Um...My name is Ellen Reece. Mr. Daniels has kindly agreed to meet with..."

Steve never turned to look at her as he was locked in a contest of wills with the security officer.

"Is...Johnson, is everything all right?" the assistant asked the security officer.

The security guard didn't answer her. He just kept staring straight at Steve.

"So, it's Johnson," Steve finally spoke out loud.

"So it is," the security guard answered.

"I'll try to remember that," Steve returned with heavy sarcasm.

"And I won't forget." As he spoke the security guard made a gesture with his right thumb and first finger as if he was shooting Steve with a gun.

Steve's temper was about to flare when Ms. Reece stepped in front of him. She had obviously seen the gesture Johnson had made, and wanted to stifle any possible outburst by taking control of the situation.

"Mr. Daniels is a very busy man and he has graciously agreed to accommodate you, despite the interruption to his schedule. I would suggest you come with me now, or I will ask you to come back another day."

Not a bad plan on her part. Unfortunately for her, the goings on of the past couple of days had soured Steve's patience and his personality to the point that he had been holding it together with the finest of threads. Now he had taken about as much attitude as he was going to take from the staff inside Pharmanetics. Steve spun toward the assistant.

"Listen to me lady, and you listen good. I am taking time out of MY busy schedule to afford Mr. Daniels the courtesy and opportunity to meet with me in a friendly and casual manner. However, if everyone around here doesn't start showing the Los Angeles Police Department some serious goddamn consideration, I will be back in an hour with a court order!"

As Steve finished, the security officer leapt up from his chair. Faster than the eye could follow Steve drew his Glock from his belt holster and placed the end of the barrel to the bridge of the man's nose.

"Sit down!"

Shock was the first thing to register on security officer Johnson's face, followed quickly with a smoldering anger building to explosive proportions as the man slowly slinked back into his chair. Other security personnel, having seen or heard the disturbance, moved in and stood around Steve with weapons drawn.

"Now are we going to be civil about this?" Steve asked while keeping the handgun aimed at Johnson, seemingly unaware of all of the men surrounding him.

Silence flowed through the room for a few seconds before Ms. Reece spoke up.

"Detective, please follow me." She held her hand out in the direction of the elevators.

Steve lowered and holstered his weapon. The mass of security personnel looked to Ms. Reece, who gestured for them all to stand down. Johnson was still fuming, but to his credit he kept his mouth shut.

Steve turned and nodded in a polite manner to Ellen Reece.

"After you, Ms. Reece." The two set off toward the elevator.

They stood in silence in front of the doors, Steve could feel all of the eyes in the building watching them, especially Johnson, whose anger was practically palpable.

As the doors opened and Steve walked into the elevator, he raised his hand and gestured to Johnson with the same thumb and first finger he had faced earlier. Steve pressed his thumb down and dropped the hammer on the security man who turned away as the doors to the elevator closed.

"That was an interesting display in our lobby," Ellen Reece said as they rode to the top floor. "Johnson is a brutish man, but he is extremely loyal to our company and only doing his job, albeit in his own way."

That stung a little bit. Steve realized he had barged in unannounced and, although politely, demanded an audience with one of the top ten most influential men in Los Angeles. He had never been rebuffed, at the worst he had been made to wait, and he had gotten into a pissing contest with a security guard over his turf. He was about to apologize when the elevator doors opened directly into a large penthouse with floor to ceiling windows overlooking the entire valley. The room was incredibly lush, with high-end electronics and boardroom furniture. Directly across from the elevator was an enormous mahogany desk with two dozen leather chairs. Standing on the far side of the desk with his back to the elevator, peering out the window stood a man.

Ellen walked out of the elevator and directly toward the man. Steve followed, but found his attention drawn to various art pieces and plasma televisions. Ellen stopped short of the large table and pulled out a chair for Steve. His attention was so distracted he almost walked into the woman.

Stopping abruptly, "Whoops, sorry." Steve smiled as he spoke to Ellen.

She returned the smile, "Won't you have a seat?"

Steve looked to the man, "Mr. Daniels?"

The man turned. "Please have a seat, Detective. Mr. Daniels will be coming in from his office shortly. My name is Kunnert, but you may call me Kenneth."

He looked at Kunnert who extended his hand in a friendly greeting. Steve shook the man's hand and found his grip to be powerful but not overbearing. Kunnert was well-dressed in a red short-sleeve, golf shirt and black slacks. He carried an air of authority.

"Forgive me Mr. Kunnert, but who are you exactly?"

"I am in charge of security for the Pharmanetics Corporation, and I am Mr. Daniels' partner, although I admit I am a very small partner, in this company." Kunnert smiled a blatantly obvious false smile and released Steve's hand. Kunnert's phone sounded off and he looked to his belt to read the display screen.

"Ah, I see Mr. Daniels has left his office and is on his way here now."

A few seconds later Alex Daniels entered the room talking on a cell phone.

"This is the second time your company has let me down and let me assure you it will be the last. I am stopping payment on the check, so come and get your equipment."

Alex Daniels looked up from his conversation and nodded to the three people in the room as he hung up the phone. Ms. Reece walked over to her boss and made the introductions.

"Mr. Daniels, I would like you to meet Detective Steve Jacobs of the Los Angeles Police Department's Homicide Division. Detective Jacobs, this is Alex Daniels, the founder and CEO of the Pharmanetics Corporation."

Mr. Daniels extended his hand, "A pleasure detective."

"Thank you for meeting with me on such short notice, sir." Steve stood and warmly returned the handshake.

"Oh please, drop the 'sir', we are all rather informal here. Now, please sit down with me and tell me the reason for your visit to our humble halls."

Steve hoped he could be "politically correct" enough to cut to the chase without causing any offense, at least for the moment.

"Thank you again. Well, I am investigating the incident which occurred at *The Inferno* three days ago, and I was hoping to gain a little insight into your company's position regarding the incident."

Mr. Daniels tilted his head slightly. "The company's position? I'm not sure what you mean."

"You are aware of what happened at *The Inferno*?"

"Of course. Our scientists assisted in the clean-up, and are now monitoring the area for any further outbreaks."

"Clean-up and outbreaks of what?"

Smirking as he answered, Mr. Daniels continued, "That's the sixty four dollar question isn't it? We still haven't ascertained what caused the catastrophe, however our trained professionals are on the lookout for any signs of a bacterial, viral, or chemical agent which might still be lingering in the area."

"Forgive my ignorance of such things, but don't you have to figure out what you are dealing with before you can go in and clean up?"

"That would be an ideal situation, however, there are also established methods for entering an area to determine exactly that. We used these protocols until we determined each area was free of danger."

"So you're saying you went in and after doing the necessary tests, didn't find anything?"

Daniels looked as if he had just said more than he had intended, but he continued, knowing it was too late to change the story now. "Yes, that's true. I suppose you could say that, in actuality, our teams were 'clearing' areas as being safe as opposed to 'cleaning' them."

"I see. How did your company get involved with the 'clearing' of the area?"

Daniels started to look uncomfortable. "One of the drugs we produce is an antidote for nerve agents used in chemical warfare, and we produce it for the government. This gives us certain ties to not only the U.S. government, but to worldwide organizations such as the World Health Organization. When the crisis happened the WHO contacted our company, knowing we had the equipment and trained personnel, with a request for our assistance. Pharmanetics, of course, was willing to help in any way possible.

"And with what exactly did the WHO say they wanted your help?"

Daniels started to sound irritated. "We weren't told what was going on, as no one really knew anything. We were only asked to go in expecting the worst and report our findings."

"I see. So a worldwide organization asks you and your company for help with some potentially lethal threat they knew nothing about, and you expect me to believe you casually sent your people, people for whose well-being you are responsible, into the area without any information?"

"Well…it was hardly casual. We have procedures for going into 'hot zones' of activity without knowing what we are up against, procedures for safely assessing, stabilizing and containing whatever the dangers."

Mr. Daniels was constantly glancing at Kunnert, becoming more ill at ease with each passing moment. Kunnert seemed unfazed and did not react in any way.

"Very commendable, I'm sure you are very proud of your crew."

"Yes, we are indeed."

"Just so I understand, why does the corporate headquarters for a company that manufactures medicines and other pharmaceuticals need a Haz-Mat team? Especially, when it turns out that your closest manufacturing plant is in Iowa?"

"Well, we…I don't see how any of this has to do with what happened at *The Inferno*. Who or what are you really investigating, Detective?"

"I checked with the business license department and your company is not licensed to have a lab or research facility on site here in Los Angeles. So I guess my real question is, if you didn't have a crew of researchers and scientists here, then where did they come from?" So much for the politically correct approach, Steve thought.

Mr. Daniels looked as if he might have a heart attack, but before he could respond Kunnert stepped forward, "I am sorry Detective, but as head of security for Pharmanetics there are some pieces of information we must keep confidential, as a result of our government contracts. If you feel the information is crucial to your case I would suggest you contact members of the federal government for the release of the information. Otherwise, I am afraid there are some questions regarding the company that will have to go unanswered."

As Kunnert spoke, Daniels seemed to have a transfusion of authority. "Detective, most of your questions seem to be an investigation into my company as opposed to an investigation into what happened at *The Inferno*. So, I ask you again who, or what, are you here to investigate."

Steve knew he had pushed too hard at this point, but there was no going back.

"If you must know Mr. Daniels, I have my reservations about the presence of a public company doing the work of the Federal government. I have worked with the Feds, and I can tell you from experience, they don't let anyone play in their sandbox without having some serious leverage or need. So that leads me to your company and whatever may be Pharmanetics' angle in the situation."

Daniels was now completely composed and under control. He stood and slowly walked over to where Steve was sitting. "I appreciate your candor Detective, however, in light of what you just told me, I believe any information you need regarding Pharmanetics is a matter of public record. Any other information Pharmanetics, or its employees, may or may not have should be requested through the proper channels. At the very least I would expect the company's attorneys to be present during the meeting. Now, please forgive us as we have no more time to spend with you today."

Astonished by the blatant stonewalling, Steve could only think to say, "Mr. Daniels, do you really want me to get the court orders? After all I was under the impression the city and the LAPD were at your disposal."

"Pharmanetics will happily provide anything it can to help the LAPD and the city, but we would appreciate the consideration of not being hounded as we perform our charity work. That's all the time I have for you Detective. Mr. Kunnert will show you to the door."

Steve stood up from his chair. "Thank you, but I can find my way out." He turned and walked to the elevator where he pushed the down button. Looking back into the room, Steve saw the two men watching him leave as Ms. Reece walked toward him.

"I appreciate what time you were able to give me Mr. Daniels. I'll be in touch." A threat was audible in Steve's voice.

"I look forward to it, Detective," came the unfazed response from Daniels.

The elevator doors opened and Steve stepped inside, followed by Ms. Reece. Steve never saw Kunnert nod ever so slightly to Ms. Reece as the doors of the elevator closed. The room was silent for a moment before Daniels turned to Kunnert, "What did you make of that?"

"He's fishing. You were right to cut the meeting short when you did," Kunnert responded.

"What did you think of the court order he brought up?"

"I think he's bluffing. He has nothing to go on, and getting a court order against this company would not be easy under the best of circumstances. The Detective is operating solely on conjecture."

"I agree. He's off the mark, but not far off enough for me to be comfortable."

"Do we make an example of him?"

Daniels thought for a moment, "No, I don't think so. Not yet anyway. However it may be prudent to keep an eye on him, just in case."

Chapter 14

In the elevator Steve paced like a caged leopard, his head starting to throb. The residual effects of his concussion manifested when he was in any heightened state of emotion. This physical problem put him in an even worse mood than he would normally have been in after such a meeting. He definitely considered the Pharmanetics group, or at least its executives, suspects in this case. The problem was the motive. Why would a multi-billion dollar company risk something as public as what happened at *The Inferno*? Steve thought it more likely they had some kind of "bug-or-drug" that had gotten away from them and the whole clean-up they "volunteered" for was, in reality, a cover for something else.

Steve stopped in his tracks and looked at the woman sharing the elevator space with him. Her whole disposition had changed. She seemed smug and patronizing as she looked at him from where she leaned against the elevator wall.

"I guess you didn't get what you wanted, did you?" she chided.

Steve didn't answer, instead he looked away and tried to focus his thoughts.

"Aw, what's the matter Quickdraw? Having a hard day?"

Steve couldn't believe this. She was actually goading him. Oh, he so did not need this.

"Careful lady. I'm not in the mood," Steve warned.

"Well, I am always careful and in the mood. I suppose I should tell you I wasn't impressed by your little display in the lobby earlier and if you ever try something like that with me I'll make you eat that gun."

Steve chuckled at the remark, "Is that so?"

"Yes, that is so." All humor had left her voice. "Johnson is a friend and believe me when I tell you I will be taking the issue of your threatening him at gunpoint to your superiors."

"Go ahead," Steve said without interest.

"I intend to have you suspended." Ellen was getting riled.

Exasperated with the woman, Steve rubbed his eyes. "Lady, do whatever you want or feel you need to do, but in the meantime would you be so kind as to shut the fuck up."

This had the opposite effect as Ellen started screaming at him.

"Who do you think you are? And who the hell do you think you are talking to?"

As the car continued its descent, Steve turned to Ellen and pointed an accusatory finger at her face.

"What are you doing here? I said I could find my own way out."

Ellen moved past the finger and stood nose to nose with Steve without flinching.

"Frankly Detective, this is my job and I don't give a rat's ass what you do, or do not, appreciate."

Slack jawed and beside himself, Steve was unable to respond.

"The fact that the CEO has asked you to leave the building means I don't have to be polite anymore, so let me tell you what is going to happen from this point forward."

Steve noted Ellen was talking with the command of a basic training drill instructor, which was actually quite disconcerting.

Ellen continued, "You are going to walk out of this elevator and I am going to walk out next to you. We shall pass through the lobby and exit the building where we will shake hands and you will then proceed to get the hell off the property!"

Ellen let the force of her words sink in, as Steve remained too stunned to speak.

"If you decide to stray in any way from this plan I will see to it that badge or not, Johnson and his thugs will get you off property by force. Do we understand each other?"

Steve regained his composure and began to respond, "Lady, I don't know who…"

Ellen cut off what he was saying by punching him with a right hook that rattled his teeth. Steve gripped his chin and spat blood into his hand. The inside of his lip had been cut on his teeth from the blow.

"This is not negotiable, Detective. Speak again and I'll drag you out myself."

Steve looked at the blood on his hand as he stood up straight and reached for Ellen. She blocked his grab and twisted Steve's arm behind his back in a hammerlock, forcing him face first into the elevator wall. The car rocked slightly from the impact as it continued its descent.

"Some men never learn," Ellen warned as she wrenched upward on Steve's arm.

Steve found himself pinned to the wall by the blonde Amazon behind him. Damn, she was another one. She was another member of Pharmanetics security and probably some well-trained mercenary who had been covering him since she had come out of the elevator earlier. He had completely missed all the signs, possibly because she was female and attractive. He had been caught off guard and underestimated her so severely she was now in complete control, really putting it to his arm. It felt as though it might pop at any moment.

"Too bad you had to attack me in the elevator," Ellen pulled out a small two shot Derringer and placed it against the back of Steve's head, "self-defense, ask any one of the witnesses."

The deadly seriousness of the situation became immediately evident. Steve let his body go slack under the woman's grip in mock surrender as he reached for the Emergency stop switch, pushing it from left to right with a click and a snap. The elevator car lurched to a stop, sending Steve and Ellen toppling onto the floor as alarm bells blared.

Steve recovered and rolled to his feet as Ellen kicked herself up to a standing position. The concussion he had suffered a couple of days earlier screamed to life as the effort of regaining his footing shot pain into his head and sent his equilibrium into a tailspin. His head cleared enough for him to realize that Ellen had maneuvered behind him and encircled an arm around his throat.

Steve could feel her bear down and try to sink the chokehold on his neck, however her efforts were suddenly laughable compared to the strength and skills he had at his command. Effortlessly, and almost mockingly, Steve flipped her over his shoulder and threw her against the far wall of the elevator. Ellen groaned as her body collapsed motionless to the floor and Steve stood over her as he flicked the emergency stop switch back to the off position. He felt the elevator come back to life as it once again continued its descent while he watched the illuminated numbers count down toward the lobby.

A sudden sound explosion erupted within the elevator car. Steve felt an intense burning in his side. As he reached down to his right flank just below the rib, his hand came away wet with blood. Steve turned to see Ellen holding the tiny Derringer she'd just fired, one of its two .38 caliber rounds had struck point blank into his side.

The elevator made a "ding" sound as it came to a full stop and the doors opened to reveal Chris standing there waiting to get on board.

"Oh!" Chris smiled when he saw Steve, "What's....?"

Chris' words caught as he saw Steve collapse to his knees and then shifted to the corner of the elevator where a woman was pointing a tiny handgun directly at Steve's head.

"Wait!" Chris cried out, but Ellen was either too stunned or was simply ignoring him as she used her thumb to cock the hammer, ready to shoot again.

"No!!!" Chris awkwardly leapt forward. Ellen finally took notice of him as her eyes went wide with surprise and shock. Chris' momentum carried his body into hers like a ton of bricks, flattening the startled woman and smashing her head into the wall of the elevator. If she were dead or simply unconscious was unimportant to Chris. He quickly picked himself up and began to drag Steve out of the elevator. Steve stifled a scream of pain as Chris pulled him into the lobby. A wave of dizziness washed over him, Steve's eyes closed and total darkness ensued.

Chapter 15

The smell of detergent and bleach gave Steve the unusual impression that he was in a Laundromat. Something else lingered in his mind about his surroundings, something he noticed in the air, something foul. Groggy, he opened his eyes and immediately shielded them from a blinding luminescence created by a tower of floodlights directly over his head. Spots flashed in his brain, as the impressions left by the powerful lights began to subside. He kept his eyes closed and fumbled for a handhold to help pull himself into a seated position. He was lying supine on top of some kind of smooth metal table that was cold to the touch.

Finding the edge of the table, he grasped the side with his right hand and struggled into a seated position. Ever so slowly he opened his eyes in order to survey his surroundings and the sight only exaggerated his disorientation. He was in what appeared to be a large surgical theater, complete with stainless steel trays and medical cases. But, instead of electrical monitoring equipment surrounding a single operating table, there were several tables evenly spaced throughout the room. Stranger still, each table looked more like a giant washbasin or sink with hoses attached to showerheads hanging overhead. It all seemed vaguely familiar, but his head was still swimming.

"Hello?" Steve called out. And his voice echoed slightly through the room.

He tried to clear the fog from his head as he thought back to the last thing he could remember. Rubbing his eyes, he winced when he touched a sore spot on his nose. He immediately remembered the fight in the elevator and getting punched and then shot by the Amazon.

Steve reached for his cell phone, which he discovered missing from its usual place on his belt. Without warning, reality settled in and his situation fell upon him like a ton of bricks. He was in the morgue and the tables were autopsy tables! Steve's stomach turned as he realized he was sitting in the place where he had seen corpses eviscerated and prepared for burial. Desperate to get out of the table/sink, he flailed as he tried to squirm over the rails, which sent him and the table crashing to the floor in an explosion of sound. He landed shoulder first on the linoleum floor with a thud. He grunted as he landed, being especially careful to keep his head from hitting anything as he rolled with the force of the impact.

The door to the morgue shot open and Chris stood there with a panicked look on his face as he observed Steve on the floor near the fallen table.

"No! Don't move!" Chris screamed as he ran to Steve's side. "I removed the bullet, but I haven't had a chance to close the wound yet. Just lie still…."

A look of intense fear and confusion covered Chris' face as he viewed Steve's exposed side. The wound had closed on its own and although still raw and angry looking, it was basically sealed.

"That…that should have taken at least two weeks to get to that stage of healing!" Chris looked up at Steve and for the first time in all the years he had known him, Chris looked frightened.

"Maybe now would be a good time to tell me again that you aren't *really* a vampire."

Steve pressed his lips together in frustration because he had never had the courage to be fully honest with Chris, or anyone else for that matter. It wasn't all mistrust though, and the truth was that he didn't have all of the answers either. The only person who might was Alpha. Steve had promised himself he was done with that part of his life and would eventually discover the answers on his own, although he hadn't had much luck in the last ten plus years, since he had gone his own way.

"Okay, would you mind finding me a chair?" Steve asked meekly, his tone slightly alleviating Chris' apprehension. Chris nodded and retrieved a folding aluminum chair from across the room.

Steve sat in the chair and proceeded, "Chris, what was I doing in a sink?"

With a mildly confused look on his face Chris answered, "After your incident at the Pharmanetics building, some people wanted to take you to the hospital and others wanted to take you to the police station. I was granted custody and brought you here."

Steve thought about it for a second then asked again, "Why was I in an autopsy sink?"

"You needed to sleep it off, so I put you in one of the sinks."

Incredulous, Steve repeated what he had just heard. "You put me in one of the sinks so I could sleep off the effects of the concussion."

"Yes. What's the matt-"

"You put me in an autopsy sink so I could sleep?!?"

Recognizing that Steve was reacting poorly to his little maneuver, Chris responded with "I uh, well...I...that is...I made sure it was perfectly clean before... Stop trying to change the subject!" Chris was getting that fearful look again.

Steve held up a hand, "Okay, okay. Calm down."

"I will as soon as you start talking." Chris reached under his shirt and pulled out a necklace bearing a small crucifix. "Here, touch this."

Steve's face screwed into a disbelieving frown that quickly reformed into a half smile, "Seriously?"

"C'mon, it'll make me feel better."

Steve let out a long exasperated sigh as he reached over and gently closed his hand around the crucifix.

Chris' eyes were fixed on Steve's hand for a few silent seconds before Steve asked, "Happy now?"

"Happier than I was a minute ago. Start talking."

Steve nodded. "All right, okay, so I guess I should start by telling you I don't have all of the answers, but I'll tell you what I do know. When I've talked about my 'family' in the past, I have been referring to a collective group of people who share a similar genetic disease called Porphyria. From what I *have* been able to learn, the clan was formed in the early 15th century and was founded by Count Alphonso Diemo."

"You have got to be shitting me! An actual 'Count' started a vampire clan?"

"Yeah, Bram Stoker wasn't nearly as creative as people gave him credit. Anyway, people with our condition do need to take in blood, as you know, but in the 15th and 16th centuries my kind were hunted down as vampires and demons. Alphonso Diemo gave dozens of us a place to live and we were formed into a kind of family. For decades Alphonso and his followers thrived in London, where they worked as barbers."

"They were hair stylists?" Chris interrupted, "I didn't know they had those back then."

Steve gave Chris a flummoxed look. "No Chris, they worked at a type of hospital, where Alphonso performed bloodletting services for his clients. Remember that back then this was a widely accepted form of healing the injured and the sick."

Chris was wide-eyed at this revelation. "That...that is friggin' brilliant! They became respected members of the community, while taking the blood they needed and without anyone batting an eye."

"Exactly, but as I said, the whole thing eventually came crumbling down, after which my people traveled from place to place, always staying on the outskirts of society and totally off the grid."

"How many were there when you lived with them?"

"Nearly two thousand."

"Two thousand! Where the hell could two thousand people live and manage to stay off the grid?"

Steve's face contorted, he felt torn between telling his friend everything, and revealing those few secrets he still felt obliged to keep. Chris noticed the turmoil on his friend's face and held up his hand.

"No, don't tell me if it's going to make you uncomfortable. Sorry to interrupt the history lesson, please continue."

Steve shook his head, "Not too much more to tell really. I was born into that community and learned how to adapt to life with my condition. It was a good life really, maybe a bit more rural than the urban existence I've since adopted, but a good and happy life nonetheless."

Chris looked at Steve as if waiting for something. When Steve was obviously done speaking Chris said, "I am still waiting to hear the part about how you are not *really* a vampire. All you have really told me so far is that there may be as many as what, two thousands of you."

"What else do you want to know?"

"C'mon Steve! Look at your side! How is it you managed to heal up without stitches or staples? How is it I have seen you do over two hundred pull-ups without even breaking a sweat? Strength and speed healing aren't exactly textbook traits of Porphyria."

"The strength is explainable," Steve said in a confessionary voice, "but the healing part is something I only have theories about."

"Well start with the strength part."

Steve nodded. "All right. Remember how I said my people were living outside of society and off the grid?"

"Yes."

"Well, deep running cave systems and abandoned mines serve that purpose extremely well."

"And how does…ah, I see."

Steve carefully stood and walked over to a wall where a planter shelf was cut in the junction between the wall and the ceiling. Steve jumped and grabbed on to the shelf with one hand. He hung there suspended by his four fingers and looked at Chris expectantly. Then he released his little and ring fingers and began to pull his body up and down the wall using only his index and long fingers. When he reached thirty he dropped himself back down to the floor.

"Rock climbing wasn't a sport or recreation for me growing up. It was a vital part of life and I was doing it to some degree before I could walk. A couple of decades later I seem to have developed an above average level of strength, which I try to maintain as best I can. It helps in my work as well as the fact that someday I...."

Steve's words trailed off as memories of his childhood flooded back to him.

Chris watched Steve's face change and finished his thought. "Someday you might want to go home again?"

Steve looked up from his daydream as his eyes began to well up. He turned away from Chris and sat back down on the bed.

"No, I can't go home. That part of my past is dead to me."

Chris looked down at Steve, as the two men remained silent for a long moment. The he said simply, "I'm sorry."

Steve looked up. "For what?"

"For doubting you, I mean, you still haven't explained the healing thing which still makes me wonder about you being a real 'dyed in the wool' vampire, but I shouldn't have called you out like that. If there is one thing I know about you, one thing I am absolutely sure of, it would be that you're my best friend... vampire or not."

Steve looked at Chris skeptically then a smile broke out across his face. "You're gonna try to kiss me now, aren't you?"

Chris lifted one eyebrow as if pondering the idea: "No, a quick reach around maybe, but no kissing."

They both laughed until Steve raised a hand to his temple at the effort.

"So what's our next move?"

Steve thought a minute, "What time is it?"

"Close to 10:00 P.M., why?"

Steve shrugged. "At this point I want to stake out *The Inferno* and see if anyone turns up."

"Why?"

"Plain and simple, I don't have anything else to go on at the moment. Maybe we'll get lucky."

With a nod, Chris helped Steve out of the chair and steadied him as the two walked to Chris' office outside the operating theater. Chris helped Steve into a soft leather chair and began to scurry around the room collecting papers, a laptop computer, cellular phone, a messenger bag and a long rectangular case. Steve knew what the case held and he couldn't believe Chris kept it in his office in the morgue.

"Can you manage, or should I put this stuff in the car and come back for you?" Chris asked.

"I can manage. I think my sea legs are coming back to me."

The two walked from the building and into the underground garage where Chris had parked his car. Chris bought and sold his cars at an astonishing rate, always seeming to have a new car. Steve looked around for the Ford Excursion he'd ridden in less than six months ago, but saw no sign of it. There were only a few cars in the garage at this hour, Steve shook his head and laughed as they walked directly toward a brand new metallic green Hummer H2. GM made the automobile but they had now somehow managed to create a super SUV for the general public, retaining some of its bulletproof, industrial aesthetic from the original military Hum-Vee.

"What?" Chris asked when he saw Steve laughing.

"How long do you keep your cars anyway?"

"Long enough, and not one moment more," Chris responded as he unlocked the rear hatch and loaded the equipment from his office into the back of the H2. Setting the rectangular case in the rear compartment, he snapped the latches open and withdrew a sawed off pump shotgun, cut way below the legal limit. He also removed a box of shotgun shells and a pair of leather gloves.

.

Steve walked up next to Chris and peered into the H2. Sitting in molded foam was one of the most exotic looking rifles he had ever seen.

"I've been on the force for years now and I haven't seen anything like this."

"And you never will anywhere else. That baby is a completely custom Colt LE 901-16S rifle with multiple capabilities. depending on what you want it to do. I can put a short .223 caliber barrel on the end and use it as an assault rifle or I can stick on a high velocity 7.62x51mm NATO caliber barrel, and it becomes the most accurate hunting rifle I have ever had the pleasure to shoot."

"Hunting? When did you start doing that?"

"I haven't ever shot at anything other than targets, but I am a dead shot at over 500 yards with the telescopic sight."

"That's sharpshooter range!"

"Yeah, I'm not sneaky enough to be a sniper, but I guess a sharpshooter would be an accurate description. Of course, the only handgun I've used in the last few years was the one that came with my PlayStation game."

"Ergo the sawed off?"

"You got it."

Chris loaded two shells into the shotgun and placed a handful of shells in the cover flap of a messenger bag. Most of the papers, and a laptop computer, rested inside the main compartment of the bag, which Chris checked after he placed the shoulder strap across his body. He then tossed the keys to the H2 over to Steve without looking where he was throwing them. Steve caught the keys cleanly in his right hand.

"Good. Your head seems to be clearing pretty well."

"I feel pretty good, but should I be driving?"

"No. Absolutely not." Having said that, Chris walked around to the passenger side of the H2 and jumped into the front seat.

Steve nodded and without another word walked around the side of the car, climbed into the driver seat, started the vehicle and drove toward the exit of the garage.

As they were about to pull into traffic Steve said, "This may be the most conspicuous vehicle we could have chosen for a stakeout."

"Probably, but remember what Dennis Miller said: 'When a person is driving up the side of a hill in a tropical rainforest, a

116

Hummer is a tool. When a Hummer is cruising up Rodeo Drive looking for a parking space, the driver is a tool.'"

"And your point is?" Steve queried.

"There are a whole lot of 'tools' in LA. No one will pay us a second thought."

Chapter 16

The Inferno
10:45 P.M.

Steve parked the H2 less than a block from *The Inferno* on the opposite side of the road, staging the vehicle in the proper position so that he and Chris could keep an eye on the front of the deserted club. The two men sat quietly as they watched from the street. After about 45 minutes Chris began to get restless.

"So...this is a stakeout, huh? Well, at least you get paid by the hour." Chris said.

"What? You thought it was all action? Hot cars, hotter women and secret agent stuff?"

"Honestly no, after all I've seen your car, however this is really tedious. How long do we wait for something to happen?"

"A stakeout can last for hours, even days with a proper team or support system."

"Oh, great," Chris said without trying to hide his exasperation. Reaching into the backseat he pulled out some papers from his messenger bag. He sorted through the various documents and quickly became totally engrossed in whatever was written on the pages.

"Well it gives me time to look into a couple of theories I have about what might have happened to those catatonic people from the other night."

Steve waited, and when Chris saw the interest on his face, he continued.

"Based on what information I was able to gather before I left the scene, I have a couple of working theories on what could be the cause for the condition of the victims."

Steve nearly jumped out of his seat. "What! All of the victims were taken to quarantine before any of our medical people could examine them. We've had nothing to go on and no leads to follow."

"Right, but remember, I was at the scene and was able to do

some cursory examinations on a couple of the victims before I was shooed away by the Captain."

"And?"

"Well, from what little I had to go on I would guess that something, and I have no idea what, basically shut down the part of the brain that controls all skeletal muscle function."

"Skeletal muscle function?" Steve repeated.

"Exactly. You see, with the exception of the heart, there are basically two types of muscles in the body, smooth muscle and skeletal muscle. Smooth muscles are controlled by the brain and keep our body processes operating without us having to think about it. Skeletal muscles, on the other hand, are muscles we consciously control in order to produce movements and perform tasks. A good example of each type of muscle would be the combination of skeletal and smooth muscles in the esophagus. The top third of our throat is the part we consciously use to swallow our food. After that we don't think about moving the food we swallowed from the throat, down and into our stomachs. It just happens because the brain senses there is substance in the esophagus and it sends impulses for the smooth muscles within the lower two thirds of the esophagus to push the food down into the stomach."

"I remember this from science class."

"Okay, without getting too technical try to imagine the brain being a fuse box with several hundred different fuses. Now if the sense of smell is controlled by one fuse and you flip the switch to the 'off' position the body would no longer be able to process any stimuli for smell. All other functions in the body, unrelated to smell, will function normally but the body will be totally devoid of the sense of smell."

"So far I am following you."

"Good, now let's look at what happens when a person has a stroke. A stroke is caused by something cutting off the blood supply to a part of the brain. It is usually caused by a blood clot blocking a specific blood vessel in the circulatory labyrinth of the brain. This leads to ischemia, or lack of blood supply, to which the brain is highly sensitive and will quickly begin to deteriorate if the blockage is not removed. The damage to the brain is usually permanent and whatever part of the brain it controlled will be compromised by the damage. Still following this?"

"Everything except how this relates to those people at *The Inferno*."

"Skeletal muscle is controlled by that part of our brain responsible for conscious thought. It happens to be in the lower aspect of the brain close to where the brain becomes the spinal cord."

"The *medulla oblongata*?"

"Uh, well, more or less."

"I told you, I remember some of this stuff from science class."

"Well, that's basically correct. Anyway, what I am thinking is that something managed to flip the switch on the part of the brain which regulates the conscious ability to control the skeletal muscles of the body, without disrupting the remaining brain functions."

Steve thought about it. From a layman's perspective it did sound like what the victims he had seen could have been experiencing. He asked: "Any idea how that could be caused?"

"It could be caused by that aforementioned blood clot or a tumor or something else blocking off the blood supply to the brain. The transmissions from the brain could be normal, but the message could be cut off somewhere along the nerve pathway before reaching its destination. Such is the case with spinal injuries. The brain is working fine but the impulses it sends to the body never arrive as the nerve pathways have been severed."

"Could some kind of chemical or biological agent make blood clots?"

"Sure, but the distribution pattern and severity of the injuries would not all be the same, as is the case for *The Inferno* victims. I don't see how only a specific area could be targeted. If an outside agent caused the blood to form clots, then the clots would be everywhere in the body and you would have various levels of destruction. Many of the victims would die as clots formed in the lungs, along heart tissue and throughout the brain. The type of injury would be as random as rolling a pair of hundred-sided dice, with no way to control the outcome. Tumors would act in a similar fashion and take time to grow."

"What about cutting off the transmissions like you said?"

"The problem with that scenario is how *The Inferno* victims presented. The first tests performed in the field when dealing with an unconscious person, after checking their breathing and heart rates, involve checking the brain for injury. Some of these tests require examining the integrity of the cranial nerves. Several of these nerves innervate the skeletal muscles of the head and face and originate directly from the brain. The only way to cut off the transmission of these nerves is at the source, which means the brain. In the case of the victims at *The Inferno* I couldn't detect any skeletal muscle function anywhere, including the muscles innervated by cranial nerves. It was as if that entire aspect of their bodies had been shut down, and as far as I could tell, there was nothing else wrong with them."

A frightening thought occurred to Steve. "You said that the part of their brain allowing the conscious control of skeletal muscle had, in effect, been shut down. Right?"

"That's the theory, but I have no idea how to specifically target an area of the brain like that on such a multiple level."

"Right. Is there any chance the victims' thoughts or self-awareness has been compromised?"

Chris' face melted into an expression of sorrow.

"I didn't see any evidence that would confirm that but…"

"Just say it."

"While I was taking the pulse of one of the victims, one of the EMTs asked if we should try to inject adrenaline directly into the heart to "jump start" those affected. As he spoke, I felt the victim's pulse jump in speed and intensity as if he had heard what had been said and was afraid of the injection. At the time I thought the victims were comatose, yet it has been recorded that people in comas can hear. Now, I am afraid that maybe they are conscious and completely aware of everything going on around them, but they are completely powerless to do anything about it."

Steve could feel his anger building at the thought of those poor people being trapped within their own bodies. He remembered reading short works of fiction written about people who were in coma-like states, completely immobile and yet their minds functioned normally. Mercilessly they waited and listened to the world pass them by as time crept forward. Steve's heart began to beat faster as his anger swelled.

"I'm sorry," Chris spoke quietly.

"What?" Steve had been so lost in his anger. Chris' voice brought him back from the depth of his thinking.

Chris spoke with empathy in his voice that was written all over his face.

"I'm sorry for laying all of that on you. At this point everything is just theory. Don't take it as fact yet. You look as though I really upset you, but try to remember that I may be completely wrong about everything."

Steve was only able to weakly reply, "I'm no expert, but somehow, I don't think you are wrong."

Chapter 17

The "secret lab" wasn't really much of a secret to anyone who worked for Pharmanetics. Everyone in the company knew there were several floors within the building, which were off limits to anyone who didn't have the proper security clearance. The mystery was that no one really knew what was being worked on behind those restricted doors. Most of the day-to-day employees thought it was simply quality control, for the multitude of pharmaceuticals the company manufactured, and that the security was merely in place to prevent industrial espionage. If the truth about what was actually happening behind those closed doors ever came to light many of the Pharmanetics employees would find themselves in a very difficult moral conundrum.

Alex Daniels passed through the last security checkpoint and entered the main lab. As he surveyed the room he took in the massive number of refrigeration units with glass doors packed to capacity with plastic IV bags of glucose solution and other food supplementations. On the far end of the lab were the limited number of lab technicians and nurses brought in to care for *The Inferno* abductees. Apparently they were all taking a simultaneous break from their duties as they watched Dr. Whelan prepare a slide and place it under a microscope. Once the slide was properly inserted Dr. Whelan moved to a computer screen and clicked the mouse to bring up a live feed from the camera housed in the microscope.

Alex moved quietly behind the techs and looked at the images on the screen. He couldn't decipher anything he saw.

"Find what you are looking for?" Alex asked and startled a few of the techs in the process.

"Not really," Dr. Whelan replied as if he had known Alex had been there the whole time. This brain tissue shows only a trace amount of change as a result of the anesthetic, otherwise, it is completely within the parameters of normal brain tissue."

"And that means what exactly?"

Dr. Whelan turned away from the computer screen and spoke to the techs. "Could you all excuse us for a moment, maybe run a few diagnostic tests on our guests upstairs?"

Silently the techs all nodded and walked to a rear door, leaving Alex and the doctor alone in the laboratory.

When the last of the techs had exited Dr. Whelan said, "I think the subject who was immune to the anesthetic must have somehow been shielded from the effects as opposed to having some kind of genetic predisposition which made him immune."

Alex shook his head. "We picked *The Inferno* precisely because of the way the place was wired. There was no section of the club that should have been able to block the process."

"I agree, but there is nothing special about the subject's brain tissue, DNA or any other biological aspect that might have led to his immunity. No chemical components were in his blood that would have dulled or subdued the effect and his vision was more than sufficient to receive the input. The only possibility left is that he was shielded somehow."

Alex was trying to figure out how Phillip Devereaux managed to evade the effects of the anesthetic when a stray thought entered his mind.

"Brain tissue?" Alex asked. "How did you acquire the brain tissue samples from Phillip?"

"Dissection, of course." The doctor looked confused, as if the answer should have been obvious.

"But I thought you said the pathway the anesthetic affected was deep within the core of the brain."

"Yes...It is."

Alex frowned. "Then how did you manage to retrieve a sample without killing the subject?"

The doctor simply shrugged his shoulders.

"You killed him?"

Dr. Whelan looked thoughtful for a moment then said, "I like to look at it as he didn't survive the surgery, however, the end result is, of course, the same."

Alex sighed. "Did he even have a chance?"

"His well-being was never of any real interest to me. My only priority was the collection of the tissue I needed in order get the information required." Dr. Whelan frowned at Alex. "Most, if not all, of the great breakthroughs in medical science have always had a particularly nasty, yet necessary, dark side to them. Now is not the time to get squeamish, Mr. Daniels."

Alex suppressed a chill traveling through him at the coldness in the doctor's tone of voice. He changed the subject. "So how could he have been shielded?"

"We're working on that, but I would surmise there was a private area cut off from the rest of the nightclub, despite all of the plans and schematics we looked at prior to running the test."

"But we don't know, do we?"

"No, the police were alerted too quickly for me to properly search the entire club after I dropped Devereaux with the mobile device. Perhaps after things calm down a bit more we can use the cover story Kunnert put together to get another look inside the club."

Alex nodded. "Good idea. I think I'll have him get on that as soon as you all return from this second test of yours."

Dr. Whelan smiled. "All my bags are packed and I'm ready to go."

Then he started singing in one of the worst Elvis impersonations Alex had ever heard.

"Viva, Las Vegas…Viva, Las Vegas… Viva… VIVA… LAS VEGAS!!!"

Chapter 18

"Hey! Oh my goodness. Who the hell is that?" Chris bounced in his seat with excitement as he spoke.

Steve's head whiplashed back to the street to see a woman, deliberately avoiding the direct beams of streetlamp light, walking alone down the opposite side of the street. Her back was already to the H2 as she moved away from where they were parked. Long, luxurious raven hair reflected an almost metallic sheen as ambient light flashed across her mane.

Initially, Steve felt a surge of panic, but as the woman passed under a streetlight he realized it wasn't Lei.

Chris was excited at the enticing garb the prostitute was wearing. His mood instantly changed for the better. "Damn, I need to do more rides-along with you!"

Steve chuckled, "Still thinking with that part of your anatomy are you?"

"Well c'mon bud, you know I spend most of my nights looking at…Uh, oh." Chris sounded suddenly alarmed.

"What?"

"Look a little further down the street."

Steve turned to scan the darkness and saw them immediately. Two young men were cruising right for her and, from the look of their gait they were clearly hopped up on some kind of pharmaceutical.

The woman had noticed them and initially moved into the shadows in an attempt to keep from being seen. Too late she realized the men had already seen her and were now changing their course to move where she was hiding.

Steve killed the interior light of the H2 and opened the door. He could immediately hear the three separate voices speaking anxiously. Realizing the scene was going to turn violent, Steve drew his weapon and exited the H2.

Before he could take a step, Steve recoiled from an sudden

ear-splitting scream. He spun around just in time to see the two men dragging the woman into an alleyway between *The Inferno* and the neighbor building. The woman was fighting them. Kicking, screaming and slashing with long fingernails, as she desperately tried to escape their hold on her. She connected with her nail weaponry across the left cheek of one of her assailants. This small triumph was rewarded with a hard right cross to her jaw. Her body went slack as she moaned from the blow to her face. Steve was running full speed toward the commotion as the three disappeared around the corner and into the shadows of the alley.

"Freeze, Police!" Steve shouted toward the darkness. No response came from the void.

He rounded the corner to find one of the two men lying in a heap on the ground with his neck displaying an unnatural angle. Steve cautiously approached the body and immediately knew something was terribly wrong. He knelt to check for a pulse at the neck. The slightest touch to the neck caused the head to roll back and away. The man's neck had been fatally broken. Steve aimed the weapon in front of him as he moved further into the alley.

The alley split into two possible outlets, both leading back to a street. Steve noticed a door in the brick wall to his right standing slightly ajar. He squinted into the darkness but could not see any evidence of anyone moving. Deciding the remaining man must have been looking for a private place to take the woman, Steve reached for the door.

Steve jumped as Chris slid to a stop next to him with a completely uncoordinated flailing of hands, arms and shotgun. To his credit, Chris kept his graceless dance quiet as he read Steve's body language about the door. Chris stood to one side of the door with his back to the wall and readied himself as Steve again reached for the doorknob.

Swinging the door open quickly each man took his position, weapons aimed, and moved through the door. The room was a large empty warehouse with no visible hiding spaces. Still, the darkness could be enough to conceal two people, especially if one was unconscious. Steve and Chris moved carefully though the facility. After finding a staircase on the far side of the room, the two men completed their cursory search of the warehouse floor, and then moved up the stairs onto the next level. This floor was almost identical to the first floor, however, there was a great deal more ambient light illumination as a result of several large windows facing the street at the far end of the warehouse. The extra light made the reconnaissance of the room instantaneous with the end result revealing no woman or second assailant. Chris moved to the windows and scanned the street below.

"Over here!" Chris called out.

Steve ran to the windows and looked down to the street. At the mouth of the alley the second assailant stood in a fighting stance. The woman he and his partner had accosted was leaning against the alley wall, clearly terrified yet none the worse for wear. The man was circling someone else who was out of sight from the window. Judging from his footwork, he had spent a good deal of time inside a boxing ring. The man was about six feet tall, probably two hundred pounds, and apparently in excellent shape. He lunged forward toward the unseen individual and immediately staggered backward as if he had been hit with a jolting punch. He regained his composure as he moved back from the alley and further into view, again staring at whomever he was fighting.

Steve's breath caught as he felt something tug at his insides. He wanted to burst through the glass and jump the distance to the street below. Fortunately, his mind and body didn't function as a whole and he instead leaned against the wall to one side of the window.

It was then Steve could see Lei confidently walk into view. She was wearing a schoolgirl outfit complete with white-buttoned shirt, unbuttoned to expose her overly ample cleavage, and an extra short plaid skirt. Her incredibly long hair was actually in pigtails, bound by bright red elastic   scrunches. She skipped forward in white knee high stockings and patent leather loafers. Placing her arms behind her back and grabbing her wrists, she leaned forward toward the man and said something. Steve and Chris couldn't hear what she was saying but it incensed the man who lunged for her again. Lei casually reached for the man's striking arm and grabbed him by the wrist. With ridiculous ease she twisted and launched the man against the near alley wall where he struck with such impact his body bounced nearly five feet as he landed in an unconscious heap.

Both women stared at the unconscious body for a few seconds then looked at each other. Lei moved to where the woman was standing against the far wall and placed a reassuring hand on her shoulder. From their vantage point, Steve and Chris saw the woman begin to speak to Lei in what looked like a relieved string of "thank you's."

To his utter amazement Steve heard the words the woman spoke in his head as clearly as if he had been standing next to her." I don't know how you did that, but I really don't care."

Lei nodded and caressed the woman's cheek. The woman tried to look back to the motionless man lying less than ten feet from them, but Lei's hand gently guided the woman's face back to hers as they locked eyes. Moving closer to the woman, Lei pressed her body up against the woman who looked initially as if she was going to panic and push her away.

"What are you...?"

Lei locked eyes with the woman as she took hold of the woman's wrists and raised her arms above her head, pinning her to the alley wall. She kissed the woman fully on the lips in one strong, sensual motion. She heavily mashed her perfectly enhanced breasts into the woman's own natural bosom.

"You were looking for me weren't you?" Lei whispered into the woman's ear. "Well here I am."

"Wait. I'm not, I mean...I don't...I've never..." The woman's voice trailed off into heavy short breaths. The startled woman didn't resist, but was clearly overwhelmed by what was happening.

So were Steve and Chris.

"Uh, wow," was all Chris could manage to say as he watched

through the glass in disbelief.

Steve could only mutter under his breath, as he had to use all of his will power to keep his own body under control. "Damn it Lei, don't you do it!"

Neither woman broke eye contact, as Steve began to feel an irresistible pull at his core. Now he could feel the woman's body against his as if he were the one on the street below moving against her. He knew there was no logical way to hear what was going on beneath them, but the words were clearly audible to his ears.

Lei straddled one of the woman's legs and with incredible control, began to almost imperceptibly gyrate her entire body against the unbelieving woman who appeared to become more enthralled with each passing moment.

Letting go of the woman's wrists Lei stroked the back of the woman's neck with her left hand and gently traced her fingertips down the bare flesh of the woman's left arm. The caress continued over the woman's shoulder, neck, sternum, left breast, flank, and finally came to rest in a grip around her left hip.

The woman, who hadn't dropped her arms as they were released, closed her eyes and began to move with the gyrations of her savior. Steve could feel the woman's body trembling with never before known excitement as her inhibitions eroded under Lei's ministrations. With a sudden, assertive, yet gentle manipulation, Lei raised the soft part of her thigh up, between and across the woman's pubic area. Electricity shot through the woman as her hands shook uncontrollably with the combination of ecstasy and uncertainty. Releasing a hot breath across the tender skin of the woman's neck, Lei teased at her flesh with gentle neck kisses and slight tongue licks. Finally unable to keep herself in check the woman surrendered as her hands dropped down the Lei's back then disappeared under the short schoolgirl skirt. Moaning aloud and totally lost in the enthrall, the woman held tightly to her hero as the intensity of what was happening threatened to send her into unconsciousness.

"No." Steve said, but the words came out hoarse, little more than a whisper as he "felt" the small intense contractions of the woman's torso against his own hip and abdomen. He sensed the intensity building within the woman, an intensity that felt like a rise in energy from the woman's core, soon to be discharge in a physical explosion, which should not have been possible. Steve turned away from the window as the sensations became too strong. Averting his eyes however, did not diminish his connection to what was going on.

Steve turned his gaze to Chris who was lost in the site of the whole spectacle. He looked as if he was excited, ashamed and completely unnerved all at once. Steve turned back to the scene on the street to find Lei in complete control of the woman's body. She held one of the woman's legs aloft from the underside of the knee, while the other leg swung limply across the pavement, supporting no weight. The woman was moaning so loudly a minute amount of noise could be heard through the glass, although Steve heard everything with a clarity akin to having the woman screaming in his ears.

Then a sound as eerie as Steve had ever heard drowned out all other sounds and commanded his attention. It came on subtly at first, but grew in intensity until it was all Steve could concentrate on.

A heartbeat.

"Oh God! Lei stop!" Steve actually managed to get the words out, and it broke the spell Chris had been in.

Chris turned away from the window, "Steve?!? What's wrong?" Steve couldn't hear his friend any longer as his ears were filled with the deep and resonant thrum of the woman's heartbeat increasing in speed with each moment. Steve placed his hand on the wall for support. He wanted to move away from the window despite his last failed attempt to sever any connection to what was taking place on the street below.

The woman was tearing at her own clothes, desperately wanting to feel her champion's soft skin against her own. She wanted to kiss the mouth so perfectly sending electric impulses down from her neck into the very center of her being. She wanted so much to be a part of what was happening except most of her strength was gone. All she could do was hang on.

The woman sensed it happening, the building intensity she had only experienced in a similar but wholly different way before. Her face began to flush and her legs began to vibrate as she pulled her rescuer tighter into her body. Lei began to gently bite at the flesh of her neck increasing the eroticism of the moment. Each small, tantalizing nibble sent tidal waves of pleasure into the woman. Lei bit down only slightly harder and the woman had to concentrate to keep breathing. Reaching up with her right arm the woman grabbed a handful of hair near the back of Lei's head and forced that amazing mouth down hard on her neck with all of the strength she had left in her.

Upstairs, Steve swooned as the taste of the woman filled his mouth. He became severely dizzy and slumped to the floor, closing his eyes in an attempt to clear his spinning vision. Behind his closed eyes the scene continued to play out in real time as if he had never taken his eyes off of the window.

He felt the building, building, building of energy coming from the woman. Straining, indeed begging, for its release.

Then it happened.

Lei bit down hard on the neck of the woman and latched on to her. Every fiber of the woman's body exploded with orgasmic contraction and crackling nerve conduction. Arms flailing and legs convulsively kicking as the contractions arrived in wave after wave with no indication of any cessation.

From the window above, Chris saw the eruption of blood and immediately went into panic mode. "What the hell? Oh, holy shit! Steve! Wake up, we have to get down there!"

Steve rolled to his knees and peered out the window to see blood pouring from where Lei had latched onto the woman's throat. The woman's skin had turned a pasty white and her eyes rolled drunkenly in their sockets, her grip on Lei's head appeared stronger than ever, refusing to allow separation of Lei's mouth from her throat.

Chris bolted for the stairway as Steve fought to regain his footing. On the ground below the woman had grown weak from blood loss and her arms dropped to her sides as she gasped for breath. Her face was not one of terror, but exhaustive ecstasy as her mouth tried to form words while her vision went white.

A door banged open on the street below and Steve heard Chris screaming for Lei to release the woman. Making no attempt to dislodge herself from the limp woman, Lei continued her sexual undulations as if she had never heard Chris. Steve watched Chris raise the shotgun and point it at Lei. The life suddenly flowed back into Steve's body as Lei dropped the unconscious woman to the pavement.

Lei's beautiful mouth and chin were now covered in crimson, her face distorted into a frightful countenance of rage as she faced Chris. Steve wanted to scream in protest when a blur of black leather and white hair snatched the shotgun from Chris' grip. Realizing he had lost his weapon Chris tried to throw a punch into the larger figure only to find himself in a chokehold a mere second later.

Panic forced him into action as Steve fired three rounds through the window, showering the figures below in shards of glass. Bolting out of the way of the sharp rain, Alpha released Chris and dove toward Lei. Chris hit the ground and rolled in the opposite direction as Steve launched himself through the window, landing with a roll, to the pavement some 14 feet below.

Crouching to a stop with his weapon aimed directly at Alpha, Steve spoke in deliberate, murderous tones.

"Don't...fucking...move!"

Alpha was facing him, looking down through yellow eyes and barred teeth.

"Steve, look out!"

Steve heard Chris' call, but couldn't react swiftly enough as Lei kicked the gun from his hand. Rolling out of the way of her next kick, Steve increased the distance between himself and the two members of his former family. He assumed a fighting stance as he began to defend himself from an onslaught of punches and kicks from Alpha which resonated with a force of impact more powerful than anything he had ever felt before.

Steve was able to efficiently block and parry each blow shot toward him until he sensed an opening where he countered with an uppercut to Alpha's abdomen. The blow landed with a thud and Alpha froze upon impact. Steve was sure he had placed the punch perfectly in the solar plexus and expected Alpha to respond more than he did. Instead Alpha took two steps back, looked down to his abdomen and said in a sort of reverent disbelief, "You've improved."

Alpha's voice was musical, deep and heavy with a European accent of unknown origin. "Let's try that again, shall we?"

This time Steve had no chance of blocking the perfectly placed right cross that landed squarely on his left temple. His head felt like it was going to burst as he tried to roll with the blow. Steve managed to keep conscious despite the pain.

"Alpha, leave him! I have the girl. Let's get out of here!"

"You need to learn to finish what you start Lei."

"We need answers, now isn't the time to settle old scores!"

Spinning to Lei, "We wouldn't have this kind of trouble if you showed more control." Alpha had turned his back on Steve and seemed to scold Lei in a patronizing fashion.

Alpha turned again to face Steve as Steve tried to square his shoulders to his mentor. From behind him a loud ratcheting sound broke the standoff, as Chris loaded a round into the chamber of his now retrieved shotgun.

"I think we all need to calm down and have a little talk," Chris spoke in an even and level tone.

Alpha didn't move, but his eerie yellow eyes darted from Steve to Chris and back to Steve. Steve put his hands on his thighs and bent over in an attempt to catch his breath. Chris moved to Steve's side, "You okay?"

"Yeah, just give me a minute."

"Sure, I..."

Suddenly, although he was well out of striking distance, Alpha kicked one leg out at them. Realizing what he was doing, both Steve and Chris instinctually turned to protect their eyes as several small shards of broken glass flew off the ground and sped toward them. Having been able to shield themselves in time, the glass bounced harmlessly off their clothes. Steve and Chris turned back to find both Alpha and Lei running a good distance away down the lighted street with the unconscious woman over Alpha's shoulder.

Steve picked up his gun and took off after them with Chris tight on his heels. Rounding a corner, Steve saw Alpha effortlessly open a manhole cover about fifty yards down the street. Lei jumped in the manhole first as Alpha looked up at Steve, then carefully dropped the woman feet first into the hole. Steve and Chris both stopped in their tracks knowing they were about to lose their quarry. Chris raised the shotgun, but Steve placed a hand on the barrel causing Chris to lower the weapon.

Never taking his eyes off of Steve, Alpha pointed a long gloved index finger at him.

"Until you remember where your loyalties should lie, stay out of our way boy!" Alpha's voice resonated through the deserted street. "This isn't personal, at least not on my end, but don't make me wish to change that situation!" Then, with barely a sound, he jumped into the open manhole.

Chapter 19

Downtown - Las Vegas, Nevada

It is a rare and rather unpleasant experience to feel the outside temperature still tipping the thermometer at 105° at 10:30 in the evening. There is no such thing as a cool breeze at that temperature. Instead the wind gives a sensation more unto that of opening the door of a convection oven and getting blasted by the hot air.

The "Fremont Street Experience" is a project built several years ago in the downtown area as a major undertaking to bring back the once former glory of the current "low end" area of old Las Vegas. The project resulted in the closing of three blocks of Fremont Street, which was the downtown area's main street, and a distant cousin to the Las Vegas Strip, which was now the outside world's vision of Las Vegas. The production included an enormous metal and glass canopy bridging the street between the hotels on each side. This covering was filled with millions of multicolored lights, Surround Sound speakers that stretched over the entire three blocks and a computer system to coordinate them both. All this technology culminated in a spectacular light show of sight and sound, supposedly unlike anything else in the world.

Unfortunately, the high end production of the "Experience" did not prompt the various casinos in the area to modernize or improve their facilities in any way. For reasons known only to their owners, the downtown casinos languished in their current run down, filthy and past-its-prime décor, as the standard for the area. Only the Golden Nugget Hotel could claim any of the magic that could be seen from the newer mega-resorts on the famous Las Vegas Strip. This apparent apathy from the downtown casinos left the area in the same dilapidated state on the inside, despite the high dollar and admittedly extraordinary facelift for the street outside.

Kunnert stood at the street corner with an earpiece resembling a blue-tooth wireless phone as he waited for one of his agents to call in. Dr. Whelan's second test was underway as of five minutes ago and once again, the doctor had insisted on performing the test himself. The only difference between this test and the last was that this time Kunnert had sent an agent of his own to tail the doctor and report back as the test progressed.

Kunnert's agent's voice now broke over the earpieces: "Visual of target acquired. Target is going into the Glitter Gulch."

Kunnert replied, "Understood. No one move except on my orders."

For years the Glitter Gulch was an extremely successful slot parlor-type casino, that is until the owner envisioned a change for his highly lucrative business that would generate even more profit than the slot parlor. The owner of the Glitter Gulch simply turned his successful slot parlor casino into a large topless strip club and watched as his expenses diminished and profits multiplied. The location of the club was now set dead in the heart of the elaborate "family friendly" Fremont Street Experience. Despite several attempts on the part of the city's public relations team to shut it down, the club still remains open 24 hours, 365 days a year.

Kunnert's agent, former Sergeant Nick Morris, entered and moved through the dimly lit, smoke filled club, completely ignoring the young buxom women sauntering around him. He removed a roll of one dollar bills and stuffed three or four of them into a G-string whenever he was propositioned by one of the girls who worked the club. After giving out a few bucks it was easy to shoo them away and they moved on, hoping to find other men who might be larger fish.

Initially, the agent had no luck pinpointing the target after his first search of the club. He started to check the VIP room when a huge bouncer blocked his path. Putting the singles away he reached into another pocket and pulled out a few one hundred dollar bills and requested a chair in the VIP room. The now friendly bouncer politely escorted Kunnert into the reserved area and he immediately located the doctor.

The target, Doctor Phineas Theodore Whelan, was sitting at

his table with two practically naked women grinding their bodies over his in a manner that would probably get them arrested if the doctor turned out to be a vice cop. The agent sat at his table and the bouncer asked what type of girl or girls he would like to have sent over. He requested instead to watch a few of the girls first before selecting anyone in particular. The bouncer nodded, said he would send a waitress over and returned to his spot by the door.

No one in the club had noticed that the good doctor had been placing hockey puck sized discs throughout the club as he entered the establishment. By the time he reached his table he had spread nearly half a dozen discs from the front to the rear of the club. The music began to fade and the two girls slid off whatever part of the doctor's body they had attached themselves to and collected their money. The doctor shifted in his seat while handing the girls their bills and the first girl disappeared into the club, but the second must have sensed the doctor had deeper pockets to delve into, she sat back down on his lap without putting her top back on.

The doctor slipped one hand into a front pants pocket and fumbled around for something. The girl's faced contorted in a concerned countenance as she probably thought he was trying to "adjust" himself until the doctor removed his hand and revealed a dark round object which he dropped to the floor.

"Oh, what's that?" the confused dancer asked as she watched the object roll slowly away from where they were sitting.

Agent Morris had felt more than heard the disc land on the floor and he tried to get a glimpse of whatever it was, before he returned his attention to the doctor, who had donned a strange looking pair of sunglasses resembling laboratory goggles. In the hand previously holding the round object was what looked like a keyless entry remote for a car. The doctor's thumb was resting on one of the buttons.

"Those glasses are pretty weird, kinda neat too, but weird." The dancer was commenting as the doctor cupped his free hand under one of her breasts.

It was then that something bumped against Sergeant Morris'

foot. He looked down to see the round object the doctor dropped sitting on the floor next to his feet. Agent Morris' eyes went wide with shock as he realized what he was looking at. Before he could react the doctor pressed the button on the keypad igniting all of the discs in the club simultaneously. Each disc exploded in a cacophony of sound and light that reverberated through the club and could be heard outside on the street.

The explosions from the doctor's modified flash-bang grenades were similar to the more traditional type. Typically, the large explosion from such a grenade would produce an immense amount of sound and light without force or projectiles, considered a humane weapon that attempted to disorientate and subdue. The doctor had modified the light to explode in a predictable, rapid flash pattern similar to what he had programmed his "camera" to emit. Bodies fell from stages, poles, barstools and wherever they stood. Others slumped limply in lounge chairs, or fell across the small tables behind which they had been seated.

The flashes ended almost as soon as they'd begun and the doctor found himself on the floor screaming in agony. In his zeal to ignite his latest creation he had forgotten to place the earplugs in his ears. The tumultuous sound rendered him in abject misery, even though the glasses had protected him from the lights.

Dr. Whelan never considered himself to be physically graceful or coordinated, but the stagger he exhibited with his first step made him realize just how much his equilibrium had been sent asunder. Dizzy and slightly nauseous, post flash-bang grenade, he braced himself on a hand railing and waited for the room to stop spinning. After a few moments the pain and vertigo had subsided, although it would be some time before his hearing would return completely. He stood to survey the scene. Men and women were strewn about the club and, as far as he could see, no one had been unaffected. He removed the glasses and placed them in his fanny pack then removed the mobile anesthetic device he had created from a modified camera with a more powerful than normal flash.

Switching a knob on the top left side of the device it once

again became an actual camera. The doctor moved through the throng of inanimate bodies on the floor and in chairs, taking snapshots as he meandered. That is, until he found Kunnert's agent lying on his back in a wide-eyed stare at the ceiling.

"Can you see me? I know you can." The doctor mocked him as he spoke, "How long do you think it will be like this? Will it last for a few minutes, a few hours, a few days? Well, I'll tell you a little secret. So far, there is no limit to how long a person can stay in this state. If I were to make a prediction, I would guess you could very well spend the rest of your life trapped in that body of yours with your mind perfectly clear and cognizant." The doctor turned to walk away, but after only a few steps he stopped and walked back to the agent on the floor.

"Wouldn't be sporting of me to leave one of the team like this, I'll let Kunnert know you are down, but when you come out of it, please let him know I don't like having a chaperone."

Chapter 20

Outside the club, on the street, the explosion of sound and flashing of light had not gone unnoticed. The people who were standing in the doorway of the Glitter Gulch, and could see the lights generated by the grenades, collapsed like marionettes whose strings had just been cut. Others ran from the sound of the explosion as it rocked the entire three block area. Kunnert was in the process of swallowing a mouthful of water from a squeeze bottle when the flash bangs detonated. He nearly choked on the liquid as his body contorted from the explosive sounds.

He immediately started giving orders as his security officers transformed themselves into the elite soldiers they actually were. Drawing automatic weapons from specially-made concealed holsters within their uniforms they rushed to the club's entrance but did not enter the facility. Armed Las Vegas security guards lumbered into action and drew their weapons on Kunnert's men who returned the greeting with raised weapons of their own. A free-for-all gunfight was about to ensue as Kunnert hollered for his men to lower their weapons. Reluctant, but ultimately loyal to their commanding officer, Kunnert's men lowered their weapons as Kunnert spoke with the Las Vegas security guards.

Tourists ran in every direction still having no idea what had happened or where. Someone screamed "Terrorist attack!" and the whole scene deteriorated into a full-fledged panic. The general tourist population went into chaos as word of the explosions spread through the crowd.

Las Vegas Metro Police would soon be arriving, Kunnert however, had dealt with this contingency earlier. Previous work in the military and on a federal level in law enforcement had taught him how to accurately forge the necessary documents and identification he needed to give him instant credibility with the locals, something he should have done in advance in Los Angeles. Had he warmed up the LAPD to his presence, *The Inferno* incident would have had his team working with the police instead of containing them.

The Las Vegas Metro officers who arrived on the scene would have orders from their superiors instructing them to assist a federal terrorist task force already in place. As they arrived, Kunnert set the local police officers to the task of controlling the crowd knowing they would have their hands full and wouldn't accidentally be witness to anything incriminating his team or Pharmanetics.

Once Kunnert finished speaking with local law enforcement he made a beeline for the Glitter Gulch. Stepping over the bodies lying in disarray, Kunnert quickly moved through the front doors and found Dr. Whelan inside taking pictures with elation.

Kunnert moved up next to the doctor, "I take it from your demeanor the test was a complete success?"

The doctor's smile was so wide Kunnert thought it might cause the man's lips to split.

"I checked every room and no one eluded the effect. We have a completely successful test!" The doctor pumped one fist at his side in triumph as he finished his statement, then looked to Kunnert as he remembered the agent on the floor. "Oh, your guy is over there." The doctor pointed absently in the direction of Kunnert's downed man as he resumed taking photographs.

Kunnert nodded and walked over to where his man was lying on the strip club floor. "Can you wake him up here?"

"You know he's actually awake at the moment, right?"

"That's not what I'm asking Doctor."

"Sorry. Yes I could get the proper equipment easily enough, but it might be a better idea if we took him back to my lab in Los Angeles."

"Why?"

"Just in case anything unusual happens when we bring him out of it."

"Understood." Kunnert lifted his radio from his pocket and

pressed the send button. "Evac for one." He didn't waste another moment of concern for his man, as his mind was already thinking ahead.

"So we are a go for phase two?"

The doctor slapped Kunnert on the shoulder. "Oh absolutely! By all means go out and start bagging and tagging our 'volunteers.' The sooner we get them back to the lab with the others, the better." The doctor raised the camera up to his eyes and resumed clicking away at the lifeless forms on the floor.

Kunnert began to move off when the doctor called out to him. "This is so stimulating. Can you ever remember having this much fun?"

Chapter 21

4:30 a.m. Los Angeles, California

Steve and Chris had dropped down into the sewer in pursuit of Alpha, Lei and the woman they had carried off. They instantly lost the trail, as Steve had suspected they would, and the two climbed back out of the sewer and replaced the manhole cover a few moments later.

As they made their way back to the H2 Chris broke the uncomfortable silence.

"So, at the risk of repeating myself, now might be a good time to tell me again that you are not *really* a vampire." Chris wasn't afraid when he posed the question this time. In fact, he actually seemed more amused than anything else, teasing Steve with the repetition of his earlier request.

"After what you just witnessed I'm not sure I can anymore." Steve paused and shook his head, "In fact, I'm not sure I can convince myself of that anymore either."

Chris' mocking expression vanished as soon as he heard the tone of Steve's voice. The two walked in silence until they reached the H2. Chris held his hand out to Steve who silently handed the keys over and moved to the passenger side of the vehicle. The two climbed in and buckled up as Chris turned the key in the ignition. He left the H2 running in idle as he turned to Steve.

"Okay, let me see if I can make a few educated guesses here. You knew them didn't you?"

"Yes."

Chris nodded. "Well you've told me enough about Alpha for me to guess that was him?"

"Yes."

"And he's the leader of your people and a direct descendent of the original founder of your clan, or coven or whatever you call it?"

"I call it my family Chris. We've never looked at ourselves as anything other than a large family and community. As far as Alpha's lineage is concerned, the rumor is he's a direct descendant of the family patriarch Alphonso Diemo."

"And he's your father?"

"Yes…no…well, basically yes. He's not my biological father, I don't know who that man might be, but Alpha is the one who raised me and taught me just about everything I know."

"Lovely. What kind of name is Alpha anyway?" Chris wasn't bothering to hide the sarcasm in his voice.

"It's more a title than a name. 'Alpha', you know, like the first in charge kind of thing."

"Oh sure, that makes perfect sense." Chris rolled his eyes as he spoke. "Now, on to the more important things. As far as I can remember you've never mentioned 'she of the magnificent rack' before. Who was she?"

Steve turned to Chris, his face a mask of rage. "After all you saw her do, all you can comment on were her breasts?!?"

Chris only reacted with a shrug of his shoulders and a smile. "You should know by now a good set of tits are, and have always been, at the top of my priority list."

When Steve's face didn't lose its edge Chris said only a little more seriously, "I haven't forgotten the rest, it's just my nature to make a snide sexual remark whenever I can. Although it would be remiss of me not to point out that this type of humor is usually well received by you. Why are you so sensitive all of a sudden? Who is she?"

Steve's face calmed and he pressed his hands to his temples as if fighting off a sudden headache.

"We were engaged." As he spoke the words Steve felt like all the air had suddenly been let out of him.

"WHAT?!? You hit that?!? Oh good God in heaven tell me you hit that!"

Steve immediately raised his head with an incredulous look on his face as Chris' response couldn't have been anymore

145

inappropriate. Then again, it was Chris, and the goofball expression he was shooting Steve cut through his memories, a small laugh swelled from somewhere deep inside his core. By the time it reached the surface the laugh was rolling out of him and Chris had started laughing as well. When their laughter finally ebbed, Chris put the H2 into drive and pulled the vehicle out from where they had parked.

"That's better," Chris said victoriously after having broken Steve out of the funk he'd been in. "Now about the vampire thing?"

Steve asked the question out loud as if talking to the universe in general, "Am I a vampire?"

Chris waited, trying not to let his own excitement of the impending answer show in his expression.

"The simple answer is, Yes."

Chapter 22

The silence in the H2 lingered for a time, before Steve felt ready to continue.

"People, and I do mean 'people' like my extended family and myself, have existed throughout history. Why? I don't know. Maybe nature decided humans needed a natural predator, or maybe it truly is as simple as a genetic mistake, which caused the condition. Regardless, our history would read something like this, and please note this is more legend than fact."

"Initially, the madness caused by our Porphyria claimed the sufferers around puberty and they would become little more than animals. Some basic instinct we have however, tells us what we need in order to survive, hence the legendary attacking of people and the drinking of their blood. Some of my kind even embraced the condition and thrived despite the serial killings they were perpetrating within their own society. The one commonly perceived characteristic was that all of us were monsters and deserved little more than the gruesome deaths we eventually received. My kind were hunted down and killed in the most heinous way the primitive villagers, or tribesmen, could conjure in their depraved and theoretically justified minds. Even the church got involved and proclaimed us demons, and they even had special branches employed to hunt us down. I suppose it's no surprise that these branches included the Inquisitors, during the Spanish Inquisition, but I reckon that it's not relevant at the moment."

Steve paused for a breath, and in order to collect his thoughts, when he realized Chris was just driving in circles.

"Where are we going anyway?"

"Nowhere. Keep talking."

Steve nodded and continued. "Anyway, the way the story goes is that one of my people was able to overcome the madness. How he managed it has never been figured out because, even to this day, if any of my kind goes into the madness there isn't supposed to be any way to recover. Still, according to the legends, this one man recovered and began to collect as much information on the condition as he could. Initially he could only use his own life as data, but eventually he found another like him, who was on the brink of insanity and he helped him recover. Together these two men went on a bloody crusade of sorts, in order to save others like themselves. This is where the modern day legend of the vampire may have started. Alphonso and William treated anyone not like them as little more than cattle. They were brutal, secretive and incredibly efficient in their abilities."

Steve paused at this point and stared off into space as if telling the story had caused him to drift into his own memories.

Chris grew uneasy in this moment of silence and prompted, "So when did this Alphonso go from being a serial killer to your benevolent patriarch?"

Steve awoke from his daydream with a start, and looked around as if confused by his surroundings, until his eyes fell on Chris and he seemed to regain his wits.

"Right. Sorry." Steve rubbed his face and continued where he had left off. "After a while, Alphonso and William had gathered so many of us together they couldn't take enough blood from unwilling victims without running the risk of exposing themselves. They had been run off a few times, when angry mobs began hunting them down, and they knew they needed to find a better way than killing indiscriminately. It was Alphonso who came up with the answer to the problem, when he began working as a barber in England. He set up a makeshift hospital/barbershop, and began to perform bloodletting services to the English Aristocracy. Word spread and soon Alphonso had set himself and his extended family up in the heart of London, where he was known to be an advisor to several of the English Kings from 1450 through 1528."

"Wait, wait, wait!" Chris interrupted. "That's 78 years! How could he have worked for..." Chris looked at Steve, and then thought to himself before saying, "Oh, vampire...right."

"We're not immortal Chris, in fact, we're not even ageless."

"Then how do you explain it?"

Steve shook his head. "In Alphonso's case, I can't. Try to remember that everything I've told you is more legend than hard fact. I would be remiss however, not to mention that there are some factual aspects of being a vampire, some that are pure fiction, and some areas that are quite…grey."

"So the facts are?"

"Well, we all have Porphyria and need to take in human blood products in order to survive without going mad and dying in extraordinary pain. We are all exceptionally long lived if our condition, or something else, doesn't kill us first, however our life spans are not outside the realm of what a normal human could attain. We are also extremely hard to kill, but this has more to do with our unusual blood chemistry than anything supernatural. That's basically it. Those are the things we know about ourselves, the facts of us would-be vampires."

"So the fiction would be the stuff about turning into bats, smoke or demons." Chris volunteered.

Steve chuckled, "Yep, but that's only the beginning of the fairy tales. For example, crosses, holy water and the like, are all bogus. Some of the people I grew up alongside are quite devout and wear crosses and other religious paraphernalia on their person at all times. Garlic is one of my favorite foods, and the reason a wooden stake through my heart would kill me is simply because, well, someone had thrust a wooden stake though my heart."

"Fair enough," Chris said, "so what are the 'grey areas?'?"

"Okay, here is where it does get a little weird." Steve seemed to notice something up ahead as the H2 was traveling. "Get on the I-10 going east."

Confused, Chris asked. "We going somewhere?"

"Yeah, but it will take a while to get there, and I need to make a stop at my apartment first."

"Sounds like you have a plan."

"Not really, but I know where Alpha and Lei are going to take the woman."

"And where would that be?"

"Home, Chris. I swore to myself I never would, but I'm thinking that I'm actually going to have to go home."

Chapter 23

The needle on the RPM meter of the H2 fell just under the red zone as the engine growled like an angry animal speeding down the highway. Chris tried to coax more speed out of the massive V8 engine, although they were already moving at full speed, and nearly overtaxing the H2's capabilities. The sun was still behind the horizon and despite the fact that the highway was practically abandoned at this early hour, the road seemed endless and monotonous as the miles crept along.

They had made their stop at Steve's apartment over an hour and a half ago. Steve had rushed from the vehicle and returned minutes later with a large flask in one hand and a dusty army duffle bag over his shoulder. After throwing the duffle bag in the backseat he jumped into the front passenger seat and the two were once again underway on the I-10 East. The freeway was still practically empty as they reached the I-15 North connection in record time.

"I-15 North? Please don't tell me we're going to Vegas."

"Just outside the city limits, actually."

"And that's 'Home?'"

Steve only nodded, as the H2 continued to hurl its mass down the paved road.

"So what are those 'grey areas' we spoke of earlier?" Chris asked literally out of nowhere.

"You don't let-up do you?"

"Nope. Too interested."

"And afraid?"

Chris turned his eyes from the road to give Steve a sarcastic frown. "Please, if I were still afraid of you I'd have abandoned you in LA."

Steve smiled, "Fair enough." He cleared his mind and thought about how to best answer Chris' question.

"Remember that thing I said about our blood chemistry making it difficult to kill people like me?"

"Sure."

"Did you wonder what I meant by that?"

"Of course, but you were on a roll, and I didn't want to break your train of thought."

"Okay, well the reason why we are so hard to kill is actually because we heal so quickly. Now, the reason we heal so quickly is because our blood chemistry isn't a compatible environment for viruses and harmful bacteria to survive in." Steve paused to let that sink in before he asked,

"Understand?"

"No. What does that mean?"

Steve laughed. "I thought you were supposed to be a doctor?"

"I am, and I understand what you said, except for the small fact that it's impossible!"

"Not in our case."

"So what you're telling me is that you have complete immunity from all viruses?"

"And most harmful bacteria as well."

Chris looked like his head might explode with the prospect of that information.

"How…how is that possible?"

Steve shrugged his shoulders. "No idea. I don't know the science behind it, but if I were to take a guess I'd say it's some kind of evolutionary thing. I mean, how could my kind have survived on human blood down through the ages of non-existent sanitation, not to mention times of plague and other disease, if we weren't able to develop some type of immunity? Those of us who didn't develop a natural immunity to the cesspool people lived in then, probably died off. They must have succumbed to the diseases they contracted from their victims, but those who weren't susceptible lived on, and passed those traits to their children, in the same way as any other species on the planet."

"This sounds suspiciously like theory as opposed to fact."

"My take on the origins of our immunity is completely based on my opinion, but the fact that my people are still immune is exactly that…fact. Remember when you recently said to me how you've never seen me sick a day in all the time we've known each other. That's why."

"And the bullet wound?"

"Think about it in simpler terms. If you cut yourself it takes a certain amount of time for the wound to heal. If you tend to the wound and keep it clean it heals faster. If you apply anti-bacterial cream to the wound on top of that it will heal faster still. Now imagine how efficient the body could work if it didn't have to deal with *any* bacterial or viral infiltration at all."

Chris could only shake his head. "Wow."

"It's not instantaneous by any means, but it is far faster than what is considered to be normal in a human."

Chris began thinking out loud. "So, unless the damage to the system is lethal at the onset…"

"We will be able to recover from virtually any injury." Steve finished Chris' thought.

Chris stared ahead at the seemingly never-ending road ahead when his eyes suddenly went wide.

"Steve…"

Something about Chris' voice was disturbing to Steve but he answered without letting it show in his voice. "Yes?"

"How old are you?" Chris said almost meekly.

Steve began to shift in his seat uncomfortably. "Why?"

"You told me your people are extremely long lived. If what you just told me about your immunity is true then your longevity would be a result of your body having undergone significantly less cellular damage over time. This cellular damage is what the anti-aging docs think is the cause of aging in the first place."

Chris turned and looked at Steve's relatively wrinkle-free face before turning back to the road. "I always thought we were around the same age." Chris waited. When Steve didn't answer right away, he said, "I'm thirty eight."

The time dragged on, as only the sound of the H2's engine and the tires on the road filled the interior of the vehicle.

Then, quietly, Steve said. "I'm seventy three."

Chapter 24

The sound of Steve's cell phone ringing erupted within the interior of the vehicle.

"Who's calling you at 6:00 in the morning?" Chris asked as Steve removed the phone from his pocket.

Steve frowned as he looked at the screen. He didn't recognize the number illuminated within the small rectangle.

"Jacobs here."

"Jacobs? It's Paul Meyers."

Steve stiffened. "Yes, Captain."

"Where are you?"

"Oh boy," Steve thought. He knew the fact he was on his way out of town without letting his superior know ahead of time was not going to go over well.

"Sir, that's a long story…."

Meyers sighed on the other end. "Never mind, just make your way to the airport. You and Barnes will find tickets at the security desk for the first flight to Las Vegas. Whatever happened at *The Inferno* just happened at some strip club out there."

"Uh…sir?"

"What?"

Deciding there was no good way to get around the reality of the situation Steve simply said, "Chris and I are currently driving toward Vegas at the moment. I estimate we are just over two hours out from the city limits."

"What?!?"

"Yes sir. Some events that occurred tonight suggested the need for us to do some investigating out near Las Vegas."

"And you were going to inform me of these "events" when exactly?"

"Would you believe me if I said I didn't want to wake you, sir?"

"Don't get cute Jacobs." The acting Captain sounded more

flustered than angry, as he mumbled something under his breath. "All right, they have some victims from the scene this time. When you get to Vegas have Barnes go to the hospital and start working with the docs there. See if he can learn anything about what we are dealing with. I also want you to coordinate with locals and see what information you can get from the crime scene."

"Sir, the lead I am following is on a timetable and I need to follow through on that before I check in with local law enforcement."

Meyers was silent for a moment then said sternly, "I would very much prefer it if you were to tell Las Vegas Metro who you are and what you are doing before you run off and get caught up in something that wouldn't shine well on this department."

"If it makes you feel any better Sir, the lead is outside of the Las Vegas city limits, therefore, outside of their jurisdiction. I won't be stepping on any toes checking it out ahead of time."

Meyers seemed to consider that before he said, "All right. Can you send Barnes ahead to make the introductions?"

"That should work."

"Tell him to behave."

Turning to Chris, Steve said. "Chris, behave."

Chris rolled his eyes and raised his hands momentarily skyward. "I haven't even done anything yet!"

Chapter 25

About fifteen miles outside of Las Vegas Steve had Chris pull off the main highway and onto a dirt road leading west toward a small mountain range. Chris had some difficulty keeping the H2 from sliding around on the loose gravel of the desert floor at the speed they were going, and the bumpy terrain bounced them around inside the vehicle. The road ended when a large log, or possibly an actual telephone pole at some point, blocked any further travel that the H2 could manage along the dirt path.

"We need to find another way around?" Chris asked.

"Nope." Steve unbuckled his seatbelt, "We're here."

Chris raised his eyebrows, as he surveyed what appeared to be nothing more than the undisturbed flora and fauna of the Mojave Desert.

"Steve I don't think we are anywhere."

"That's exactly the idea. I have to hoof it for a quarter mile."

"What happens in a quarter mile?"

"There's an entrance to an abandoned silver mine."

"A silver mine?"

"Yep, Home Sweet Home."

You mean to tell me, your people are all living in an abandoned silver mine less than fifteen miles from Las Vegas?"

"And have been for over fifty years. It was the perfect place really. Access to utilities and water had been created for the miners, the tunnels were all pre-dug and several large excavations several stories deep into the ground were pre-made for us. These mines are all over southern Nevada but once we found one large enough to meet our needs, all we had to do was make it livable."

Chris didn't seem convinced. 'You're sure you're going to be okay out here?"

"Absolutely, stick to the plan and see what you can find out from the local authorities and the victims from the incident at the strip club. I'll get back to you as soon as I can."

"How long will that be?"

"Might be as long as twenty four hours, keep your cell phone with you in any case."

"I don't like this, you're really on your own out here."

"I'll be fine. Really!" Steve pulled his duffle bag out of the backseat and placed his flask in a pocket along the side of the bag. Then he removed his Glock and his back-up pistol and checked to assure both were loaded and ready.

Chris watched and shook his head. "And everyone says I'm the nut bag."

Steve smiled as he closed the door and then slapped the side of the H2, as Chris began to back the vehicle away from the log to turn around and head back to the road.

Steve watched the H2 raise a dirt cloud behind it, as Chris drove away, and then he slung the duffle over his shoulder and started walking along the path he had committed to memory decades ago.

Steve had only walked for about ten minutes when he saw the sign he knew would be there, accompanied by a picture of a male restroom-style stick-figure falling, and placed above a skull and crossbones below:

DANGER!!!
Do Not Enter Abandoned Mine!
Area unstable and trespassers risk severe injury!
DANGER!!!

As Steve had told Chris, southern Nevada was once a major source of silver. It has an enormous network of silver mines surrounding its outskirts. Most of these mines were supposed to be empty of any worthwhile amounts of silver, and they had been abandoned decades ago. Adventurous hikers, spelunkers, or treasure hunters who were prone to try their luck in the mines, usually ended up falling into the open mine shafts where they suffered severe, if not fatal, injuries. As a result, signs like this one weren't uncommon to happen upon, in the wilds of the southern Nevada desert. For Steve however, this was like seeing the mailbox in front of the family home, where he grew up. He carefully walked to the mineshaft opening and peered down through its mouth, seeing only darkness in the abyss.

Steve stepped back a few paces and pulled the duffle bag off of his shoulder. He quickly removed his flask and put it in his back pocket, and then removed a series of rock climbing necessities including a rope, harness, clamps and leather gloves. Moving to the warning sign Steve found the concrete reinforcement securing the sign into the earth. He tied the rope through the torso harness checking to make sure it was secure and attached the other end of the rope to the base of the sign. He proceeded to remove and check the special flashlight he had stored in his duffle bag. The lantern had been created for those in the pest control industry with a high intensity halogen flashlight on one end that could burn through the darkness like a laser beam. The other feature of the lantern was a pair of long ultraviolet light bulbs housed in the body of the device. The purpose of the UV light was to reveal the Desert Scorpion indigenous to the southwestern United States. Although he might be immune to bacteria and viruses, Steve was not immune to the venom of these small arachnids, which was potent enough to potentially kill human beings.

Shining the flashlight down into the mineshaft Steve could see the base, which appeared to be scattered with plastic grocery and trash bags. Decaying food and the silver metallic wrappers of protein bars were evident all around. Apparently the nature lovers who hiked the area considered these mineshafts good places to dump their garbage. Then again, he was in the middle of nowhere. Who would be hiking out here?

Carefully, Steve moved to the edge of the mineshaft opening. The ground groaned and began to slip away from under foot as he reached the edge. Quite suddenly, all the earth near the edge collapsed and fell into the shaft taking Steve down with it. Desperately he pulled on the rope trying to stop his free fall into the abyss. The rope went taut with a snap and Steve was thrown into the side of the shaft from the momentum.

He dangled like a spent yo-yo for a few moments as he fought to control his breathing. It was very clear why so many people were hurt or killed when wandering too close to the old silver mines. Dirt and debris fell on top of him as he remained suspended on the line. Then a faint case of claustrophobia had him scrambling to switch on the lantern. The dark, close quarters were playing tricks with his mind. Steve imagined dozens of scorpions crawling all over his body and a wave of panic began to wash over him. In the seconds before he ignited the UV lantern Steve had the ghastly fear of the lamp revealing a living, swarming mass of the poison barbed arachnids maneuvering their way around his body and crawling underneath the base of his jeans then up his bare legs underneath. Certain that, at the very least, the bugs would be covering the inside of the mineshaft like a ghostly ant hill of fluorescent white, a nauseating chill passed through him. He laid his finger on the switch.

The fear became so intense and palpable Steve had to shake himself of the mental images filling his mind. Waking from his arachnophobic daydream, he looked up the thirty feet he had fallen to the mineshaft opening and the blue sky shined above. The sight of the sky calmed him and in this more relaxed state, gave him the strength to switch on the lantern. The UV bulbs gave off a low-level purple-blue illumination, which filled the shaft with enough ambient light to see details within the ancient excavation.

Surprisingly, no fluorescence shone back at him. No scurrying, or crawling, or even stationary critters were anywhere to be seen. The white plastic grocery bags glowed with a spectacular brilliant white-blue, far brighter than any glow given off by the little creepy crawlers he dreaded to see.

Crawl factor, negative. One critter down and one to go.

Strangely, Steve didn't dread the presence of the far more dangerous rattlesnakes that he expected to find, nearly as much as he did the scorpions. This was strange, because the venom of the desert rattlesnake was far more potent than the sting of scorpion's tail. Life in the caves had taught him to bring along another tool for the vipers, Steve removed the telescopic snake stick he had clipped to the harness. Given the ample pre-strike warning that nature had provided to the snake, and his experience at having handled an abundance of snakes in the past, he would rather deal with the snake than the scorpion any day.

Steve grasped the clip on the front of his harness, which had halted his fall, and slowly began to let rope slip through, thereby controlling his descent. He only had another twenty feet or so to go before hitting bottom and he was anxious to get his feet on the ground. With a deft swing of his arm, Steve held the snake stick away from his body, and dropped it down to the floor of the mineshaft. He aimed for the spot where he believed he would most likely place his feet first when he reached bottom. The stick landed with a soft crinkle on the plastic bags and immediately the sound of a snake's rattle began to reverberate about the chamber. The first rattle was followed by another less intense rattle of a second snake seemingly coming from further in the chamber.

The eerie sound didn't startle or alarm Steve, he calmly looked in the direction of each of the two sounds. He switched from UV light to flashlight and was able to quickly locate the two snakes, which to his pleasant surprise were not directly beneath him. The snakes were actually about ten feet further inside the mine away from the vertical drop of the opening. Eyeing the snakes, which were each about three feet long and on opposite sides of the chamber from his landing spot, he realized they posed no initial threat to him as he continued his descent to the floor.

Reaching the base, Steve's feet gently sank into the soft refuse that yielded under his bodyweight when he finished his descent. Picking up the snake stick, he noticed the descent had dropped him into a circular clearing, opening into a new, and this time horizontal tunnel, leading into the mine at a very gradual downward slope. Moving cautiously into the tunnel, he approached the location of the first snake, which had coiled in a classical defensive position.

Steve took a careful step forward toward the reptile when something crunched under his foot. The unexpected sound startled the viper and resulted in the animal's rattle reverberating with greater speed and intensity. Without taking his eyes off the snake, Steve slowly lifted his guilty foot and retraced his steps in reverse to see what he had crunched. Using the high beam Steve glanced down to see his foot emerge from a partially exposed human ribcage. His shoelaces snagged on the now broken rib bones as he shook the remains from his foot.

Moving the flashlight to a midway point between the snake and his current position he used the ambient light of the beam to illuminate additional partially clothed bones. The bones were clad in khaki shorts and what looked to be a cotton tank top. The skeleton was small, with no visible anatomical features indicating gender, however, a small backpack near the remains could provide one possible explanation.

Conspiracy theories have been a popular fad within the general population ever since the release of the X-files. These days, people are more apt to believe a cover up is in place, to hide the motivations of the ulterior motivated government. In the case of silver mines, backpackers and other adventure seekers were renowned for believing that the warning signs were mere distractions, to the fact that there were indeed large caches of silver still within the mines. The warnings and rumors of the mines being empty were therefore, false. All a ploy on the part of those who owned the deeds to the mines in order to keep their silver safe. Truth be told, there was some silver left within the mines, the problem was that the cost of excavating the metal was more than the metal was worth today.

Many tried their luck with the integrity of the mineshafts, and most were victims of their own fatal mistakes. The fall was always traumatic and usually fatal, with death occurring from exposure, if not from the initial impact. The bones were not part of the usual modus operandi of his people, nor were the piles of trash at the bottom of the mineshaft opening. Was there any connection between the bones and whatever was happening at the nightclubs?

The victim's backpack was green canvas as opposed to the brightly colored nylon most packs had been over at least the last decade. There was no scent of decay in the dusty air and the bones did snap dryly when Steve stepped on them. Obviously the body had been down in the shaft for a long time. Reassuring himself the skeleton could not suddenly animate itself, while realistically a live rattlesnake could, Steve turned his attention to the nearest snake, still positioned directly in the path he needed to take to enter the tunnel in front of him.

Steve moved forward as the snake's rattle intensified and became more audible. He slowly closed the distance between them. Having recovered the snake stick, he now reached out to the middle rear of the animal. The snake recoiled into tighter spirals as the stick made contact with its scaly body. The snake didn't try to strike out as Steve ever so gently looped the blunt hook around the viper's body and lifted it up and off of the pathway. With slow and deliberate movements, Steve lifted the entire snake off of the ground and moved the animal behind him, setting the snake back on the ground. Evidently the snake realized the large mammal was not a predator and the rattle subsided to a mere hum. The animal slithered away from Steve and disappeared under the garbage bags where Steve had initially landed, about fifteen feet behind Steve's current location.

Suddenly, from deep within the chamber the sound of the second snake grew louder and more urgent than it had before. Steve moved deeper into the tunnel using his flashlight to illuminate the way, until he stopped short and held his position. It occurred to Steve he might not have been the cause of the second snake's agitation, since he was still a good forty feet away from the sound. Steve guessed that whatever agitated the animal might have a similar agitating effect on him so he drew his sidearm, aimed the beam further down the expanse and cautiously continued his advance.

Breaking through the rhythmical rattle was another sound of something heavy landing on soiled earth. The impact was so forceful Steve could feel the vibration of the impact. A faint crunching sound was followed by the rattle falling quiet. The chamber went deathly silent. Fear slipped up the back of Steve's spine, except this time it wasn't claustrophobia or arachnophobia. This time the fear was of something much larger watching him just beyond the reach of the flashlight beam.

Who was it that said you can't ever go home?

Steve stared into the shadows while shifting the beam of the flashlight from right to left, up and down with no success of viewing whatever was in there with him. He felt very much like a blind person swinging a cane back and forth to find his way. Deciding it was too late to turn back, Steve moved forward, continuing to swing the flashlight back and forth, searching for any indication of life. Then he heard footsteps approaching from far down the shaft. Someone was coming and coming fast!

"Alpha! It's me! It's Steven!" When no reply came Steve lifted his Glock and dropped to a shooter's stance. He aimed with both the flashlight and the sidearm ready for whoever or whatever was about to make an appearance. Desperately, Steve swung the flashlight beam across the darkness in front of him trying to get a glimpse of movement. Everything went silent. No footsteps. No sound of the breeze. No rattles. No crickets, nothing. All sound just went dead.

The sudden silence unnerved, but did not break Steve's concentration on the tunnel ahead. He could feel the presence of eyes upon him. It wasn't Alpha in the tunnel with him, Steve had a feeling of a multitude of presences in the darkness before him. The feeling was as real and as tangible as was the salty taste of sweat now copiously falling from his brow to his lips.

Steve became aware of a faint shallow raspy sound, like quick short breaths and realized it was his own breathing. Fighting to control each breath his need for answers diminished as his instinct toward self-preservation kicked in. This was getting to be too much, and a deliberate and expedited retreat was now in order. Carefully, gingerly Steve took a slow step back. Barely a sound could be heard as he placed his left foot behind him.

Deep, crunching footsteps began to move closer toward him. Damn! Steve thought. He should be able to see whoever was out there by now. To make matters worse, a distinct second set of footsteps now combined with the first. The footsteps picked up their pace as Steve took another step backward, frantically swinging the flashlight beam left and right. More footsteps, all sounding like they were running straight for him.

Something should be visible by now! The beam of light extended thirty yards into the tunnel. A body part, a face, a shadow, something should be distinguishable. The footsteps were growing resoundingly loud, Steve realized all sounds were amplified by the stone walls of the mine making the persons heading his way sound far closer than they actually were. Still the flashlight beam revealed nothing of what was coming. He remembered the flashlight was part of a lantern that would illuminate everything around him in a blue all-encompassing glow. There would be no way anyone could approach without being seen in the lantern's revealing aura.

The sound of the footsteps was becoming deafeningly loud as he fumbled for the switch to change over from flashlight to lantern. His fingers searched without luck. Frustration and desperation overwhelmed Steve as he briefly took his eyes off of the tunnel before him and, using the peripheral glow of the flashlight beam, located the switch on the side of the lantern. Looking back up, and into the tunnel, Steve thought he could make out silhouettes of men running toward him as he pressed down on the switch.

Instantly the entire area of the mine was washed in the glow of the blue light. Steve screamed with astonishment as he brought the pistol to bear on three men, all of whom skidded to a halt at the sight of the blue light and the man holding said light in one hand and a Glock 17 in the other. All three men were less than five feet away as they stared in disbelief at Steve, who realized he was equally disorientated at the sight of them. Seconds ticked by as everyone held their ground. Steve noticed a growing look of apprehension on the face of one of the three men.

"Drop to the ground, NOW!" Steve hollered in his best cop voice.

The reaction he received was completely unexpected. The man with the growing look of fear immediately covered his eyes and screamed in a wail of pain that bounced off the walls of the chamber. Another of the men dove to his friend and caught him as he crumpled to the ground.

What the hell was this?

The screaming man was flailing, convulsing and clawing at his face with frenzy. The second man tried to cover and control the man in his delirium. Steve suddenly panicked, realizing he was so enthralled by the strangeness of the two men on the ground he had forgotten about the third man.

Raising his weapon to head level he turned and came eye to eye with the third man who was now aiming a particularly large caliber revolver between Steve's eyes. The third man was saying something but the wailing of the man on the ground made whatever it was inaudible.

His police training took over, "Police! Drop your weapon! Now!"

The third man was now screaming something back at Steve.

"Shut off that light!"

Ignoring the seemingly inane request, Steve persisted.

"Drop your weapon now or I will kill you!"

"Turn it off!"

"Drop it! I mean it!"

"You're already killing him!"

Did he hear that right?

"Put your weapon on the ground! And shut him up!"

Both men were yelling at each other, though neither was listening to the other. The third man was highly agitated and less concerned about the gun being pointed at him than he was for the light.

"Turn off the goddamn light! You're killing him!"

Against all his training, Steve eyed the man on the ground who continued convulsing in pain. Blisters were forming on every exposed area of his skin.

"Turn it off now or I'll have to shoot it out!"

Steve retorted, "I won't shut anything off while you are pointing a gun at my head."

A moment passed with the only sound being the moans of the wrenching man on the ground and his friend trying to cover him.

"All right, I'll drop the gun and you switch that thing back to the high beam I saw earlier. Agreed?"

"How do I know your friends aren't armed?"

"Dammit! He'll be dead before any of your trust issues can be resolved. Here!" The third man tossed the weapon in front of Steve's feet.

Not wanting to bank on this small victory, Steve replied. "Okay, move over to your two friends so I can keep all three of you in the flashlight beam."

The third man readily complied. Dropping to his knees by his fallen comrade he quickly removed his shirt exposing a corpse-like pale flesh that almost fluoresced in the ultraviolet illumination. The man ripped and wrapped his shirt around any remaining areas of his comrades exposed skin which, to Steve's amazement, had begun to blacken and crack as if being severely burned.

Turning back to face Steve, the man hissed, "Turn the lantern off!"

Steve would have preferred to leave the light on, but he was in search of answers, and not out to make enemies if he could help it. Reluctantly, he switched the lantern setting back to flashlight. The area instantly went black except for the intense ray of white light capturing the three individuals in its beam. The blistering man calmed and relaxed, but still moaned quietly from the pain of the injuries he had sustained.

The third man never took his eyes off of Steve, he stared

directly into the center of the flashlight beam. His eyes shone in bright orange circles like an animal's eyes caught in the high beams of an approaching car.

"We have to get him to the healers now!" the other man said urgently as he continued to tend to his friend.

"I know. Calm down," the man watching Steve said with measured control.

"Calm down?!? You saw the burns! You know what that can mean for him!"

"I saw them, and I am well aware of the need!" He angrily responded.

Steve and the man studied each other for the next few seconds, assessing their next move. Steve noticed a shift in the man's expression for a fleeting instant before it was gone.

When the man spoke again it was with a disconcerting confidence that unnerved Steve.

"Nathan, get Samuel to his feet."

The man on the ground looked to his friend, "I don't think he can stand, Jeremiah."

Purposefully the man turned his back to Steve and, with the help of the man he called "Nathan," lifted the man named Samuel. With quick motion Jeremiah hoisted Samuel onto his shoulders in a fireman's carry and took a couple steps back toward the depths of the mineshaft.

"HELLO?! Man with a gun over here!" Steve called out in a voice that belied his incredulity. Had they completely forgotten he was there?

Steve warned, "You take one step out of the light and I start shooting!"

Nathan immediately froze in his tracks, but Jeremiah continued moving.

Calling back over his shoulder Jeremiah said, "C'mon Nathan, he isn't going to shoot."

"Are you so sure?" Steve racked the slide of his Glock. The sound of the weapon being made ready to fire echoing off the walls

168

of the mine.

Jeremiah turned back toward Steve, "Actually, what I meant was you aren't going to be able to shoot. Alpha's got you."

Then the man turned and proceeded further into the tunnel closely followed by Samuel.

"Hey Freeze! No one's going anywhere until..." Suddenly the name Alpha registered. Steve had been so preoccupied with the three men and the unusual scene he hadn't grasped the significance of hearing Alpha's name.

"Oh crap, not again." Steve felt an intense pain at the side of his neck and lightning seemed to erupt before his eyes. Then everything went black.

Chapter 26

The sounds and smells of his surroundings slowly began to register, as Steve's mind struggled to consciousness. Unfortunately, the more he became aware of himself, the more he realized how much trouble he was in. He was lying on his side in a near fetal position, completely unable to see. He could feel something wrapped tightly around his head and covering his eyes. As he attempted to reach up to his face to remove the wrapping he discovered his hands were bound at the wrists, loosely connected to what felt like straps binding his feet at the ankles. Steve twisted and arched his body until he was able to set himself in a seated position. He listened for any evidence of a presence in the area. The only noise was a slow drip of what sounded like water from a high elevation falling into a pool or puddle. Steve guessed he was still within the cave, judging from the loudness of the drop as it hit the pool. The area felt like some kind of large cavern comprised of cold stone as opposed to the loose earth he'd experienced when initially descending into the mine.

Steve had no idea how long he had been unconscious. His head and neck throbbed terribly as he tried to stretch himself out as far as his bonds would allow. Every movement or scuffle along the floor was amplified by the cave, threatening to announce his consciousness to his captors. He did everything he could to keep quiet but, realizing it was a losing battle, he redoubled his struggle to free himself from his bonds.

The floor felt smooth like river rock and probably wouldn't create enough friction to wear through the bindings. He tried to wriggle his hands to create some space, thinking he would use it to loosen the restraints, but the knots held fast. Dipping the side of his head to one shoulder, he even tried to push free of the blindfold. He had some success, but not enough to raise the wrap to the point where he could see. Steve abandoned this effort as he realized no light was coming in from the perimeter of the blindfold. He was in pitch blackness and would be unable to see regardless of the mask.

The sound of multiple footsteps approaching resigned Steve to the fact that he would not be able to free himself in time for any kind of escape. He decided to conserve his strength, which served as a morale booster and a tiny measure of optimism, considering that was pretty much all he could do anyway. Dwelling on his extreme helplessness certainly wasn't going to be useful.

Shifting and scooting with tremendous effort, he was able to push himself in reverse and away from the approaching footsteps until his back struck a solid wall. He had no real idea whether or not he was in any kind of contained area and the fear of scooting right off the edge of some unseen ledge haunted him prior to striking solid rock. Tensing as the footsteps grew louder and closer, Steve did his best to stifle any new noise which might alert whoever was approaching. The sound of the footsteps was becoming so loud it was if they were now walking inside his head.

Then, unbelievably, Steve thought he heard the sound diminish slightly and the footsteps sounded as if they were moving away, quieting and distancing. Realizing he had been holding his breath, Steve slowly let the air out of his lungs as his whole body relaxed.

"That was quite an effort."

Steve's head shot up so fast at the sound of the voice he struck the back of his skull against the rock wall he had worked so hard to scoot up against. He hadn't heard or sensed anyone near-by, and the thought of someone having watched him the whole time chilled him.

"Alpha?" Steve said aloud, almost reflexively.

"I have to say boy, we seem to be having a terrible time, always running into each other." The voice was low, rhythmic and harmonic with the accent Steve had always thought to be musical. Now the effect of the room caused his voice to echo in as menacing a manner as it was once melodious.

"Knock it off Alpha and let me up." Steve tried to sound intimidating but really felt ridiculous given his bound state.

"You are a little bit outside your jurisdiction, officer, to be giving anyone orders," the voice chuckled.

"You're not really that mad at me are you?"

"How could you bring an ultraviolet light into our home?" Alpha spoke in a low tone, which Steve knew meant he was beyond furious.

"I hadn't meant to use it as a weapon. Who were those three?"

"New arrivals of course, triplets, all of whom share our common fate. Unfortunately one of the brothers suffers from XP as well."

"Oh God!" Steve gasped. *Xerotogenous Pigmentosa*, or XP as it is more commonly known, is a genetic defect where the melanin in the skin isn't functional in absorbing ultraviolet light. Steve knew this weakness is rare but not uncommon among those living in the silver mine, although those affected usually keep to the darker and deeper sections of the cavern system.

"Alpha, I swear I had no idea."

"Of course you didn't, but you should have known better than to bring a UV light into the community."

"I wasn't in the community yet. I was still in the tunnels. Besides, since when are you making one of us with XP into a hunter?"

"It was a favor to his brothers. I was against it but the boy was so capable otherwise. Anyhow, someone had to take your place."

171

Alpha spoke with distaste. "And if you didn't bring the lantern in as a weapon then why…?"

"You know I hate scorpions."

Alpha was quiet a moment then said softly, "Actually, I had forgotten."

The voice came from a completely different area around twenty feet to his right and yet Steve hadn't heard a single footfall.

"It has been a while, hasn't it?" The warm manner in which Alpha now spoke made the situation all the more disconcerting. Steve felt a quick tug at his ankle and then his wrists.

"All right, you can get up now."

Steve slowly raised his hands to his face and slid the blindfold from around of his eyes. Warm light from two firelight torches filled the room as Steve inspected his surroundings. The room he was in was enormous, with its high ceiling, rounded walls and floor all carved from solid rock. The room itself was as open as a large cathedral with sparse wooden beam supports throughout the central area. The rock appeared to be polished to a semi-gloss shine, which assisted the fire from the torches in illuminating the area. It was primitive, but the effect was also magnificent. Steve actually felt as though he was inside some kind of ancient royal chamber.

"You've been busy in my absence," Steve said with a certain amount of awe in his voice.

"Amazing, isn't it?"

Steve looked toward the direction of the voice. On the far side of the room was a large stone carved throne with Alpha seated casually within. "Sometimes I feel surges of guilt when I take for granted the enormity of this room and the craftsmanship it took to construct it."

"Where are we?"

"This?" Alpha chuckled again. "This is a place where we do some of our most important work."

Steve scanned the room noting a few patterns in the floor that were far from random. He also noted the shape of the floor was slightly conical, with the perimeter of the room rising slightly higher than the center of the room.

"What work would that be?" Steve found himself asking aloud.

"You will find out soon enough," Alpha said cryptically. "First, I have some questions."

"Well, I have several questions as well," Steve said honestly.

"I'm sure you do, however, my interest lies less with enhancing your knowledge as with assuaging my need to learn what I can from you."

Steve gazed directly at Alpha's uncompromising amber eyes.

"That may have been the first inhospitable statement you have made so far. Is this trend going to continue? I thought we were going to have a friendly dialogue." Cynicism oozed with his every word.

Alpha's face twisted and contorted with a ferocity Steve had never seen in his former mentor. He drew back a few paces.

"Fool! You have no idea what is happening, do you?" Alpha burst from the chair and closed the distance between him and Steve with unbelievable speed. The very chamber seemed to quake as he spoke.

Steve heard the sound of panting and quickly realized it was coming from his own heaving chest.

"How long was I out?" Steve thought his words sounded weak and desperate as he spoke them. Remembering the pain he suffered before losing consciousness, he rubbed the sore area on his neck.

"Not quite a full day." Alpha's voice had become melodious and polite again. "Not surprising really after the nerve strike I gave you."

"Nerve strike?" Steve couldn't believe what he had heard. "You hit me with a nerve strike?!? Are you insane?"

"I didn't realize it was you until after I hit you."

"What? My yelling 'Alpha, it's me, it's Steve' didn't clue you in?" Steve asked with more than a trace of sarcasm in his voice.

Alpha seemed excited by the reference. "Ah, I must not have heard you."

Ignoring the evasive answer Steve pressed for more: "What's going on Alpha? What did you mean when you said I wasn't aware of what was happening?"

Alpha casually walked back to his throne chair and as he sat down his whole body seemed to deflate. He rested his forehead in his hands. "We're being hunted."

Steve frowned. "You and Lei?"

"No, all of us. Some of our people have gone missing recently and several others have been attacked when they ventured out of our home."

Steve moved closer to Alpha. "Do you know who is behind it?"

"In a way." Alpha looked at Steve, took a deep breath and continued. "Three years ago we sent some emissaries to a small medical research center in Philadelphia. The idea was to open a line of communication between their hematology department and our people in the hopes of finding a more efficient serum, than what we are currently using to stave off the effects of our condition."

"After arranging the meetings we sent a sample of our blood to the center. Their initial skepticism about our existence and our need was soon replaced with intense scientific curiosity."

"Curiosity about what?" Steve was getting wrapped up in the discussion.

"They didn't tell us, they simply seemed astounded when they heard the blood came from a fully functioning adult. The researchers were requesting, almost demanding to be able to help us. Many of our people took their enthusiasm for charity and altruism, but something about their requests, to see an actual 'patient,' sounded a little too…aggressive to me. With a steady dose of cynicism, we accepted their help and told the Research Center of our special needs, for complete privacy, anonymity, and daily injections of our serum, etcetera. We were told all arrangements would be taken care of prior to the volunteers' arrival within a special facility.

We sent three of our people to the research center: Jonathan was thirty-two years old, Tiffany was twenty-three, and Jackie was eight. Their first week at the facility the Center had found consisted of what I am told was routine testing and was relatively uneventful. All three were able to communicate with us and actually seemed to be enjoying their stay. I suppose the facility was catering to them in a way they had never before experienced. Then, in the middle of the second week, we lost all contact with our people. Every time we asked the researchers about our people we were reassured they were involved in some more extravagant testing and were unavailable. By the third week the researchers cut off all lines of communication between, not only our people, but with their own Center."

Steve listened intensely as Alpha began to shiver.

"I went to investigate the facility with Lei only to find the space had been abandoned. Contacting the landlord revealed that what I had thought to be a small and reputable company, was actually the research and development branch of some anonymous corporate superpower. The corporation had paid off the remaining two year lease of the space, folded up their tents and left town without a word. When we asked the name of the corporation the landlord said he didn't know, and the check he had been given for the rent was in the name of the old facility so there was no paper trail to follow. We had no leads, no one to guide us and no way to involve the authorities without risking exposure to the entire community. We had no idea why such a big company would want to kidnap or kill our people. It was a place of science, not of religious persecution like the old days."

"Six weeks later we heard from Jonathan. He had managed to escape and called us long distance from Washington D.C. We instructed him to hold up in a low rent motel until we could pick him up. He told us to stay away. He was being pursued by security from the facility and he would find his own way home. Jonathan

175

was a hunter, like you and Lei, and was well versed in the art of the kill. Normally, I would have had every confidence he could survive and manage his way back to us, but I could hear the weakness in his voice and decided to go after him. I could tell he had been without the serum for too long and he was going to need to feed in order to survive.

After that it was only a matter of following the body trail. Jonathan preferred a certain type, mostly drug dealers and other street criminals. I suppose it appealed to his sense of morality to drink those people. His first couple kills were more like an animal mauling compared to the neat and tidy manner in which he normally struck. I was incredibly concerned by this and with the frequency at which he appeared to be working. Just before I caught up with him in Denver he had killed a particularly nasty drug dealer in his usual, neat and organized fashion, which revealed to me he was recovering and led me straight to him. When I found him he was still in a desperate state, even after all of the blood he had taken. I shudder to think what he had been like before I found him."

"I was able to take him home and eventually he recovered. Once he was well enough to recount his tale, he told us of how, after about a week into the research, the staff at the facility was herded out to be replaced by all new technicians. The tests became uncomfortable and the three of them were refused their serum. Each of my people became more like lab rats than volunteers. Tests were performed mercilessly, and by Jonathan's account, felt more and more like torture. By the third week there was no question that it had become pure torture for them. They were strapped to gurneys and exposed to different intensities of UV light to determine how fast their flesh would reach the third degree burn stage. They were injected with strange drugs that caused excruciating pain. Each was subjected to endless hours of torment followed by the extraction of more blood samples."

"In the end Tiffany was exposed to ghastly chemicals which always made her very sick. Jonathan said they had injected her

176

with bleach to see if she could survive it. She couldn't and died about four days into the third week. Little Jackie was strapped to a table, placed under florescent lights and denied her serum. Jonathan overheard the techs saying they were to document the girl's rate of deterioration. One asked how long they were going to allow her to decline and was told to test her until she went into cardiac arrest. Then they were to revive her and continue the test. The test didn't last very long and the third time they tried to revive her, she died. Not a single person there took pity on one as small and kind as that little girl. Fortunately, her soul was able to escape her tormentor's grasp."

Alpha was shivering violently and seemed on the verge of collapse. When he spoke again his voice was filled with such pain Steve could feel tears welling in his eyes.

"I was present when both of those girls were born, and you know how I hold a particular fondness for those who are born here, though all who share my home are dear to me."

Alpha looked like he might start weeping, but after a few moments he straightened himself and continued in his original tone.

"Jonathan was exposed to several different diseases for which there are no current cures. Obviously, with what we know of our own blood chemistry and our immunity to virus and bacteria, Jonathan never suffered any effect of the diseases, however, he was wise enough to feign illness until he managed to escape when they left him unattended. There's more boy, much more, but the point is we tried to seek outside help and were rewarded with a cowardly betrayal of the most foul. Oh, what I would give to find those responsible for Tiffany's and Jackie's deaths, but the name of the corporation has ever eluded me."

Alpha went silent, while Steve remained speechless at the horror perpetrated on Alpha's people.

Steve broke the silence, "I don't…I don't know what to say."

Alpha nodded, "There's nothing to say. The human race has always visited horrors on us. We may be no direct threat to the outside world, but the outside world is a direct threat to us. As you know, for that reason we stay safely invisible."

His voice trailed off as he seemed to lose himself in contemplation. Within a few moments he regained his composure as his body straightened: "That bastard Daniels betrayed us three years ago, and ever since we have been hunted on a grand scale. This time the inquisition comes not from priests but scientists and…"

"Alex Daniels?!?" Steve blurted out before he could stop himself. The name hit Steve's ears like a slap across the face.

Alpha stopped mid-sentence and stared at Steve is disbelief.

"You don't mean Alex Daniels, do you?" Steve asked, still in shock and confusion.

"What do you know of him?" Alpha's voice was a hushed whisper, oozing with malice.

Chapter 27

The ground on the earth's surface paid witness, as rubber soled shoes, barely hissing or making any sound at all, trod over the desert terrain. Dozens of pairs of padded feet advanced hurriedly toward the opening of several different mineshafts spread out over a nearly five mile circumference. Their black clothing covered them from head to toe while night-vision goggles supplied the illumination necessary to traverse the landscape. Blue tooth technology allowed each member of the team to keep in constant communication, while speaking in otherwise inaudible whispers. Having reached their initial destinations apparently unnoticed, they quickly began the assembly of their equipment.

Every team waited for the last to finish their set-up of repelling equipment, followed by a thorough weapons check. While final confirmations came over the blue tooth from each team, Kunnert stood in front of a fallen wooden pole studying it and the attached repelling gear as it descended into the darkness of the mineshaft opening. The gear looked brand new and was clearly not the leftover of a hiker or cave diver from the past. Despite being born an American citizen, Kunnert shared a common German/South African trait of being overly organized. Everything he did was completely according to plan. Thinking through every possible contingency and contending with them prior to execution had made him a very effective officer in the military, before his retirement to the private sector. However, he had not expected this repelling gear, which meant he had an unknown in his plan, and Kunnert did not like unknowns.

* * *

"Alpha, do you even know who your enemies are?"

Alpha said nothing, he just kept staring at Steve with suspicion.

"You don't, do you?"

"How do you know the name Alex Daniels?" Alpha's tone was now a malevolent threat and his whole body was tensing as if getting ready to spring.

Steve was too lost in his own thoughts to notice the change in Alpha. The wheels were turning, puzzle piecing the mystery together with every passing second.

"I know who is after you." Steve finally said. "What I don't know is why."

Steve told Alpha everything about what had happened at *The Inferno* and what he had heard about the Glitter Gulch. Alpha seemed keenly interested in the static state of the victims in each occurrence, who remained static and were captured in the aftermath of the attacks.

"You mentioned your people started disappearing right after you dealt with this research facility, right?"

"Yes."

"Alex Daniels owns a corporate pharmaceutical company called Pharmanetics, and is the CEO of the company."

Alpha looked as though he was going to start shaking uncontrollably. Instead, he winced and sighed, running his fingers through his white mane, while he began to pace the room.

Steve watched as the connection he had made burrowed into Alpha's mind. Clearly this had a far greater meaning to him than he had expected.

"Our fears have come to fruition. My fault. All my fault." Alpha sounded near tears as he spoke. Recalling he was not alone, Alpha asked, "And the men who took your fellow officers at *The Inferno*?"

"As far as I can tell they work for Daniel's, but something doesn't make sense about them. They are too well-trained to be run of the mill security or hired muscle."

The explosion cut off any further words Steve was going to

say and the force of the blast sent the two of them reeling.

Part III: Harvest

Chapter 28

Kunnert watched as his team dragged the limp bodies of those they encountered back to their insertion point for evacuation, as each team followed the orders they had been given. The immobilizing tranquilizer they were using was a particularly potent brew, and would keep the victims docile for hours. Each team member had been made to understand that every inhabitant was valuable but, with the exception of the young, expendable if necessary. No word of a kill had been heard over the radio, which gave Kunnert the impression that, for the time being, everything was going according to plan.

Each team member had already silently subdued dozens of targets, who were being prepped for extraction. The remainder of his vast insurgents pushed deeper into the earth toward the core of the silver mine. Kunnert knew the mission would not stay on the quiet for much longer, but he hoped to keep the advantage of surprise for as long as possible. The people living in this place were sheep for the most part, but they did outnumber his teams by approximately 100:1. He was concerned about a stampede effect, should the sheep ever get wise to the small number of wolves amongst them.

Kunnert hadn't expected to hear an explosion, so when the sound of it blasted through his earpiece into his naked ears, it came as a complete surprise. He reacted as swiftly and efficiently, as he did back in his military days when he'd come under fire.

"Take them to the surface and secure them!" Kunnert bellowed, as his men dragged the unconscious behind them and carried those children small enough to be most easily expedited. "If any resist beyond a controllable level, shoot them!"

One soldier called back, "With the tranqs or lead, sir?"

"Either! Those who come quietly can live. Those who do not still have value but are ultimately expendable from this point forward!"

Kunnert was visibly uncomfortable with the chaos swirling around him and his men. The unfamiliar fingers of claustrophobia began to work their way up his back, even though the underground cavern he currently found himself in was vast and open. At this point he could have been inside an arena. He watched his men hustle figures of all ages up and out of the cavern, to be taken into the tunnels leading to the ventilation shafts where they had entered. One soldier wrenched a toddler away from its wailing mother who screamed and grabbed for her child as another man knocked her to the ground and kicked her as she tried to rise. Her cries grew more insistent as the soldier pinned her to the ground by placing his boot on her chest, she pleaded with the man to give her child back while the masked man regarded her through his goggles. The soldier pulled his sidearm from its holster and shot the woman in the head twice, before swinging the butt of his weapon to brain another adult who tried to bolt past him.

Information poured into Kunnert's earpiece as he moved. The current number of "volunteers" that had been removed had just hit eight hundred and Kunnert knew that he and his team were sure to reach the goal of one thousand within minutes. Kunnert began walking toward the extraction point. He left the open cavern for the more restrictive tunnels when another call came over the wireless.

"Sir! We have located our missing operative."

"What's her condition?"

"Unconscious, but stable."

"Is there any indication whether or not she might have compromised us?"

"Nothing in the room but medical supplies and machinery. Looks more like they were trying to heal her rather than torture her."

"Roger that. Get her out with the rest."

"Yes sir."

Another soldier's voice came over Kunnert's earpiece along with the sound of automatic gunfire.

"Older subjects being eliminated as ordered." The soldier's

voice started out calm but that quickly turned to abject panic. "My God! Someone just dropped on us from above! What the...holy shit!!! We need back up now! Some...thing is tearing through us! Can't risk a shot, target not clear ...N-NO!!! The sender began to scream in a shrill, soul tearing wail, which was quickly replaced by a wet gurgling sound and a background noise of inhuman growling.

By the time the soldier's radio went silent Kunnert had sprung into action. He called for all men with "viables" to evacuate with their captives, while those without captives were to pinpoint the location of the signal from the downed radio and purge the area. Each man was given directions to the location from the surface where satellite technology had mapped the entire cave system beneath the ground. With organized precision the men filed into the area and awaited orders before entering the adjoining cavern, where the sounds of men dying were emanating in eerie moans.

Requests to proceed went into Kunnert's ear as he held his position just inside the mouth of a tunnel that emptied into the cavern he had previously come from with a dozen of his men on his heels. Kunnert told the men to hold position until the remaining reinforcements arrived, but as he spoke the sound of gunfire and the screams of men boomed back to him from another location within the labyrinth. Then his radio went silent again. Kunnert stopped in his tracks, as did the men behind him. He listened to the sounds, or the lack thereof, coming over the open channel. A sound like the scraping of a microphone over stone burst painfully into the sound piece in his ear. A guttural rumbling and heavy breathing could be heard. Kunnert frowned as he listened to what sounded more like an animal breathing into the receiver than a man. Whatever was on the other end suddenly bellowed out a roar that exploded into the earpieces with such volume all the men wearing earpieces around him raised their hands to their ears in pain.

From all outward appearances Kunnert did not react to the sound coming from the speakers, but if anyone of his men dared to look closely enough they would have seen recognition flash over his chiseled face…recognition and terror.

"Everyone out now! Fall back to the extraction point and terminate all non-personnel as you exit. Anyone not out in ten will be left behind!"

Not a single man hesitated with any iota of indecision, nor remorse regarding their fallen comrades. Orders were followed as each man from Kunnert's team hastily retreated to their extraction points, shooting anyone who wasn't wearing the commando gear they were wearing. Each man moved forward and covered the others as they ran passed, taking up a shooters stance some fifty feet ahead and covering the men from the rear as they repeated the drill. At one point a lone woman tackled one of the advancing men with such force the sound of bones breaking could be heard as he hit the ground. The woman sprang to her feet and lifted the man off the ground as if he were a mere child, placing him between her and the rest of the commandos like a human shield. Kunnert ordered his men to open fire and the men complied instantly, filling their fellow soldier and the woman full of high velocity rounds before she had any chance of realizing her plan wasn't going to work.

Further down the tunnel they were attacked again, this time by a trio of nearly naked women who looked as though they belonged in the Playboy mansion, not in a modified silver mine. The women's nakedness shocked the men for the briefest of moments, and the women used this hesitation to attack. Blood was flying and necks were breaking as the women tore a brutal path toward Kunnert and his main host of commandos.

"Hunters!" Kunnert yelled as the majority of his remaining men reacted to the call with professional precision.

The tunnel was immediately thrown into a blinding series of light flashes as Kunnert tossed one of Dr. Whelan's prize flash bang grenades. The special goggles each of the mercenaries wore filtered out the light. The three women immediately fell to the floor.

The women were secured and removed with several other inhabitants as Kunnert covered their escape, until he was the last

186

man in the tunnel at the base of the mineshaft. He was about to take hold of the rope ladder when he was hit full force by another woman. She wasn't nude like the others, but she avoided his blows as if she could read his thoughts and react to his attacks faster than his own body could.

Kunnert quickly realized the woman had a greater than expected level of strength. When she grabbed his wrist and pressed his gun hand to the tunnel wall he found he could not free himself from her grasp. The fingers of her other hand encircled his throat and twisted his head to the side. With his free hand Kunnert grabbed the woman's long black hair and pulled. Even his best efforts only slowed her oncoming teeth toward his neck. He grunted and strained with the effort, but to no avail. He could feel her warm breath on the skin of his neck.

The sound of something heavy striking bone filled his ears and the woman fell slack to the floor of the tunnel. Kunnert shook himself back to the moment to see one of his men standing next to him with the girl at his feet.

"You all right, sir?" One of Kunnert's mercenaries asked.

"Fine. She alive?" Kunnert asked taking in the full vision of Lei lying sprawled on the ground.

"She'll live. That is, unless you say otherwise." The mercenary pointed the barrel of his rifle at Lei's head.

Kunnert considered a moment, then said, "She's no longer a threat and is still valuable, take her too."

"Yes sir."

Chapter 29

The sound of the explosion was amplified through the rock walled chambers of the room where Steve and Alpha stood. From the spot on the floor where he landed, Steve covered his hands over his head and ears in a protective gesture as he watched the dust and debris settle back to the floor. The sound of automatic gunfire replaced the ringing in his ears, when his sense of hearing returned.

The sound of gunfire stopped as abruptly as it had started. Steve felt a pang of relief until the shrill piercing sound of people screaming replaced the explosion of gunfire. More gunfire erupted from within the labyrinth as Alpha bolted toward the chamber's only opening, shouting commands to others who seemed to materialize out of the air. Steve ran after him through that sole entrance/exit and was able to see the vastness of what had taken place below the earth, inside the old silver mine. Everything had been chiseled from solid rock, complete with stairways and vast bridges, which stretched what he estimated at three hundred feet at the widest point.

The platform Steve stood on was part of a spiraling ramp running along the outside of the open area and serving as a gradual ascent and descent. Steve stood on the sloping spiral perhaps fifty feet above the bottom of the cavern with a view of the entire chamber. It rose another hundred feet to the rock ceiling above. Electricity was available on every level, along with what Steve guessed to be thirty-by-thirty square depressions, cut into the rock walls in a honeycomb fashion, evenly spaced at every second revolution of the spiral.

"Damn Alpha!" Steve thought out loud as he took in the majesty of the scene. "You have *really* been busy!"

These spaces must be living areas. Each was sparsely furnished and decorated with completely different styles. Some had fabric coverings, others had elaborate wicker doors. All were flung wide open as people gathered their belongings and, in some cases, children and pets. A familiar flow of air ruffled his hair slightly as if he were standing in a light breeze, but Steve knew this was refrigerated air devoid of humidity. The overall scene looked like a grand national park or museum filled with amenities.

Steve moved to the railing that protected walkers from the fifty foot drop down to the floor of the cavern. He ran along the railing and peering over the side, to see men in full combat gear shooting automatic weapons directly into the crowd of people. The callous, cold-blooded horror of the scene turned Steve's blood to ice. Without thinking he ran down the circular ramp, which spiraled to the bottom.

Steve realized he had no way of saving anyone and had less of an idea of what he might do when he reached the people or the gunmen below. His instincts as a former hunter for his people, and a current LAPD Detective, overwhelmed his ability to register conscious thought. He had barely made it down one full circle of the ramp when something large and black fell past him, hurtling down to the bottom of the cavern in free fall.

Initially fearful that a second group of assailants may have reached the floors above him and were throwing people over the railing, Steve quickly realized it had been Alpha dropping the remaining fifty feet into the melee below. With his black leather coat fluttering behind him as he descended, Steve watched as Alpha softened his fall by landing on two of the assailants and rolling with the remaining impact. Instantly, Alpha was in motion, ripping rifles from the hands of the gunmen and bringing them back around to smash the flesh and bone of their former owners. Steve watched in utter amazement as the heavily armed gunmen, who were now holding their fire for fear of shooting their own, fell around the whirlwind that was Alpha.

Steve had been sprinting down the spiral ramp without realizing it and completed the rest of the descent as the last man hit the floor. Ignoring both Alpha and the soldiers, he began checking the victims who had been gunned down mere moments ago. The sound of gunfire in another area of the labyrinth sent Alpha off through another tunnel and out of the cavern, leaving Steve alone with the multiple mounds of humanity. The first six bodies Steve checked were dead, an apparent mercy from the brutality the ammunition had rendered unto them. The next few were either dead or clinging to life, but far beyond the ability to help. When Steve checked the last victim his heart sank. The body of the young teenage boy was already starting to cool.

Steve's eyes searched the cavern floor and found one of the automatic weapons Alpha had wrenched from the grasp of the soldiers. He picked up the weapon, ejected the magazine, found it to be empty and tossed the magazine aside. Bending to the nearest soldier he rifled through the man's pockets until he found three identical fully loaded magazine clips. Quickly, Steve tried the first one in the automatic rifle and it clicked into placed with a machined perfection. As he placed the remaining two magazines into his pockets a moan came from the man on the ground beneath him. Surprised, Steve jumped back at the sound. The man's moan was a wheezing rasp, Steve noticed bloody foam coming from his mouth as he struggled to breathe. Apparently, Alpha had broken the man's ribs with enough force that one, or several, had punctured a lung. Not an immediately fatal wound if treated quickly, but very painful and frightening for the sufferer. The man extended a hand out to Steve, a plea for help, but Steve backed away, cocked the rifle and fired once into the man's head, blowing his brains out the back of his skull.

Chapter 30

Steve didn't move after he fired the shot. He just stood there looking down, still pointing the rifle at the man he had just killed, completely shocked and confused by what he had just done. He had just fatally shot a helpless man. Never, even during his years as one of Alpha's hunters, had he killed so callously as this. His body had taken on a will of its own. He glanced over at the dead boy on the floor. The boy had received four rounds to various places within his torso. The damage was so extensive he'd practically been eviscerated by the entry and exiting trauma of the bullets. It was then Steve understood what he had done and why. He had taken a measure of revenge for his people, who had been gunned down.

More screams were coming from the tunnels, more gunfire erupting in the distance. Steve broke from the open area of the cavern and ran into the tunnel where he had seen Alpha disappear. The tunnels were a complicated maze and Steve worried he might not remember his way and start traveling in circles. Electricity was still available in the tunnels, but to a minimal degree, especially compared to the main chamber. The lights spaced throughout the tunnel were red, perhaps as a shield against the UV light the people living here were so careful to avoid. Unfortunately, these lights only gave off enough brightness to make travel possible. Any details were lost in the eerie red glow.

Steve stalked forward carefully, barely able to hear the gunfire and raised voices in the distance. He hadn't seen any evidence that he was in the right tunnel, which would lead him to either civilians or commandos. Bodies began to appear on the ground. More victims, a mass of unarmed people shot with high velocity bullets from an automatic rifle at close range. Steve's anxiety and confusion over killing the soldier ebbed as he surveyed the scene, which was becoming more gruesome with every step. No one, it would appear, was to be spared. The dead included the elderly, but

Steve noticed there hadn't been any children under nineteen in the area of the initial slaughter.

He walked further down the tunnel, stepping carefully over the bodies until he glimpsed a commando sitting with his back propped up against the tunnel wall. The man seemed peaceful as if to be resting, but judging from the way his arms and head hung slack, Steve could tell the man was either unconscious or dead. He pressed forward. The number of civilian dead dwindled as the commando casualties began to increase. Alpha had found them. Deeper within the tunnels the sound of gunfire and men's screams grew louder. Alpha had found some more of the commandos.

Keeping the barrel of the rifle pointed in front of him, Steve moved more quickly toward the sound of the conflict. The gunfire stopped, at least in the area toward which he was moving, and now only the desperate cries of men could be heard, along with voices pleading for mercy. As Steve rounded another corner he was faced with a fork in the tunnel in an area he didn't recognize. Desperately, he looked for some clue as to which path would take him to the source of the sounds. Nothing presented itself, or at least Steve wasn't able to find any clue to the best direction, and the dim light only increased his heightened state of anxiety.

Then, as if on cue, a commando staggered out of the darkness of the tunnel to the left. His face was so pale it rendered a sickly grey pallor even in the red glow. When Steve brought the rifle up and hollered for the man to freeze, the man didn't seem to hear. He walked uneasily around the tunnel as if he might fall over at any moment. When he was close enough for Steve to see him in the remnant light, Steve observed the man was missing his right arm. The wound was jagged and the flesh was torn in an unusual manner. Bone extended from the wound, which Steve recognized as part of the shoulder girdle and not the arm. This type of wound was not a result of an extremity being blown off from artillery or chopped off with some kind of blade. This man's arm had been wrenched out of the socket and torn from the body by sheer force.

The man staggered a few more steps then collapsed either in

shock or from blood loss. Oddly, Steve didn't have any more pity for this man than he had for the one he'd shot back in the main chamber. Moving cautiously into the left tunnel Steve now found himself in total darkness. Aware of his vulnerability in the blackness, Steve retreated to the fork in the tunnel where the armless man had collapsed. Finding exactly what he was looking for, he removed the night vision goggles from the man's head, checked to verify they were still working and looped them over his own head. He would have to wait until he was in perfect darkness before he could activate the goggles or risk being blinded by the remaining light.

The commando on the floor began to moan softly, "My arm feels asleep. Hey, did I fall asleep on my arm again?"

The man was talking to Steve as if they knew each other.

"I feel really cold. It's dark and dirty down here. Can I go home now?" he asked Steve in a boyish voice.

"Soon," Steve answered though he wasn't sure why until he spoke again.

"Did you complete your mission soldier?" Steve asked in as much an authoritative voice as he could muster. It had the effect he was hoping as the man straightened his back, or tried to, and spoke in a soldier's voice.

"Yes sir! I extracted the minimum total of twenty targets before the final execution order came in. Once the order came in I stopped the extraction and began the cleaning protocol, but..."

The man's voice trailed off as his eyes began to glaze over.

Shouting like the police boot-camp drill sergeant he had encountered when first entering the LAPD, Steve bellowed, "What do you mean 'but'??!!! There are no 'buts,' except of course *your* 'butt' which I am personally gonna fill with my perfectly shined boots granted to me by the government and paid for by the taxpayers for a grand total of twenty-nine-ninety-five."

As he hollered the man fought to regain his composure, so Steve stayed at him. "Those self-same individuals gave of their hard earned money to buy said boots, so that those boots would

193

help me protect them in their time of need. Soldier, those poor people would cry in their respective diapers if they found out I soiled their gift to me by embedding one in your ass! So you better answer me truthfully now! Did you complete your mission?"

"The children were extracted as ordered. I purged as many of the adults as I could before…before…"

"Before what soldier?!"

Steve would have questioned the man more but as the commando spoke his last word he fainted. Steve turned his back on the dead or dying man and bounded heedlessly into the tunnel. When it got so dark he couldn't see his hand before his face, Steve lowered the night vision goggles into place and switched them on. The whole world took on an eerie green glow. Steve followed the path until he ran across another, far smaller, cavern that appeared to have been used to house computer equipment. All the remaining equipment had been shattered or destroyed.

A light emanated from another tunnel at the far end of the cavern. As best he could tell, no one stood between the light in the distance and the opening of the tunnel. Still Steve proceeded cautiously, checking every shadow for movement, carefully placing each footstep where he planned, while intently listening to his immediate environment.

Eventually Steve reached the opening of the tunnel without being attacked or molested. As he entered the tunnel the glow inside the night vision goggles was becoming uncomfortably bright. He checked to see if there was enough ambient light to see by, and determining that there was sufficient light to work, without putting himself at risk, he returned the goggles to the top of his head and moved forward.

The sight of the trash on the ground told him he was near a vertical mineshaft opening like the one he had dropped down from earlier. The topography indicated it was not the same one. Finding a rope conveniently left behind by the commandoes, Steve began to climb up to the surface. Since finding his way back through the darkness would not be possible, Steve looked up, and estimated the distance to the surface to be around seventy-five to ninety feet and an absolutely vertical climb. Steve ignored the rope and found his first handhold on the side of the mineshaft and began to climb the vertical rise as quickly as if he were a lizard scurrying up the side of a tree. Memories of his childhood flooded into him, as he instinctively found the next hand hold and foot fall. He continued to climb as muscles he hadn't fully used in years obeyed his commands and brought him further and further to the surface as the floor of the mineshaft fell out and away from under his feet.

It still took longer than it should have for Steve to reach the surface. Just when he thought the burn in his arms would make finishing the climb impossible, his hand cleared the tunnel and found purchase on horizontal earth. Struggling to raise himself through the opening, he finally succeeded and breathed in the night air, unspoiled by the pungent smell of dirt and death.

Steve rolled to his feet to find Alpha standing, with his back to him, by the opening of the mineshaft he had initially descended.

"You see what I was trying to prevent, boy? Do you understand the stakes?" Alpha sounded weak and defeated as he spoke.

Steve watched Alpha in silence.

Alpha sat on the ground next to Steve, placed his head in his hands and began to weep.

"It's happening again. God help me it's happening all over again." Alpha kept repeating miserably.

Chapter 31

Steve stared at Alpha and studied the man more thoroughly. As Alpha sat there, trying to regain his composure, Steve noticed three areas on Alpha's black leather coat that appeared to shine more than the rest of the garment.

"Are you wounded?"

Alpha looked up at Steve and followed his gaze to the splotches of wetness on his person. Lifting the fabric up and away from his body Alpha peered inside his clothes.

"No, I'm all right. Must be someone else's blood," Alpha said confidently. But even in the darkness Steve was pretty sure he could see blood coming from underneath the material. It certainly didn't look like splashes from others.

"What about you?" Alpha said and gestured to Steve's temple.

Steve abruptly raised his right hand to his temple and felt the crusting of dried blood. When his fingers pressed harder, pain seared the side of his head and his fingers sank into a shallow wetness, which he discovered when he pulled his hand back, was blood.

"What? When the hell did that happen?" Steve said, amazed a bullet had so nearly killed him. Only a couple inches to the left and it would have turned his lights out like a light switch. He would have never known what hit him. Hell, he hadn't even been aware of being under direct fire.

"Alpha we should go. Are there any vehicles we can use?"

"Several, but I have to stay and search for any who may have survived."

"Alpha…"

Alpha held up a hand. "What would you do in my place?"

Steve hated to admit it, but Alpha was right, so he said, "All right, let's see if we can find anyone."

Chapter 32

The macabre scene they witnessed as they returned to the tunnels was overwhelming. Frustration and sadness overcame them as each body they checked was lifeless and cold. For hours they searched, turning bodies over and checking for pulses, only to be met with more silence and death.

Sounds of footsteps came from the distance and intensified until a dozen figures appeared before them. Alpha cheered as he rushed towards the men. Steve had to push himself to keep up with his former mentor. Steve recognized some of his former fellow hunters, each wearing huge smiles in response to seeing Alpha alive. The smiles quickly faded at the sight of Steve, replaced with uncertainty about how to react to the familiar face that used to be one of their numbers.

Alpha noticed the uneasiness and said, "It's all right. The boy's come home." Each hunter looked from Alpha to Steve and immediately the smiles returned to everyone's faces.

Everyone's but Steve's, who whispered angrily to Alpha, "We'll settle that later."

"There's something else boy." Alpha said hesitantly.

"What?"

"Look around for who is missing. They have Lei."

* * *

Despite his appearance for having trekked through the desert, not to mention the copious amount of dried blood on his clothing, Steve had no problem passing undetected through the hospital. The fourth floor was quiet. Only the hum of computers and the soft tread of a nurse's rubber soled shoes on the linoleum floor echoed gently through the halls. Steve made his way to the only nurse at the nurse's station to ask where Chris might have set up a temporary office. The woman was busy on the computer and never even looked up to observe the state Steve was in.

When he asked about the M.E. from Los Angeles the nurse let out an exasperated sigh.

"Oh, him." The sound of disgust in her voice was unmistakable.

"I see you've met him."

"I can't wait until my shift replacement arrives in the morning to release me. He keeps wandering the hospital. Last time we found him in the children's wing, after visiting hours! If you ask me, we should have him bound to his desk or sedated him until morning. If he's back where he's supposed to be, then you'll find him in room 140 West."

Steve had no good response for that tirade, so instead he thanked her, and began a search for his troublemaking friend.

Chris was actually in his makeshift office when Steve looked in. His body was hunched and he appeared on the verge of falling asleep on his laptop.

"Hey." Steve said softly in an attempt not to startle his friend.

When Chris raised himself up and turned to Steve his eyes immediately shifted into a wide-eyed look of panic and concern. "Steve! Jesus, what happened?"

Steve raised his hands, "I'm fine Chris, but if you wouldn't mind, I wonder if there is a place where I could clean up?"

"This is a private room with a shower. Chris stood and gestured. Help yourself...or do you need help?"

Steve reasoned he must look a whole lot worse than he realized, if Chris was treating him with kid gloves. He was about to give Chris a run down about the entire evening when he caught a glimpse of himself in a mirror and was stunned into silence. The sight shocked him. He was more than dirty and disheveled, he looked absolutely ghoulish. Dark circles had formed around his eyes and his skin was very pale to the point he appeared deathly.

"Steve?" Chris asked gently. "Where's your flask?"

"I…I don't know." Steve said in honesty.

Chris studied him, "Are you wounded?

Surprised by the interrogative tone, Steve answered directly, "I'm fine, but I was grazed."

"You may not be wounded but you are far from fine. Have that shower then I'll see to that cut on your head."

As Steve turned to face Chris, his peripheral vision sensed, more than saw, movement in one corner of the well darkened room shadowed by the low lights.

"Steve don't…" But Steve held up a hand to cut off Chris' statement.

Chris read Steve's face and realized something was awry. Alpha emerged, materialized out of the shadows of the room. It was an improbable sight to witness. How could someone so large suddenly take shape out of such a small space? The power and the sense of threat Alpha conveyed combined, with his own grizzled appearance, would cause the dead to shiver.

When Chris saw Alpha he stumbled backward in surprise. He tried too quickly to right himself, lost his footing and fell on the polished linoleum floor in a reverse ballet of coordination. Unable to find his footing, Chris pushed himself backward away from Alpha as fast as he could until he slammed himself into the far wall of the room.

The vaudevillian act was enough for Alpha and Steve to turn their concentration to Chris, as he rubbed the back of his head.

A rasping cough emitted from Alpha. It was low and rhythmic but growing in intensity. Steve looked back at Alpha as did Chris, who kept rubbing the spot on his head.

The neutral expression on Alpha's face was usual, but his body bounced and writhed with every cough. The speed of the cough increased until it became uncontrollably rapid. Steve watched Alpha as the sound changed to less like a cough and more like…

Laughter.

It wasn't until Chris started chuckling that Steve began to relax. Within seconds he too was laughing along with Chris and

Alpha, who was now smiling like an idiot and pointing at Chris in full frivolity.

Chris shook his head and said, "Okay, I know a truce when I see one. Since both of you are apparently in need of stitching and I'm the only one in the room with any medical training, I'd suggest someone help me up before I have the two of you to take off your pants, bend over and sing *Moon River*."

Chapter 33

Steve let Chris stitch him up, and then showered while Alpha underwent more rigorous treatment, including a bullet removal from his side. He then dressed in a fresh pair of scrubs that had been provided while his clothes were being cleaned, the fresh smell and feel of the simple fabric on his skin was heavenly, after having been grimy for so long.

As he left Chris' room a nurse informed him that he should report to the lab, where Chris had set up his makeshift workstation. Steve wandered through the halls of the University Medical Center and wondered why all hospitals had to have the same plain, boring and antiseptic look about them. Silently speculating why the floors, walls and ceiling always had a vanilla wash, with a smattering of pastel color that was what passed for design, within the healthcare industry. The banality of the atmosphere, Steve was sure, was detrimental to the healing process of the patients within the walls. Certainly it would dampen the spirit of anyone wafting through the establishment and hoping to receive friendly care.

Taking a moment to consider whether physicians ever considered that an unpleasant, colorless setting could, in fact, cause a person's health to deteriorate, Steve moved through the doors denoting the laboratory where Chris had been working since he had dropped Steve off in the desert some 36 hours ago.

Steve hated hospitals, although not for the same reasons as Alpha, and he did everything he could to avoid them. The unease he felt stemmed from his desire for raw blood, the smell of which was still pronounced within the hospital, despite the antiseptic cleaners that were used on a regular basis by the janitorial crew. The smell mixed with his self-loathing, over having the desire in the first place, but nevertheless, Steve stifled his combination of emotions and quickened his pace to Chris' lab. When he arrived he found Chris hunched over a stack of medical files and reference books, most of which had the word "Neurology Department" embossed on the side of the jacket.

When Chris looked up, Steve froze. The apprehension on his friend's face was evident, and although Steve could tell he wasn't the cause, he couldn't imagine what would make such a carefree soul as Chris look so concerned.

Steve finally found his voice. "Jesus Chris, you look as though…well you've looked better. C'mon, I'm getting you out of here." Steve motioned as if he might lift his friend out of the chair when Chris jumped back as if afraid of his friend's touch.

"NO!" Chris was wide-eyed with intensity, then realized his reaction was out of place and physically calmed. "No. Not yet, not yet. Let me show you what I found first." Chris looked past Steve, "Where's the brute squad?"

"Alpha? He's still cleaning himself up."

Chris hesitated before he spoke. "Don't be mad, but I took some blood swatches from both of you and sent them out."

Steve was more confused than upset. "Why'd you do that?"

"Just the M.E. in me, popping up with questions, when I hadn't intended to ask any."

Steve sighed. "I don't have any more secrets Chris, not from you in any case."

"I believe you. Maybe there is something in your blood that will give us answers as to why Alex Daniels wants your people."

"Is that all that's bothering you at the moment?"

Chris looked to his computer screen and shook his head. "No. At the moment that is the least of my concerns."

"Chris what's…"

Chris held up his hand, cutting Steve off. "I know. I know. I am a little freaked out at the moment, but let's just leave it alone for now. I think I have an idea of what kind of weapon is being used to put people into "stasis.""

It was Steve's turn to offer a wide-eyed look, masking his excitement for the breakthrough and apprehension for whatever the findings might be. Steve couldn't help but feel animated, but he tempered his emotions, based on whatever was bothering his friend. The look on Chris' face told Steve that Chris was determined to be heard, so he compromised his need for answers regarding Alpha's condition, and nodded for Chris to proceed.

"Just promise me that as soon as you're done explaining you'll tell me what's up with you."

A wry smile crossed Chris' lips but his eyes still conveyed his anxiety. He took a deep breath and composed himself before rolling his chair to his laptop computer. He positioned the laptop on the edge of the table and scooted the chair about two feet from the edge. He checked the area surrounding the desk and chair, then placed a small leather rod, about six inches long and half an inch in diameter on the table next to the computer. Steve looked dumbfounded at the leather rod with several small indentations about a third of the way down the shaft on either side. Before Steve could ask Chris spoke:

"Okay, stand on the other side of the desk."

Steve looked and felt confused, but he complied with his friend's request. Chris typed something on the keyboard then leaned back in the chair. The desk chair was high backed and had padded armrests Chris stroked his palms across. Taking in another deep breath he closed his eyes and let out a jittery exhale.

Steve frowned, his mind screaming to ask questions, but he recognized Chris' intensity and attributed whatever was going on with Chris to be the result of the exhaustion he must be feeling.

"All right. Everything seems to be ready." Chris looked up at Steve. "I could go into some long thesis about the whole theory I have, but I think it's better to show you my theory and the basis for what I believe might be happening."

Chris reached for the keyboard as Steve asked, "How can I see the computer if I am facing the back of the screen?"

Chris looked up at Steve as if to say something reassuring, but the words caught in his throat and his hand shot away from the keyboard.

"WHOA!" Chris reached over to the desk and picked up a pair of dark goggles. "I'm sorry, I almost forgot these. I guess I'm more tired than I realized."

Steve looked at the goggles as Chris held them out to him.

"What?"

"Put them on."

The goggles were oversized, round and rather silly looking. Steve looked at Chris skeptically.

"Why?"

"For protection, you're going to need them."

Since Chris only had the one pair, Steve grew even more skeptical. Apparently Chris was not going to don a similar pair.

Chris bounced the goggles in his hand impatiently.

"C'mon! The sooner you put these on, the sooner I can get some rest," Chris urged.

With obvious disapproval, Steve took the goggles from Chris and placed the lenses over his eyes, cinching the elastic strap that gave the eyewear a sealed fit on his head.

Steve turned to Chris who was looking at the goggles on Steve's head.

"What?"

"I wish I had a camera," Chris snickered. Thinking Chris had just pulled a prank on him, Steve raised a hand to remove the glasses.

"Don't!" Chris commanded with all seriousness. "I'm sorry I ribbed you. You really do need those."

Steve was losing his patience, "For what Chris?"

"For what I am about to show you." All humor had drained away and Chris now had a pleading look on his face. Steve dropped his hand to his side.

"Thanks." Chris sighed. "Okay, when I hit the enter button a program I designed will run and, if everything works as I suspect, you'll have a real idea of what may be going on."

Steve waited as Chris began to shiver.

"Steve," Chris said, "don't panic, everything will be fine."

Without further warning Chris depressed the "enter" key and sat back in the chair. The lights in the room went out, which left

Steve in an unusual amount of darkness, given the glasses he was wearing. A moment of amazement passed through Steve's mind as he realized Chris had placed the lighting system of the laboratory under the remote control of his laptop.

"Chris what..?"

"Just wait. Trust me." Chris' voice came eerily out of the darkness.

Steve could hear the disc drive on the laptop began to hum as the program Chris had prepared sprang to life. The glow of whatever was on the computer screen cast the only illumination in the room and onto Chris' face. Steve could see Chris watching the screen with unblinking concentration. A few seconds went by and Steve found himself holding his breath in anticipation, of what, he didn't know. Then, without noise, a series of strobe like flashes lit the room as efficiently as any discothèque special effect. The flashes continued and Steve watched as Chris' face was lit with every flash. Steve noticed a change on Chris' face. Chris began to look sleepy and was having trouble looking at the screen. He wavered slightly in his chair and Steve thought he might fall asleep any moment.

After about twenty seconds the program ended. The flashing lights ceased and the lights of the lab switched back on. Steve looked around the room as he removed his glasses and tossed them on a nearby chair.

"So what was I supposed to..." Steve gasped and bolted toward Chris who was violently convulsing in the chair. His eyes were rolled back into his head and white frothy foam was oozing from his mouth. Every muscle in his body seemed to spasm and release with an immeasurable ferocity.

Steve screamed for help as he tried to gently lay Chris on the linoleum floor. Hearing his calls for help, nurses and orderlies sprang to life, some rushing to Steve while others went for a physician.

"Chris!"

Desperately he tried to control the spasms his friend was

experiencing while a gurgling sound discharged from Chris' throat. Suddenly, the leather rod Chris had placed on the table made sense to him. He turned to the table and grabbed the rod from the desktop. He pried open Chris' mouth and inserted the rod between Chris' teeth like a horse's bit. Steve could feel hands pulling him up from the floor. He was about to resist when he realized it was the various health care professionals trying to move him away so they could get to work on Chris. Steve was led away from the lab and told to wait in one of the generic waiting rooms. He sat worrying for nearly an hour before a nurse walked into the waiting room.

"Excuse me, are you Steve?"

Steve didn't know how the nurse knew his name but his concern for Chris took precedence over his "why do you ask and who wants to know" mentality.

"Yes?"

"I need to ask you a few questions about your brother."

"My...brother," Steve repeated out loud, pausing at the insanity of the statement. Then he guessed what was going on and hoped his words hadn't sounded like a question. Instead of giving the nurse a chance to ponder his confusion he distracted her with another question. "How is he?"

"He's stable and coherent. How long do the attacks normally last?"

Steve had no idea what was going on, but he played along.

"Not very long."

"You don't time them?"

"I'm not always with him."

The nurse frowned but continued undaunted.

"How long has it been since his last episode?"

Steve knew he hadn't answered the first question to the nurse's satisfaction so he tried to seem casual about his answer, as if this wasn't an unusual occurrence.

"I honestly can't remember the last time this happened." Steve smiled to himself as he realized that Chris would have liked that answer.

The nurse found this to be encouraging.

"Well, it's a good thing the episodes aren't frequent. By all indications he's just fine, a little tired from the ordeal, but none the worse for wear. I'll need to get a full medical history from your brother at some point, but for now he's awake and asking for you. The doctor would like to keep him overnight for observation, would that be acceptable?"

"What did…uh…my brother have to say about that?"

"He refused." The nurse looked a bit annoyed when she mentioned Chris' response.

"Well, I'll talk to him about it, but I think the final decision will be his. That is if he's going to be all right."

"Yes, yes he's fine. The doctor gave him a muscle relaxant and a mild sedative along with a prescription for *Neurontin*, so he shouldn't be driving."

"Uh, of course." He couldn't take it anymore and had to ask the obvious question. "Do you know why this happened to him?"

The nurse looked sympathetically at him.

"No, I know it's hard. I had a cousin with epilepsy and there didn't seem to be any specific rhyme or reason for her episodes either. She'd just tell everybody that if an attack occurred they should stand back and let her thrash about. She'd come out of it in a few minutes and be fine. Tired, but fine."

Steve was so taken aback by what he was hearing all he could do was nod his head as the nurse led him to the room where Chris had been taken. What was going on?

Chris wasn't an epileptic.

Was he?

Chapter 34

As the nurse walked Steve to Chris' hospital room, Alpha came running around the corner and nearly scared the nurse into cardiac arrest.

"It's okay, he's with me."

The nurse looked at Alpha with some concern, "I'm sorry, but the patient has only asked to see his brother."

Alpha looked confused, "Brother?"

Steve immediately spoke up, "They have rules that only family members are allowed to see certain patients who've been admitted." Steve turned to the nurse as he removed his police badge from his belt, "Listen ma'am, I don't mean to throw my weight around, but this man is part of an investigation and it is very important he be included on the visitation list."

The nurse started to protest but Steve cut her off, "He's harmless…really."

The nurse looked at Alpha then shrugged her shoulders and said, "He's your brother, so as long as he doesn't object then I guess I won't either."

The nurse walked off mumbling as Steve and Alpha walked into Chris' room.

"Hey, look whose come to see me," Chris said weakly as Steve and Alpha entered the semi-private hospital room. "What? No flowers?"

Steve didn't smile or take heart at the comment, although out of the corner of his eye he thought he could see Alpha suppressing a grin, which was more than a little out of character for him.

Returning his attention to Chris, "How do you feel?"

Chris could see the mood Steve was in and became serious. "Pretty weak, but none the worse for wear. They say the first episode is the worst so…"

Steve kept glaring at him until Chris spoke in a conspiratorial whisper.

"See if the guy in the other bed is out."

Alpha moved to the other bed and checked the patient lying supine and motionless. Alpha moved to the foot of the bed and checked the chart. After studying the front page for a few moments Alpha said, "The man is heavily sedated and probably won't wake up for a few hours."

Nodding, Chris began his explanations. " Okay, so I guess you have a lot of questions and are wondering about what really happened. Let me ask you first. Have you ever seen those little plaques outside of nightclubs or certain amusement park rides warning people with epilepsy about strobe lights?"

"Yeah, so what? What was this, Chris? I know you don't have epilepsy."

Chris nodded, "Actually, you don't really know that."

"So you do have epilepsy?" Alpha asked.

"No." Chris was shaking his head now. "It's just that epilepsy can come on at any point in life."

"But that's not what happened to you," Steve volunteered.

"No, but it is possible to start having seizures in adulthood."

"Chris what does this have to do with…"

Chris continued, "You know, I had a cousin who, one time…"

"Chris!" Steve called out in exasperation.

In a very exasperated and affected tone Steve drawled, "Would you *please* try to focus."

Reluctantly, Chris conceded. "All right. Jeez Steve, you're no fun anymore."

Steve placed his thumb and first finger on opposite sides of his nasal bone and squeezed into the headache his now alleged brother was giving him.

Chris composed himself and continued. "What I meant was that epilepsy isn't a specific disease or dysfunction which occurs at a certain time in your life. Sometimes it just comes out of nowhere and most of the time no one knows why."

"And your point is?" Steve said with impatience.

"You saw the program I was running back at the lab. Even

with the dark glasses covering your eyes, you must have seen the series of flashing lights coming from the computer screen."

Steve nodded.

"Okay, as I said earlier, I don't have epilepsy, however, I was looking at the lab work of the victims from the strip club who were in stasis and couldn't find any foreign substances in their blood or systems that could account for the state they were in. It occurred to me that perhaps the microbe or chemical causing the problem had been metabolized by the body or it was undetectable with current technology."

Steve and Alpha were totally entranced and hanging on to Chris' every word like Boy Scouts, listening to their first ghost story around a campfire.

"We were using some pretty high tech equipment in the lab, but we still couldn't find any traces," Chris continued. "Then I thought, what if we were looking for the wrong thing altogether."

Chris looked at Steve and Alpha to let the words sink in.

"We just assumed it was some kind of chemical or biological agent, but what if it wasn't a microbe or chemical. What if it was some other common denominator directly affecting the brain? Nightclubs in general are dark places with various neon and strobe lights, loud music and fog machines. I considered what kind of person would be least suited for that environment. For some reason, I remembered the little plaques in front of some of my favorite amusement parks. Immediately epilepsy jumped to the top of the list."

Chris paused to reach for a glass of water, which he sipped before continuing.

"If a person with a particular type of epilepsy walked into one of these places, he or she would probably drop with a seizure in a matter of seconds, as a result of the flashing lights. The drop could be as quick as what happened to all of those people at *The Inferno* and at the Glitter Gulch."

Steve and Alpha silently took in all the information.

"There's a flaw in your theory," Steve volunteered.

"I bet you're going to say something to the effect of 'why would two clubs be packed full of non-epileptics, all of whom spontaneously suffer epileptic seizures at the same time?'"

Steve nodded, "That and the fact that this 'stasis' they are in doesn't resemble an 'epileptic seizure.'"

"Right. That's what I was testing. Obviously, all who were affected in the clubs couldn't have been epileptics so I began to wonder if it were possible to induce a seizure in a non-epileptic with the proper strobe light stimulation."

Steve interrupted Chris: "I hate to be the one to say it, but I only know epilepsy as a person having a seizure. Could we slow down a minute, and get an explanation about what it is?"

Chris smiled as he explained, "Epilepsy is a group of disorders characterized by unprovoked and recurrent seizures. These are caused by sudden, transient disturbances of electrical activity in the brain, disrupting its normal neurological functioning. The symptoms are dependent on the type of epilepsy, and the location of the disturbance in the brain. Loss of consciousness, loss of motor function, psychic disturbances, or aberrant sensory phenomenon can all be symptoms of epilepsy."

Alpha leaned over to Steve and spoke conspiratorially, "My mind has never truly accepted the technology of this world. What did he say?"

"I think if he had spoken in English it would translate into 'something causes a break in the brain's ability to communicate with the body, and a seizure, or some other symptom, is the result'."

"A little basic but that's the general idea."

"So where do the flashing lights come in?" Steve asked.

"The reaction to the flashing lights is a type of epilepsy called Reflex Epilepsy, in which seizures are triggered by an individual's sensitivity to sensory stimulation in the environment. The most common form of this is photosensitive epilepsy, in other words, seizures caused by exposure to intense or fluctuating levels of light. People who suffer from this condition have seizures triggered by flashing lights or rapidly alternating light and dark patterns. A flickering fluorescent light, the flicker of sunlight while driving past standing trees, certain video games, or flashing strobe lights can trigger seizures in photosensitive people. In these cases the herky-jerky type seizure can occur, but there's also a type of seizure called an Absence Seizure. In this case the person shuts down and stares off into space."

Steve contemplated this "absence seizure" since it sounded like what was happening to the victims of both *The Inferno* and the Glitter Gulch.

"But you said you don't have epilepsy."

"That's true. What I wanted to do was test whether I could induce a seizure in a non-epileptic by stimulating the nervous system with a specific pattern of strobe light flashes. And, as you saw first-hand, I was successful."

The full weight of what had happened to his friend after his exposure to the flashing lights in the lab, came crashing down on Steve with an impact akin to having a piano dropped on his head.

"You actually caused yourself to have one of these reflex epileptic seizures?!? Are you insane!?!"

Steve was beyond furious with Chris' recklessness.

Holding his hands up in a submissive gesture, Chris answered, "It's not like I could have asked for a volunteer, and we didn't have time for any other alternatives."

"You seriously endangered yourself, not to mention me!"

"The polarized sunglasses with blue lenses I had you wear are a widely known as adequate protection from this type of photosensitive seizure. You were never in any danger."

Alpha seemed to be keeping a more rational temperament than Steve. He calmly asked, "What causes epilepsy?"

Glad to change the subject, Chris answered Alpha, "Sometimes various diseases or syndromes, resulting in brain damage, can cause the condition."

As Chris spoke Steve riveted his attention to his friend and a

212

grave look of concern crossed his face. Noticing Steve's reaction, Chris continued, "No, I didn't cause any permanent brain damage by conducting my little experiment."

"No," Steve said under his breath. "No more than was already there."

"I heard that. Anyway, in about 85% of the people who suffer with epilepsy, the origin is idiopathic, or in other words, there is no known cause for the condition."

"So how did you do it?"

"My theory, is based on a theory for the cause of the Reflex Epilepsy. Since the eyes are linked directly to the brain, visual stimuli is hardwired directly into the vision center, without having to travel through the periphery of the nervous system, as do most of the sensations we experience. This means the stimuli are unfiltered prior to reaching the brain, which then receives the full impact of the stimuli. The vision center of the brain is actually in the back of the skull, the furthest point from the location of the eyes. My conjecture was that with the proper sequence of strobe lights directly stimulating the brain, one could disrupt and negatively impact the electrical impulses within any desired area of the brain. Through this disruption, I believed I could induce a seizure similar to the ones suffered by those with Reflex Epilepsy."

"Apparently you were right," Alpha concluded.

"Only on the surface," Chris said modestly as he went on with his hypothesis. "Now you guys are going to have to make a little bit of a leap of faith on this one, but what if someone else had already been on this track and made modifications to the sequence and intensity of a particular strobe light. If I could do what I did, then someone more brilliant and focused than me could, theoretically, design a strobe light with a specific sequence and intensity, to have any given desired effect on a person's brain function that they wished."

Chris remained quiet for a moment to let that sink in.

Steve was the first to speak up, albeit skeptically.

"So you are saying that you think the victims in both clubs

were all zapped by someone with a special strobe light? What? Did he carry it around with him in his jacket or pants?"

Chris thought about that for a moment.

"No, to have an effect on all of those people simultaneously, the culprit would have needed to tap into the club's special lighting effects in order for it to be powerful enough to get *The Inferno* results."

Something nagged at the back of Steve's mind, fighting its way to the surface.

Alpha asked another question. "Would the effect be possible to create with a flash bang grenade?"

Chris bolted upright in his hospital bed.

"What?!? Maybe. Why?"

Steve volunteered, "There is evidence at the Glitter Gulch that flash bang grenades were detonated."

"As well as in our home last night," Alpha growled softly.

Chris nodded. "Those grenades do give off a powerful and disorienting blast of light and sound. With the right expertise in munitions a person could modify the grenade to explode with a series of light flashes. It would be similar to making a giant firecracker for the Fourth of July."

"There was no evidence of flash bangs in Los Angeles," Steve said dryly.

"That means the only way the theory would work in LA is if someone sent the impulses out through the existing lights at *The Inferno*," Chris postulated.

"Which makes sense since Pharmanetics agents were officially helping with the clean up, that would enable them to remove all evidence of their involvement."

"Seems a little bit of an obvious and convenient suspect," Chris speculated. "Also, how could they have overridden the FBI and the WHO?"

"Good question. And a now that we are good conspiracy theorists, the answer would have to be some kind of payoff or favor from, or to, an agent of the government."

"So we are actually going to be taking on our own government?"

"I doubt it," Steve consoled. "Not directly anyway, but considering that the three of us are the only ones who know there is a potential connection, things could get a lot worse before they get better."

Either encouraged or genuinely excited, Chris announced, "So 'Athos', what would our next move be?"

Steve was somewhat amused by the reference.

"Simple, my dear 'Porthos.' We return to the scene of the crime and see if any of the Cardinal's spies arrive."

Alpha had not caught the reference. "So where do we go from here?"

Steve looked at Chris, "How soon before that blood work is ready"

"What blood work?" Alpha asked Steve.

"Should be any second now, why?"

"What blood work?" Alpha turned and asked Chris.

"Because we've had two mass abductions and it stands to reason the best way to keep that many abductees under control would be to make them all sleep through it."

"Excuse me. What blood…"

"You think *The Inferno* and the Glitter Gulch were just tests for some other true purpose?"

"Exactly, but I don't know what that purpose might be, perhaps the result of the blood work will…"

Alpha slammed a fist down so hard on the nightstand the wood shattered and the metal bent under the weight of the blow.

"WHAT BLOOD WORK?!?"

Steve and Chris looked at each other.

Quickly Chris said, "I'll be outside." Chris started to roll out of the hospital bed and yelled at Alpha. "Aramis! Get me my pants!"

Steve put a hand on Chris' chest preventing him from getting out of bed. "Easy boy, you're not going anywhere."

Chris looked at Steve with incredulity and exclaimed, "Nonsense! Aramis, the pants!"

Alpha still didn't understand why Chris was calling him "Aramis." And then it connected.

"Perhaps you should rest and tell me about the blood work... Porthos."

"Damn you both. Well that's fine, at least let me get dressed."

Reaching out, he pressed the "Call Nurse" switch and a female voice crackled over an intercom.

"Yes Mr. Barnes, are you all right?"

"Hello my little nightingale, how I have longed to hear your voice again." Chris was making a show of swooning into the intercom, but he sounded more like Pepé Le Pew than Casanova.

"Are you all right sir?"

Chris quickly shifted gears and grew indignant, "No, I am not all right! These heathens are vexing me, and I shall require wine and my tailor, post haste!"

Steve couldn't help but smile at Chris' antics, unfortunately, Alpha looked as though he might blow a gasket again.

After a brief pause the nurse responded, "No alcohol is allowed on this floor sir. Besides it wouldn't be a good idea while you are still catheterized."

The room immediately fell into an awkward silence. Chris' eyes looked up from the speaker and darted from Steve to Alpha and back to Steve. He then looked at the "Call Nurse" button as if it had suddenly turned into a hunk of uranium. Slowly, Chris extended a shaky finger and depressed the button.

"...Excuse me?" Chris' face was ashen and all traces of the romantic had faded.

Both Steve and Alpha watched Chris, eyes wide.

"That's right sir. You have a catheter in your urethra. You probably don't feel it as a result of the relaxants the doctor prescribed for you."

Completely bamboozled, Chris stammered, "I have a 'what' in my 'where'?"

"So this is Karma," Alpha said as Steve patted Chris on the shoulder.

"Take it easy drippy dick, you'll be all right."

As Steve and Alpha sat in a couple of folding chairs that the hospital had provided, a stunned Chris slowly raised the sheets of his bed to nervously peer at himself under the covers.

"My God, that tube is huge! How can I possibly not feel that?!?"

Chapter 35

For the next hour, Chris attempted to explain to Alpha why he felt the need to have their blood analyzed. Alpha was furious at first, but the truth in Chris' explanation overwhelmed his anger so that he reluctantly acquiesced. A doctor arrived to check on Chris, performed a few cursory evaluations, and had a nurse remove the catheter while he signed a release so that Chris was free to leave. Most of the drugs were out of his system by now, but Chris was still moving sluggishly, as he started dressing. He was having trouble tying his shoes, when an orderly arrived with two manila folders. Chris immediately opened the folder on top and began reading the lab reports.

After a few minutes Chris' face took on a look, which gave Steve the distinct impression he had read something raising a red flag. "Steve…I…?" Chris' voice was hushed and in a rasp that added to his already disturbing demeanor. Chris looked down at the medical chart containing figures looking to be a lab report, searching for where to begin.

"Steve, you told me that you guys weren't susceptible to viruses and certain harmful bacteria, right?"

"That's right. Why? What's up Chris?"

Nodding, Chris replied, "Well, there actually are several aspects of your blood that were unusual, but I think I know why Pharmanetics is interested in you and your people."

"What?" Steve said with alarm.

"Steve, your blood has no antibodies. The white blood cell count is zero, however, your T-cell count is normal."

"Yes, the T-cell count would be normal and there would be no antibodies in the blood if we assume there are absolutely no viruses within our systems now, nor will there ever be," Alpha said cryptically.

Chris shook his head. "That's completely impossible. Viruses are present in everything we eat, drink, breathe, touch or absorb.

Even though most are controlled by a healthy immune system and pose no threat, they can't be avoided."

Alpha countered, "Viruses are structurally one of the most simple, and yet most complicated, life forms on the planet, simple strands of DNA. Yet some of them target, attack, consume, reproduce and ultimately evacuate their host organism, just to go on to attack another host. Somehow, there is an inherency within those simple strands that recognizes a suitable environment in which to thrive.

"And that's why Pharmanetics is interested in you and your people!" Chris suddenly announced. "If they could develop an absolute cure for viral infection, like an antibiotic does for bacterial infections, the patents would be worth billions, perhaps trillions of dollars. Everything from the common cold, the flu, even AIDS and…"

"Biological warfare?" Alpha finished the sentence for Chris.

Steve blanched. "What?"

"It's far easier, and more affordable to produce a biological or 'dirty' bomb, than it is to produce a nuclear one," Alpha stated matter-of-factly.

"Pharmanetics is harvesting what they need from Alpha's kidnapped people. That's why they took the children first and why they created the device that puts people into stasis. Chemically induced comas can be detrimental to health over time, and Pharmanetics can't afford to have their only resource for the medication dying too soon. "

Chapter 36

There was dead silence in the room after Chris gave voice to the revelation of Pharmanetics' true agenda.

Steve thought for a moment then spoke: "The question is, 'what will our next move be?'"

"The remaining hunters and I will be going to Pharmanetics to get back our children, and whomever else they may have taken. And we will destroy anyone who tries to get in our way," Alpha said with cold confidence.

"Easy Alpha, we don't want to go on a killing spree."

Chris jumped back into the conversation. "What we need now is a way to get those people back without getting them or ourselves killed in the process." Chris caressed his chin in thought then raised his index finger to the ceiling and shouted, "I say we storm Pharmanetics!"

"Uh-oh" Steve thought, "There he goes."

Steve spoke as calmly as he could. "Uh…Storm, Chris?"

"Yes STORM! Like a hurricane!"

All eyes were on Chris now as he began to rapidly pace the room.

Alpha turned to Steve. "I like this one."

"Don't encourage him."

About a minute later, Chris stopped and turned to the duo.

"Okay, I'm pretty sure I can hack into the city's zoning offices and the Pharmanetics security computers. Give me one hour to put a plan together and I will describe in detail how we are going to storm the Bastille."

Chapter 37

The room Lei woke up in was dark and cold. It was also dry with a sterile, though not wholly unpleasant smell, easily identifiable as refrigerated air. She tried to rise from the cot she lay on but found her wrists bound by police issue handcuffs. Testing her restraints briefly she realized she wasn't going anywhere, so instead of struggling or panicking, she relaxed her breathing and let her eyes adjust to the surroundings.

She was supine on what she eventually comprehended was a hospital gurney, not a cot. Her wrists were shackled to the framework of the bed placing her in a crucifixion position. The rest of her body was free to move. Her eyes continued to adjust to the darkness and memories of a ride in a large vehicle, with the bodies of her people stacked around her like discarded clothing, played like a movie in her fading mental haze. She remembered lapsing into and out of consciousness, as if continuously sedated. When she felt she was regaining clarity during the ride, she would suddenly become groggy and nod off for another period of time.

Her mouth and throat were parched and held a foul taste, further confirmation of having been drugged. With a concentrated effort, she shook off even more of the effects of whatever had been introduced into her system. The increased clarity allowed her the realization that she was naked on the bed. Lei hadn't initially been aware of her nakedness because the room was adequately warm, and she hadn't experienced any kind of chill. She knew captors stripped their captives to give them a heightened sense of vulnerability, but in her case, her body and the intense allure her appearance could evoke, had always been her armor. Through her training, as well as the fruits of skilled cosmetic surgeons, she felt at her most powerful in as little clothing as possible, or even better, nude.

In the next moment, she sensed she wasn't alone in the room, feeling someone's eyes on her, as she had so many times in the past, but no amount of adjusting her eyes to the dark of the room revealed another person.

"So who's there?" Lei said in her most seductive tone.

No answer.

Okay, time to play the game she had never lost since she had completed her training.

"C'mon, come closer...You know you want to take a better look." She shook her breasts gently from side to side. "It's so dark in here, you can't possibly see me as well as you would like."

A slight creak sounded behind her, as if someone shifted their position in a chair. It came from directly behind her which, given her bound state, was the one area she couldn't see.

"Are you watching me?" Lei asked as she arched her body so more of her could be seen from the position of the sound.

"I like to be watched. What's your name?"

Lei heard a slight chuckle come from the area where she suspected the voyeur to be. She couldn't do anything with him from that position and needed to draw whoever it was in close, to engage them, to draw them nearer. She would easily enthrall them and encourage her new conquest to free her, even protect her as she made her escape.

"This isn't usually how I go about finding a partner to watch me, but..." She began to breathe with a bit more effort, as if she was getting aroused by the thought of someone watching her.

"You know sometimes if I squeeze my thighs together just right..." She bent her knees while keeping her feet planted on the mattress, slowly arching her back and lifting her torso up into a pelvic thrust as she pulsed her hips and thighs together. Her body shuddered slightly as her muscles tightened, she began grinding her pelvis in slow circular motions, occasionally jolting her body as if one particular spot sent an electric impulse through her.

Lei let out a small gasp and a quick intake of breath as she repeated the performance, gradually increasing the speed of her gyrations, and this most erotic dance. As her breath came out in labored need, the effort caused a slight sheen of perspiration to form on her cappuccino colored skin.

Moaning as softly as a whisper, she continued her dance. Lei's heart skipped for a fleeting moment when she heard sounds of someone rising out of the chair. She spread her feet further apart and planted them firmly on the sides of the mattress. She raised her legs and completely exposed herself to the opposite side of the room from where the voyeur was sitting.

"God, I love being watched...Do you like what you see?" She breathed heavily, "I think you do." Her voice was perfected and she sounded lost in the moment. In truth, she was actually starting to lose herself in the moment, just a little bit. Her best performances always came when she could 'feel' the role she was manipulating.

"Please..." She huffed, "Please, I am so close. I need to be touched...I need to feel someone touching me all over."

No sound.

"Please," she begged as her movements became more desperate and her breath more erratic. "I know you want to touch me. You've been watching me all this time, going out of your mind with the need to touch me. Do it! Please! I want you to! I need you to!"

Lei never heard the man approach. Suddenly two large, leather-gloved hands reached over from behind her head and caressed her lower waist and abdomen. The surprise of the contact sent shivers through Lei, although she hid the surprise with a barely audible cry of pleasure.

The powerful hands flowed over her flat stomach, down the sides of her hips then back up and over the large curves of her breasts, where they stopped and pinched firmly on her erect nipples.

Lei almost laughed out loud when the hands stopped on her breasts. Men were so predictable. The only reason she didn't laugh was her breath caught in her throat, the pressure registered an exquisite sensation, sending a tremor through her.

She was getting into it now, almost regretting that once her goading put the voyeur into her thrall the fun would have to end. It was so easy now. Any doubt in her ability had left her mind years ago with the culmination of all of Alpha, and his clan's teachings. She could seduce and enmesh anyone, at any time, mostly because she knew how not to play fair.

"Can you reach me down here?" Her voice was in gasps and heavy swallows as she raised her hips even higher to further display herself to the assumed man.

Placing the palm of his left hand on her right cheek the man gently, yet firmly, pressed and turned Lei's head to the left while walking around to her right.

"Hmmm," She thought. "This might be a slight complication."

The act was a surprise but a maximum turn-on for Lei who'd always liked a bit of the "top and bottom" play in her personal time. The man's left hand firmly, but non-aggressively held her head away from him while his right hand continued its exploration of her body, slowly caressing her breasts and working its way down...

Down...down...down...

Then the leather-gloved fingers parted through her very small, well-groomed patch of pubic hair. For her part Lei began to push up into the right hand while moaning slightly louder than previously.

Lei felt the tip of his little finger graze against that most sensitive part of her and the whole experience became *very* real. Recognizing that she was getting too far lost in the moment, she gently tried to turn her head back for a look at the man who, for the time being, thought he was in control of her. Her efforts were resisted with a minimal increase in pressure on her cheek, countering her attempt to turn her head.

The hand rotated and all four fingers moved down and covered her sex, pressing gently while rotating softly over the whole area.

"Damn," Lei couldn't help but think "this guy has got a clue."

She could feel her moisture making the leather slick, increasing her pleasure with each slight circulation.

Effortlessly, a finger slipped deep inside her. She gasped loudly as her body reacted with exquisite submission to the penetration. Lei gyrated and undulated her hips around the finger, squeezing the finger all the while, with muscles well-trained for this optimum pleasure giving purpose.

"Take off the gloves," she cooed between breaths. "Don't you want to feel me? Feel me on the inside?"

The hand had gone slack as she worked her body around it, opening and closing her thighs in a type of primitive intimacy.

"Feel my warmth and wetness? Feel my body grip onto yours?" she moaned.

The left hand eased the pressure on her cheek and the right hand slipped from inside her.

She turned her head slowly to face the man, but just as her eyes found his he threw his leg over her body, placing himself into a mounted position. The movement pinned her with each of his legs on either side of her hips, and his feet interlocking around her inner thighs. His left hand held her face under her chin, and when Dr. Whelan brought up his right hand it held a small but wicked looking knife. He moved it within centimeters of her right eye.

"You think I don't know you bitch?" The doctor said with unrestrained lusty anger. "Oh, I do want to penetrate you. Oh yes, I do. But not with just any part of me. Oh no, no."

Fear overwhelmed her as she recognized, not the man, but the type of man now straddling her body. She acknowledged she'd made a horrible mistake. This type of man took his pleasure in a very different way. This type of man was to be avoided at all costs. His pleasure was not merely the inflicting of pain, it was in the kill, the rush from stealing life, and the power derived from the act. The type so many sexual predators emulated.

The doctor seemed lost in some brutal lust, until instantly the entire scene turned from a seduction with Lei in control to a kind of sadistic torture in the hands of a knife-wielding madman.

"No one I have ever met can sharpen a blade to the extent I can. See?"

The doctor ran the flat of the blade across her cheek. It didn't cut the tender flesh of her face, but Lei could tell from the way the razor itched to grip her skin the blade was indeed, exceptionally sharp.

Dr. Whelan traced a path down Lei's face, across her throat and over one breast, stopping briefly at her nipple. Lei panicked knowing the mere flick of a wrist could effortlessly and cleanly amputate it. Instead the blade continued down her chest to her belly, she felt the coolness of the blade travel to the inside of her navel and stop.

"I have found the best place to work the knife while prolonging life is within the abdomen. As long as you don't perforate the intestines the bleeding is minimal, and death can take days upon days. Unfortunately, I don't have that kind of time with you, but I do have a few hours to kill."

The doctor chuckled at his little joke, then grew serious.

"Shall we begin?"

The knife was indeed sharp, Lei felt the cold steel, as its tip sank unimpeded into the flesh of her stomach.

Chapter 38

It took longer than an hour, but when Chris rejoined the group he had everything they needed pertaining to Pharmanetics: printouts of blueprints for the building submitted to the city, security systems filed with the police and fire departments, in case of an emergency, even the specs for the phone, electricity, plumbing and sewer systems. All were laid out neatly on a large conference table in the executive offices, where the crew had been waiting.

"My God," Steve exclaimed, viewing the sheer mass of detailed information before him. "You couldn't have come into all of this information via the normal channels."

"I didn't," Chris said nonchalantly. "In fact I'm sure I violated an enormous amount of privacy and communications laws in the process of acquiring it."

Steve looked at Chris, unsure if his friend had been kidding him. The idea of deliberately breaking the law to do...well... anything, didn't initially sit well with Steve. He was still a cop after all. Then again, here he was about to storm into a major corporate building with potentially lethal force, and without going through the proper channels, which made the entire event a highly irregular and illegal action.

"You know what?" Steve said.

"What?"

"I just don't want to know, so spare me the details from now on."

Chris considered it a moment, then said "I think that would be best."

Alpha was scanning the plans as Chris and Steve talked, shaking his head in apparent disbelief.

"This information is incredible! How could you have achieved this when all of my resources could not?"

Steve spoke up before Chris could reply, in an attempt to spare himself the dissertation Chris would provide on the subject.

"Chris has always been a relatively well accomplished hacker."

"Relatively well accomplished?" Chris said as if greatly offended. "I'm one of the best! If it weren't for my desire to be a legitimate member of the common good I would be living in the Bahamas draining corporate slush funds and living like Hugh Hefner."

Chris shook his head, "Three girlfriends...at his age, unbelievable!"

Stunned, Alpha looked at Chris, "And I thought you were an idiot."

Chris looked slightly chastened, "Well, it's okay. I thought you were an albino."

Alpha cocked his head, confused, "But...I am an albino."

Nodding, Chris replied, "Well, there you go," and immediately turned his attention away from Alpha and began reading through the security installations, from the blueprints he had acquired.

Alpha looked to Steve for enlightenment, but Steve only shrugged his shoulders and went back to work at the table.

They worked diligently, finding out as much information as they could about the weaknesses of the massive skyscraper, and a plan began to come into focus.

"Okay," Steve started, "it appears the first and second floors are information desks and offices, which are open to the public. The third through ninth floors are research and processing labs, while the tenth through thirteenth floors have been opened up into one large production warehouse."

"It's a big, open, empty space. Why do you say this is where Pharmanetics produces their products?" Alpha asked.

"See all the high voltage electrical lines running directly to this area, and nowhere else in the building? That tells me they have equipment on this level requiring beefed up power way beyond that of simple research machinery."

"Actually, some of the machinery used in the Pharmanetics' research labs can use, and generate, a great deal of power. An electron microscope for example, would practically need its own power plant," Chris explained.

"Wouldn't the machines which produce the drugs be extra heavy as well?" Alpha asked.

"Yes they would, and I believe they are," Steve answered. "You'll notice on the blueprints, that each floor from three through nine has added structural reinforcement, albeit minimal. And the floor still runs on normal electrical circuits. I believe the base products for the drugs are made in the labs on these levels, and then sent to the upper floors for assembly."

Each man silently studied the schematics as they considered Steve's theory.

"I think you're right Steve," Chris interjected. "Look how the third through ninth floors all have special safety features and yet minimal security. Sprinklers and foam fire protection, special ventilation and unique drainage, all very standard for a working laboratory. Now look at the open area on the tenth through thirteenth floors. They have minimal safety and much higher than normal security. Given your theory this particular set-up makes sense. The creation of the basic products within the pharmaceutical world is no secret, but the combination of chemicals, and the ratios which make the drugs effective, are highly guarded. Not to mention the finished products themselves need to be protected until they are shipped to the suppliers."

"How does this help us?" Alpha asked impatiently.

Steve recognized the irritation in his voice. As far back as he could remember, Alpha was about action as opposed to planning.

"Bear with me for a second Alpha. We can see that the rest of the floors, fourteen through eighty are either showroom floors or straight office space, with the top floor being for the exclusive use of our good Mr. Daniels. The floors below ground appear to be the usual boiler room and other utility areas for the building."

"Is this normal for a company to use their buildings to not

only house their corporate people, but also house their production facility?" Chris asked. "I would think the costs of warehousing and research could be more efficient at lower real estate rates."

"True, unless you want to keep you're activities extremely private and monitored the tightest security standards, which is far more difficult to do in multiple areas."

"Again I ask you, how does this help us find our people?" Alpha demanded with a little more volume than before.

"The high security Alpha."

Alpha looked at Steve realizing the answer was forthcoming.

"What if…and this is pure speculation now, but what if instead of major production equipment putting drugs together in combination, the area has been converted."

"Converted?" Alpha said. "Converted to what?"

"We've already determined that our blood supply was what Pharmanetics wanted for its ability to make a human body an adverse environment for viruses and bacteria."

"Yes," Alpha agreed.

"How long does the effect last?" Steve asked Alpha.

"Like you and yours, I would think that the benefits of the drug would alter your blood chemistry permanently," Chris responded.

"Then I would ask you, where's the money in a permanent cure?"

Steve let the question hang for a short period of time then continued.

"If a person received a cure derived from the blood of our people for a common cold, and was never going to get another cold for the rest of their lives, how does Pharmanetics continue to make money?"

"So…you think they are converting the permanent curative aspect of the blood to something more temporary?"

"As Chris Rock used to say in his stand-up routine 'There's no money in a cure', I think they have reversed the process. They acquire the blood supply in the heightened security room and transport it to the other floors for refinement into a more profitable product."

"But the sheer mass of people who would be on that floor would require constant maintenance, food supplies, bathroom facilities, and etcetera."

"This brings us full circle to what happened to those people at *The Inferno* and Glitter Gulch. A new technology which keeps a person in a coma-like stasis without the harmful side effects of chemicals would mean a body could produce more products over time before…"

Steve stopped himself from saying what he was going to say and altered his words before he continued, "Before the person is no longer able to produce additional product."

Alpha stared wide-eyed at Steve, as he heard his finishing words.

"I will see the building burned to the ground and render the fat of all of those involved as the fuel for the fire." The look in Alpha's eyes made it clear he meant every word. This was not an idle threat.

Trying to ignore the frightening revelation, Chris said, "So we can assume our LAPD brethren are there as well?"

"It's our best guess, but it is still only a guess."

"So," Alpha asked while still studying the documents on the table, "how do you intend to get in the building and remove all of those people without having any idea how to bring them out of the state they are in?"

"I don't plan on bringing them out."

Alpha looked up from the documents on the table sharply and faced Steve.

"I only intend on exposing Pharmanetics for who and what they are, then we'll let those far more brilliant than we, figure out how to help the prisoners."

"That would mean exposing our people to the whole world!"

"Hoo-boy…" Chris whistled.

With a calm Steve hadn't expressed since this entire escapade had begun, he said, "I know."

"You know? That's it?!?" Alpha was yelling again.

"Yes, I know and I'm sorry for that, but I see no other way to accomplish this."

"That is completely unacceptable!!!"

"If you have another plan for how to remove over three thousand comatose people from a building in secret, then now would be a good time to share."

Alpha balled his fists and for a moment appeared as though he might strike Steve. Then his head dropped and his hands went to his face and rubbed his forehead.

"It's all coming apart and, you're right, it is too big, for me to stop it from happening."

A nervous moment passed before Alpha spoke again.

"I need you all to promise me something." Alpha spoke so quietly Steve had to strain to hear him. "I need you to promise me that when this news breaks, you will use whatever influence you have to help keep these parasites and vultures of humanity away from my children."

Steve looked at Alpha, understanding the weight of what was being asked.

"I know it may seem an impossible task, and all I am asking is that you try. Try your best, please."

"I promise," Steve nodded.

Alpha's eyes were red and moist as he gripped Steve's hand in both of his.

"Thank you."

Chapter 39

"Doctor?" The voice cut through the silence as clearly as if it had been amplified through a speaker system. Unfortunately, the person it was directed toward was so lost in the slice he had made in Lei's abdomen he never heard a sound.

With the care and precision of a master craftsman, Dr. Whelan glided the impeccably sharp blade further toward Lei's right hip. She was pinned in near immobility, quaking in small tremors as the knife passed through her skin as easily as a hot knife through soft butter.

"DOCTOR!!!" Kunnert's voice was an explosion of sound and command. Dr. Whelan's head snapped up upon hearing Kunnert that time.

"What...are...you...DOING?!?"

The doctor was visibly shaken, as if waking up from a dream, looking from Kunnert, to what he had done to Lei, and back to Kunnert in a confused manner.

"I...She..." He was completely lost for words.

Kunnert studied the situation before he spoke again.

"She's mine. Put the knife down and get off of her." Kunnert's voice was calm and there was even a twinge of understanding and compassion mixed in with the command and unspoken threat.

The doctor hopped off Lei immediately, walked over and stood next to Kunnert who studied him. Kunnert made a small gesture with his head, and the doctor nodded and left the room.

Kunnert walked over to Lei and observed the incision the doctor had made. It ran three inches horizontally from her navel toward her right hip, splaying her open in surgical exactness. There wasn't much blood, but what blood was present was pooling in the open wound, gently flowing over the side and down her body with every rise of her chest for a breath of air.

"Lie still." Kunnert spoke to Lei in soft tones that sounded remotely like compassion. "I will get something to clean and stitch the wound."

Slowly Kunnert turned his back to Lei and walked over to a wall cabinet, removing a small white box that appeared to be a first aid kit. Pulling a standing tray behind him, Kunnert walked back over to Lei and began removing items from the first aid kit, placing them gently on the tray. Among the items Lei could see were three rolls of sterile gauze pads still in their packaging, forceps, a long curved suturing needle and a tube of what she believed to be antibiotic paste. Kunnert removed other things but she couldn't make out what those things might be.

"I must apologize for my associate. He lacks some of the more social graces, and has particular tastes which can be somewhat disturbing."

Lei didn't respond, the pain in her abdomen had finally registered and she strained with her bonds in order to alter her position and cover her wound.

"He is also quite skilled in the use of that blade of his. He sliced through your skin and the minor amount of subcutaneous fat you have, but he didn't penetrate deep enough to sever the muscles of your abdomen."

Kunnert began to gently clean the area around the wound with a dark yellow-brown liquid Lei recognized as iodine. Then he opened a package of the gauze and mopped up the excess liquid while he dabbed at the blood pooling inside her incision.

Lei winced as Kunnert pushed the gauze into her open wound. She knew this was the proper procedure for caring for the kind of wound she was enduring, and knew he was doing what he must to properly care for and close the incision. The anxiety she felt about still being incapacitated made the pain even more intolerable.

"Why are you helping me?"

Kunnert looked up from his work, "Helping you?" he asked, momentarily confused. Then a look of clarity washed over his face. "Ah, I see. Well, I would imagine I am dressing your wound because there is a great deal I wish from you and an infection to the abdomen would not serve my purposes in that endeavor."

Lei remained quiet as Kunnert began to squeeze some of the antibiotic cream onto his fingers.

"I suppose infection isn't something your kind suffers from given that miraculous physiology you and yours possess, but I am nothing if not a creature of habit, so you'll indulge me, won't you?"

Lei didn't answer the question and instead asked one of her own: "Where are the rest of my people?"

"You don't remember your little ride here?" Kunnert nodded, "Yes, many of your people are with us now. Rest assured, they are completely safe, and their every need is being attended to by the staff of this building. You have no need to worry."

The memory of the battle in the caverns came flooding back to her. She began to tremble as Kunnert reached for a set of clamps along with the needle and thread.

"How many are here?" Lei was rambling at this point but hearing her own voice was calming to her.

Kunnert again turned away from his work to face Lei.

"Is that what you want to know? Or would you like me to answer the question you are really asking?"

Lei was astonished the man had picked up her little deception, but pressed forward innocently, "And what question would that be?"

"How many were killed that night in the mine?" As Kunnert spoke he inserted the needle into the point of the incision furthest from her navel.

Lei's breath caught in her throat from the shock of pain from the needle, and because of what Kunnert had just stated. She grimaced as he slowly weaved a thread through each side of the cut and fastened a knot in the first stitch.

"All right," Lei continued, "how many were killed?"

Kunnert faced her again and looked directly into her eyes, "By my best estimation nearly five hundred and fifty-two."

"Five hundred…and…" The number caught as tightness ensnared her breathing.

"And fifty-two." Kunnert finished the sentence for her and inserted the needle into the flesh for the second of a series of stitches.

Lei winced again, but the pain wasn't as bad as it had been previously.

"And how many of my people are here?"

"We have beds on the security floor for thirty-five hundred, most of them are full, in fact, I believe we are at capacity."

Lei wanted to scream but held it in. "That's…that's not possible. There are just under three thousand people in our community."

"True enough," Kunnert responded amicably, "but if you count all of those from Los Angeles, then the numbers work out."

Everything Alpha had feared might happen had come to pass. The entire clan was either dead, or abducted to this hell, wherever this place was. If there were indeed thirty-five hundred people lying in beds, on what this man called the security floor, and over five hundred dead, then the few who remained would number in the dozens, and far too few to form any kind of rescue effort. Those dozens would be mostly civilians, she knew, as she had been watching when most of her fellow hunters were cut down. At the moment, she realized the last thing she remembered was having attacked this man before something struck her from behind.

She turned her eyes to face the man who had now closed her wound halfway across the incision.

"You know, I would have killed you if I hadn't been interrupted," she said in a mocking tone.

Kunnert had been looking at her nakedness, but his eyes darted back to her face as the jibe registered. He just looked at her and Lei returned the look with a glare that would have killed, if looks could actually kill.

Kunnert pursed his lips and nodded, in what appeared to be agreement then reached over to the tray with the hand not holding the suturing needle and retrieved a probe from inside the kit. The tip of the probe was blunt, rounded and bent at a forty-five degree angle. Kunnert held the instrument over the wound briefly, as Lei's eyes shot from the probe to Kunnert's face and back to the probe.

Kunnert never looked at Lei's face as he hooked the probe inside her wound near her navel and stretched the broken flesh upward.

Lei screamed as she felt the probe penetrate the inside of her body and mercilessly pull at something unyielding under her skin. The probe had hooked onto a part of her insides resilient enough not to tear, but a searing pain unlike any she had ever felt before ran through her body.

The look on Kunnert's face was one of pure and unbridled wrath, as he jerked on the handle of the probe, which caused the pain to increase with each manipulation.

When he finally relented Lei was panting and tears flowed freely, but she did not sob. Kunnert noticed this and appeared to be a little impressed by her resistance. He placed the probe back on the tray and resumed his stitching of her wound.

"Maybe someday, if you play your cards right, we will be able to test your skills when you aren't jumping me from behind. In any case, and I know this may come as a bit of a shock for you to hear, but the rest of your people are being utilized as nothing more than a resource for the creation of our product. Vegetables to be harvested, as they ripen on their silicone vines, I however, am going to offer you an alternative to that fate. Accept it and you will be able to continue in my service, refuse me and you'll join your people in their silicone garden."

"Don't bother even asking, just take me to the rest of my people and turn me into a turnip, or whatever. I'd rather be a brainless vegetable, than be anything to you."

Kunnert chuckled, "Are you so sure girl? You know you might enjoy your position, or positions, as the case may be, after a time."

"I doubt it. When I was a little girl I spent some time in Mexico. I supported myself by performing in the novelty shows…a low point in my life. It all happened before Alpha found me, but I'd rather go back to those shows before I'd agree to do anything with you.

"What?" Kunnert looked shocked.

"Yes, that's right. I fucked donkeys more appealing than you."

Immediately losing his patience, Kunnert's fist slammed the right side of her face and Lei felt a tooth loosen. The back of his fist slammed the other side of her face, and her head whipped back to the right, and then a straight punch drove into her abdomen, right where he had just finished stitching her wound.

The pain of the punch to her stomach was heightened by the pain of the thread pulling at her fresh wound, yet to her amazement, none of the new stitches broke or tore.

Attempting to regain his composure, Kunnert said, "If that is the way you want to play it, fine. I require information, so answer my questions and I will leave you to think about your fate."

Lei offered a short quick laugh, "This is going to be a long night...and you hit like a girl."

Chapter 40

"You're already inside?" Alpha said with surprise. "Excellent! Make yourselves scarce until you hear from me again."

Alpha clicked the mobile phone shut. "Good news, the remaining hunters are infiltrating the Pharmanetics building now, they'll conceal themselves and await our arrival."

Alpha, Steve, and Chris were on a corporate jet Alpha had somehow secured for them, along with a pilot and a flight plan. They were en route to Los Angeles International Airport. The large amount of automatic weapons and ammunition they were sorting through and assembling en route precipitated the need for the private plane. Steve snapped the weaponry together with military efficiency, while Chris loaded multiple magazines with the ammunition he had spread out on a towel in front of him. No one spoke or looked up at Alpha as they worked their tasks. This was not a time for words. This was a time for action.

"Gentlemen, listen to me. I have several of my people inside the building. They will assist us when, and only when, the time is right."

"How many?" Chris asked.

"Fifteen."

"That means they're probably going to out-number us pretty severely." Chris volunteered.

"Each one of my hunters is worth at least three to four of their soldiers," Alpha said with considerable pride.

"They didn't do too well earlier in the mine," Steve stated.

Alpha nodded. "Those pigs surprised us all, with their sneak attacks and automatic weapons. Now we shall surprise them!"

"Are your men armed?" Chris asked.

"They do not need to be, they are hunters trained in the old ways. Believe me, what you will see tonight will show you how technology can be as much a burden as a benefit."

Chris looked at Steve skeptically.

"I promise you, my people will be there when you need them and the blood will run."

"I want no unnecessary bloodshed Alpha." Steve said with authority.

"You know the discipline. The hunters have their orders and will not attack," Alpha gestured in an overly exaggerated manner, "until absolutely necessary."

"And when will that be?" Chris asked without looking up from what he was doing.

"When you give me the signal, I will give them the signal."

Steve nodded, "Okay, good…good."

Chris looked at Steve with one eyebrow raised in a question.

"What?" Steve asked.

"You're one of them aren't you?"

"I thought we established that some time ago."

"No, not the vampire part. You're one of these 'hunters' Alpha keeps mentioning."

When Steve didn't answer, Alpha chimed in. "He's far more than that."

Steve shot Alpha a look.

"Hunters? Doesn't sound like a very benevolent job description." Chris said sarcastically.

Alpha nodded. "Perhaps not, but they were definitely necessary in the past, and given our current circumstances, even today."

Turning to Steve, "What did you hunt?" Chris asked.

"Nothing. I was the lead tracker. It was my job to find any of our kind who may have been in the throes of the madness, and bring them back to the fold or…"

"Dispatch them." Alpha finished the sentence when Steve hesitated.

"You killed them?"

Steve could only nod in response.

Chris began to react when Alpha chimed in.

"When one of our kind goes into the madness there *is* no

return. Their end was a merciful hastening of the inevitable, while protecting the public at large."

"Protecting the secret of your existence as well I would imagine," Chris surmised.

Alpha looked directly at Chris in an uncompromising and unrepentant glare. "Yes, that too, I suppose."

Chris raised the palms of his hands in supplication and Alpha's demeanor eased.

"That was only one of the job descriptions," Steve offered indignantly. "There were also hunters who served as security for our people. In the early years both groups lived up to their names, and were responsible for the collection of kidnapped victims who were returned to the collective as living food bags, hence the title 'Hunter.'"

"In the early years?" Chris asked.

"Or so I had been taught. I was instructed in the old ways, but I had always thought it was something we had to learn to improve our skills for the protection of our people and ourselves. I never knew this 'serum' we live on is derived from the blood and organs of innocents."

Alpha regarded Steve, and shook his head, "He was one of the most talented hunters I have ever trained. His only weakness was an unfortunate, overabundant sense of morality. It was, and still is blinding you to the truth. How you ever managed to become a detective is beyond me."

"That's enough Alpha." Steve's voice was as cold as Chris had ever heard it.

Alpha did not back down, instead he intensified his fervor and faced Steve unflinching. "No it is not nearly enough. You are prideful, stubborn and so ready to believe the worst that you have never given me the opportunity to defend my actions from all those years ago."

Steve stood his ground as he returned the intense glare Alpha was giving him. "What's there to defend? You kidnapped and

241

drained the blood of those people into the same collection bags I'd seen used to create the serum! I heard their screams and… "

"NO…I…DID…NOT!!!" This time when Alpha spoke his voice was low, resonant and guttural. In fact, it barely sounded human. Chris felt an unnatural chill grip his spine, he desperately felt his instincts tell him to run away.

Chris noticed Steve was also taken aback, but he couldn't tell whether it was from the change in Alpha, or the denial Alpha had just made.

"I know what I saw." Steve said with a bit less confidence than he had moments ago.

"No, you don't. That is what I have been trying to tell you but you have never given me the chance. And since I have you trapped at the moment you will listen to me, NOW!"

Steve slapped the bolt closed on the rifle he was holding. The weapon was loaded and he clicked the safety switch to off.

"Uh, Steve. Maybe firing a high powered automatic rifle inside a pressurized airplane isn't such good idea?"

Steve aimed the rifle at Alpha's head. Alpha stood firmly with an unimpressed look on his face.

"Hello?" Chris called out to Steve.

"Crap." Steve lowered the rifle, engaged the safety and tossed it on the seat next to him.

"Excellent. Now, the first part of your story is correct. All of those people were kidnapped and, yes, we did drain them, but they were not sacrificed."

"That's not…" Steve started to object but Alpha quickly cut him off.

"SHUT YOUR MOUTH, and listen. They were all like us. They had been retrieved and were on the verge of madness. Yes, they were taken without consent, but that was necessary because they had no idea who or what they were. They knew they were sick, but the outside medical world couldn't pinpoint their ailment. So when we took them they were obviously afraid, despite our reassurances to the contrary. You experienced this several times in your own duties did you not?"

Steve was dumbfounded. "Well...yes, but I hadn't retrieved..."

"You were not our only trained tracker. How could you have ever thought you were?"

"What?!? Why wasn't I ever told there was another?"

"Because you knew how dangerous one of our kind could become when in the grips of the madness. You would have been... conflicted...if you knew the other one was facing such dangers."

"Oh God no." Steve whispered. "Not Lei."

"Exactly. She was perfect for the job, and between the two of you we always had the right combination of skills, depending on the situation presenting itself. Where you used subterfuge and guile, she used allure and wile."

"But that night in the caves?"

Alpha shrugged his shoulders. "We were doing what used to be called a 'direct transfer.' In the old days we'd force the blood down their throats. In the last century we found that draining the inadequate blood from the body and then transfusing the strong blood from a hunter had better results. We saved many lives that night."

"But the bags and the organ removal?"

Alpha nodded. "Some lives could not be saved, we harvested the blood and organs of the doomed in order to run tests that would further develop our serum. Those who were beyond salvation were given dignified and pain-free endings, just as you gave to the similarly afflicted on the outside. Admittedly, it was quite a macabre scene, which is why I never blamed you for your misunderstanding. But I never dreamed you would be so obtuse as to never let me explain, or that you would abandon Lei as a result."

Steve felt a wave of vertigo threaten to overwhelm him and he had to grip the armrests of his chair to keep from swaying.

"This can't be true." Steve muttered miserably.

Alpha looked stern yet sympathetic as he peered at his former protégé. "I assume my credibility has diminished in your eyes over the years, but you used to know that I do not lie. In any case, if Lei were here instead of in the arms of our enemies, she could confirm the truth."

Steve remained silent, lost in his own thoughts when Chris said. "Fine then. You can ask her once we get her and the others out of there."

Chapter 41

When the plane arrived an oversized limousine approached the hanger. As it stopped next to the three men the trunk popped open. Alpha didn't miss a beat loading their gear into the trunk. Steve hesitated briefly, but Chris had followed suit and dropped two laptop computers and his rifle case into the trunk, and then climbed into the rear passenger seat.

"It seems our friend Chris is very sure of himself in this." Alpha said to Steve. "How about you?"

"I'm fine....Let's go break some of the laws I'm sworn to uphold."

Alpha chuckled. "That's the spirit boy!"

The limo stopped less than a block from the Pharmanetics building. The three men quickly jumped out and retrieved their gear from the trunk. Chris immediately ran to the nearest manhole cover, dropped a lever into the one hole in the center of the lid, and wrenched the heavy circular cover from the ground. Without missing a beat, he covered his boots with plastic garbage bags, tied a strap around his calves and descended into the sewer. Alpha and Steve repeated the process, and followed after Chris with Alpha being the last to descend. After Alpha descended a few steps he gripped the manhole cover with one hand by its edge and effortlessly dragged it over his head, and back into its former resting position.

When Alpha reached the other two he found Chris studying a printout of the sewer system and caught the conversation mid-sentence.

"...two hundred yards that way and then left twenty yards to the ladder." Chris finished.

The three men walked quickly through the shallow sludge and reached the ladder, which would bring them up to an area near the entrance into Pharmanetics. More importantly, their exit location was in an area housing multiple wireless routers for public use, powerful enough to allow Chris access to the Internet. From there the security system would succumb to the assault Chris was about to hack into it.

Chris set up the first of his two computers and his fingers began to fly across the keys. This computer was going to remain at the location, in order to hack into the security system and render it inert, while they assaulted the building. He informed the rest of the group, that the display on the screen depicted several individual red buttons, which meant the alarms were armed and locks engaged.

Then with a grandiose flurry of arm movements Chris announced, "Breaking the law!" and pressed the 'enter' key.

Alarms formerly in operation were silenced, as the button they represented flashed from red to green. Electronic locks on doors clicked open, while still appearing on the screen to be shut and secured. Next, Chris explained that a specific type of power surge was being sent, and in such a way that the normal protection would be ineffective throughout all of the internal security systems. The result would be irreparable damage. However, once the power surge began to fry the circuitry, the security personnel would most likely be immediately alerted to the fact that their system was impaired, and would take steps to lock down the building.

Chris gave a thumbs-up sign and waited for the word to send the surge.

Chris used the second computer to tap into the security cameras. They revealed minimal personnel, all of whom would need to be incapacitated and secured before they moved on to the labs on the third through ninth floors. The plan was for all three of them to assault the first and second floors. They would each clear a floor and subdue any resisting personnel, until they reached the warehouse spaces on the tenth through thirteenth floors. At this point Chris would fry the second set of security systems and then…well, then the "shit would hit the fan" and they would have to play the rest as it came at them.

It was agreed that if, and only if, things went really south would Alpha signal his men and lethal force would be used. Steve said a quick prayer that it wouldn't come to that, but he sensed the reality of the situation, and knew it probably would.

"Okay," Chris said, "everybody ready?"

The others nodded their agreement. Looking at his watch, Steve calculated there was about another four hours of darkness before sunrise.

"See you all in the penitentiary showers," Steve remarked as he turned to Chris, "Okay, do it."

Chapter 42

Lei sucked on her bottom lip, split under the barrage of punches that had pummeled her since Kunnert had begun questioning her. Her face was a mangled mess at this point. One eye was swollen shut, and she couldn't see clearly out of her other eye. Blood flowed freely down her throat every time she tried to breathe through her nose.

When Kunnert tired of hitting her face he switched to hitting her in the ribs. Lei felt a painful grinding with every intake of breath, rendering her in a state of perpetual hyperventilation. Kunnert had released her from her bonds to prevent her own blood from drowning her. As he rested from his latest beating, Lei cowered naked, broken and bloodied in a corner. She had tried to enthrall him, but his rage, and the pain he dealt her, made the strategy impossible. All the while he had been asking her questions, most of which she had no clue of the answer.

"How many survived the attack on the mine?"

Lei recoiled at the question. She had been knocked unconscious in what she believed to be the middle of the battle, so how could she possibly know.

"How many 'hunters' were there to begin with and how many were alive when you attacked me?"

This one she knew the answer to but she decided not to share it with him. She mentally steeled herself for the coming abuse and made her decision to die before giving anything to this man, who killed and kidnapped unarmed men, women and children for nothing more than profit.

Her thoughts turned to Alpha, who replaced the father she never had. He will see this place brought down to rubble when he finds this location, and he will find out. Maybe not before she died, but he would find out and everyone involved would get a preview into the hell awaiting them.

"Get up girl." Kunnert's voice was quiet but still sounded

angry.

The last time he told her to get up and she hadn't, he had kicked her in the ribs. She covered her potentially broken ribs with her arms and slowly rose to her feet, standing awkwardly before Kunnert.

"It could have been so much easier for you. Easy or not, I promise you *will* answer my questions," Kunnert said a bit patronizingly.

Lei wanted to shoot an insult back, but her body hurt so much it was all she could do to remain standing.

Kunnert picked up a kitchen towel he'd been soaking in the sink and began cleaning the blood that had smeared across her face.

"Now there is one question I must insist you answer. And I warn you girl, on this I will tolerate nothing but the truth from you. If you don't answer this then you are of no further use to me."

Lei could see from the look in Kunnert's eyes he was serious. Whether he would put her in stasis with the rest of her people or simply kill her on the spot she didn't know, but whatever question came next would be the last one for which he would not get an answer.

Kunnert moved very close, "The albino, who is he?"

Lei didn't have an inkling of what kind of an answer Kunnert wanted. Did he want to hear that "the albino" was the leader of her people, the one who was saving them from society and from ourselves? Did he want to hear about her relationship to the man? She didn't know any origins or history about Alpha, she had never asked. She was about to brace herself for the end when a realization sparked in the darkness.

Kunnert had asked "who is he?" Not "was" but "is." Alpha was still alive! She hadn't known for sure until this moment and her heart swelled with relief.

"Why? Is he giving you trouble?" Lei said with a smile.

She never saw Kunnert unsheathe the blade but the next thing she knew the tip was inches from her right eye. Kunnert grabbed her hair from the back of her head and held her in place.

"Last chance girl before this gets very, very bad for you."

"He's in charge."

"I didn't ask his position in the hierarchy of your little cult. WHO IS HE?"

Lei realized she had no answer for that. Even if she wanted to answer, she couldn't. This was it, she knew from this point forward all the future held for her was pain and death. She spoke back to Kunnert with words she hadn't expected to say.

"I don't know anything about him that can help you."

Lei felt the grip on the back of her head loosen slightly, but the tip of the knife held firm an inch or so away from her eye.

"Then tell me what you DO know." Kunnert said calmly.

"Alpha will try to destroy this place and kill everyone here if…WHEN… he finds you." Lei chuckled, "You don't know what you are dealing with."

And then, there it was. A not so subtle shift in Kunnert's expression spoke volumes. The knife was lowered from her eye and the grip on her hair went slack as the stern face of Kunnert widened into shock. She had surprised him, even scared him, but how would that be possible unless…

Kunnert looked away from her as he spoke out loud to himself.

"N-No. It can't be." Then with sudden fury he grabbed Lei again.

This time Lei actually started laughing as he grabbed her.

"I see, maybe you DO know."

Kunnert studied her face, his eyes darting back and forth as if reading a hidden message in the context of her contours.

After a moment his eyes widened again. He released his grip on Lei and backed slowly away from her, as he whispered the same word over and over again.

"Impossible…Impossible…Impossible."

Chapter 43

Kunnert screamed into the radio he'd removed from the clip on his belt, "I want everyone! No exceptions! Meet in Daniels' office NOW for an emergency briefing! That means you too Daniels! Anyone not there in five minutes, will deal with me directly."

Multiple responses squawked back at Kunnert, all confirming their being en route to the executive's office.

Turning back to Lei, now lying in a bloody heap on the tile floor she'd slithered down to, he said in a voice thick with malice, "You'd better be wrong girl." He then locked the door behind him as he left the room and sprinted into the hallway.

Kunnert arrived in front of the large double doors to Daniels' office, and was in the process of reaching for the doorknob when he noticed his hand trembling. He made a fist and took a few deep breaths to slow his heartbeat. It would not do for his men to see him in a state of near panic, so he concentrated on calming himself, despite the urgency he felt to mobilize his crew. He could feel his body easing to a more relaxed state. His heartbeat quieted and his breathing slowed to a normal pace after several moments. He would have been better to continue his meditation for a few more moments, but the urgency of the situation prompted Kunnert to open his closed eyes and reach again for the doorknob.

That's when, quite literally, the lights went out.

Chapter 44

The three men stormed the front door of the Pharmanetics building with weapons drawn and attitude to spare. Glass doors shattered under the force of Alpha's impact making the entrance for Steve and Chris. Each immediately found cover from what they expected would be an onslaught of security personnel and gunfire.

To their breathless surprise nothing happened. The first and second floors appeared to be deserted. Silence screamed at them as Chris, Steve and Alpha all stood and looked around the space. There had been at least a half dozen security personnel roaming the floor less than 10 minutes ago when Chris hit the button sending the surge.

Alpha looked around and then to Steve whom shrugged his shoulders in confusion.

Chris said, "Ah, okay. What the hell?"

"I know you wanted to keep casualties to a minimum, but…" Alpha said guardedly.

Steve thought for a moment trying to regroup. They had come too far and the lack of resistance didn't change the desired outcome.

"Okay, we move forward as planned. Chris, is there any way they may have been alerted to our presence before the system went down?"

"I don't see how, but anything is possible."

Steve's mind was drawing a blank.

"All right, Alpha hit your floors. Maintain radio contact. Be careful. It would be the strangest one I've ever seen, but this whole scenario could be a type of trap. Chris, see if you can re-establish a link with their security system and cameras. I'd really like to find out where everyone is."

"On it!" Chris sprinted to the computer terminal where the security personnel should have been stationed and began hooking up his own computers in a frenzy of wires and hand movements.

"Chris, once you're in, give a shout and let us know what's up."

"Okay, you'll be hearing from me soon. Go find our people."

Alpha and Steve rushed to the stairwell, and then cautiously proceeded through the door. No sounds were coming from inside, as Steve let out an anxious sigh, "C'mon, let's move."

The third through fifth floors turned out to be exactly as they expected: working labs which, despite the heightened security measures, were relatively easy to access, after Chris had permanently damaged their systems. The machinery was moving at what appeared to be full operation, an unmanned operation at the moment, with no evidence of base materials nor any indication of the final product.

Steve was on the fourth floor when Chris' voice echoed into his earpiece.

"Okay my fellow "B and E"ers, I am up and running. Security cameras coming online now, give me a second to check each level."

Steve waited through the silence as Chris studied each floor.

"Weird…" Chris's whisper could be heard over the com-link.

"Want to let us in on what's so weird?" Steve responded.

"Sorry, yeah, the first seven floors are completely deserted. I have a good visual of each space, these levels show nothing but assembly line type machinery. No security or scientists or any of our people."

"That's what we've found as well," Alpha confirmed.

"And it seems that's all you guys are going to find on the next few levels. My recommendation would be to start moving directly to the tenth floor. It may yield some new discoveries."

"Prudence would dictate clearing each level as we went," Steve warned.

"Yes, but we don't know how much time we have before someone is alerted to our being here," Alpha replied. "My people are also saying we are clear on these levels. I say we hit the stairs and move to the tenth floor," Alpha spoke up from his position.

"You're still in contact with the hunters?" Steve asked incredulously.

"Always," Alpha said with a slight tone of indignation at the thought he would be out of contact with his few remaining people for even the slightest moment.

"How?"

Alpha turned his head to the side, pulled his white hair over his ear and pointed to a small earpiece practically invisible inside his ear canal.

"When the hell did you start using those?"

"A lot has changed since you left youngster." Alpha smiled.

"I'm not that young anymore." Steve grumbled.

"Compared to whom?" Alpha chided.

Steve changed the subject and spoke into his hand held radio. "Chris, how sure are you that we aren't going to have any unexpected company on the remaining four floors."

"Right now I am one hundred percent sure. If anything changes though, I'll let you know."

Steve really didn't like the idea of moving forward without clearing each level, but the reality of their time constraints weighed more heavily.

"All right Alpha. Let's move straight to the tenth floor. Chris you be our eyes and let us know if any bad guys pop up."

"You got it."

With that the two men began the long ascent to the tenth floor, totally unaware, and blind, to anyone who might be waiting for them.

Chapter 45

The manner in which the highly trained and disciplined mercenaries reacted when the power initially surged off, could not accurately be described as panic. Controlled chaos perhaps, but not panic. Kunnert fired two rounds into the ceiling, thereby restoring order among his currently agitated security force.

"Now listen to me, and listen good. There is a fair chance the building has been breached by the remaining force of what we all faced down in the silver mine. Their numbers are unknown, but there couldn't be more than a handful of these people left alive, so this should not be a difficult undertaking. However, it has been brought to my attention that a new player may have entered the fray. This individual is *not* to be engaged in any way. Do I make myself clear? If you want to live to see tomorrow, do not engage this individual."

One of the security staff spoke up from the crowd, "Sir! How will we know who to engage and who to avoid?" The man was large and gruff, looking totally out of place in the jacket and slacks of the security uniform.

"If you see someone who looks as though death itself has come for you, that'll be the guy to avoid. Believe me, you'll know him." Kunnert left it at that and changed the subject.

"Your priority is the lockdown and removal of any aggressors within the building. Lethal force is authorized, so collect your weapons and resume your positions."

Kunnert looked around the room and realized Alex Daniels was absent from the rest of the group.

"Oh Goddammit! Where the hell is Daniels?"

Dr. Whelan, who had arrived with the rest of the security personnel, spoke up. "He went into his private office where his video feeds are connected, to see if whatever shorted the power also crippled the rest of the computer systems."

Kunnert knew it had. There were no coincidences in this

world. He doubted that whatever had sacked the power would spare the systems.

"I'm sure he will find the system's well-fried. I want those of you with the appropriate skills to go to Daniels' office and see if you can get the system up and working again. You will be our eyes as we move through the building."

Two men and a woman stood and walked from the conference area, heading toward Daniels' private office. Kunnert watched them go, wondering if he should go with them to see what state Daniels was in. No, that could wait.

"Okay people, move out!" Kunnert finished, and then called Dr. Whelan over.

"Do you have enough of your equipment in a mobile state, to make a hasty getaway if it comes to that?"

"Well, no, not really, however I could get all I really need in a couple of minutes, if it becomes necessary."

"Really?"

"All I need are the research files. Everything else, equipment and the like, can be purchased anywhere in the United States." The doctor studied Kunnert, and could see the man was worried. "Are you thinking I should start packing?"

Kunnert thought about it for a second and replied. "I think that would be prudent, especially if it would only take a few minutes. If we can contain this then you will have only lost a small amount of time. If not…"

"No problem then, I'll get started."

With a questioning look Kunnert said, "Check your cell phone. Are communications out?"

The doctor reached into a pocket and pulled out his cell phone. Normally his phone had full connectivity, however, as Kunnert had predicted, the line was unable to connect with a signal for use.

"Dead as a doornail…whatever that means." The doctor replied.

"I thought so. All right, get going, but meet me in Daniels' office when you are done."

Once the doctor left the room Kunnert walked through the double doors to Daniels' private office. The enormous suite was shrouded in darkness save for the flashlights being used by the techs overlooking Daniels' server. The entire system was down and a faint smell of burning was in the air.

For his part, Daniels was nervously pacing around his office, looking on the verge of losing control.

Ignoring Daniels for the moment, Kunnert turned to the three techs, "One of you go with the group heading to the lobby and see if you can get something working from the first floor. Your priority is the reactivation of the security cameras."

"What about the security locks in place on the tenth floor?"

"No, those are supported by redundant systems separate from the main. Even if everything else shorted out I guarantee they are still functioning at full capacity. Get the cameras up and running. We need to be able to see our enemy."

One of the men grabbed his tool kit and sprinted from the room to catch some of the security personnel before they reached the elevators.

"We're under attack! We are actually under attack," Daniels moaned miserably. "This is not how business is done! We move through the courts and legal systems. We can fix those things. What the hell is going on?" Daniels was rambling.

Kunnert walked over to him, "Relax Mr. Daniels. Everything is under control. We will have the computers and security systems functioning again soon and anyone found in the building who isn't part of the team will be dealt with most severely."

"Kunnert! Don't you get it? We are under attack!!! My God! They aren't here to arrest us, they are here to kill us! We have to call the police!"

Kunnert slapped him so hard he thought he could hear the man's neck pop. Alex Daniels went sprawling to the floor. He made no attempt to get up, only looked up at Kunnert with disbelieving eyes.

"You want to call the police?!? Are you insane? We have over three thousand donors and volunteers being held in this building, some of whom *are* the police."

Alex Daniels looked away from Kunnert and at the floor.

Kunnert turned his back to him to walk away then stopped, turned back around and said, "What did you think the ones we didn't take were going to do? Just sit around and try to explain to the authorities who they were and why all of those people were kidnapped and killed?"

Alex whined out, "But, but they couldn't go to the authorities without exposing themselves so..."

"So what? You thought they'd just lie down and die?" Kunnert asked rhetorically, watching Daniels' face and realizing that's exactly what the man had thought would happen.

"Oh, you are kidding me?" Kunnert sighed.

"What could they do? They had no one to turn to and nowhere to go. They should never have been a threat to us."

"Damn, you are so naive." Then Kunnert softened, "All right Daniels, just stay up here in your office where it's safe. I'll call you when it's over. You do understand that when communications come back online you CANNOT call the police?"

Alex Daniels rose to his feet, dropped his head and mumbled "Yes."

Kunnert added, "Good, keep your eyes on the prize Mr. Daniels. This night is the only obstacle left."

"Sir?" one of the techs spoke up.

"What is it?"

"We have restored partial function to the security database."

"Partial?"

"Yes sir."

"Which part exactly?"

"Enough to run a diagnostic on the system."

"And you found?"

"The security systems are all down with the exception of the tenth floor, as you predicted. The video feeds are also active but I am unable to get a picture on any of the floors appearing to be operational."

"And why would that be do you think?"

"The only thing I can think of is that someone is piggybacking the signal and has accessed the currently active video cameras."

Kunnert felt the rage inside him begin to boil. "They are using our own equipment against us?"

"It would seem so sir."

"Can you stop this?"

"If I send a double loop feed...hmm." The tech seemed to consider an option then said, "No, I can't completely shut them out, but I can work with their signal and share the same information they are seeing. I could also shut down the feed for everyone."

"How interesting..." Kunnert's mind raced as he considered how he could use this to his advantage. "Will they be able to tell we have gained access to the cameras?"

"Electronically no, but our responses will ultimately make it obvious."

"And by that time it will be too late for them. Make it happen."

Chapter 46

Upon reaching the tenth floor Steve and Alpha were greeted by an ominous looking security wall. It was similar in appearance to the outside wall of a bank vault and had the same impenetrable feel.

Steve spoke into his radio, "Chris we found some pretty heavy security here, any luck in over riding its system?"

"Hold on."

Steve could hear the rapid clicks of the keys on the keyboard as Chris worked furiously on the other end of the radio.

"Chris? I don't mean to rush you, but time is a factor here."

"Have you tried saying 'Open Sesame' yet?"

Steve sighed, "No not yet."

"Well try it a couple of times, if that doesn't work wait five minutes and try again. If you still get no response then wait five more and try saying it with a different accent, I recommend Irish."

"Chris…"

"Okay, I'll try a different tactic with you. It will be open as fast as possible so…SHUT UP AND LET ME WORK!"

With that Chris cut off the conversation and his radio.

Steve chuckled under his breath while Alpha's countenance looked stern as always.

"He's…uh…working on it," Steve said to Alpha who had obviously heard the entire conversation.

They walked to what appeared to be the door and waited nervously for something to happen. In less than a minute Steve's radio squawked with Chris' voice.

Steve picked up the small box, "That was fast, from the way you sounded I thought…"

"Nope, still haven't got it, but I'm close. Thought you'd like to know you have a serious number of angry looking individuals spreading out from the eighth floor working their way up to your level. Looks like they came out of the elevators below you to cut off any chance of escape."

"WHAT?!? I thought you disabled the elevators."

"I did. And what is more disturbing is that I didn't get any kind of online warning they had come back. Regardless, the reality of your situation is that you need to find some cover and fast."

Steve regained his composure while Alpha, having again heard the entire conversation over the shared radio frequency, was already on the move.

"Are you secured on your end?" Steve asked as he followed Alpha.

"So far the only activity seems to be heading your way, but I never saw them coming to you so…" Chris let the unspoken words hang in the air.

Concern swept through Steve as he responded to what Chris was telling him, "All right, keep working, but if you have to abort in order to protect yourself you do that."

"Got it," Chris said with a little too much cavalier in his voice for Steve's liking.

"I'm serious, if it gets too hot, get out."

"Yeah, got it," Chris said, with a tad more conviction in his voice than the first time.

Steve bolted after Alpha who had re-entered the stairway and assumed a shooter's stance, holding his preferred weapon, a .45 automatic pistol, in each hand.

Steve looked to the large weapons, "Not exactly 'old school'."

Alpha turned quickly to Steve then cocked his head while considering something. "Remember we have allies within these walls. Perhaps now would be a good time to call for them?"

Before Steve could respond the sound of automatic weapons reverberated through the stairway. Steve began to shoot back but had to immediately cease fire when Alpha leapt over the railing and dropped to the stairway one floor below landing between the two gunmen who had fired. The two startled men hesitated as Alpha landed and in that moment of hesitation Alpha pistol-whipped them into unconsciousness.

Steve made his way down to the ninth floor and moved from the stairway to the seemingly abandoned hallway. They were working their way down the hall when Chris' voice erupted over the radio.

"I got it!"

Each man jumped at the sudden sound.

"What you got Chris?"

"The door is on a timer. I couldn't override the security system, so basically I accelerated the timer. Instead of opening at seven tomorrow morning the system will disengage itself in approximately five minutes. Are you still on that floor?"

"No we moved to the ninth floor."

"When that door opens, the heavy reinforcement of the structures in the room will give you the most protection. Not to mention that whatever is inside has to be highly valued by our adversaries. They would probably prefer it intact versus the alternative."

"Good call, we'll make our way back to…"

Steve wasn't able to finish his sentence before Chris cried out, "Oh shit!" The sound of automatic fire proceeded Chris' voice, followed by an eerie and unnerving silence.

"Chris!" Steve yelled into the receiver.

Silence was all that was coming from the other end. After a minute or so a voice came back to Steve, far more ominous then the silence. The voice did not belong to Chris and had a cold and merciless air to it.

"It would appear as though your friend has been seriously wounded. I've seen abdominal wounds before and I can tell you he has some time to receive care before it is too late. If you and your associates act quickly, he has a chance. Stop where you are and surrender yourselves to the security forces headed your way. You will not be harmed and we will make every effort to save your friend's life."

Steve went numb. For a moment he couldn't even draw breath reflecting on what the man had said. Was Chris really wounded or was he already dead? Hell, for all he knew Chris might have escaped. It's not as though he had any kind of confirmation either way.

Alpha whispered to Steve. "Go back up to the vault. I will head to our friend Chris."

As Alpha turned to go, Steve managed. "Alpha…"

Alpha held his position, "Yes?"

"If they've hurt him…give the hunters the green light. Do it your way Alpha. Do you understand? Do it your way."

Alpha stood slightly straighter and looked at Steve, nodding ever so slightly before bolting down the stairs.

"I have never been known for my patience!" The voice yelled over the radio, "Make a decision!"

Steve knew he had no choice. Slowly he turned the dial on the radio until it clicked off.

Chapter 47

Dr. Whelan looked at the radio dumbfounded. He hadn't expected such an abrupt and expert disconnect of communications. No negotiations were made, no requests or even threats thrown around, just the simple act of quietly killing the radio.

The doctor turned to where Chris lay in a pool of his own blood and said, "Wow, that was good. You guys are pros, that's for sure, but you look as though you also understand the significance of your injuries. You know what it means to be gut shot, don't you? Well, just in case you don't, it means your own shit is leaking out of your intestines and will slowly poison you to death. You'll hang on for quite a while though, and that excruciating pain you feel won't dull with time."

The doctor knelt beside him, his face inches from Chris', "I'll tell you what I'll do for you."

The doctor pulled his knife from its sheath. "I'll make this quick for you, but only if you tell me how many people you brought with you."

Chris' face was contorted in extreme agony, but he managed to look at the doctor then back to the floor.

"Oh come on." The doctor mused, "It shouldn't matter to you anymore. Do you really want the last moments you have to be filled with this kind of agony? Come on, just give me a number and I'll help you go quick."

Chris looked up again, but this time he didn't even glance at the doctor or the dozen well-armed men surrounding him. He was searching for a sound he actually felt more than he heard. Dr. Whelan and the rest of his men were oblivious to the low growl, but Chris recognized it immediately.

The look on the doctor's face changed from mild amusement to confusion as a smile broke across Chris' face.

"I wouldn't want to miss a moment of this," Chris grunted through clenched teeth.

Dr. Whelan looked around in a confused state to his men, some of who chuckled at Chris' apparent audacity.

To the doctor, Chris said, "Guess what Bunky? You are about to have a very, very big problem."

Frowning, Dr. Whelan stood and said, "You'll change your mind with a little bit of time. When you are ready to talk let me know, otherwise, just die quietly." Then Dr. Whelan turned to the computer tech Kunnert had sent from Daniels' office.

"See if you can get the systems back online."

"On it," the tech replied.

"Uh...sir?" One of the security men beckoned to the doctor then to the building's stairway.

Standing just inside the doorway was an enormous man, clad head to toe in black leather. He remained absolutely motionless as Dr. Whelan and the rest of the security force realized he was there and brought their weapons up to bear upon the man.

Although he was a few feet inside the doorway, Alpha's frame filled the space making him look larger than in actuality. The face staring back at Dr. Whelan and the security force was emotionless to the point of looking lifeless as a corpse. And he never moved. Never turned his head to survey his surroundings, never looked to Chris, nor to the guards or even to the weapons they were holding.

Surprisingly it was the doctor who came out of the momentary bedazzlement that Alpha's presence initiated.

"Shoot him down!" Dr. Whelan yelled as he ran for cover.

Perhaps there was a hesitation in the men because Kunnert had warned them not to engage...someone...at the cost of their own lives. This had to be that man, however instinct and years of training, along with an ingrained response of following immediate commands, found each man mentally making the choice to fire. Unfortunately, their slight hesitation was all Alpha needed. Before the first shot could be fired, he barreled forward and was on them.

The doctor did not enter the fray. Instead he brought his sidearm to bear and fired wildly in Alpha's direction while running for the stairs Alpha had just exited. Alpha fired his weapons point

265

blank into the bodies of the security guards, they crumpled to the floor broken, unconscious or lifeless.

The onslaught continued for mere moments. When it was over only Alpha remained standing, figures strewn all around him.

"The stairs…" Chris grunted. "He went…the stairs. Everyone else is on… tenth floor." Chris realized the difficulty he was having drawing in the shallowest of breaths, but he forced the words out despite the white hot pain paralyzing him.

Alpha slowly turned his head to Chris, then to the slowly expanding pool of blood. Alpha moved to Chris' side and knelt before him.

"You know what these injuries mean too, don't you?" Chris asked with little surprise in his voice. "And you know you have to go help Steve right?"

Slowly, reluctantly, Alpha nodded his head.

"Good, good…Use the elevator, they don't know we have access to it. Steve's trapped up there….get him into the vault…it's the only safe place."

With those final words Chris passed out from the pain, blood loss and exertion. Alpha gently caught him as his body began to slump to one side. He propped Chris into a seated position with his back supported by the side of a desk and left him looking as if he had simply fallen asleep.

Alpha started toward the elevator doors when he suddenly stopped, glancing back at Chris, lying unconscious against the office furniture. An idea had occurred to him, which he only considered for the merest of moments, before returning to Chris' side.

Chapter 48

The vault door was surprisingly quiet as soft clicks sounded and the latch releases disengaged. The door opened effortlessly under its own mechanics, and Steve watched impatiently as it slowly swung open and was wide enough for him to slip inside.

What he observed as he walked in froze him in his tracks.

Hundreds...no, thousands, of bodies lay in industrial looking, makeshift cots, stacked like some surreal bunk bed/filing system. The sheer mass of people piled like parcels in a warehouse was unsettling, as was the apparent indifference to the humanity of those lying there. The scene became all the more devastating as Steve realized the majority were children, ranging in apparent age from as small as two years old to early teens, each naked save for the loose fitting hospital gown printed with serial numbers across the chest. Transparent tubes held clear liquids which flowed into one arm while red, presumably blood, barely trickled out the other arm. The blood was being collected by a small cylindrical device attached to the opening of each cot. Each body was catheterized to a tube that flowed away from the body and connected to a large collection duct shared by multiple users.

"My God..." Steve barely managed.

Steve also realized from the look on the faces of each immobile figure, that this was everything Alpha had feared and that he had only suspected. Each individual lying in their space was under the same "stasis" state as those who had fallen at *The Inferno*.

Steve wanted to start searching through the faces, and he had a sudden desperate need to find Lei. Where were the adults? The room was so vast it seemed to go on for miles. The combined number of bodies stacked on the gurneys made the number impossible to count. As far as Steve's eye could see, all of the victims here were children. His mind raced to figure out the whereabouts of the adults from the mine, as well as all of those people taken from *The Inferno* incident, including his fellow LAPD officers.

Steve was not going to get the chance to find any answers. A small group of security guards moved into the vault behind him. They were not subtle as they proceeded, and Steve heard the sound of their footfalls as they entered the vault. He was caught out in the open and expected the guards to open fire as he dove for cover. None of them fired a shot.

Steve's thoughts went to Chris and his earlier prediction that the guards wouldn't risk damaging their prizes stacked so meticulously inside the vault. Despite the fact that the guards were not shooting, they were advancing. Steve knew it was only a matter of time before he would be pinned down and a safe shot could be made.

Steve only counted three guards, he could see them now, heavily armed and gaining steadily on his position. The weapons were high caliber assault rifles, and he knew their ordnance could easily penetrate the cover he was hiding behind. Steve peered around the bunk, and to his surprise he saw Alpha sprinting around the corner of the vault. The man launched himself into the air, a feat which always seemed to defy gravity and never ceased to amaze Steve.

Alpha crashed into the three guards. With brutal efficiency he rendered each guard unconscious before any of them could fire a shot. He was about to motion to Steve when he realized his surroundings and what it contained.

The man deflated physically, and the look on his face was so heart-wrenching Steve thought Alpha was going to fall to the floor and wail. Instead the look, and any physical weakening, quickly vanished as the man straightened to his full height, looking both powerful and determined. Reaching to his belt, he removed the small cell phone and flipped it open. He pressed a button on it and waited.

Nothing.

A look of concern crossed his face and then Alpha remembered, "We're jamming the cell phones. Damn!"

"Chris can get them back online. You need to get your people…"

Alpha looked at Steve with such sorrow Steve's voice caught in his throat.

"I'm sorry son, but Chris won't be able to help us anymore."

The great expanse of a room was completely quiet, with the exception of the softly humming mechanical equipment.

"No! No, you couldn't have gotten to him and back again so quickly," Steve said more to himself than to Alpha.

"I'm sorry, but I'm not lying to you. I found him downstairs with a bullet wound in his stomach. He was propped up against the information desk in the lobby. If it is any consolation to you I dispatched his killers."

Suddenly security forces materialized around each corner and wildly opened fire with high velocity ammunition. Apparently they were no longer concerned about the collateral damage, and the vault door was the only cover Steve and Alpha had for protection. Fortunately for them, it had sufficient stopping power for what was being hailed against it.

Steve brought up the barrel of his weapon aiming as the ricochets exploded against the door to his side. Alpha turned and began shooting as well, causing the security force to momentarily seek cover of its own.

Alpha reached for the heavy vault door and to Steve's amazement was actually able to cause the astoundingly heavy door to slowly swing shut. The door was almost completely closed when Alpha suddenly jerked back, struck by a bullet to his side. The wound was superficial but still had enough force to send the man spinning. The heavy door continued to close in well-designed efficiency from the force Alpha had previously exerted, until it closed with a thump, but did not lock.

Sounds of men running forward to the door could be heard along with shouts of "Get that door open!" As hard as the men outside tried they couldn't get a decent grip on the smooth exterior surface, winches or other devices could not be hooked to the door in order to force it open.

Steve ran to Alpha, "How bad are you hit?"

"I'm fine!" Alpha stated and with what little blood was coming from the area of the wound Steve believed him. "I'm also spent." Alpha tossed his two pistols away and went oddly silent as he completely ignored his wounds, got to his feet, and moved to the bedside of one of his people. Alpha peered down at the tiny form lying motionless on the cot. Steve watched him from his position of cover.

More than he saw it, Steve felt a change occur in Alpha at that moment. Nothing obvious or dramatic, but significant, like all the warmth had suddenly been sucked out of the room. Before Steve could raise a question about the strange occurrence, the door to the vault began to swing open.

Men poured through the open space and pointed their weapons at the first enemy they saw. In this case it was Alpha who still stood motionless peering at the likewise immobile children in their makeshift beds.

The security force looked at each other, uncertain of their next move. A deep guttural sound began to come from where Alpha stood, accumulating pitch until it was a voluminous wail of such anguish and torment it did not sound human.

Steve stared in confused disbelief. The guards fired their weapons and Alpha, without further hesitation, exploded into action.

Chapter 49

Steve never saw where the gothic looking knives had come from, their appearance was as if, in a moment of extreme force and speed, they had materialized in Alpha's hands. Alpha moved so swiftly that as the first shots were fired, he had moved out of the line of sight of the weapons, and was carving his way through the two dozen or so security forces. Steve watched in awed disbelief as Alpha managed to be one step ahead of the gunfire, cutting down the team in a graceful, yet brutally expert manner. Despite their best efforts, the guards couldn't bring their weapons to bear on the whirlwind of death Alpha had become. A crazed panic found footing within the resolve of these exceptionally trained guards who began to shoot aimlessly into each other, in an attempt to land a hit on Alpha.

More than a half dozen of the guards had already been fatally stabbed, the cuts deliberate and purposeful toward the end of delivering certain death in the most prolonged and painful manner. Mercenaries to the core, those guards with their bodies still intact began a hasty retreat to the stairwell, abandoning their comrades to Alpha's blades. With a sickening "thud" one of the great blades found a resting place inside the abdomen of the last remaining guard. The blade must have severed the abdominal artery for the blood came spurting out of the man in an explosion of liquid red. His body contorted then slumped onto the knife and draped over Alpha's arm. Alpha kept the man otherwise aloft as he again howled in similar inhuman fashion.

Steve was holding his breath so as not to draw the attention of the monster Alpha had become. Alpha was snarling demonically as he ripped the blade from the corpse he was holding. The sound of a woman's scream diverted their attention and had a clearing effect on Alpha's mind. He turned to Steve and shouted, "This way!"

Alpha shot forward and turned down a hallway. Steve ran after him, finding himself following a bloody trail with no indication of its source. When he caught up with him, Alpha was slamming his body with tremendous force against a reinforced door in an attempt to break the door down. Voices could be heard behind the door, one was a man's voice telling whoever was outside the door to "back off" and that he'd "kill the girl if you don't back off." The other voice was female and screaming, not in fear, but in fury, regaling the walls with obscenities of such vulgarity it would make a sailor blush. The gist of her tirade was that the person trying to break in should redouble his or her efforts and essentially mutilate the not very nice man inside.

Alpha paused in his attempts to smash his body against the door to let out a roar. It was exactly that, a roar completely animal in nature, and akin to that of a tiger. Noticing Steve had joined him, Alpha's body relaxed and he regained some of his composure.

"Lei is behind that door isn't she?" Steve asked Alpha who nodded his confirmation.

"One of the guards retreated and locked himself in there with her. Why they were holding her in this room, and not in a comatose state inside the vault, I can only guess." Alpha looked down at his cell phone on his belt. "Damn, if my cell phone worked I would have loosed my people on all of these men and this fight would be close to over by now."

"What the hell happened to you back there? I've never seen anything like that from you or any of our other people."

"We'll have time for explanations later. We have to get word to the hunters before we are overwhelmed." Realizing the truth behind Alpha's words, Steve dropped the subject and began searching the surrounding offices for anything that could take the place of Alpha's cell phone. The search was almost immediately interrupted by the sound of multiple footsteps rapidly approaching them, and growing in intensity as a second wave of guards arrived on the tenth floor, and began closing in on their position.

"Damn! Throw me a weapon!" Alpha called out as he moved into the hall, his two knives at the ready and covered in crimson.

Steve was about to join him when he noticed a traditional landline phone sitting on a desk in the office he had been searching. Chris had disabled the landlines by electronically severing the connections outside the building, however, another specific function of this particular phone had intrigued him.

"Alpha! In here, quick!" Steve yelled with urgency.

Not wanting to limit their movement inside a restrictive office space, Alpha moved reluctantly to Steve and looked at the phone Steve was pointing to.

"I couldn't find any working cell phones, but maybe they would be able to hear an intercom?"

Alpha nearly ripped the phone out of the wall as he grabbed the handset and yelled into the speaker, "Hunters, to me, NOW!"

Having neglected to press the button to engage the intercom would have made Alpha's hollering into the phone comical, except the second wave of guards were now visible, and sprinting to their location.

"Press the button marked 'intercom'! PRESS THE BUTTON!" Steve screamed.

"WHERE? I DON'T SEE IT!!!" Alpha hollered back as he furiously pressed miscellaneous buttons in random fashion.

Guards burst into the hallway and into the office screaming "FREEZE!" and "DON'T MOVE!" and "DROP THE WEAPONS!"

The reality of being cornered in an office was overwhelming to Steve who slowly lowered the barrel of his weapon. Alpha was now only armed with the handset of the phone to his ear, still, one of the guards closest to Alpha called out orders to him.

"You!" The man pointed to Alpha, "Put down the phone!"

Steve turned to Alpha who just stood there with the phone to his ear, but in the periphery of Steve's vision he saw an illumination on the keypad of the phone that had not been there before.

Alpha raised a hand in apparent surrender and made a gesture as if to hang up the phone. Instead, he spoke calmly into the receiver, "Hunters to me now."

The sound of Alpha's eerie voice and accent was amplified and boomed from multiple speakers throughout the hallway, and perhaps the whole building. The sound seemed to even surprise Alpha at first then he calmly, slowly, hung up the phone and looked patiently at the clearly disquieted man who had ordered the phone down.

The man controlled his rage as he ordered both of them to lie on the floor. Each was in the process of complying with the command when a soft rumbling of noise began to grow in intensity. It sounded like something falling through a laundry or garbage chute.

"Bang, clang, bang, whoomp, bang, clang.".

Steve and Alpha were already lying on their stomachs but looked up to try to find the source of the sound.

From parts unknown within the building the sound continued to grow.

Bang! Clang! Bang! Whoomp! Bang! Clang!

Another sound was now emanating along with the first, like white noise initially, but slowly identifiable as human voices raised in a sort of battle cry.

"AAAAAAAAAAAAAAAAAAAAAAAAAHHHHHHHHHHH HHHHHHHH!!!"

Where the voices were coming from was impossible to distinguish. The guards looked up one hallway, then down another. No attackers could be seen. Steve watched as guards spoke into radio receivers in an attempt to coordinate what was happening with others, who were probably watching from the security cameras in the same manner as Chris had been.

The sounds were coming much faster now and growing louder.

"BANG! BANG! CLANG! BANG! BANG! BANG! BANG! CLANG!!!"

All hell was breaking loose at this point. Whatever was making the sound was right on top of them. In a moment of revelation, the guard who had ordered Alpha and Steve down to their stomachs looked up to the ceiling, just as the ceiling fell upon them.

BANG!!! BANG!!! BANG!!! BOOM!!!!!!

Down they came, practically raining from the ceiling, snarling with teeth flashing as they bore down on the guards. The hunters overwhelmed and sank their teeth into the throats of their prey in a similar but much more savage fashion than Lei had done in the alleys of Los Angeles. Each time a guard avoided, or threw one of the hunters off of his person, another was waiting to launch himself, full force, into the unattached guard, to continue ripping at the flesh of the guard's neck.

All attention turned to the gothic scene in the hallway, a fatal mistake for the guards in the office. Alpha sprang to his feet and joined in the fray. There were three guards inside the office, the rest were being attacked in the hallway. Alpha grabbed two of the guards, spun them around and launched them out of the office and into the hallway where they were instantly set upon by a hunter. The last guard turned to face Alpha who quickly dodged behind the man, grabbed a fistful of the man's hair, and wrenched the man's head to one side so he had easy access to the man's neck. Alpha sank his teeth in deep on the side on the man's neck then shook his head in a kind of spasmodic vibration to assist in the tearing out of the man's jugular vein. Steve stood mesmerized by Alpha's savagery. When Alpha wrenched his head away, an enormous half-moon shaped crater was formed along the side of the man's neck. Something deep within Steve screamed to be let out, and Steve felt his will dissipate.

Alpha spat out the flesh he had removed, then clamped his mouth down around the wound and the steady stream of pulsating of blood that pumped from the man's severed jugular. Alpha apparently held the man in a death grip as he flailed about uselessly while Alpha drank his fill.

Grown men were screaming in terror, automatic weapons fired from pinned hands. Multiple hunters latched on to them and

275

pointed them out of harm's way. Each guard had at least two hunters attached to different parts of their bodies with merciless teeth and exploring tongues wrenching flesh free. They remained alive as the hunters fed upon their life blood.

A guard who had broken free of his hunter was about to spray the room with automatic fire when Steve came back to life and slammed him to the floor, the force of impact sending the man's weapon out of his grasp. Steve pinned the man's arms with his body and one hand while he ripped the man's shirt open with his free hand. He sank his teeth into the man's throat, just as Alpha had taught him to do nearly sixty years ago. The guard screamed in agony as Steve tore chunks of soft flesh away from the man's neck and began to drink the warm blood from the wound.

Alpha was feasting on a new mercenary, his snow-white hair becoming stained by the bright red blood, looking as ghastly as any ghoul that Hollywood could ever have dreamed possible. In the end, the hallway was filled only with the violent snarling and undulations of the hunters tearing away at their victims who, their blood sapped, flailed helplessly while the last moments of their lives slipped away.

Alpha rose slowly to his feet. As he moved so too did all of the eyes of the hunters, even those still feeding. Without a word, the hunters abandoned their victims and stood at a kind of attention. With a royal grace, Alpha raised an arm and pointed to the door behind which was Lei.

Steve watched as the hunters moved toward the door. Alpha cut them off with a grunt, pointing up. Each of the nearly two dozen hunters shifted positions and began to form a human ladder until a few of them were again moving within the crawl spaces of the ceiling.

A muffled crash emanated from inside the room followed by an animal like snarling and the pleading screams of a man begging for mercy. Then there was only silence until the sound of the locks on the door "click/clacked" as they were all released. The door swung open slowly and revealed Lei standing in all regality, completely nude with a smear of blood running from her chin down her neck, between her breasts, and to her navel. The bruises on her face and the small stitched area to one side of her abdomen didn't take away from how impressive she was visually.

Rage welled up inside him as Steve took in the sight of her injuries and a strength filled him as he moved forward, effortlessly shoving his fellow hunters aside before taking Lei into his arms and holding her tightly.

Lei returned the fierce embrace, clinging to him in a more possessive manner than in an act of receiving comfort.

Steve broke the embrace and put his hands to her face as he peered deeply into her eyes. He didn't speak, instead he gently ran his fingertips over the welts on her cheeks and the split in her lip.

"I'm all right." Lei whispered. Her voice was soft, barely a whisper, and in it Steve heard the years of loneliness and longing she must have felt ever since he had left her all those years ago. He would spend the rest of his life making it up to her...if she would let him.

Lei looked up into his eyes, "You look awful." She chided.

Steve smiled and was surprised that he could find his voice, "I'm better now."

Alpha cleared his throat and removed his trench coat, offering it to Lei. Lei reluctantly dropped her arms from Steve's waist and took the coat but merely held it in her hand, making no attempt to cover herself in any fashion, then moved to Alpha's side. The hunters gathered around Alpha, who beckoned to Steve to come over to the group.

"Gentlemen, and lady," Alpha began, "our people are located inside the room which lies beyond the vaulted door. All are alive and in no immediate danger, however, they are hooked to machines, and rest in a state akin to a coma or a suspended animation of some sort. At the moment I have no idea how to revive them. You are all my hunters. You have been trained in the old ways to act as leaders of our people in times of need, so I put the question to you. Do we try to disconnect our people from the machines and bring them to a safe location where we can attempt to revive them? Or do we call upon those not of our community? Those of the outside world, and pray they are both willing and able to help?"

The hunters looked genuinely distraught at the idea of asking for help from anyone not of their world.

Steve listened to Alpha and could not keep quiet, "You can't try to revive them or even move them unless you know what you are dealing with here. You could easily do them more harm than good." Steve's voice softened, "I'm sorry, but we need to bring people in on this for help."

Alpha responded with a calm and passive question, "And if the people brought in are successful in reviving my people Detective, what then? Will they be locked up for observation? Will they be imprisoned on the premise that it's 'for their own good'?"

"I seriously doubt the LAPD officers, who are presumably locked up around here somewhere, will arrest those who just rescued them, as well as these other poor souls," Steve said with confidence.

Alpha was clearly ill at ease with the idea, but Steve thought that, to his credit, Alpha would let the group make the final decision.

To Steve's surprise, Lei spoke up first, "All those in favor of calling those not of our kind for help?"

Not a single person moved, no hunter spoke up or said anything as Alpha scanned the group.

Then the unbelievable occurred. Alpha stepped forward and raised his hand into the air. All of the hunters, including Lei were visibly taken aback by the gesture, too stunned to move or respond in any way.

Lei walked over to Steve and wiped blood off of his chin.

"You back home now?" She asked as she wiped the blood on her fingers across her lips. Steve looked deeply into her eyes then at the red slick down the front of his shirt and back at Lei. He removed his badge from where it hung on his belt and tossed it aside. No words past between them as Steve pulled Lei in, and kissed her deeply, each of them tasting the blood on the others lips.

Alpha rolled his eyes, but smiled at the reunion. After the merest of moments Lei's hand went up as well, her lips still locked on Steve's.

When the pair finally separated Lei shook out the trench coat Alpha had handed to her and in a graceful sweeping flourish, swept the coat around like a cape, pushing her arms into the sleeves. Using the belt attached to the back of the jacket she tied the coat closed in the front, and then slapped Steve across the face.

"That's for making me wait." Lei exclaimed, giving Steve another quick kiss.

The hunters regained their animation and each walked up to stand with Alpha and Lei until the vote was unanimous in favor of the group reaching out for help from a world that had only ever exploited them in the past.

"All right," Alpha began, "Tracker, I want you to organize my people. Protect the innocent and get communications back online so we can get the help we need."

Steve chuckled as he heard Alpha call him by his old nickname. "What are you gonna do?"

"I am going after Daniels."

Chapter 50

Alex Daniels' mouth hung agape, in combined horror and astonishment at the scene he had just witnessed on the security monitors in his private office.

"Oh God!, Oh God! They're eating them! They're actually eating them! They are the real deal! Real vampires, and they are eating my security team!"

Daniels tried to think. Kunnert had told him to stay put, but he had to get out of the building. Besides what did that buffoon know? This wasn't some clandestine operation or demilitarized zone. This was his skyscraper. A building he had bought through all of the hard work he'd put in over the years, while making his fortune.

Well, in truth it was a fortune he had made on the hard work of others, but it was his vision that had made the company. All of the money those inept intellectuals spent would have been lost, if they were allowed to keep to their own ideas and other devices.

Yes, that was right.

It was *his* genius, *his* vision that took the information, and used it properly to make billions. And think of all of the people who have benefited from the mass production of the drugs he had "acquired" All those who would not have been helped, if the medicines had been produced on a smaller scale.

Yes, that's right!

This wasn't fair. These demons were going to kill him for doing no more than trying to make the world a better place. Clearly they didn't understand this view, so he had to make sure they didn't find him. He wasn't threatened at the moment, the security cameras showed all of the demons on the tenth floor. Daniels moved away from the monitors, and to the safe on the wall where he kept all of the computer files regarding the "Donor Program."

What Daniels didn't see was the blur that passed under the camera located just outside his office door.

Frantically, Daniels spun the tumbler on the combination lock, nervously failing to get the door open on the first, or even the second try. The third time, as the saying goes, was a charm, and with a snap the fastening latch disengaged and the door could be pulled wide open. Daniels shoved stacks of money out of the way as he groped inside the safe for the small diskettes. These were the only records indicating his direct involvement in the project. These diskettes were also crucial to the company.

They were encoded with Daniels' business and marketing plans for the new anti-viral drug to be developed worldwide. Daniels kept these files separate and secure in his own safe. He knew from experience that every company, from time to time, is subject to investigation. Proper police procedure would always call for warrants to be filled out ahead of time, which gave his paid people from the courts and law enforcement all the time they needed, to give him a proper warning of any pending investigators. Daniels had always used this time in the past to hide or destroy any incriminating evidence against himself, or the company. Having set up these particular destruction procedures well in advance, Daniels had minimal work to do, in order to gather the material and decide how to best hide or dispose of it.

His fingers touched, then grasped the diskettes. He was placing them in his pockets along with a handful of the stacks of hundred dollar bills when a low voice called politely from across the room.

"Going somewhere, Mr. Daniels?"

Daniels whirled around with such speed he almost fell.

"What?!?" Daniels stammered out before recognition came, "Dr. Whelan? What are you doing here?"

"Just following orders like a good soldier," the doctor chuckled as he spoke. "Funny to think of me as a soldier, isn't it?"

Daniels broke in, "Doctor, I don't know if you realize but this isn't a good time for..."

Daniels would have continued but he noticed the doctor's eyes had shifted to the open safe and the stacks of money inside.

"Listen to me, you can have the money, as much as you can carry, but we have to get going." Daniels began to stuff some of the money he had taken out for himself into a briefcase and searched his desk for his car keys. He was ready to leave, and this fool wasn't going to slow him.

"Thank you for the gift. I will of course accept such a generous attempt at compensation, however, it is too little, and too late."

The doctor removed something small and shiny from his pocket, and a small amount of light glinted off the metal, catching Daniels' attention.

Daniels froze. "Is that?"

"A smaller, portable version of the flash box? Why, yes it is!"

The predicament he was in now registered. Daniels was barely able to protest when a blinding white light flashed in front of his eyes. The next thing Daniels knew he was sitting in his office chair, albeit somewhat uncomfortably, with the doctor looking down at him with a compassionate and concerned look on his face.

"Are you all right Mr. Daniels?"

The doctor's low voice was always so unnerving, especially coming from such a slight man. The look on the doctor's face was pained, as if he were reluctant to tell him something, but the doctor placed a hand on Daniels' shoulder and in a caring and calm manner he proceeded.

"I want you to remain very calm and try not to move." The doctor sighed, "Regrettably I see you were leaving with my research diskettes. I wondered what happened to them when I found them missing from my personal safe just now."

Daniels tried to move but found himself completely immobilized by the device.

"Betrayal is a very foul act Mr. Daniels. It represents not only an act of deceit, but a fall from grace, in the eyes of those who had put their faith in you."

The doctor brought a small knife into view and twisted it before Daniel's eyes. There is no greater crime to perpetuate against the faithful, than betrayal."

The knife dropped out of view. Alex Daniels suddenly felt horrific pain across his abdomen then a dropping sensation as if he were descending rapidly on a rollercoaster.

Chapter 51

Kunnert looked in disbelief at the radio he held in his hand as words played over the speaker. Everything was going south in a hurry, and a strategic withdrawal was looking more and more like a prospect worth considering. At this point Kunnert reasoned his best move would be to collect Daniels and the doctor and beat a hasty retreat to the parking garage.

The techs had been producing the anti-viral medicine non-stop for two days and had it prepped for shipping. With a minimal amount of help he could get a truck loaded to capacity, and escape with enough medicine to make him millions on the black market. Sales to certain terrorist organizations would be extremely lucrative since its effects make their soldiers immune to their own dirty bombs.

"Doctor, give me your position."

The doctor quickly responded, "At this point I am just cutting loose ends."

"Copy that. I want you, and only you, to break off and head for the loading dock."

"Oh?"

"When you get there use the forklift to load as much of the product as possible into one of the newer trucks, and get the motor running."

"Live to fight another day?" Kunnert could hear strange amusement in the doctor's voice, and it disturbed him.

"Exactly. I'll meet you in the loading area unless you hear otherwise from me. Out."

"Oh indeed. Out."

Kunnert clipped the radio to his belt and thought about his next move. The first step was to collect Daniels then figure out the best way to get the two of them down to the loading dock without attracting attention.

Kunnert ordered his remaining men to set up a defensive

perimeter, with the assumption that any hostile force would be coming out of the stairwell. As the men took their positions in front of the stairwell door, Kunnert moved into the hallway and jogged to Daniels' private office. Gripping and turning the doorknob, Kunnert entered the office without knocking. The smell hit him first and fast. It was a coppery, noxious smell that had filled his nostrils so many times before.

Blood…lots of blood.

With a swiftness and efficiency that only come with years of training and practice, Kunnert simultaneously drew his sidearm and dropped to his knees in a shooter's crouch. He surveyed the room. Nothing moved. Slowly Kunnert crept across the floor to Daniels' desk. Deciding to take the offensive, Kunnert crept to a position of best conjecture, held his breath and counted to three. On three he quickly stood and whipped the barrel of his weapon to bear on the first thing that moved. Nothing moved, but Kunnert peered at the ruin of what was once Alex Daniels. The man had been completely disemboweled.

The sheer insanity of the sight made Kunnert start to shake, and it took a great deal of concentration for him to re-holster his sidearm, without potentially shooting a hole in his foot. Kunnert looked from the mangled corpse to the open safe in the wall, which reset his head to work analytically again. What had been in the safe that was so important to Daniels? Carefully, Kunnert moved to the body, pushed aside the gore and felt over Daniels pockets, finding nothing of interest.

"Breathe," Kunnert told himself, "breathe," as he tried to still the unbridling fear shooting through his entirety. Kunnert heard gunfire coming from somewhere on this floor. He raced back to the elevators to find Alpha cutting down the men he'd stationed there.

Kunnert could only stare as he watched the man move. Every motion flowed seamlessly into the next, as if the entire battle had been choreographed ahead of time. Kunnert had watched enough masters to recognize the expertise in the white-haired man, who was literally taking his men apart. Men who were armed with automatic weapons being carved to pieces by one sole individual armed only with knives.

The area where most of the bloodletting had been occurring was a good thirty-to-forty feet away from where Kunnert held his position. Kunnert ran several possible scenarios through his head regarding how he might get past the fracas without having to join in the melee. Deciding on his best plan, Kunnert moved into the fray anticipating his path. To his surprise, Alpha leapt out of the space and into the hallway leading to the elevator. This maneuver ruined Kunnert's escape route, although it did open the possibility of the stairs as an exit point.

As Kunnert bolted for the stairway door he turned to see Alpha spinning with arms outstretched. With timing, strength and a speed that seemed humanly impossible, he placed his right hand horizontally on the last guard's throat. The guard's neck cracked sharply and his body toppled over as Alpha came to a complete halt. He stood facing Kunnert and the stairway door.

At first Alpha either didn't see, or didn't recognize Kunnert, frozen in place under the glare of a face completely masked in crimson. Kunnert remained motionless as Alpha regarded the heap of bodies he had left in his wake. Kunnert's breath caught in his throat, as he fumbled desperately for the latch to open the door. Alpha's hands tightened into balled fists at the sound and he charged toward Kunnert.

Kunnert's training took over. He instinctively drew his sidearm and fired at Alpha. Alpha had seen the motion, broke his charge and darted into one of the side offices for cover. The bullet whizzed past his head and exploded into the wall behind him. Kunnert's entire countenance quaked as he realized his shot had missed. He never missed! How could this be? It was impossible to dodge a bullet. How could this freak have managed it? Kunnert screamed as he fired aimlessly into the office, praying he could somehow hit and, at the very least, incapacitate Alpha with one of his shots.

As the last bullet was spent, the bolt of Kunnert's automatic ratcheted to the open position and paused. With practiced efficiency Kunnert ejected the magazine, and lifted a full clip from his pocket. He slammed it home reloading the weapon in less than a second. While aiming his gun back into the area where Alpha had disappeared, a rush of air whistled past his ear. Something very solid and heavy slammed into the door behind him and stuck there with loud impact. Kunnert turned to see what had hit the door and was horrified to view a metal letter opener sunk deeply in the door. Alpha had thrown the opener with such force it penetrated a steel, fire resistant door!

Alpha moved back into the hallway. Kunnert aimed and pulled the trigger on his weapon, not bothering to look where his shots were going. He bolted through the stairway door. Had he looked he would have seen one of his shots graze the side of Alpha's thigh, an insignificant wound, but enough to secure Kunnert's getaway into the stairwell, as Alpha twisted with the impact and fell hard to the floor.

Chapter 52

Steve was back on the first floor, where Chris Barnes' dead body lay peacefully on the ground, with his head propped up on the jacket he'd been wearing. Steve stared at the body of his friend, overcome with grief at the sight.

Alpha had directed half of his hunters upstairs with his people on the tenth floor to protect them from guards looking to escape by using the innocents as leverage. The remaining hunters, including Lei, were searching the building for any opposition.

Earlier the hunters had located a tech, hiding in one of the bathrooms on the first floor, and brought him to Steve. The man was sufficiently terrified, and set to work on the system with ferocity.

"I have restored the security cameras throughout the building. We can see every floor in full detail. I have also removed the block on the cell phones so everyone should be getting the maximum signal available to them at this point forward."

One of the hunters watching the monitors called out: "We have movement in the loading dock."

Lei ran over to where the hunter was standing, "No, they're not..." Alpha had given Lei his cell phone before he went after Daniels. She quickly used it to call the other hunters. "We have activity in the loading dock. Who is checking that area?"

When no one responded Lei slammed the phone on the desk and ran for the exit.

The noise stirred Steve from his mourning and yelled after her, "Take some help with you!"

"I can take care of myself, keep everyone else on task," Lei responded coldly.

Steve reluctantly got up from where he'd knelt beside Chris and moved to look at the security monitors. He could see someone loading a truck with several boxes, but not wearing a security uniform. Then a second man came running into view, Steve glared

288

at the image on the screen.

"Lei, a second man has just arrived. It's that security guy, Kunnert. Do not attack on your own!"

No response came from the other end.

"Lei? Did you hear me?" Steve repeated.

Chapter 53

Kunnert watched as Dr. Whelan loaded the last of the pre-packed boxes into the truck. As he climbed into the driver seat, Kunnert pulled down on the truck's rear overhead door, latching it closed and securing the valuable contents.

He had just jumped down from the truck's bumper when Lei casually walked around the corner still wearing only the trench coat Alpha had given her earlier.

"Going somewhere my darlings?" she breathed heavily to Kunnert, and the doctor.

Kunnert flinched, quite surprised to see her. He quickly regained his composure and shot back, "Yes, as a matter of fact, but it can wait for another minute or two."

"Is that all it takes with you? Oh come now stud, you wouldn't get it off that fast and leave me wanting more, now would you?"

Dr. Whelan looked in the side view mirror of the truck and saw Kunnert and Lei in a stand-off in the back of the loading dock.

"Ken, leave her!" The doctor shouted from the driver's seat.

Kunnert yelled back, "Get out of here Doctor, I'll meet up with you later at our destination."

As he turned back to Lei he removed a large folding knife from the holder that was clipped to his belt. "I've wanted to get into you all night."

Kunnert flicked open the blade and charged at Lei who gracefully danced out of the way. Kunnert attacked again, but this time he feigned right, before lunging left. Lei's reaction was too late and the knife sliced through the leather of the trench coat as easily as if it were made of silk. Fortunately Lei's movement had been in time to prevent her flesh from being cut. Kunnert pursued his attack, but instead of dodging the knife, Lei blocked the arm wielding the blade, and launched a sidekick to Kunnert's knee. The blow knocked him off balance, but it did not hyper extend his knee as she had hoped. Kunnert quickly regained his footing and threw a front kick of his own, which connected solidly into Lei's abdomen, knocking her off of her feet.

The tie around her waist loosened, and as Kunnert lunged for her she flipped the coat open, blocking his view as she struck with her hand at an exposed area of Kunnert's back, slashing her fingertips across his flank. Kunnert winced with surprise and stumbled away from Lei to gather himself. He stood facing her, running his hand along his side where he felt the pain, and discovered his shirt had been sliced and several shallow, stinging lacerations on his side were oozing thin streams of blood.

Looking at the blood now covering his hand Kunnert respectfully said, "Now that was clever."

"You're lucky I wasn't cleverer. My nails are usually poisoned," Lei shot back.

"Indeed. Lucky me, but unlucky you," Kunnert murmured as he charged again, the knife flailing as he rushed toward her, but instead of retreating, Lei ran forward, meeting his attack head-on with the trench coat flying behind her like a cape.

The vision of her running completely nude with black leather flapping in her wake created Lei's desired effect and she concentrated on Kunnert's eyes, as the distance between them diminished. Lei clawing her fingers into a Shaolin style position, and Kunnert positioning his blade for a strike at shoulder height. Each was aiming for the other's neck, and the vulnerable structures that lay beneath.

Lei never took her eyes off Kunnert's, and the world was moving in slow motion, as her fingers approached his throat, while his blade crept ever closer to hers. Then she saw it, as Kunnert's eyes flickered from the spot on her throat, to the lower part of her anatomy, as four million years of male instinct took over his brain for the tiniest of moments. All the physical training, and the surgical enhancements, molding her into the human siren she was, paid for themselves ten-fold as Lei used the moment to shift her weight, and the blade passed harmlessly to one side of her neck, while her fingers continued on course for the man's throat. In that split second, Kunnert realized his mistake and desperately tried to correct his body's trajectory.

Lei's fingers penetrated fabric and flesh. Her fingers pierced into Kunnert and the warmth of blood ran down her digits and across her hand, but the desperate shift of position on the part of Kunnert caused her fingers to penetrate the muscles of his chest and shoulders instead of his throat. Painful as the wounds would be, Lei knew they were neither fatal nor incapacitating.

Kunnert backhanded her with such force the blow sent her head back and her body reeling like she had suffered a knockout punch in a boxing match. It threw her off her feet, into the air, and spiraling backward some five feet, before she crashed onto the cement beneath her, resting haplessly on the ground.

From the shadows where Lei had appeared earlier came the sound of feet approaching. Kunnert turned to see two hunters sprinting toward him. Reaching down, he grabbed Lei by the hair and lifted her up enough to slide his blade beside her throat.

"STOP! Or I'll slit her throat!" he called out. The men instantly slid to a stop, some twenty feet away.

Dr. Whelan, who had reluctantly waited to see the outcome of the fight, was shifting the truck into first gear as Kunnert dragged Lei back to the vehicle. Her eyes were blinking rapidly in an attempt to regain her senses. Kunnert leapt up onto the loading step and grabbed hold of the balancing handle outside the overhead door. The truck started to roll out of the loading dock as Kunnert held Lei awkwardly to his chest with knife still at her throat. The hunters began to run for the truck, a gesture that made Kunnert laugh out loud.

A loud explosion, a flash, and a cloud of smoke plumed from the loading dock, at about the same time a fountain of blood erupted from Kunnert's right leg. His laugh turned into an immense scream, and he was rocked off balance, as both he and Lei flew off the truck and down onto the pavement of the parking lot, just outside of the Pharmanetics building.

Rolling with the impact, Kunnert controlled his fall, and then quickly sat up to examine his leg. A large caliber bullet had gone in one side of his thigh and out the other. Ignoring the intense pain Kunnert was reaching for his knife, where it lay on the ground next to him, when he remembered his 3 inch barreled Smith & Wesson Model 13 .357 Magnum, still in its ankle holster on his left leg, and he reached for the gun instead.

As he looked up from his ankle toward the loading dock Lei jumped on top of him, wrapping her legs around his body at the waist and locking her ankles, then encircling his neck with her right arm, she grabbed the inside of her left forearm, to locking her grip. She fisted the hair at the crown of Kunnert's head, wrenching his head back, as she simultaneously ground her naked body intently against his. With incredible force she drove her head down, sinking her teeth into the center of Kunnert's throat, crushing and tearing at his Adam's apple. Kunnert struggled and punched at her in order to get this crazed woman off of him, but Lei had locked her body so efficiently he couldn't find the slightest leverage to remove her, as she chewed continuously on his throat.

With a sickening crunch, bones and cartilage splintered, as Lei ripped at the damaged area. She tore loose a huge chunk of flesh to open Kunnert's windpipe then spat out the chunk of meat and bone before covered the wound with her mouth. She didn't drink the blood flowing in a torrent, instead, she sucked on the side of the man's windpipe, forcing it to remain open while Kunnert's own blood to ran down into his lungs. Kunnert's eyes widened in shock, pain and fear and he began to sputter and gurgle at the realization that he was drowning on his own blood. He desperately grabbed hold of Lei's hair, trying to pull her off of him, but the loss of blood made his efforts too feeble to overpower her.

Lei had completely pinned him to the ground, and she tightened her total lock around Kunnert's body much like a serpent constricting its prey. She mouthed, tongued and generally played with the inside of the man's throat, just to prolong his agony. When Kunnert's final undulations ceased, Lei removed her mouth from the man's throat, gazed into his eyes and ground her pelvis into his groin.

"Come on now, give it up, baby." She purred at the dying man who had gone hard beneath his jeans. She teased her hips in a circle over his hardness, holding his eyelids open as she pleasured herself faster and faster until her body released in a giant climax, at just the same moment his body released his dark soul.

Lei ran her hands up and down her body briefly as her muscles contracted and released in post-orgasmic spasms. She rose off the body and glared angrily at the dead man, while running her index finger over the stitched incision next to her navel, where she had suffered with Kunnert's earlier torture on her chained and naked body.

She didn't hear Steve approach and she jumped, at the sight of him standing beside the body pointing Chris' rifle at Kunnert's head. Alpha came running onto the loading dock, as Steve and Lei walked back to the entrance.

"Kunnert?" Alpha said to Lei as he looked out to the street and the mess she had made of him.

Lei smiled, "He's fucked."

Chapter 54

As Alpha, Steve and Lei returned to the security station on the first floor Alpha announced, "All right, let's go and tend to our people."

Lei headed straight for the elevator, along with the rest of the hunters in the lobby, as Steve went back to Chris' body. He wasn't sure why but he began to collect all of Chris' things.

"Tracker?" Alpha called from the corridor by the elevator.

"I'll be right up." Steve's voice broke slightly as he furiously collected and packed Chris' computers into the carrying cases his friend had used to bring them in. Various tools were spread out over the security system panels, Steve snatched them up as if they might be blown away on some strange wind.

He finished his stuffing and paused. Uncharacteristically, Steve dropped to his knees and began sobbing, covering his face with his hands.

"Chris, I am so sorry," he managed between sobs.

He felt a reassuring hand on his shoulder. "In moments like this boy, there aren't any words that can truly give us comfort. But I will say I believe your friend has left his pain and worry behind him now. He's gone to a better place where he will be safe and taken care of. Try to find some comfort in that."

Every fiber of his being wanted to grab Alpha, throw him to the ground and start pummeling his face with punches.

Instead, Steve simply nodded and responded, "I want to believe that. You know that I've never been overly religious."

"Me either." Alpha replied with a smile, "but I do believe, what I believe."

Steve smiled and the two men finished collecting Chris' belongings and headed for the elevator. As they stepped inside the elevator car an envelope fell out of Chris' computer carrying case. Steve bent down to pick it up and saw it was addressed to him. Alpha pressed the button for the tenth floor as Steve opened the envelope and read its contents.

Hey Steve,

This is a tough one to write. If you are reading this, it means one of two things. Hopefully, it means I was hurt, lost consciousness, and am now on my back heading to the hospital for some, "don't worry Steve, he's gonna make it, it's just a flesh wound" type of emergency medical care. If not...well then... let my ex know that the haunting is about to begin. Either way I think I've found something that may be of help in the resuscitation of the victims of the "stasis."

See, the method of delivery putting them into the stasis condition was a photochemical reaction within the eyes, delivered to the brain via the optic nerve, which in essence short-circuited the normal neuro-electrical signals that normally allow one portion of the brain to communicate with another.

I know. I know. He make-um big words. But if the brain was in fact short-circuited maybe it can also be jump-started. I know on the surface this may sound a little crazy, but the method under which the human nervous system operates isn't really all that different than an electrical system found in a car or a computer. If you could somehow send a jolt into the central nervous system strong enough to accomplish the jump-start, maybe the victim's neurological pathways would be re-booted into normal operation.

What kind of jolt or how this jolt can be administered...Well, that I don't know, but if you and yours can find a way to do it, I believe it will be the cure.

Anyway, I just thought this info may be too important to lose, hence the letter. Also, if this is good-bye...Well, I'm not much for saying good-bye. I'll say instead "see you again my friend."

How's next Thursday? I'll look for you! I'll also make sure to haunt you a little bit, after I scare the bee-Jesus out of my ex.

Your friend with much love,
Chris

Steve was crying again as the elevator doors opened onto the tenth floor.

Chapter 55

Alpha and Lei read the letter, and began to discuss the "jolt" while Steve wandered into the room where all of the people in stasis were lying in their beds.

"What do you think the jolt he was talking about might be?" Lei asked.

Returning, Steve said, "I don't think he knew. I think he was just speaking hypothetically."

"Well, maybe a search of the computer systems can tell us something," replied Alpha, "although that could take quite a bit of time."

Lei asked, "What about those heart paddles? You know the ones on TV where they yell 'CLEAR' then shock the guy and his body bounces in the air?"

"A defibrillator?" Steve said aloud. "I don't know, isn't it only supposed to affect the heart and surrounding muscles?"

"Do we have a defibrillator?" Alpha asked.

"I saw one in the lobby."

"In the lobby?" Alpha and Lei both commented in unison as their puzzled faces turned to Steve. "Why would there be a defibrillator in the lobby?"

"It's not all that unusual for big companies to have emergency defibrillators on the walls of their buildings, like fire extinguishers. It's actually saved quite a few lives since it became a customary practice in Los Angeles. Maybe if we set the device to its lowest setting…"

Alpha bolted for the stairwell.

"Wow." Lei said with genuine incredulity. "Could the answer be that simple?"

Chapter 56

Steve and Alpha watched as Lei and some of the hunters began to revive the victims lying in stasis, including the LAPD officers who had been taken the night of *The Inferno* incident. Alpha had found them in a separate area, where they also had been hooked up to feeding tubes and catheter bags. They were being used as test subjects for the medicines produced from the blood drawn from Alpha's people. Pharmanetics techs had been infecting them with different strains of the flu and measuring the effectiveness of the drugs, and the side effects with various dosages. Fortunately, the facility did not appear to have access to the more frightening viruses, such as Ebola or AIDS, or they would have undoubtedly tested those as well.

"So is it always like that?" Steve asked Alpha meekly.

"Is what always like what?"

"Living blood. I…I had no idea how powerful…"

Alpha seemed to grow concerned. "How do you feel?"

"To say I feel completely satisfied for the first time in my life would be a serious understatement. I feel like a literal weight has been taken off my shoulders. My vision is clearer, each breath I take is more satisfying, my body feels nearly weightless and all sorts of small aches and pains I took for granted are simply gone. Poof!"

"Yes, it can be a very intoxicating, first time experience." Alpha said knowingly. "But part of the sacrifice we make in order to live unmolested from the majority of the world requires our kind to endure certain small 'uncomfortables' in exchange for our solitude.",

"Is that why Lei…"

Alpha regarded him briefly. 'You mean the woman from the alleyway?"

"Yes."

Alpha nodded. "The taking of living blood is very addicting.

Lei had been in a position where she could act on her desire for living blood against an enemy, and saw no reason to hold back."

"Where's that woman from the alleyway now?"

"She was with our healers when Pharmanetics' people attacked, so I would imagine she was removed by her comrades. There was no sign of her body when we were searching for survivors. Either way, she was one of them and I have little sympathy for her."

Steve silently agreed with Alpha's sentiment toward the people involved in this conspiracy. He looked out over the sea of people still waiting to be revived. He noticed a particularly surly man sitting upright in a chair away from the rest of the victims. When Steve realized who it was he immediately hustled over to the man.

"Captain?" Steve asked, "How are you feeling?"

"How do I look, Jacobs?" the Captain's gruff response made Steve smile, as anything less would have caused him concern.

"So what is happening around here?"

"Quite a bit has happened since you left *The Inferno*."

"I'm sure. So tell me, what..." the Captain stopped himself mid-sentence as Alpha approached and stood beside Steve.

Steve saw the Captain reach for his sidearm only to be shocked not to find it at his side. Steve immediately spoke up to reassure the Captain.

"He's with us, sir."

The Captain's eyes slowly drifted away from Alpha and fell back on Steve.

"You vouch for the guy?"

"Completely," Steve said with absolute confidence.

The Captain considered this for mere moments before he spoke again, "Good enough for me, Detective."

Steve felt his whole body relax at those words.

"Now Jacobs, I think I'm gonna need to lie down. Why don't you start telling me a long, detailed, bedtime story?"

Chapter 57

Channel 3 News @ Nine:

Our top story tonight: Pharmaceutical giant Pharmanetics has been seized by Federal authorities and shut down earlier today, after overwhelming evidence of illegal human testing and white slavery surfaced from anonymous sources.   Robert Keppler reports.

Robert Keppler:

In the past few weeks the Los Angeles Police Department, in combination with a task force from the Federal government, has been investigating the corporation Pharmanetics, after an anonymous tip led investigators to believe the corporation was conducting illegal drug testing on human beings. What makes this story all the more frightening is that it now appears the test subjects were not volunteers.

Police Captain Lincoln:

Our investigations have led us to uncover evidence that Pharmanetics was operating illegally, with those on the executive level having full knowledge that the individuals being subjected to the human test trials, were not participating voluntarily and had in fact, been kidnapped by Pharmanetics own security force.

Robert Keppler:

These trials had not been submitted to, nor received the approval from, the FDA, which is what prompted the FBI's involvement in the case. However, as the case developed, a frightening correlation to another case, also being investigated by the Los Angeles branch of the FBI began to take shape.

Senior Agent William Van Ness:

We have been investigating the possibility that a white slavery organization has been operating out of Los Angeles for some time. The investigation came to a conclusion today when the Federal agents, working in conjunction with local authorities, stormed the Pharmanetics offices and made several arrests of key individuals.

Robert Keppler:
Many of the company's employees were unaware of Pharmanetics sinister agenda. Executive officer Alex Daniels is unavailable for comment, and police believe he has apparently gone into hiding as of this time. The state and national government have put out a nationwide alert for the arrest of Mr. Daniels, and authorities are hopeful he will be in police custody very soon.

The names of the victims have not been released by police, however the authorities are encouraged that they have identified all of the people who were being held inside the building. They are all in good health, and are cooperating with the police. They will soon be reunited with their friends and families.

This is Robert Keppler, for Channel 3 News @ Nine reporting.

Chapter 58

Santa Monica, California
Three weeks later, 2:00 AM

Steve walked down the hardwood stairs to the first floor of the Old Spanish ranch house, set on a hill overlooking the ocean, in the Pacific Palisades. The house was built near the turn of the nineteenth century, and had been restored in the early eighties by an elderly couple who had lived there until their deaths in 2000. The children of the couple had no need for the home so it was put on the market, where it sold for ten million dollars to an anonymous buyer working through a realtor.

Checking the refrigerator, he opened a bottle of orange juice, took two long pulls directly from the bottle and savored the refreshing quality to the juice as it coated his dry throat. He screwed the cap back on and replaced the bottle in the fridge. He removed a small insulin needle and an ampoule of medication then turned to climb back to the bedroom when he heard a noise come from down the hallway.

Setting the drug and needle on the kitchen counter, Steve pulled a key off a hook on the refrigerator, opened one of the kitchen cupboards and inserted the key into a lock. The lock turned easily, opening to reveal that the lockbox was holding a small, but powerful handgun. Steve checked the weapon, assured it was loaded and switched off its safety mechanism, and proceeded into the hallway, in the direction of the noise he'd heard.

The house was quiet with the exception of some soft rustling coming from the end of the hall. Steve approached the far end of the house where only a spare bedroom and the basement were available, as hiding places for anyone breaking in. A quick scan of the bedroom revealed no one inside. The basement was going to be a more difficult check, since the elderly couple had turned it into a wine cellar. Although all of the wine had been removed prior to the sale of the home, the multitude of wine racks, humidifiers and other such wine paraphernalia provided ample places to lay in wait, out of sight.

The basement door had been replaced after the home was purchased and it now opened and closed in noiseless perfection. Steve quickly threw the door open and aimed the gun into the darkness. He couldn't see anyone, but then again he couldn't even see the last two of the ten steps descending into the basement. Carefully, he navigated each concrete step, trying to use his peripheral vision as his guide, knowing this area of human eyesight acclimated to the dark faster than normal sight. When he reached the bottom of the steps he waited momentarily so his eyes could fully accommodate the lack of light. Seeing as well as he knew he was going to, he continued into the space.

The basement expanded beneath the entire length and width of the house, just as traditional basements did in mid-west and north-east homes. He had a lot of ground to cover before he could be certain no one had intruded. Walking between two floor-to-ceiling wine racks, Steve realized his vision was improving beyond the point of his eyes simply adjusting to the darkness. He continued forward and, as he came out the other end of the wine racks, saw the very small, flickering, illumination of light.

Someone had lit a candle.

It was Alpha, sitting at a desk that Steve had been using since he had taken possession of the house, looking intently at his reflection in the mirror. Steve lowered his weapon to his side and was about to walk up and greet the man when Alpha reached up with one hand and jammed his fingers into his own left eye. Steve froze as he watched Alpha grimace and work his fingers and thumb around the inside of the eye socket. Blood dripped slightly from Alpha's explorations and, with a slight sucking sound, Alpha removed a large, round semicircular contact lens from the front of his eye socket.

Steve had been about to shriek, thinking Alpha had removed his own eye, but when Alpha looked back to the mirror the reflection revealed something far more disturbing than self-mutilation.

Alpha faced the mirror, his right eye was the same amber yellow color that the rest of his people shared, but his left eye was completely black…no whites, no pupil, just a deep ebony ball, that Steve initially mistook for an empty eye socket. Two teardrops of blood ran from the left eye. As Steve unconsciously backed away from where he was standing, his foot caught something solid on the ground, scraping the floor.

Alpha's head twitched in Steve's direction as he spoke with a sigh, "Ah, good evening…or should I say morning?"

Steve moved from the shadows and faced the man with the mismatched eyes, then looked to the mirror and back to Alpha.

"What the hell is up with your eyes?" Steve said calmly.

"I have never submitted to an examination so I don't really have any factual explanations. It began about fifty years ago and I've been hiding it with sunglasses and contact lenses ever since. I can see just fine, but it definitely appears unnerving to most people." Alpha sighed, "I have been alive for nearly seven hundred years. That's far longer than any of our kind has ever lived, and I fear I am moving into an area of the unknown for our people."

"My God, seven hundred years?" Steve was genuinely shocked at the revelation from his mentor. A connection struck him and he blurted out before he had any chance to think.

"Count Alphonso Diemo?!? YOU are Count Diemo and not simply one of his descendants, as all of our people have been led to believe?"

Alpha smiled, "The first one to ever come back from the madness and so forth and such like?

Yes."

The revelation filled Steve with a million questions, and he mentally tripped over his sentences, wanting to ask all of them at the same time, but all that came out was, "How?"

"That my boy is information which has been lost to time. Not surprising really, if you think about it. After all, I am supposedly the first of our kind to return from the madness that destroyed the minds of all who came before me. If this is truly so, then those who lived before me wouldn't have remained sane long enough to record our origins, the need to consume the blood of others, the sensitivity to light, the alteration of the normal physical traits of humans, such as an unusual eye color, are all the traits separating our evolution from regular human beings."

"But no one else has lived as long as you either. What does that make you?"

"Actually, there were only two others I ever came across who shared the same traits as me. Unfortunately, they were killed in London while helping the rest of our kind flee the Inquisition, when it came to our door one horrible night."

"Who were they?"

"Their names were William and Abigail. They were my most trusted aides, and dearest friends. William was the first person I ever "saved" from the madness, but the truth of it was he was coming out of the dementia before I ever did anything to assist in the reversal."

"And they were killed?"

"Yes, but their sacrifice saved the lives of everyone who lived under my roof, including their baby boy."

Alpha looked directly at Steve expectantly.

Steve stammered in confusion. "I...I couldn't be that boy. I'm nowhere near that old."

Alpha chuckled. "No, you are not that boy. He grew up and had a family of his own, and they had families of their own, and so on. What you are Tracker, is a direct descendant of William and Abigail. A great, great, whatever-great grandson of the two people I loved the most in this rotten world and, as such, that makes you my grandson as well."

"That's why you took such an interest in me as a baby."

"Partially, yes, but I also saw the traits in you that were in your parents."

"Meaning?"

"Meaning you are like me. I have no idea how long your lifespan might be, and you have strengths you haven't even begun to tap into yet. I would have taught you when the time was right, but after that fateful night, you ran away."

"I had lived with you over fifty years, when exactly was going to be the right time to tell me?"

"I didn't know, but in retrospect I think probably about the time this began," Alpha gestured with one hand toward his discolored eye, "that would have been about right. I am afraid I may soon become someone/something not suitable to be the leader of our people. I may become something that instills fear as opposed to faith among the very people I have devoted myself to protect. I don't know what is going to happen to me, but whatever does, I would wish to leave the others in capable hands, hands that have gained the proper experience to sufficiently lead our people. That would be you, my boy."

Steve was stunned…more than stunned to be precise. He hadn't even made the decision yet to return to the fold.

"Alpha…I don't…"

"Don't worry yourself for now. This isn't something that has to happen immediately, in fact, I think I still have a few decades in which to teach you a thing or two, before my public exit becomes necessary. I just wanted you to know how special you are, not only to me but to the whole of our kind."

Alpha turned back to the mirror, raised his hand up to his right eye and removed the prosthetic in much the same manner as he had removed the left one earlier.

"Ahh, that's better." Alpha sighed.

Steve thought the initial appearance of both eyes being completely black would be even more disconcerting. Instead, the look was strangely balanced and far less malicious than the mismatched combination. Alpha's appearance, although very unusual seemed…well, correct, for lack of better phrasing.

"There's more to tell you."

"Well, we have time don't we?"

306

Alpha nodded, "We do, but this…I should have told you this sooner."

Steve could hear the apprehension in Alpha's voice as he said, "Acute Peritonitis."

Steve's jovial mood turned sour. "Excuse me?"

"Acute Peritonitis. It's what they call the condition that kills people who have perforation injuries to the abdomen, assuming no vital organs or structures were ruptured."

Steve felt rage welling up inside of him. "Why are you saying this to me?"

Alpha raised his hands in supplication. "I'm sorry, but it's important that I know you understand the condition before I…"

"You know full well I am aware of the condition, especially under the recent circumstances,"

Alpha nodded. "I assumed as much since it was the cause of death for your friend."

"Chris." Steve whispered. Steve was well aware of the condition and how excruciatingly painful a death it was for the victim. It had made Chris' death all the more difficult to bear when he found out the truck that escaped was full of the anti-biotic and anti-viral medications Pharmanetics had been creating from the blood they'd harvested. One small ampoule of the medication could have saved his best friend's life.

"So, what of it?" Steve asked with far more force than he had intended.

"I'm sorry, but I'm afraid I took some liberty with your friend's body and had the hunters remove it from the scene."

Steve was shocked. "You lied to me?"

"Yes, and I am very sorry for having done so. I thought I was protecting you and, in a way, your friend."

"Protecting us how?"

"I thought that if there was any evidence of a death of someone not affiliated with Pharmanetics then it would… complicate the issues that were sure to arise in our negotiations with the federal government and the LAPD."

Steve was beyond furious. He was ready to lash out, but found himself asking, "The coffin that we buried?"

"Empty." Alpha said matter-of-factly.

"So where is his body?"

"He is among our own now."

"His remains are in the mine?"

Alpha hesitated. "Yes. I thought it best, as you could visit him anytime you liked."

Steve relaxed upon hearing this. He knew the care and reverence his people are given when they pass. Chris would have been given a far more respectful and proper burial with Alpha and his people, than he received from the state funded civil servant type of internment the LAPD had provided.

Steve was having trouble finding his words. "I suppose I should thank you for granting my friend the courtesy, however…"

Alpha looked pleadingly at Steve as he tried to interrupt. "Wait! There's more that…"

Steve waved a hand in front of his face. "No!" Again Steve's voice betrayed the emotions he was holding inside. He took a deep breath to calm himself before continuing. "I'm sorry but no. It's too soon for me to hear anymore right now."

Alpha stared at Steve for a long moment then seemed deflated as he said, "All right. Perhaps it isn't something you should hear from me in any case. I just want you to know it was never my intention to keep you in the dark."

Steve didn't understand what Alpha was saying, but he also had no interest in talking about it anymore so he simply agreed with a nod of his head.

The room was silent for a long moment before Alpha spoke again.

"So what are you and Lei going to do now?" Alpha said with a sly smile. "I assume she is still asleep upstairs?"

"You knew?"

Alpha chuckled. "Dear boy, the girl hasn't been home in nearly three months. In the entirety of her life only you could ever hold her interest, so where else would she be?"

"You disapprove?"

"Hardly, but I am wondering what your plans will be when the…ah…honeymoon ends."

"I've left the LAPD. They wouldn't grant me the leave I requested, so I resigned. Alpha, I need to finish what Chris and I started. I am going to track down Dr. Whelan and everything he stole from our people. I figure that while that man is still out there, well, our secret and our people will never be completely safe."

Alpha was wide-eyed in what appeared to be amazement before he said. "Yes, I think you will be a terrific leader of our people someday."

"We'll see, Lei has agreed to accompany me in this search, as well."

Alpha nodded. "Not that you need it, but the two of you have my full support. Anything you require will be provided to you, if you but ask."

Steve looked guardedly at Alpha. "I'm not making any promises that when this is over I will return to the fold and become this leader or whatever you are describing."

Alpha shrugged his shoulders. "I offer my support with no conditions attached or implied. Your success is incentive enough for me to stand with you on this."

Steve nodded. "Thank you."

Then breaking the serious mood the room seemed to have fallen into Alpha said, "Oh, I have something for you Tracker!" Alpha reached into his jacket and pulled out two long brown cylindrical objects that Steve recognized were cigars.

"What's this?" Steve asked.

"Where I am from originally, we honor new beginnings with a toast and exchange of gifts." Alpha said with a smile. "These are special," Alpha indicated to the cigars with a flourish, "as they predate the American embargo of Cuba. They have been kept in pristine condition by a vendor I happen to be very fond of."

Steve had only heard of such cigars still existing in America, and he had always been keen to try one. He was also well aware of the value placed on these cigars, and knew that this was a really rare treat.

"Alpha, I'm honored. Let me go upstairs, I believe I have a good bottle of…"

Alpha pulled out a flask of the exact make and model as the one's Steve used to hold his emergency blood and wine mixture. "I think you will be hard pressed to find anything superior to this."

Alpha unscrewed the top and held the flask out at arm's length, "To new beginnings!"

Alpha drank from the flask and smiled contentedly at the flask afterward, then handed it to Steve.

Steve took the flask from Alpha's hand, he wanted desperately to check the contents of the flask before drinking. Alpha watched him intently. Steve considered the flask for a moment more before saying.

"To old, very old, friends and family!" With that Steve drank from the flask without hesitation. The scotch inside was well-aged with far more flavor than burn as it sparked his palate and rendered a feeling of warmth all over.

"That was delicious," Steve said, impressed by the fine liquor.

"I agree, very satisfying." Alpha nodded and handed one of the two cigars to Steve. Steve held the cigar with reverence, then said,

"I'm afraid I have no gift for you."

"In this case it is not necessary. "

"All right, so what happens to you now?" Steve asked.

"In what regard do you mean?"

"Will you be moving our people again? Or are you going to try to rebuild the mine?"

"No, the mine has been compromised. We will be moving, but not very far." Alpha smiled. "I think I am going to buy one of those giant casinos. Have you ever taken a tour through one of those behemoths? There is an entire city working under what you see on the surface. The spaces are even larger than what we had in the silver mine. Of course, I will have to change out all of the lighting…still."

Steve laughed, "You're going to buy a casino?"

Alpha looked dead serious and Steve stopped laughing.

"You're serious? Alpha, where are you going to get that kind of money? We're talking hundreds of millions, if not billions, of dollars."

"In a way, our very dead friend Alex Daniels has provided a viable, twenty first century solution to our housing issues. The creation of the anti-viral drug he coveted has opened up a possibility I had never before considered."

"And that would be?"

"We are going to create the medicines ourselves and sell it to the pharmaceutical companies. From the research records we found at Pharmanetics we learned, that if every one of our people were to donate one pint of blood, then we would have more than enough to stockpile the medications and vaccinations for years to come. Pretty soon we will have more money than we know what to do with. Purchasing a casino will enable us to 'hide' all of our people in plain sight."

Steve could only laugh in amazement at the brilliance of Alpha's plan.

"Sometimes things just work out for the best don't they?"

"Indeed they do Tracker. Indeed they do."

The two talked for several more hours into the morning until the first signs of sunrise began to lighten the sky.

"It would seem as though it is time for me to leave." Alpha said as he rose from his chair.

"Why don't you stay? I know Lei would love to see you."

"Unfortunately, I have business back in Las Vegas and if I am going to be in time I will need to leave now."

"I'll walk you out." Steve climbed out of his chair as well.

"Thank you. Oh! Let's enjoy those wonderful cigars before I leave."

Steve looked at the cigar Alpha had given him. "I'll save it for when you return."

"Thank you, but no. I'm afraid they don't last long when taken out of storage."

As Alpha and Steve made their way out of the basement Steve picked up a long stick lighter from the fireplace. "You know, I've always wanted to try one of these. It's a real gift, thanks Alpha."

As they exited the basement, Alpha turned to Steve, "You should know that being…what I am…what we are…does have some rather…well…" Alpha didn't seem to know how to say his next words.

"What is it?"

Alpha looked Steve right in the eye, "Just know that, the things we can do…It isn't good or evil. It's just something we can do, okay?"

Steve had no idea what Alpha was talking about, but said, "Okay."

"I know it's painful for you to think about your friend, but you are going to have to face it, and sooner than you think. Here, let me light that for you." Alpha flicked the flint on the lighter as Steve bit the tip off the cigar then held the other end under the flame. Once the tip glowed Steve raised the tube to his lips and pulled. The flavor was astounding and not harsh in any way.

"It is satisfactory?"

Steve smiled, "As I said, it's a real gift." Steve watched the smoke rise as the two men moved out of the house and into the front yard. Steve could hear the ocean break against the shore at the bottom of the hill, and turned to look into the horizon.

Alpha nodded, "I'm glad you like it. However, you should know that while the cigar may be my gift to you, it is not however, from me."

"What?" Steve turned to Alpha, but to his surprise he found himself standing alone.

Steve raised the cigar back to his lips and pulled on the end for another wonderful drag.

"Never the easy way, always so cryptic." Steve blew out the smoke again and looked up to the stars, "And if it's not from you, Alpha, then who?"

Steve took another long drag of the cigar…

"BANG!!!"

The end of the cigar exploded in a high-pitch concussion that sent Steve reeling, dropping to the ground, and looking for cover. He scanned the area, looking for the source of the explosion only to see the cigar lying on the ground next to him with the lit end burst apart. The cigar had been rigged for the old "exploding cigar" trick.

Steve was beside himself. He loved a good prank and this was right up his alley, however he couldn't see Alpha doing anything of the sort, and it was such a waste of an amazing…

Then he saw the label on the cigar.

"Montecristo."

The label jarred a memory and Steve realized there was only person who could, and would, do something like this to him.

He picked up the cigar gently, stared at the label and said out loud without even realizing he was speaking,

"Chris?"

About the Author

Michael Weinberger graduated from University of Pacific after earning his undergraduate degree in Sports Medicine, and then went on to the Los Angeles College of Chiropractic where he earned his Doctor of Chiropractic degree in 1993, at the age of 25. He returned home to Las Vegas and operated a successful chiropractic office until the fall of 2000, when a severe arm injury forced him to step away from his chosen profession. It was during his recovery that he began writing.

Michael Weinberger enjoys writing, archery, martial arts, deep-sea fishing, movies and is an unrepentant "foodie." He lives in Las Vegas with his wife and two daughters where, when not otherwise engaged, can usually be found shooting arrows into the garage, using one of the custom archery bows that he makes in his spare time.

The author welcomes all comments, reviews and inquiries at his website:

www.weinbergerbooks.com

www.ingramcontent.com/pod-product-compliance
Lightning Source LLC
Chambersburg PA
CBHW050923120626
46552CB00001B/9